MW01594772

DAWN OF CHIMERA

By Renee Butterfield

PublishAmerica
Baltimore

ISBN: 1-60672-099-6
PUBLISHED BY PUBLISHAMERICA, LLLP
www.publishamerica.com
Baltimore

Printed in the United States of America

Chapter 1

From her tower, high above the hollow, the bewitching red-head peered through the glint. The expansive window offered her the crystal-clear view of what she considered to be an insignificant valley; a meaningless and fretful cradle of inferior, agonizing humanity, hurrying to crowd their useless lives with worthless extravagance.

Like a spider, perhaps a black widow, who found her victims mildly amusing as they blundered about, mindless of their demise, blind to their impending peril even as she wove her web, fabricating their destiny. They were about to build their Utopia. Another Eden, re-born without assistance from their antagonist, the foe who had brought Eden down upon their heads the first time around because He was a capricious and irritable taskmaster. He took from them their beloved Eden, and even went so far as to transform the archangel into a hideous snake.

She touched the medallion around her neck, handling it with delicate care. The snake-like insignia which dangled over the crevice of her voluptuous breasts assured her enormous success. Still gazing through the window, her eyes fell upon a familiar figure, that of the young man in the trolley-car riding to the top of Mount Gaspar. There was nothing about Allen Carter she didn't know. While he was agreeable to look at, he was as dumb as a stick.

Unaware of the fact, he was being watched, Allen was on his way to the top of Mount Gaspar. Inspired by the breakneck climb aboard the tram to the top of the mountain.

Inside of the cable car, which swayed and creaked in the early morning breeze, he inhaled the thin air and gazed around him. As he made the ascent he saw the rugged vestige of brush and trees below him. The mountain's valley was carpeted with green fir trees and vegetation. He saw the four-footed animal, a spotted hyena, amble into the foliage. The hyena was a predator, preying upon mammals less hardy than himself. Allen compared him to certain individuals in the peculiar society which prospered at the top of the mountain. He was on his way to visit them now.

They referred to their dream-world as Chimera and they went on and on about it. No one was worse at this than Daphne Orion, the woman who had brought them all together. Their celebrated host, the seductive female who had organized the bizarre society, or, at least, this particular branch located high upon Mount Gaspar.

Aboard the trolley car, as he lifted his eyes he saw the raven which mounted the wind and soared beyond his reach. Screech was a magnificent bird. He had a loud, sinister-sounding call and long, prominent wings. For some reason Allen could not fathom, why the coal-black Raptor had befriended him, a mere human being.

The cable attached to the cage Allen rode in made a loud, grating noise and the cart plummeted several feet. It was just enough of a jolt to make the ride exciting and he hungered for adventure; more chills, spills and thrills. When the cart dropped he held onto the crossbar and his feet dangled in nothingness.

Allen had no job or money, and no transportation, either, other than an old beat-up bicycle, an artifact from childhood. Adolescence was agonizing, it crept by much too slowly and then it was over.

His adopted dad, Charlie Carter, was dead and his adopted mother, Harriet, was dying, although he had trouble accepting her death and he kept trying to convince himself she would recover; they would find a cure for her cancer. Allen even talked himself into believeing the doctors had somehow misdiagnosed her condition. When her illness progressed and she grew worse, he found he could no longer deny it. He lost his faith in a merciful and loving God.

The raven, Screech, floated through the atmosphere, free-spirited and unrestrained and finally descended to land upon Allen's shoulder. His razor-sharp talons dug into Allen's thick, black coat.

While moving through the sky in the creaky old cart, with the raven perched on his shoulder, thousands of feet above the terrain, Allen felt very much alive. His heart soared and he enjoyed the rush of adrenalin. He was fully alert to something archaic and older than mankind. Some primitive power flooded his being, flowing through the veins of both man and beast. Screech flapped his wings gently, eyeing his alter-ego.

"Survival of the fittest," Daphne had quoted to him. "Anything less than competent must be disposed of."

Included on the list to be disqualified were the aged, the obese, as well as those with severe maladies. Chimera would comprise only the most able-bodied. What, or whom, would be designated to eliminate them, Allen didn't know. By the time they realized Chimera, the infirmed might have simply passed away. With any luck the feeble would be reincarnated he supposed, and their souls would come back in more wholesome, prestigious bodies. They could then live forever in Chimera.

Like countless others who had been adopted, Allen sometimes contemplated his natural parents, who and what they were, what kind of people had brought him into the world to abandon him, leaving him to flounder in a cruel, unstable world. Charlie and Harriet Carter had been very kind, bestowing on him a name and parentage, but no roots or heritage and he always felt he didn't really belong anywhere. This may have been the major reason he went to the mountain-to search for himself. Daphne seemed to think, given time, he might fulfill his quest right there amidst group loyalty. The ambiguous, she said, quite often discovered wonderful revelation on the mountain.

"It's an exceptional part of Chimera," she sweetly enticed him.

However, thus far, he'd only encountered more questions. He'd also discovered a very odd raven and the bird, somehow realizing his aloneness, had befriended him.

Screech squawked and Allen gazed into his soul-stirring, black eyes and felt the bird was seeing straight through him.

Chapter 2

The order's white, concrete domicile at the top of the mountain always reminded Allen of a planetarium, with its dome-like curvature and sky-light roof. It was neoteric, too. 'Neoteric,' he thought. It looked like a sterile, vacant planetarium to him.

There was no welcome mat at the door, no neighborly signs displayed anywhere. Just a rather curious white, concrete building shaped like a bubble, isolated by the woodland at the top of Mount Gaspar.

Allen didn't knock because he figured they expected him. He turned the black latch on the wooden door and went inside, leaving Screech perched in a tree outside and probably eyeing him.

The luxurious interior didn't look particularly friendly either and Allen was surprised to find not a soul in the cardinal room. He was alone in the disk-shaped dwelling, panoramic paintings on all of the walls; the blue-grey elephant head with long, sharp tusks, a gold-colored lion with the feet of a bear and the body of an eagle, a black bear on his hind legs, looking vicious and ready to attack, and then, of course, the large red dragon with the words inscribed above his head,

"The Dragon Gave Them Their Power."

They didn't know it but the words came straight from the Holy Bible. Charlie and Harriet's Pastor had read that particular verse to his congregation one Sunday during his sermon and Allen had remembered it. He didn't tell the others about the Bible verse though. However, as he eyed it, he had the eerie feeling it was profoundly prophetic.

Allen gazed at the colorful pentagram drawn on the center of the tiled floor, an enormous, perfect pentagram. There were gold-plated chains attached to similar posts which circled the room a couple of feet away from the pentagram. Daylight broke through the sky-light, which was probably the chief reason the various plants setting around grew so heartily.

Allen's attention was drawn to muffled commotion coming from behind the wooden door across the spacious room. He read the director's sign on the door. It was Daphne Orion's facility and either she had forgotten to turn off her radio, or she was in there with someone else. Judging from the noise, he guessed there was more than just one other person in her suite with her.

Finally, he saw the glamorous red-head open her door and as she held it open for her assistants, he watched, as one by one, they filed through the portal.

Meanwhile, Daphne cast her cool green eyes upon him and he accorded her a polite smile. She returned it.

Allen recognized every one who exited Daphne's suite. The first one out the door was Archie Petersen. The plump man was in his early forties. Petersen was critical of any one different than himself. This building was the least likely place one would expect to find a man like Petersen.

"You finally decided to show up, huh?" Petersen grumbled at him. Allen gave him an apologetic look and answered,

"I had no idea I was late."

He was surprised his tardiness didn't seem to bother Daphne. In her sexy black jumpsuit, she appeared more animated than ever.

Behind Petersen, Allen saw Rattler Mackenzie's younger brother, Doctor Stuart

Mackenzie, a thin, bleak-looking man. Lena Guire was with the fashionable Drew Gerard, the French Olympic Medalist and they were followed by Lena's husband, Barry Guire. Barry was a big man, taller than Allen and far more robust, too. Leopold's nephew, Wesley Versuch was next in line. With a heavy Austrain accent, Wesley said,

"Hello, Allen, you should have been there today. You missed out on a great deal of information!" He managed to pique Allen's curiosity.

"I'll fill him in," Daphne told him.

The last person to exit the room was Doctor Peter Wolfe. He stopped in the door way, struck a match and lit the pipe in his mouth. At once the cherry fragrance filled the air.

Doctor Wolfe lifted his dark eyebrows, inhaled the aroma and said,

"There's nothing like it after a successful board meeting!"

He appeared very satisfied as he kissed Daphne's cheek, and gently massaged her back and said,

"The dragon will triumph! Sweet deal, Princess." he flattered her. She laughed and thanked him for his presence on this particular occasion.

Patiently, she watched as everyone left the building, leaving them alone.

"It's vacant," she sighed, "They've all gone and we're alone." she commented, but it was

not something Allen needed to hear her say. He had eyes and he could see the others had left. They had deserted him, leaving him alone with this female who baffled him. She looked at him.

"Now that we're alone, I think I ought to tell you, I want you to relinquish whatever hold you have over the raven."

"Screech?" Allen asked her, hoping she couldn't possibly mean she wanted him to get rid of him.

"Hmm," she sighed, nodding her head at him. "You've named the little meddler too?" She turned on her heels and he followed her into her office. "He's a busybody and he's not one of us, you know?" she cautioned him.

"I didn't know this," he replied. All along he'd had the idea Screech was a part of Mount Gaspar and attached in some way to their organization.

She went to the globe in its cylinder, positioned on top of one of the several desks in her large, cluttered office. She was no neat freak, Allen observed. Turning to face him, she said,

"We have to be careful because we have classified information in this building and it mustn't leave the mountain."

Who was the raven going to tell? Allen wondered; other ravens?

"Okay," he said, supplying her with the answer he thought she wanted to hear. Keeping a straight face, he added, "I'll share this tidbit with Screech."

"I'm not kidding with you, Allen and I don't want you to deride me." Without the slightest bit of humor she proceeded,"If information were to leak out a lot of people, including the president of our country, could be destroyed. Do you understand me, Allen?"

"So far," he answered her.

She knew Allen Carter and she was quite confident he didn't understand her. He couldn't possibly comprehend the amount of intelligence she referred to. There were times when she, too, found it hard to believe.

They moved to the large wooden desk where the globe was set in its pedestal.

"Spin the globe, Allen," she appealed to him.

He gave her a questioning look.

"Why?" he asked her. The adventures around this place never ceased, he thought. Chimera was a good title for the world Daphne Orion intended to establish.

"Go ahead," she encouraged him, "Spin the globe and see where it lands!"

Accommodating her, he gave the globe a whirl and then watched it revolve. Countries and continents were all spinning by so fast he had the odd thought, had it been real, entire populations would have dropped off and soared into space. Finally, the globe stopped spinning.

"What do you see?"

"Europe," he told her, gazing at the ball as if it was a game, a favorite pastime. He supposed it may have been for her.

"Put your finger on any part of Europe," she instructed him.

He put his big index finger down and mumbled, "England."

"England?" she questioned him.

He examined the globe,

"Yes, England. You know, like, 'England swings like a pendulum and bobbies on bicycles, Westminster Avenue and the tower of Big Ben...' ".

"The rosy red cheeks of the little children." She added.

"Yes, that England," he attested.

"There are Delphians there too." She enlightened him. "There are Delphians on every spot of the globe," she said. She crossed the room to the window and gazed out.

"A few weeks ago I faxed a proposal, an interesting one, to the president of the United States. Today my proposal was made into law." Daphne turned and gave Allen a crisp look, "That legislation, Allen, is Universal Health coverage."

"I had no idea you had this sort of pull in the White House." he replied, and now he was truly fascinated.

"I don't" she told him, "The dragon gave me this authority." *'I must never forget the dragon. He must always be credited for everything.'* she told herself.

"Universal Health coverage is a good thing?"

She smiled at the way the handsome man lifted his eyebrows when he questioned her statement. The dragon gave her fascinating peculiarities. The creature spoke directly to her on many awesome occasions. As long as she gave him credit and brought him pleasure, he'd continue to confide in her, too.

She drifted toward Allen, although still keeping her distance. She had a horde of assistants but no confidants. No one she trusted.

Alarmed, he stepped backward. He'd never been in the presence of anyone so mystifying. The more he thought about it, the more he appreciated the idea of universal health coverage, though. He knew both Charlie and Harriet Carter had spent their life's savings on doctor bills.

"Right now our people in Public Relations are coming up with advertisements. Soon we'll have universal vaccinations as well. The people, being so dependent upon government for their health,will go along with it. We'll never make it mandatory, though. They will have a choice. We want willing participants, people who are willing to sacrifice their lives for Chimera." she stressed.

"Yes, Chimera" he groaned. "It's beginning to sound more like Hades to me" he told her.

"Oh, for god's sake, Allen!" she complained. "Because of our chemtrails, they're already being poisoned. Every breath they take may be fatal to them."

Once again, she turned away from him. She marched to a cabinet of drawers and opened one of them. He saw her remove a closed, medium-sized envelope.

"Hell, if we didn't kill some of them, they'd soon do it to themselves. Do you prefer mass suicide?"

"You mean, like a holocaust; mass murder?" he questioned her.

None of the others had objected so much when she informed them of these things. Not even Wesley Versuch dared to make commotion. Allen was different, Allen was crazy; crazy and faultless. Two detrimental attributes which could put an end to their cherished Chimera. Still, she owed it to her beloved Rattler to inform Allen of their endeavors, she told herself.

"So, our scientists invent a virus and government tells the public to be vaccinated, injecting them with a lethal drug." She shrugged, "They'll die, painlessly, in fact, even quite euphorically. Then they will be reincarnated."

She knew reincarnation didn't quite work this way but Allen had bought her lies before because he was so incredibly naïve.

"Do the people know they've made a sacrifice for Chimera? Do they realize they are being poisoned to death?"

He wanted her honest, gut-level reaction. He wanted some kind of emotional response, preferably remorse.

"Most of them will never know and the few who do have any knowledge are simply labeled kooks or conspiracy theorists."

Her conscience wasn't pricked in the least. She plopped down in her chair, leaned back and put her feet on the desk in front of her. Resting comfortably, she continued,

"Our objective is to reduce the global population by 4 billion people. Our scalar weaponry system will help us accomplish this."

She sat up in her chair, too exuberant to rest. She placed the manila envelop she was holding on top of her desk and started to open it. She showed some dismay when he didn't rush to the desk to see what was inside of the envelope. She glanced up at him,

"Don't worry, this isn't the first time we've been the public's adversaries. Remember what you learned about the first polio vaccinations and how they were recalled? It was discovered the antibiotic gave people the virus. What? Did you think this was by accident, or wasn't planned in advance? Hardly!" she said, "They got caught trying to wreck havoc is all."

He was speechless. He heard her call to him,

"Come here, I want to show you this" and, benumbed, he followed her suggestion, but his heart wasn't in it. He wished he was anywhere else. He thought of the mountain and of Screech. She seemed far too preoccupied with her blueprints to worry about the bird any more. He was positive one raven couldn't do much to stop them now, any way.

She laid several pictures before him, pictures of the sky and clouds, heavy criss-crossed clouds.

"These are chemtrails" she filled him in. "Not only do the clouds assist NASA in their efforts to make cloudbursts, cyclones, hurricanes and other natural disasters but people with average, or below average immunity systems experience pneumonia-like respiratory problems because of chemtrails. Pretty fascinating, huh?" she remarked. "Once again, the dragon gives us our power."

"You didn't have to befriend him and you certainly don't have to follow every flippin' suggestion he makes." Allen told her.

"In order to create Chimera it's necessary to destroy the old world." she emphasized.

She collected the photos and returned them to the large envelop. Relaxing in her chair, she again put her feet up on the desk and said,

"Oh, before I forget, your mother became terribly ill earlier this morning and was rushed to the hospital." She shook her head, feigning an apology before adding, "She's either dying right about now , or she's already dead and if this should be the case then someone will arrive at your address in a couple of hours to commit you to an institution."

She said this as though she'd just received the divine revelation; maybe the dragon had spoken to her once more, Allen thought, as he turned to leave.

He knew she didn't care any more about Harriet than she cared about the other billions of people she was busy trying to find ways to eliminate. Harriet was just one more victim of Chimera. At the door, he turned around to glance at her.

"Just one more question, Daphne," he said, "Are the chemtrails responsible for Harriet's demise too?"

She raised herself to her feet.

"What do you think, Allen?" she replied.

"I think the chemtrails had everything to do with it." he answered her.

"I'd say you're probably right but don't forget about reincarnation, my dear apprentice." she smiled.

As Allen made his way down the mountain he looked closer at the sky on this trip, thinking of how he had always taken it for granted, wondering if it was the last cloudless sky he'd ever see. On his way to the tram the bird joined him again, flying high over his head. Daphne said Screech wasn't part of their society.

As the raven sailed the sky like an ace pilot, Allen watched him.

"Who are you and what do you have to do with this place?"Softly, he questioned the bird.

Chapter 3

Harriet's Pastor stood in her hospital room. Holding her weak hand with his own, he questioned why the Almighty hadn't intervened and put an end to her suffering.

The God he counted on and believed in was big enough to do anything, he imagined. Yet, this was the third time this week the Pastor had stood by and watched another one of his parishioner's die. All of them were senior citizens, healthy at one time before their bodies were stricken.

Harriet was the only one with cancer, the others had died of what their doctors called chronic obstructive pulmonary disease. Their lungs so debilitated breathing became far too laborious and they died.

He struggled to choke back his tears. As he swallowed hard, he felt Harriet squeeze his hand and he heard her whisper,

"Don't you weep for me. I am going to see my Lord!"

For a second he saw her countenance brighten before the cancer jabbed her, raising it's cruel fist and ripping the smile from her face. The beacon of light which had shown so long in their midst smoldered and threatened to burn out.

"I've arranged to have Allen put in an institution," the dying saint uttered with difficulty.

"Yes, I know," he replied.

Harriet still had custody of her adopted son, Allen. Although he would soon be twenty-four years old, she still retained supervision of him. Every one knew Allen was mentally unbalanced. Harriet claimed he was her cross to bear. She cherished him as if God had personally reached down and planted him in her care.

The decision to have Allen transferred to the County Mental Hospital, *Saint Vincent's,* was not an easy one for her to make. There were no alternatives though.

Paul didn't blame the members of their church for their reluctance to encumber themselves with an insane young man. Even Paul declined to take Allen into his home. His plate was full and he had many responsibilities already. Then, too, he had three daughters he was determined to protect.

When Harriet decided to have Allen put away, he didn't disapprove; he thought it was best for everyone. However, as he gazed down into her piercing eyes, he couldn't deny the twinge of guilt he felt over Allen's sorry fate.

"Harriet," he sighed, "You know, if I could I would take responsibility for Allen but there's Kastanje and the girls to think about, too." He shook his head at the thought. "They wouldn't get along," he tried to explain to her.

"Just hear me out," she begged her Pastor and long-time friend.

He was sure the heavy dosages of morphine made it even more difficult for her to articulate her thoughts.

"Toby!" she murmured, and he clearly heard the rattle in her voice. He knew she was almost ready to go toward the light.

It's what they called it in books he had read on the subject of dying. People who had returned to life from death claimed to have seen a shining light, which they said came from inside a tunnel. They had to go through the tunnel to reach a glorious place on the other side of it.

"Would you take Toby into your home?" Harriet asked him. It was such a simple favor she asked him to do. He couldn't refuse such a meager request. Toby was an ugly Boston terrier. Paul thought the dog resembled an old wrestler he once knew. The wrestler was clipped in the mug several times too many.

Harriet's profound aptitude of caring for ugly dogs and injured people had always amazed Paul.

"Of course, I will, Harriet!" he told her.

"Allen will want to visit him, too" she told him. "He loves the dog."

"Sure, he can visit Toby all he wants," Paul assured her. He'd make space in his busy schedule to personally see to it.

Harriet squeezed his hand one last time. Then she closed her eyes.

"Pray with me," she invited him. It was the last request Harriet ever made of her Pastor.

Paul turned away and with blinding tears, he saw the white-uniformed nurse enter the room. He didn't see her face, he couldn't know her emotions concerning Harriet's departure. His own grief was overwhelming. He had

16

visions of Jenny, George and now, Harriet; all of them had died this week, one right after the other. He'd stood by them, held their hands, tried to sound cheerful when he felt dejected.

Jenny, God rest her soul, needed to talk about her afterlife.

"I know my Lord will raise me from the grave when He returns," the eighty-seven year old managed, somehow, to say as she fought for every breath. "Pastor, is there a Paradise for me until then?"

"There was for the thief when our Lord was on the cross, wasn't there, Jenny?"

Jenny, who had embraced her Savior as a little girl and had dedicated her whole life to Him, had to have more clout than the criminal who hung on the cross beside the Lord.

"Yes, Jenny, I believe you will be in Paradise today, too!" Paul assured her.

Jenny seemed relieved. She closed her eyes and with a smile on her face, she went to sleep.

Paul now stumbled from Harriet's hospital room and leaning against the wall, he struggled to gain control of his emotions.

He heard commotion nearby and turned to gaze down the long corridor of Intensive Care where he saw four elderly people at the end of the hallway. One of them was sickly and the others gathered around him. They argued with the nurse whose counsel obviously wasn't appreciated.

"Sir, you're sick" the nurse told the old man. "You need immediate care!" Paul heard her inform him.

"He doesn't want your help!" one of them, a female, told her. The woman may well have been the sick man's wife.

"Don't crowd him!" one of them shouted at the others. "Stand back and let him breathe! Don't you see, he's having trouble breathing?"

Paul heard the familiar voice and realized it was Roosevelt Schuyler. Then he recognized them. They were all members of his church. Although, they were senior citizens, they were not senile; not one among them could be considered demented. Perhaps forgetful, and irritable at times, but not feeble-minded. He hurried to see what the trouble was.

The nurse spotted the man dressed in black slacks and shirt, with the white clerical collar, as he came toward them. Calling to him, she said,

"This man should be hospitalized!"

She referred to the old man leaning against the wall having a difficult time trying to breathe.

"I'm alright" he tried to tell her between gasps for air.

Andrew Martin didn't look all right to Paul and he told him so.

"You're not alright, Andy. You look like you need help."

Paul's eyes searched the man's face and he could see he needed urgent intervention.

"Andrew doesn't need any care I can't give him at home," Lorraine Martin insisted as she took her husband's hand.

Paul remembered Andrew and Loraine were both naturopaths who tackled viruses with natural, vitamin-enriched foods from their garden, along with herbs and other supplements.

"You can't hospitalize him against his wishes!" Roosevelt Schuyler said, lowering his voice and speaking directly to the nurse. "You may not be aware of this, young woman," he said as he inched closer to her, closing the gap between them. "But senior citizens are being killed. Someone or something wants us dead and out of the way!"

Paul looked at Roosevelt, the conspiracy theorist. He seemed to be the spokesman for this assembly.

"Roosevelt," Paul addressed him, "You're not helping matters here. You're a paranoid old coot" and he gently tugged at his arm.

He was confident Roosevelt meant well, but he was presently leading his peer group astray.

"He's not overly suspicious, Pastor." Joseph Elvio spoke up. "Harriet Carter was the third senior from our church to die this week. You know as well as we do, this isn't a coincidence."

Paul looked at Joseph; he didn't know any such thing.

"We're all under a great deal of stress" he said, sympathizing with them.

Andrew seemed to be recovering from his spasm, at least well enough to once more inform the nurse he did not need to be hospitalized. He was adamant about it. The nurse passionately disagreed with him.

"I don't believe your health is something which should be left to amateurs to flounder around with, Mister Martin," she advised him in no uncertain terms. "When you come to your senses, you know where to find us!" She said and then turned away from the assembly of geriatrics and took off down the hall with an angry stride.

The geriatric crowd turned their attention to their Pastor then.

"We don't mean to be difficult, Pastor Paul" Lorraine said and she sounded firm but friendly. "But we've a hunch there's something in the air."

"Yes" Roosevelt chimed in, "We're dropping faster than flies" he exaggerated.

"It's not natural" Joseph agreed.

While the pastor still stood in the hallway of Intensive Care, attempting to convince this portion of his congregation there was nothing strange going on, he saw a man, dressed in black suit and striped tie step out of the elevator.

As soon as he saw Paul, his pale face lit up with an expression of delight and there was a look of sincerity in his blue eyes. He came right to him, stuck out his hand and said,

"Good day, Pastor. I'm Wesley Versuch from the financial department of Mercy Hospital. I want to discuss Harriet Carter's outstanding bill with you." He informed him with a heavy German accent. "In private, if I may" he inquired.

"No, you may not," Roosevelt answered the young man. He was obstinate. "We were close, personal friends of Harriet's. We refuse to be ignored and kept from knowing the details of her death now." The others nodded in agreement with Roosevelt.

Paul glanced at the employee from finance,

"If you don't mind," he politely said, even while still clutching his hand. "We needn't alienate Harriet's church friends who've been like a family to her."

Mister Versuch gave them an ambiguous look but nodded his head.

"Okay" he replied but his face showed he was averse to the idea. "Follow me" he told them.

They went to the elevator which took them to the bottom floor where they disembarked and continued following after the man who hurried down the hall. Andrew made loud gasping noises as they went.

The hall was deserted and it flashed through Paul's mind Mister Versuch could have been just about any one; a real heavy who might not have been altogether above-board. He realized it was silly to have such thoughts but with all of this talk about some drive to exterminate the elderly, Paul was already feeling a little spooked.

Young, Mister Versuch turned the corner and disappeared into a room and Paul was right behind him, followed by patriarchs of his church.

Paul was surprised to see their Senior Pastor, Barry Guire was one of the two men inside of the office. When the big man, Barry wrestled out of his chair to greet Paul, he sighed,

"Oh, Paul; it's foolish to drag the entire church into Harriet Carter's private affairs! I thought you'd have more sense then to turn Harriet's exclusive matters into some open-door spectacle."

Paul immediately felt put down. Roosevelt interrupted the senior pastor.

"I believe the first church, in the book of Acts, shared all things in common." Lorraine, who lead her sick husband to a chair, muttered, "It's long past time for our church to bear each other's burdens." she declared.

"I'm impressed by your demonstration of support, however, there's no need for you to trouble yourselves!" A man behind the lone desk in the room, stood up and hurried to greet them, crossing the room, extending his hand. He gave them a broad smile as he went on,

"While Mrs. Carter still owes this hospital seventy-five thousand, a debt she was unable to pay because both Carter's afflictions devoured their life's savings, the new legislation called, Universal Health Care will cover the cost." The man told them, radiantly.

"Universal Health Care" Paul asked. He saw the man nod, still grinning from ear to ear as he leaned on one side of his desk,

"Pastor, I'm Robert Costly, you may call me Bob," he said and continued, "The new legislation just came across my desk today. It also includes vaccinations to prevent this epidemic which seems to have afflicted the older citizens of our community; in fact, senior citizens through out the country."

Bob gave Andrew and Lorraine Martin a compassionate look and said,

"The antidote will prevent this illness."

"This is great news, Bob!" Barry said and he sounded very pleased. Lorraine shook her head profusely,

"No way in hell!" she said.

Chapter 4

With Harriet's dog in custody, Paul drove his car onto the cement driveway which lead to his two-car garage. The garage door was opened and he slid his car nicely into its usual spot.

As Paul opened his car door Harriet's dog was fast to disembark and scramble. Which way he took off was impossible to really ascertain for he'd managed to swiftly disappear.

He thought he heard his neighbor's dogs bark, though. He never guessed one little dog could cause so much trouble and he felt new respect for dog owners everywhere.

As he made his way out of the garage he was met by his next door neighbor, Archie Petersen, with a restrained Toby.

"Does this thing belong to you?" the heavy-set man asked, chuckling as he handed Toby to him.

Paul was grateful for Archie's kindness. Hours earlier, when he started the day, the dog was the last thing he thought he would acquire.

"He's an ugly cuss, isn't he? Looks like the poor fellow got punched in the face!"

Paul's neighbor insulted the dog's distinguishable looks with a laugh.

Archie Petersen owned two beautiful Alaskan Malamutes. Paul felt sheepish about Toby's appearance. His short coat, head and tail couldn't compete with either one of Archie's strong, well-muscled sled-dogs. The dog's mug fell short when he tried to compare it with their keen eyes and long, narrow noses.

As he reached out to take Toby from Archie, though, the dog licked his hand. This made a great deal of difference to Paul. It meant Harriet's dog was fond of him and he considered giving Toby a chance.

Paul carried Toby out of the garage and then set him down in the grass. Toby gazed up at him, barked and wagged his tail. Paul thought the little dog was going to be a handful.

Crystal was home from college for the summer and Toby wouldn't really have a lot of time with her. Right now she roamed somewhere about with Gage, Archie's son. Everyone knew they had strong feelings for each other.

Erin was interested in other activities like soft-ball. Cadence was much too young to take care of Toby. Paul was sure Kastanje would point these important facts out sometime after she gained knowledge of the dog.

"I really hope they do," Paul said but he sounded uncertain.

Kas, which was short for Kastanje, was busy with her career as a prominent lawyer. They were an active family, each of them preoccupied with other activities. Surely Harriet hadn't clearly thought things through before she appointed the Scott family as Toby's caretakers.

Paul brooded as he watched the dog lumber up his wide flagstone footpath and over to his Catmint bushes he hoped Toby wouldn't eat or relieve himself on. It took a lot of time and hard work to grow such healthy Nepeta Mussini bushes with their attractive blue flowers which grew at his garden's edge.

Behind him he heard Crystal's Cadillac Eldorado in the driveway. He turned to watch Crystal and Gage slide out from the front seat, and Erin from the back. Toby's appearance tickled Crystal and she exclaimed.

"Hey dad; How did you ever come by such an ugly dog?"

"He's not ugly," Gage disagreed with her.

Paul glanced at the attractive young man who stood shoulder to shoulder with his dad. It seemed like, maybe, Gage grasped the unique possibility of having a pet like Toby. His hopes were dashed once more when, upon closer observation, Gage called out,

"No, scratch that; He is ugly!"

Paul arrested the victim of their parody and held him. Erin saw Toby and immediately fell in love with him, though.

"Dad, let me hold him!" she begged him.

Paul handed him over to her and Toby whimpered with excitement. They seemed taken with each other and Paul felt encouraged. Maybe he was wrong he told himself. Maybe Harriet had in mind the perfect setting for her beloved pet, after all.

Chapter 5

Kas drove her new silver Viper into their two-car garage and she was disappointed when she didn't see Paul's beige Lincoln Navigator there, too.

When they went their own separate ways earlier in the day, Paul said he was going to the hospital to be at Harriet Carter's side. As far as she knew, it was the only activity on his schedule for the day. She'd just assumed he would be there when she got home.

Poor Harriet, she thought. She wondered about the ailing woman and if she still clung to life. Like a drowning swimmer, wrestling against the water's course until finally swept under it's waves.

Kas gazed at five-year-old Cadence, fast asleep in the passenger's seat. In these close quarters she heard her rhythmic breathing. Cadence had missed her afternoon nap in order to make it to her piano lesson on time and Kas imagined she was well worn out by now.

She didn't see the spectator who lingered in the darkness in one particular area of their garage, paying extreme attention to the pretty lady in the cotton dress with spaghetti-strap sleeves and the little girl beside her. He didn't make any noise. He just stared at them, watchful and silently amused by their demeanor.

Kas thought maybe no one was home. She knew Gage and Crystal went with Erin to her softball game and then they planned on being home the rest of the day. Maybe upon seeing their father's sorrow over Harriet's worsened condition, they had pulled strings, negotiated and did just what comes so natural for two teenage girls, sweeping him away in efforts to brighten his saddened frame of mind. Kas smiled at the concept; one couldn't easily contemplate death in a house full of animated females.

She unfastened her seat-belt and opened her door. She was quiet as she slid out of her brand new Viper. She needn't awake Cadence just yet, she thought.

The exotic sports car with 510 horsepower engine under the hood was extravagant and even Kas thought so. So what if it didn't fit the image of a

Pastor's wife? Neither did she and her Dodge Viper was a blatant statement of this.

Still hidden in obscure shadows, the spectator moved closer to get a good look at the car's upholstery. Impressed with the all American sports car, its ability to deliver breath-taking performance, its rich, black upholstery and bucket seats, the watcher mused.

Careful not to disturb Cadence, Kas didn't close her door all the way, but hurried around to the opposite side of the sleek convertible and gently pulled open the door. Once open, she worked to undo her little girl's seatbelt.

Careful, the spectator thought, *We mustn't wake the child.*

"Mommy," half asleep, the adorable honey-blond cherub moaned.

"Shh; we're home, Honey. Go to sleep. Mommy will carry you," Kas whispered to her and Cadence almost fell into her arms then.

She gathered her from the seat and turned and pressed her back against the door to close it. She thought she should leave the garage door open for Paul and their girls. There was no telling when they might return. Kas carried Cadence from the garage to the house. The entity watched but did not follow them.

With Cadence in hand, Kas struggled to slide open the back door and then cross the threshold. Cadence lifted her sleepy head and saw her sisters across the room and seated at the square kitchen table with white cloth. Crystal and Erin sat across the table from each other and before both of them there set a bowl of something hot. Steam escaped out of the deep dishes and advanced through the air and over their heads.

Kas caught the aroma of the chili Paul had made. There was one dish Paul could make better then any one else she knew. His chili was exquisite.

"Hi," Crystal called to them. "We thought you would be home hours ago."

She glanced at the clock which hung on the kitchen wall near them. The round clock with *Kastanje's Kitchen* written on it, told her it was already after six p.m. She'd promised to meet Gage at their pool at seven. Gage said he had a surprise for her and she was curious as to what it might be. She left the table and headed for the sink with her empty bowl and utensils in hand.

"I didn't think they would be home hours ago," Erin called to her sister as she added even more saltine crackers to her bowl of chili. "I knew Mom had Cadence and was taking her to her piano teacher's today." Erin said. She felt rather privileged to have information which Crystal lacked.

Kas gazed at her spacious and spotless kitchen; the huge windows sparkled, so did the everglade green and jade diamond shapes, ceramic tile. She felt grateful for Neva Paloma, her cleaning lady. Neva spoke mostly Hispanic and very little English and she didn't drive but traveled everywhere by bus. No matter the weather, Neva was there once a week to clean their home.

Kas saw something sneak out of its hiding place and follow Crystal across the floor. It was something ugly on four legs.

"What on earth is it?" Kas shrieked and pointed to the dog.

"According to Dad, it's our new pet," Crystal laughed at her Mother's averse reaction to him. "Apparently, at this time, there's a shortage of attractive dogs, so, Dad brought home the next best thing." She went on. "At least it's not robotic." Crystal made a grievous face,

"I deplore robotic dogs! They are hideous!"

"Well, at least, a robotic dog wouldn't smell, or trek dirt across the floor, or collect fleas." Kas could list at least a dozen reasons why a mechanical dog would be so much better than this misshapen creature. Wide awake now, Cadence squirmed in her arms, so, Kas put her down.

"Mom!" Erin got to her feet and groaned. "We're going to keep Toby! Dad said so!"

Quite often when Erin disagreed with one of her parent's, she would pit the other against him or her too. This was especially true when it was something like Toby who meant a great deal to her. To Erin Toby was a poor but adorable vagabond who needed their attention.

"Besides, Mom, I think Toby's a Christian dog!" She tried to persuade her to see the light.

"Christian dog or not," Kas answered her. "Toby is going on his own collar and leash outside." She gazed at Erin's heartbroken look and added, "I think Toby would appreciate his very own collar and leash, Erin. You know, it would give him some prestige around here!" She explained to her.

She tried to remember where she had put the items which Paul's older brother, Matthew had left behind him when he came to visit them last Christmas. Matthew had a large Labrardo Retriever who weighed 75 pounds and stood twenty four and a half inches tall.

He was a large part of Matthew's life and he wouldn't travel without him. Erin was a lot like her uncle.

Kas thought she could recall hanging the collar and leash in the garage on a hook near Paul's hunting gear. She turned toward the door and started on her way to fetch them when the telephone rang. She stopped and turned toward the loud jingle.

Erin shouted,

"I'll get it! It must be my umpire. Finally, he's going to apologize to me!"

Kas looked at Crystal who labored to get Cadence a bowl of chili and then seat her at the table.

"Why does Erin's umpire owe her an apology?" She wanted to know, gladdened by the fact Crystal could be very helpful at times.

"He made a wrong judgment which cost Erin's team the game today." Crystal told her as she put the bowl on the table and then helped Cadence up to her chair.

"Oh," Kas groaned and shook her head at Erin's problem. While it wasn't the most traumatic thing she'd ever heard, she knew what an avid player Erin was and how much winning meant to her.

"It's Dad, Mom," Erin said with disappointment. "He says he wants to talk with you." She told her as she gave her the receiver.

"Hello?"

"Hi Babe," Paul said. His voice sounded soft and contemplative as he went on. "I don't know when I'll be home. Rosie Schuyler and his merry band of geriatrics think Harriet's death was part of some cold calculated design to rid the world of seniors."

From his Lincoln Navigator, Paul stared at Harriet's house as he spoke on his cell phone. Roosevelt was already at the door of her house and he was determined to enter it.

"Then she did die? I wondered what had happened. Finally, it's over, Paul," Kas answered him with a lump in her throat. Harriet's battle with cancer had been so horrendous. "All of her pain is finally behind her." Kas breathed a sigh of relief.

However, she didn't understand Roosevelt's response to Harriet's death. He was an older citizen and she supposed the sad deaths of three people from his peer group severely unsettled him.

"Yes," Paul agreed with her. He wished Rosie had thought so too. Paul wished he was at home with Kas and his daughters, instead of being there, with Roosevelt Schuyler who now seemed completely derailed.

Chapter 6

Paul ended his conversation with Kas while he gazed at the backside of Roosevelt who stood at Harriet's door trying to unlock it.

His key didn't seem to fit the lock though. Paul had another one with him which did fit the door but he was reluctant to assist Roosevelt. However, as he opened his car door and slid from the seat, he whispered a prayer: *Once more, God, I seem to be between a rock and a hard place; please grant me wisdom here, All-knowing Father.*

When the elderly man, all alone now, turned to look at him expectantly he sent one more prayer to Father Providence. Finally, reaching Roosevelt, he gave him a puzzled look.

"Just what is it you hope to find here, Rosie?" he asked. It was a crazy mission and Paul was sure it would prove useless, a huge waste of their time.

The old man breathed hard through his nostrils,

"What's killing my friends and me," he answered and he seemed vague.

"You think you'll find this here, at Harriet's old address?" Paul asked as he stuck his key in the lock.

The white curtains on the window next to the door were pulled closed, as though Harriet were inside and merely asleep rather than her body being at the town's morgue and in the stages of preparation for it's grave.

When Harriet learned her cancer was terminal, she said she wanted Paul to see her plot. He recalled the day they visited it. It was a bright summer day but it paled in comparison to the smile on Harriet's face. With light-heartedness she said, "I will be buried right next to Charlie, the best place on God's green earth!"

Harriet had come to terms with death; she wasn't afraid to to die. In the end, it was the only way out of all of her misery.

Roosevelt's key probably would have opened Harriet's front door had there not been a hitch to it. Paul found he had to turn the lock and then, also, lift it just a little to open it. After accomplishing the task, he held the door open for Roosevelt and as he did he gazed down into the man's wrinkled face again. Seldom had Roosevelt looked so befuddled as he did this minute.

"You sound like one of those conspiracy theorists, Rosie," Paul told him, trying to keep it light. He didn't want to upset him ever further. "According to those kooks, an electromagnetic killed Harriet." As Paul followed Roosevelt through the opened door-way, he added, "Maybe she was on Bill Clinton's hit list?" Paul shook his head at the elderly man's naivety.

"You know as well as I do a horrible virus killed both Charlie and Harriet Carter. The virus which ended their lives wasn't anthrax, mad cow disease or small pox, but one which has been around for a very long time: cancer." He attempted to convince Roosevelt.

Harriet's place was just the way she had left it: brown leather sofa underneath the window with the throw pillows Paul and Kas had given her as Christmas presents one year, large console TV in one corner of the living room and, on top of it, a nice picture of Charlie and Harriet Carter together, taken sometime before either one of them ever contacted the loathsome virus.

On top of the bookshelf, filled with books, probably all written by Christian Authors, Paul imagined, there was a picture of their adopted son, Allen. He was a good-looking boy at about the age of sixteen. That was eight years ago, probably just before Charlie learned he had cancer and Allen went off the deep end. Eight years ago Allen Carter seemed perfectly alright to every one.

In another area of the living-room was Harriet's Thomas organ, right beside the Lazy Boy recliner. Paul remembered how just about every Christmas Harriet played carols for them as her friends gathered around to accompany her with their voices. The room brought back many warm and happy memories for Paul.

Obviously, it had the same effect on Rosie because he watched the old guy come to a stand-still, bow his head as if he was about to pray and then he sniffed back his tears.

Paul felt sorry for him and he made a major attempt to bridge the gap which existed between them. Death, he thought, had taken a great deal away from Rosie.

The aged man, in brown slacks and brown cardigan, with thin silver hair, short and somewhat stooped by his declining years, stood alone in the shambles of his life and he appeared to be confused by it. The Preacher placed his hand on Rosie's shoulder and he said to him, slightly above a whisper.

"We will see Harriet again, Rosie. Sure, we'll see Charlie, too, and Abbey as well. They've paved the way to heaven for us, you know, Rosie?"

Paul had a vivid memory of Roosevelt's wife, Abbey. They'd been married nearly fifty years when Abbey died in a mysterious automobile accident.

"Yes," Rosie agreed with him and for less than a minute he seemed almost serene until he moved away from Paul and marched across the room, while over his shoulder he muttered, "We'll see them again but we'll never know what killed them unless we make up our minds to uncover this brain twister now, in this life time!"

Once more Roosevelt sounded obsessed and half off his rocker, Paul thought.

"Where have you been for the past three years, Rosie?" Paul asked him through clenched teeth, as he felt his impatience rise like mercury in a thermometer on a hot day in the desert.

He followed after the demented old man who disappeared down the hallway.

"You were right there with Harriet the day her doctor told her the cancer was inoperable!" Paul shouted at him as Roosevelt made his way toward her bedroom. "You drove Harriet to her appointment! How can you now say you don't know what killed her?"

Roosevelt wasn't listening, but he was already in Harriet's bedroom by the time Paul reached the doorway. The bed Harriet had slept in, an antique bed with canopy, was very near to the wall and Roosevelt stood over it.

Paul saw him move the pillow encased in a gold-color pillow-slip. He watched as Rosie uncovered a diary Harriet had apparently hid beneath her pillow. He hadn't known she'd kept a diary there but Roosevelt seemed to have known this all along.

Paul wondered if they had any business going through Harriet's private belongings. He thought the task might better be left to Harriet's living relatives, her brother and sister who resided somewhere in Kansas. He was just about ready to grab the book out of Roosevelt's hands when he read to him what, at sometime, Harriet must have written down.

"I cannot blame Allen for the evil activities on the mountain. I will not blame Allen for this horrible virus either."

Chapter 7

After speaking with Paul on the phone, Kas tried to turn her thoughts away from the anguish and gloom of Harriet's departure. Guilt gnawed at her again. The opportunity of being real friends with Harriet was gone.

She hadn't known Charlie and Harriet Carter as well as some of the others from their Church had known them, the way Paul did, or the way Roosevelt Schuyler had. Her many clients took a great deal of her time away from the Church activities she would have otherwise attended.

Once more, she felt left out of their circle, like the new kid on the block, except she wasn't the new kid. Paul had been the co-pastor of their church in Althea for over twenty years now. She was the Pastor's wife, this was her title, but it was a role she knew she hadn't maintained well.

She looked at her sparkling-clean house and then she gazed at Toby, too and she made up her mind to collar the little terrier before he wrecked her spotless house. She harnessed him;

"Okay pooch," she said nicely but firmly. "Play time is over and it's time to lay down some rules." She was judicious.

Despite Erin's sad face she went to the door with Toby in check. He didn't seem to mind the situation half as much as Erin did. He wiggled in her arms as though he was on his way to bigger and better things. With one hand she opened the sliding door and once she was outside, she again encountered the stifling heat.

She took Toby to the garage, the door was still opened for Paul. She set out to uncover the leash Matthew had left behind him. She moved around her car to the shelf beside it, where she saw all kinds of odds and ends.

The spectator wasn't hidden now. After he investigated her Viper, after he slithered about in the driver's seat and tried to imagine himself as the proud owner of it, he had fled.

Her neighbor, Jessie Petersen was outside. When she spotted Kas she hurried across her back yard and over to her neighbor's garage. The slender, auburn-haired woman peeked into the garage, dimly lit by the sun's difficult efforts to illuminate it.

"Kas?" Jesse called into the darkness to her Pastor's wife whom she could barely see standing at one side of the building scouting through the items which hung from hooks and lay buried on shelves.

"Archie said you and Pastor Paul have a new guest," Jesse said, wanting to see the four-legged beast Archie described to her as being *ugly as hell*.

With caution, she entered the garage, not knowing what she might discover for Archie hadn't given her details. He didn't say if the dog was big or short, frisky, friendly, or mean. He just said the dog was ugly.

"His name is Toby." Kas called back to her as she hunted through the discarded items on the three shelves before her, each shelf directly above the other. Finally, she discovered to her happiness, the red collar which she could make fit the white dog with black spots if she cut it down some and pushed new holes in it. Beside it was the matching red leash, too.

Jesse was close enough now to get a good look at the animal Kas held.

"He's not so very ugly," she blurted out. "No-sir-ee," she said, reaching forth to take him from her.

Kas gave him to her. She was tempted to tell her, it wouldn't cost her a thing to take him home with her, but she thought better about it, and held her tongue. After all, Erin had developed strong feelings for the grungy animal.

"Why you're adorable, aren't you, Toby?" Jesse seemed really taken by him. "I've asked Archie for a smaller dog at least a hundred times," Jesse told her. "His malamutes are way too big for me to pamper," she explained to her.

Suddenly, Kas remembered about an hour ago, before bringing Cadence into the house, she had left the Viper's driver-door opened. While Jesse made over Toby, she went to close it while it was on her mind.

Jesse followed along behind her and continued making over the dog.

"If I had some sweet pup like this, well, I imagine, very soon he and I would be soul-mates!" Toby licked Jesse's face.

Being soul-mates with a dog was beyond Kas's ability to grasp, although she did have very strong feelings for her Viper. It was easier for her to imagine being a soul-mate with her all-American sports car.

As she bent over and stuck her head inside of the car, she saw a slip of white paper which lay folded on the black cushion. She was meticulous with her Viper and picked up the piece of paper to remove it and toss it away. Then she was careful to close the door, being sure to lock it, too, this time.

She was somewhat curious as to what she'd written on the paper; maybe one of her client's names, or some particular address, maybe even a telephone number or a grocery list?

Unfolding the note, she saw the coarse script. The writing was not her own and the words unnerved her:

"The rattlesnake has long been watching. Guard your treasures and in particular, take great care of the children.

Kas tried hard to make herself believe the note wasn't addressed to her. The scribbler hadn't written her name anywhere on it.

The note said the *rattlesnake* was watching. The rattlesnake had *long been watching*, in fact. She wasn't fond of snakes, especially not rattlers. They were not only obnoxious, but they were also deadly. They were similar in nature to the virus which killed Harriet. She leaned against her car for support and re-folded the note exactly the way she had found it.

Jesse went on and on about how much she adored Toby and Kas didn't hear a word of what she said. She gazed at her neighbor and the woman thought she was paying attention to her but she wasn't; her thoughts were somewhere else, far away.

There was one man, a fiend actually, who preferred being called *Rattler* to anything else. She had the unpleasant experience of once knowing *Rattler*. Once, a life time ago, she was familiar with Rattler's defiant, undisciplined ways. They were gross enemies. She stiffened with fear and swallowed hard at the mere thought of him.

She looked past Jesse and Toby to the road, the street upon which they lived. The hard black-top surface, the houses, all very nice houses; it was an affluent neighborhood. Rattler was dead and therefore, he couldn't very well be watching her or the children.

On the other hand, it was just as hard to believe a rattlesnake would observe them. There weren't any rattlesnakes on this street, this cherished and lovely street where they were surrounded by friendly neighbors like Jesse Petersen. No frightening creatures were hiding in her neighbor's yards, or inside of their homes.

She and Paul had lived on Victoria street for twenty years now. Archie and Jesse had been their neighbors for almost as long. Jesse said,

"Well, if you run across any more homeless dogs like Toby, be sure to let me know." Jesse smiled and gave the dog back to her and Kas returned her smile,

"Sure Jesse." she told her, "I'll talk to Paul. I'm not sure where he picked him up but maybe there are others just like him."

Chapter 8

Wesley Versuch knocked at the door to Daphne's suite. He hadn't any appointment with her and she wasn't expecting him. He had a tough time curbing his excitement over the wonderful way things were going though. He wanted to fill her in now.

He wanted to tell her of the gratitude he felt for the red dragon. The red dragon controlled all of their activities and he made excellent progress too. Just as they had hoped, people were dying, dying for Chimera.

Not only so, but he thought the dragon had a great deal to do with the fact he'd landed a position as the assistant to the CPA at Mercy Hospital. That was no stroke of luck, but divine intervention, he thought.

Wesley was dressed in a black suit and tie now and he held a boutique of red roses in his hand. He wanted to make a favorable impression upon the attractive she-devil.

Inside her suite, Daphne sat at her desk, before her computer and sipped Pepsi through a straw. The paper cup she held with the golden arches was from MacDonald's and one of her associates had brought it to her.

"The door's open" she called out. "Come in," she said with glee.

Wesley opened the door and immediately he saw Daphne's sparkling green eyes glance up at him. He went to her desk and offered her the boutique. In return she gave him a smile and took the roses,

"Red roses?" she inquired. "Red, like the blood flowing through out the valley now, Wesley?"

He watched her set her cup down as she stood up, left her desk and went about looking for a vase for the flowers. She found one, a crystal clear vase. She then brought them back to her desk and set the flowers down on top of it.

"I've carefully observed the way things are going in the the valley," she told him as she studied her computer. "People are making generous contributions to our new world, don't you think?"

33

"It's what I came here to tell you" Wesley said.

His entire countenance beamed. Daphne could tell just by looking at him how ecstatic he was over their success.

"It was just a matter of time, Wesley" Daphne laughed. "The new legislature was a brilliant idea, congratulations to the dragon. I'm concerned they might have introduced the vaccination to prevent the disease much too quickly though. People haven't had time to despair yet."

He read the disappointment on her beautiful face.

"They have to be made to feel completely hopeless against the pandemic, first. Do you know what I mean?" She gave him a questioning look.

He nodded his head.

"I believe so" with meekness, he responded. "You're afraid if they aren't suitably prepared with the worst then they might not respond favorably to the antidote?"

Daphne gazed at him, slid back in her chair, smiled and said,

"Yes, only I wouldn't have used the word afraid. I'm not afraid, Wesley. I've never been afraid of anything." She lifted one eyebrow, gave him an artic look, but motioned for him to sit down.

"Have a seat" she told him.

Wesley blushed at the mistake he'd made. He hoped his mistake wouldn't be held against him. She had the power and means to make his life unbearable. As she suggested, he sat down in the chair across the desk from her; swallowed his dread and loosened his tie.

"Bob saw how debilitated the old man was and he was moved with compassion for him and his wife too." Wesley attempted to explain to her the actions his executive took when he saw Andrew and Lorraine Martin and the way Andrew suffered so severely.

Daphne swiveled in her chair, then picked a piece of lint off the red, sleeveless blouse she wore.

"Bob Costly jumped the gun" she replied. "Lorraine Martin let him know it, too."

Wesley hadn't any choice but to agree with her. He was alarmed at the way she watched them so closely from her pedestal on the mountain. They couldn't afford to make any more mistakes.

"We've killed people, Wesley," she endeavored to explain to him. "We will kill as many people as it takes to establish Chimera. I believe your Uncle, Leopold Versuch, approves of our endeavors, the way we're going about it."

She laughed. "Can you imagine his exuberance as he watches us from his crevasse in Hades? Why, Leopold must be elated by all of our bloodshed! Would you not agree with me?"

"I would agree" Wesley said softly.

"Our ambition, however, is not bloodshed" she informed him."We aspire to give our new world to the youth, to share it with them. We are establishing Chimera for the able-bodied remnant"she said.

He saw the gleam in her eyes, the unfathomable depth of sheer satisfaction which brightened her face. She went on,

"The youth who well-deserve it,those whom we've educated in our schools and universities to equip them to be worthy caretakers of Chimera. Do you understand, Wesley?" She shifted in her chair and looked at him intensely. She saw him smile,

"I do." He surely did understand and nothing could have made Wesley so happy as his thoughts of Chimera. Wesley exclaimed, "I would do anything to realize Chimera!"

"Anything?" Daphne asked, and fixed her eyes on him.

Wesley repositioned himself, sensing the seriousness of his deportment, his duty to proclaim complete loyalty to Chimera.

"Yes, indeed, anything" Wesley stated without reservations.

"You would kidnap Pastor Scott's children and bring them here to Mount Gaspar, to me, to our community?"

Although abducting children was something Wesley had never done before, this was no time to hesitate. Therefore, he stated emphatically, "of course, I would!"

Chapter 9

From the doorway Jesse gazed at her son's strong, sturdy frame. Gage wore only his green swimming trunks and she admired the bronze tan he had picked up during the summer.

When Gage noticed the brown-eyed, auburn-haired woman at the door he smiled and invited her into his bedroom.

"I plan on doing it tonight." Gage confided in her. "I'm going to ask Crystal to marry me!" He was excited.

Tonight, beside Crystal's swimming pool, underneath the stars, he would ask her to be his wife. He had very few doubts she would say anything but yes. They had been neighbors as long as he could remember, and now they also attended the same University in Colorado. He couldn't picture his future without Crystal in it, and for years he had planned to ask her to marry him. Tonight, though, was his perfect opportunity.

Jesse worried a bit for him and wondered if he was old enough to obligate himself. There was never anyone else, and most of his life Gage had shown strong feelings for the girl next door.

"Are you sure you're not rushing things a bit?" Jesse asked him as she leaned against the white dresser in the slate blue bedroom.

There were posters on the walls all around them. One poster of Archimedes, another of Charles Lindbergh and, from one wall, Albert Einstein stared at her with a wild-eyed gaze.

By next year Gage would have his degree and he was already promised a position in Prosthetics at Desert Valley Surgical Appliances. She hoped they could wait until then before tying the knot.

"Couldn't you slow down just a little?" Jesse asked him. She sounded somewhat desperate to her own ears but it bothered her to think of how one day Gage would leave home for good.

He felt much too wonderful to let her concern for him ruin his evening though. He put his arms about her and danced her around the room. She giggled at his antics.

Gage was a younger and softer version of Archie. Archie was light-hearted once, too. Poor Archie never realized his dreams the way Gage was about to do. Archie was trapped at a job he didn't like, and after two decades as foreman, he was bone-tired. There was far too little fun in their marriage anymore.

"Don't rush things," she cautioned him. She was serious, although she had to catch her breath and her head still seemed to be spinning, even after he quit twirling her around. She looked beneath the boyish grin he wore, and the excited glimmer in his blue eyes, and bid him not to hurry.

"Gage!" they heard a loud voice call to him and Jesse was aggravated by the voice. The familiar intonation once filled her with happiness but now it made her apprehensive.

She wanted to restrain her first-born, and to plead with the owner of the voice. Just for tonight there should be no talk of what they called the *brotherhood*.

She hurried to Gage and caught his arm with her slender hand, gazing up at his face and into his eyes, which just seconds ago had sparkled with happy expectation.

Now his eyes had an altogether different look, a look which chilled her to the bone. The look of Gage's troubled allegiance to his father's treasonous lifestyle.

"Don't go," she appealed to him.

He smelled the alcohol on her breath, the scent of whiskey.

"Don't answer dad?" he frowned at her. "How can I possibly not answer dad? He's impossible to ignore, you know?"

"I know," she whispered to him.

He thought she was rather naïve to think they could just brush him off. Once, a long time ago, when he asked her why she drank, she told him she did so for medicinal purposes. At the time, he believed her.

He looked down into her beautiful face and made himself smile at her. She was so fragile, and she worried so much for him. Too much, he thought, and he wondered if all mothers were like her, or was this just another of her imperfections? Was she just an anxious and troubled woman and, therefore, she drank probably more than she should have?

He studied her, feeling some resentment toward her, and toward his dad, too. This was supposed to be a special occasion, an evening intended for blissful romance. He resented being encumbered by them now. Again, the manly voice called to him.

He moved around her to his bed where he had placed his towel, and Jesse watched him wrap the yellow and white striped beach-towel around his broad shoulders and chest. Archie had lots of hair all over his body but his son had very little, except for the mop of blond hair on his adorable head.

"I can't keep dad waiting," Gage told her in a matter-of-fact tone of voice, but she heard his displeasure.

Silently, she followed after him as he left his bedroom and made his way through the wide hallway with beige-rose wallpaper, and then through the opened doorway to their sanctum.

As she trailed after him, her anger at Archie's vulgarity griped her. How much she resented what Archie was doing to his son. He was determined to cheat Gage out of the boyish innocence of youth. Qualities which he no longer possessed.

The corpulent, balding, middle-aged man stood before their fireplace wearing a dark suit and bold tie, and he had a mixed drink in his hand, a Bloody Caesar.

There were three stairs leading down into the sanctum and Gage stopped before he descended the rest of the way. Jesse was right behind him. He could feel the warmth of her hands against his bare arms. She had stopped his descent.

A distance away from them, across the mahogany wood floor, surrounded by the pale berry-colored walls in their spacious living room with it's alpine ceiling and mahogany beams, Archie was standing. He looked like a man of notable wealth; rather blue-blooded, Jesse thought. She knew better. It was all a big sham.

"What kept you, Gage?" Archie enquired as he sipped his drink. He didn't wait for a reply as he continued, "Is your mother all prepared to mollycoddle you again this evening?" he asked, with a sneer.

Gage was uncomfortable with his father's disapproval and he moved away from his mother. With disappointment Jesse heard Gage reply to Archie's question,

"She was, but I won't let her."

He left her behind him as he made his way down the three steps, across the extensive room and over to his dad as well as his colleague.

Jesse hated how Archie had forced their son into siding with the devil. Dismayed over their tragic fraternity, she moved to the bar on the right side of the room and made herself another drink, whiskey on ice.

She would drink until, finally, she couldn't feel anything anymore. Until she became deadened to the voice of her own conscience which said to her,

'You have got to do something. You've got to get your children *and yourself out of here and away from him!* '

From a distance, both men seemed totally unaware of her, but she was paying close attention to them. Archie put his arm around Gage's bare shoulders.

"Are you going to pop the question this evening?" he asked him. He put bold emphasis on the word *question*.

"I am," Gage answered him.

"Good going," Archie wished him luck, gave him a quick hug, winked an eye and grinned maliciously.

"Thank you," Gage replied and Archie dropped his arm.

"Let's see the ring," he said with happy expectation.

Gage pulled a black velvet-lined box from the pocket of his swimming-trunks, opening it to show his Dad.

Archie whistled at the twenty-four ct platinum ring with the huge diamond set into it. He lifted his drink and toasted Gage with a flourish. After finishing a sip, he remarked,

"It's a beaut!"

"Yes, it is", Gage answered him.

He had worked all summer long at *'Wally's Electronics'* in order to purchase the stone.

It was the ring Crystal picked out when they stood in front of the jewelry store window, not long ago, and gazed at the diamond rings. He was sure she was unaware of what he had on his mind, and why he asked her which ring she liked the most.

Wally Graves was a full-fledged member of their society and, under the table, he gave Gage far more than he paid his other employees.

"No doubt, this will please Rattler very much," Archie said, as though moved with a great deal of pleasure. He lifted his head with delight and gleamed at Gage.

Archie counted on the young man more than he could guess. He knew Jesse would tell him he was using Gage to augment his bank account. However, if Gage succeeded to convert Crystal then this would satisfy Rattler. If they succeeded to satisfy Rattler, in turn, they would reap large dividends. Archie liked this thought and he continued considering their enterprise.

Gage saw the dollar signs in his dad's eyes. His father was forever trying to finagle a deal which would make him filthy rich. Gage's relationship with Crystal meant far more to him, though. He wasn't happy with his father's endeavor to compare the woman he loved to another one of his get-rich schemes.

"I could care less how Rattler Mackenzie feels about my relationship with Crystal Scott." Gage informed him, and caught the arctic look in Archie's steel-blue eyes which made him realize he disapproved of his flippant remark.

Gage thought his father's connections to the Delphians was a phase which, at sometime, he'd recover from. It was similar in nature to other get-rich-quick schemes he'd had.

He recalled his dad's short-term experience with Amway. He had insisted Gage learn all about building a pyramid of eager and happy Amway customers.

With far less enthusiasm than what his dad displayed, and with much less enthusiasm than what Archie would have preferred, Gage tried, but he wasn't any good at it. He certainly wasn't the avid salesman Archie was. Archie could sell Amway to bag ladies on park benches, Gage suspected.

"It's unwise of you to put anyone's feelings above Rattler Mackenzie's." Archie warned him. He turned away from Gage and took several steps toward the large, picture-window. Gazing through it, he saw his fifteen-year-old daughter beside the Weeping Mulberry tree, on her tire swing. Gage owed it to his mother and his sister to do all he could to cushion their lives, Archie told himself.

"I will let it pass for now but let's hope Rattler and Daphne will do the same." He told him. Archie accepted the fact Gage was a newcomer to their society, and he wasn't fully aware of their rules yet. There were obligations attached to their membership. A conscientious objector could wind up dead for voicing his critical objections to their society.

He turned to look at him again. Gage saw the frown on his face and, had he known then what he should have, his frown would have alarmed him far more than it did.

"In time you will learn the seriousness of your fellowship with the Delphians. It costs something, Son,"he admonished Gage. "It costs a lot, maybe? It's time you consider delivering something to them." He instructed him.

What he meant was it was time to give Rattler Mackenzie what he wanted, and what he desired was their next door neighbors.

Chapter 10

Crystal's parents had a classic, rectangular pool, with vinyl siding and a composite deck. At the shallow end of the pool the deck was four feet wide. On the opposite end it was much wider. Where the water was seven feet deep a large cedar wood, oval-shaped Gazebo decorated the area.

"Come on in, preppie," Crystal called to Gage. "The water is perfect!" she hollered at him.

He watched her dive beneath the water and then all he could see was her gorgeous feet above the blue of the pool and the clear of the water.

Perfect, he thought. Was anything perfect? In Gage's world, Crystal Scott was as near perfect as he could envision. Yet, even Crystal was not flawless his Dad had informed him earlier in the day. In his Dad's expert opinion, Crystal could not be perfect until she was a full-fledged member of the occult.

Gage waited inside of the the gazebo, out of the intense heat of the sun, for Crystal to resurface so he could look at her matchless face and hear her cheerful voice call to him again.

At one time Crystal had called him Gage. It was his name and he thought it a strong, splendid name, too. After they had started college, Crystal chose to refer to him much of the time as 'Preppie'.

He tried to imagine their wedding day. Pastor Paul would stand before them, holding an opened book in his hand.

"Do you, Crystal Scott, take Preppie to be your lawfully wedded husband?" he would ask her earnestly.

"Oh, yes!" Crystal would reply, "Of course! By all means! I couldn't live without my Preppie!" Their wedding guests would hear the Bride avow, see the Groom blush, and wonder who the hell was Preppie?

When Crystal resurfaced again, she was at the edge of the pool. As she gripped the tiling to keep her body in one place, she crooked her finger and gestured to him.

"Come here, Preppie", she flirted with him.

He followed his heart. Feeling like the eight-feet-tall abominable snowman, except without the long, dark hair Yeti had. Gage left the shade of the gazebo, strolled into the sunshine and made swift tracks to the pool where he knelt beside her. Then he considered the perfect shape of her head covered by the yellow bathing cap she wore, her perfect and very blond eyebrows, her perfect face, her perfect ivory complexion, her perfect dazzling blue eyes, her perfect cleavage, shaped even more perfectly by the yellow halter-top she wore, her impeccable, slender body immersed in the sparkling water.

She kicked her perfect legs and feet like a strong and perfect swimmer. She pursed her perfect mouth and he moved closer to her, to taste the sweet nectar of her perfect lips. She wrapped her perfect arms around his neck and engaged him in a tug of war. Both Gage and Crystal pulled against each other in a contest to see who would win.

Finally, he extracted her from the pool but she did not let him go. Inside of her arms, he was soaking wet, and she drenched everything else around them, too.

"See Preppie, didn't I tell you the water was perfect?" Crystal laughed, and then she pressed her lips against his and kissed him hard and passionately. His mind swam when he took her hand and drew her into the gazebo. He saw her remove the bathing cap she wore, and then he watched her as she shook her head to allow her sandy-blonde hair to cascade to her shoulders.

Gage had dreamed of this particular occasion for years. This specific moment when he would ask for Crystal Scott's hand in marriage. He didn't know why they called it this. He anticipated much more than her hand in marriage. What he desired was for Crystal to pledge to him her whole body, heart, mind and soul in a permanent and eternal bond.

He watched her sit down on the built in cedar bench. What bothered him was the fact he was so nervous and apprehensive with her now.

Crystal, too, was on pins and needles. Gage was so very unlike himself, she thought. He seemed so serious; so serious, in fact, he was almost grim. Gage had usually been the first one into the pool and he always managed to make her laugh with his crazy antics. Her heart went out to him now and she waited for whatever surprise he had in store for her.

However, when she saw him kneel down on one knee before her, she knew what followed was not something she at all wanted to take part in. Tears flooded her eyes and she shook her head at him.

"No Preppie! Please, don't!" Crystal begged him. She threw her arms around him and clung to him, burying her face in his neck.

"I love you, my darling Gage!" she told him so openly. "I would shout it from skyscrapers in busy, downtown Los Angeles but, I don't want to marry you!" Crystal said and she wept.

Chapter 11

Paul stretched and stood up. He'd been at his desk working on one particular sermon for hours. He'd labored over it so long, in fact, his eyes were sore and his body felt cramped.

As he stood at his desk, he bent over and lifted the mug of coffee and took a sip. It was cold. Then he studied the pages he'd written which lay on his desk. For some odd reason he didn't know what occasion the sermon was for.

Had he written it for Harriet's funeral service, he wondered. He didn't recognize the language he'd jotted down on the numerous pages of paper. He could not have written something he could not read. Nevertheless, it seemed to him as if this is what he'd done.

"I've worked at this so long. I can identify my own unique composition, but I can't decode what I've written," Paul told himself, as he further examined the pages, but it was a mystery to him.

When the doorbell rang he didn't move to answer it. He thought someone else would get the door. He had a major dilemma on his hands. As he stood there, trying to figure out what he'd been doing for hours at his desk, the doorbell rang again. It continued to ring as though the caller had decided to lean against it.

Ding dong, ding dong, ding dong, over and over the bell chimed. It made him think of the metaphysical poem, *'For Whom The Bell Tolls,'* which John Donne had written in 1624.

"No man is an island, entire of itself; every man is a piece of the continent, a part of the main. If a clod be washed away by the sea, Europe is the less, as well as if promontory were, as well as if a manor of thy friend's or if thine were. Any man's death diminishes me, because I am involved in mankind; and therefore never send to know for whom the bell tolls; it tolls for thee."

Paul stirred from his dream and opened his eyes. He was in his bedroom, in his and Kastanje's bed. Disturbed by his dream, he had a strong desire to cuddle her. When he rolled over he found her side of the bed was empty, though. His heart raced.

"Kastanje?" he called into the darkness which surrounded him.

"Over here," she answered him. Engulfed in moonlight which poured through their opened window, Kastanje stood staring out into the night.

Wide awake now, Paul sat up, slid his feet into his slippers, stood up and removed his bathrobe from the chair. As he put it on and went to join her at the window, he asked her,

"Do you recall John Donne's poem, "For Whom The Bell Tolls?"

She was in her negligee and in her hand she held the cream curtain so she could see out of the window.

"It's strange you should ask me," she whispered to him. "I do," she told him and she quoted a portion of it. "And therefore never send to know for whom the bell tolls; it tolls for thee." She glanced at him and he was alarmed by the look in her eyes. The moon's light reflected in her blue eyes made them sparkle but it was not happiness he saw there. She looked away from him, and returned to staring out the window.

He recalled the words Rosie had found written down in Harriet's diary.

'I cannot blame Allen for the evil activities on the mountain. I will not blame Allen for this horrible virus either.'

After Roosevelt read those words to Paul, Rosie said,

"See!"

It was as if he'd just proven his point to him. His point, of course, was there was some force on Mount Gaspar which was deliberately trying to exterminate the weakest segment of their society.

"It doesn't prove anything, Rosie except, maybe, Harriet felt she was being a little too hard on Allen. Maybe he spent too much of his time on top of the mountain."

"But what drew him there," the old man questioned him and Paul didn't know enough about Allen to answer him.

"The senior citizens of our congregation are positive an alien force, of some type, is intent upon killing them."

"It sounds absurd," she whispered and gazed out of the window once more. "I found a curious note in the front seat of my car today." She told him. She had read it so many times she had memorized it and she repeated it to him now.

"The rattlesnake has long been watching. Guard your treasures and, in particular, take great care of the children." She glanced at Paul. The words she'd quoted sent shivers down her spine. "Since when did rattlesnakes start watching adults or children?" she inquired.

When she turned her eyes away from him again to gaze out the window, he wondered what was outside which seemed to hold her attention.

"What are you looking at?" he asked her as he moved closer to the window to see for himself.

"There's a strange vehicle across the street and there's a man in it. I've never seen either the car or the man in our neighborhood before!" Softly, she reported to him.

From inside the black Bentley Arnage, the spectator saw the sexy lady staring at him through her bedroom window. At least, he imagined it was her bedroom window. Beneath the moon's radiant glow, through the branches of one Weeping Mulberry tree, the spectator could faintly recognize the woman who drove the posh Viper. It was dark and, therefore, she was difficult to see, but it was her. The spectator knew it was her and he clicked his teeth and mumbled aloud,

"Hi there, Gorgeous; I'm your Phantom." He sipped the hot coffee in the Styrofoam cup he held as he tried to imagine what the interior of their home was like; where they slept, where they talked, what items they had purchased, what they had for breakfast, and how they liked the puppy; what did they call him? Oh yes, he remembered. His name was Toby. Once again, the spectator felt the ache of loneliness inside his private world and he longed for their company. In total silence, one tear rolled down his cheek. "Do not reject me but invite me inside", he begged in a low and mournful voice.

He saw the woman leave the window and he wondered if she would return to her comfortable bed. The Pastor and his wife lead commendable lives.

The porch light of their expansive, brown adobe home lit up and the door opened. The spectator was frightened, somewhat like a little mouse, when the Pastor appeared on the terrace. The righteous man filled him with dread, the Believer in the incredibly droll. The phantom fled in his black sports car like the wimp he really was.

The mysterious Bentley, with the mysterious bandit inside of it, turned the corner, tires squealing and sped toward the mountain, Mount Gaspar, only fifteen miles away from the Pastor and his flush wife's adobe home on Victoria street.

More tears managed to flood his cheeks despite his attempts to keep them back. They would have been indifferent to his pain, had they known. It seemed his offspring had forgotten the way he was hunted down like a criminal, annihilated by the calloused cop, shot through the heart with the cop's nine millimeter automatic. They extolled the cop. The morning after he was shot, the story appeared in the headlines,

"Cop Honored For Killing High Bishop of the Cabal."

The cop's name was Lieutenant Cody Baldwyn. A resident of Althea, California, a clever detective with a quick trigger-finger. The bloodhound who managed to erase Rattler Mackenzie the first time around. Mackenzie thought his death was a tragedy and yet not another being shed a single tear for him. The Bentley clipped along, upward toward the top of Mount Gaspar, going much too fast for any one else, any one else but the dead Bishop behind the wheel of the automobile. The High Bishop wasn't forced to travel this way. Unhampered by mortality, he only chose to drive a vehicle and he called it, "joy-iding". Higher and higher the Bentley sped, rounding curves at much too fast a speed. Mackenzie was on his way back to the only real love he'd ever known, the enchanting red head Daphne Orion. Daphne lived to fulfill Rattler's purposes. They'd met sometime before Detective Baldwyn killed him.

Killed him for what, for bringing a swift end to his dear, little family? Back then Cody had a wife and a little boy; the reporter, Belle Baldwyn, who just couldn't keep her nose out of his business. The news hawk merited death and in the end she begged him to kill her. It was just one of the many memorable occasions in Mackenzie's mortal life, events which now and then brought him great pleasure to reflect on.

Mackenzie had always been a cold blooded killer. When he was a kid, he killed his beloved dog, dissected him, and drained the dog's lifeless body of its vital fluid and then drank its blood. Mackenzie intended to repeat the event. He never guessed how easy it would be, how others would aid and abet him with his endeavors.

One summer while visiting his Grandmother, she begged his parents to allow her adorable boy to spend the summer with her at her cottage on the lake. Unaware of Mackenzie's faddish for murder, his parents allowed it. They left Mackenzie all alone with his Grandma as they returned to their home, sixty miles away in the Bronx.

Mackenzie's Grandma loved her Grandson. She also loved picnics on the beach and long, hot bubble baths. One night while his Grandma was enjoying her bubble bath, Mackenzie crept into the bathroom and he sort of accidentally dropped her electric razor in her bath water. It was a huge tragedy, every one said.

Mackenzie said, between sobs, he didn't realize such a feat would bring his Grandma's life to an end. People said it was an accident, after all, Mackenzie was only a boy and no normal boy would ever aspire to kill his Grandma.

Mackenzie developed a gross appetite for murder. Yet there was one thing he feared. Mackenzie feared the Pastor's belief in the Most High God.

Chapter 12

In the summer time Crystal always slept in. She wasn't under the usual pressure to awaken at seven every morning, after studying all night, to make it to her eight am first hour class. Once there, she was greeted by her teacher and ordered to dissect a cadaver.

"I think there is something here you should see, Crystal!" Erin said to her as she stood with the peach curtains pulled back, peering through the window of Crystal's bedroom.

"Don't you ever knock?" Crystal asked groggily as she rolled over in bed and pulled the covers over her head.

"You're really missing something here," Erin coaxed her and she finally piqued Crystal's curiosity. She pulled the warm blanket away from her face and gazed at the digital clock beside her bed. It wasn't even noon yet. Erin glanced at her and then invited her to the window again.

"Come here, Crystal!" she egged her on.

"You know, kid," Crystal grumbled as she wrestled out of bed and over to the window, "You really are a pest at times!"

Her thoughts turned toward Gage, remembering the last time she had been with him. How sad and disappointed he was when she told him she could not marry him. It just didn't feel right. Maybe, someday it would, she told him, although she didn't think it would ever feel ethical. She loved Gage, but more like the brother she never had, and not like a woman in love with her fiancé.

Crystal took a deep breath and brushed the sleep from her eyes before looking at what-ever it was which made Erin think she could invade her privacy. There was a brand new, red Mustang parked outside of the Petersen's house and a raging redhead at the wheel of the car. Gage had quickly moved on, she guessed, and she gasped at his ability to spring back so quickly. The woman's red v-neck blouse was cut almost to her belly-button. Her large breasts threatened to escape her low-cut blouse.

"Did you and Gage have a fight last night," Erin asked with curiosity.

"Not a fight, exactly," Crystal mumbled. "He asked me to marry him and I said no." she explained to her.

She felt feverish and also embarrassed, when her rival glanced up at her and waved. She was not likewise cordial and she didn't bother to return the gesture. Her feet felt like lead and she was frozen to the window when she saw Gage come out of his house dressed fit to kill in a gray Herringbone tweed suit, red tie and dark sunglasses. He surely didn't look wounded to her. In fact, she thought he never looked so good before. He sprang over the car's door and landed on the seat right next to the redhead.

"He got over your rejection, rather quickly, didn't he?" Erin whispered.

Crystal watched her opposition cuddle up to him. She pressed her breasts against his arm and left her red lipstick on his cheek. Then, the redhead tooted the horn before she squealed her tires and took off down the road.

Shortly after leaving his house, they started up the mountain and Daphne Orion did not slow down. She took the curves going seventy miles per hour.

Daphne and Crystal were as different as night and day. She sure could teach Crystal a thing or two, Gage thought. The Pastor's daughter was pompous and spoiled.

The wind blew through his hair and the higher they ascended, the more thrilling the ride became. She drove as close to the shoulder of the road as she could get. When she steered the red Mustang around the curves his pulse raced and he had the feeling they would go flying over the embankment. He could see the valley down below grow smaller and smaller.

"Poor blind and stupid Crystal!" Daphne criticized her. Her voice was quite deep and fit the image of a more mature woman.

"Rattler isn't going to like this. He's not going to like this one bit." she told Gage.

Rattler McKenzie had invited him to bring Crystal with him when he visited the next time. Daphne told Gage how mean Rattler could be if they didn't do exactly what he said. She tried to warn him.

Gage had met Mackenzie only once. It was something he would never forget. He was a master of Black Magic who terrorized his subjects and he gave him the creeps. Yet he made up his mind to hide his anxiety. It just was not macho to give way to his fears, he told himself.

"I'll tell him she had to wash her hair." He laughed. Daphne didn't appreciate his audacity.

"He will get to you, too, Gage just like he got to everyone else." She said. "Pretty soon you, too, will hear voices and swear to god the voice belongs to Mackenzie." She promised him.

She saw the color leave his face and now she couldn't help but laugh. She laughed because he was really a naïve little boy who had no idea what awful fate awaited him. He was so taken by the fast and fancy life styles they led. He was from the idiotic world far beneath them; the world each one of them came to the mountain to escape. He didn't know the mountain like she did and, of course, the grass always looked greener from the other side.

His old man had lassoed him in. She sized him up and thought Archie's boy would produce nothing of real significance for them He was much too lily-white and he'd never adjust to Chimera. His clean hands and virginity excited her for one reason alone. She longed to debauch him. She had already made up her mind how she would do it and it wasn't going to be difficult for her either.

Chapter 13

After stopping at the stop-sign, Paul made a sharp right turn onto Victoria Street. It was a nice, clean safe neighborhood, and Paul thought a lot of his neighbors,too. There were no rattle snakes on Victoria street; no such vicious reptiles lurking about, watching them, and he assured Kas of this, too.

The house across the street from him was owned by the bachelor, Mark Mandarin. He was seldom ever home. Paul thought he worked in New York and only came to the desert on weekends and holidays because he enjoyed the hot, dry climate.

Paul slowed down and parked his car along-side the curb. As soon as he got out of his vehicle Archie called to him.

"I tried to gain his attention," he pointed at the young man who was circling Paul's driveway on an old beat up bicycle. "He ignored me though," he shrugged as if he couldn't understand why.

"He came to visit his dog." Paul said.

Archie had deceived the Pastor. Maybe it was blasphemous, but it didn't matter to Archie.

"Oh," Archie said, and gave him a puzzled smile, "So, he's the person who gave you the ugly mutt?" he chuckled. The actor in him was bucking for an award.

"No, his mother gave him to me." Paul further explained but wondered to himself why he bothered. Finally, Paul's neighbor excused himself and strolled away.

Paul stared at the familiar figure in his white-washed cement driveway. He saw him gaze into the sky as though searching for something there. Allen had spotted Screech and with intrigue he watched the raven soar high over their heads.

"Allen," Paul called to him, "Did you come to visit Toby? Would you like to see him now?"

Allen turned his gaze from the sky to Paul and stopped the twenty-seven-inch bicycle with his feet because he didn't have brakes.

"Is he here?" the young man inquired. Harriet's Pastor, Pastor Paul Scott mistook Allen for a lunatic and Allen saw no reason to convince him otherwise.

"If you follow me," the Pastor directed him, "I will show you where I think Toby might be!"

Allen droped his bicycle, leaving it behind him in the driveway. On his way, he paused once to gaze at Mount Gaspar from Pastor Paul's backyard. It was the closest he had been to the mountain for some time. The mountain seemed more like home to him. The only home Allen had, now, for Harriet was buried at Desert View Memorial Park and Cemetery.

Allen thought about the people he knew who lived on the mountain and, in particular, he thought about Daphne Orion. The last time he'd seen the gorgeous redhead. How she'd explained the chemtrails to him. The chemtrail's grave affects upon the less healthy and frail of their society.

The pastor lead Allen to their kitchen door, and through the sliding glass window, he saw Toby. The dog waited on the kitchen tile floor for him. He wagged his tail with wild enthusiasm.

Paul removed his key from the pocket of his blue denim jeans and inserted it into the lock.

Seconds later Allen fell upon his knees beside the dog and gathered him into his arms. Toby licked his hands, ears, neck and face. He was a real bundle of energy.

"Mrs. Scott is bound and determined to keep him outside," the Pastor told him as he watched the young man gather up Harriet's dog in his arms. The dog was all he had left of his adopted parents now.

"Erin is opposed to keeping Toby outside and she and her mother go round and round about it all of the time." Paul told him.

Suddenly, Kastanje appeared from the driveway. She caught her breath and said to the young man, through the screen door,

"Allen, I am so very sorry but I just ran over the bicycle you left parked in our driveway!"

Paul looked at her. He really hadn't expected her home until evening. She was supposed to be in court, he thought.

"I'm completely serious; I just hit Allen's bicycle with my car!" She repeated and wondered why her message failed to raise any appropriate response from them. She glanced at her wrist-watch and continued.

"The girls went to Erin's game and won't be home for another couple of hours. Meanwhile, we could go get another bike for Allen?" It was a brilliant idea, she thought.

Allen swallowed the lump in his throat. He'd always found the pastor's wife beautiful but bewildering. There was something about her, something he couldn't quite put his finger on. Something which at the time, escaped him.

"Can I take Toby with me?" he asked.

Allen could share nothing about the cult only fifteen miles away from them. If he said anything about the Delphians Rattler would rattle. Even from this distance they would witness his venomous anger.

Yes, he should definitely take the dog, Toby, along with him. It would be good for him to accompany them to the department store, she said. Well, not in those exact words. Maybe he made too much out of the simple nod of her head.

"We'll take Paul's Navigator," she said to them, and they let her lead the way. "It's big enough for a brand new bike!"

Paul wanted her to drive, and he turned in his seat to gaze at the way Toby responded to his owner's every touch. He didn't know how he could separate them when the time came today for Allen to leave. He didn't ask Allen about what Roosevelt had discovered in

Harriet's diary, or if and why he was attracted to the mountain. He didn't want Allen to even know someone else had been snooping through Harriet's private belongings.

Toby was content and never left Allen's lap. Not until they arrived at the store and they left Toby behind after telling him they would hurry back. The dog made no comment which they understood.

Allen looked over the plain two-wheel bicycles. All of them were new and so much better than the one Kastanje had hit with her car. She actually did him a favor, he thought.

She called his attention to the bike she liked. It was a twenty-six-inch men's red and white Mountain bike with an HG-22 Derailleur. She told him it was a steal at two hundred and ninety-eight dollars.

Allen was shocked by the price tag. He immediately wished he had something to give her in return. He had no employment, though, and he didn't have a dime to his name.

"I have nothing to give you," he grumbled. He badly wanted the bicycle. It would be his only mode of transportation, at least for the time being.

"Don't worry about it," she told him. "I just want to see you on a nice, safe bike! After I ruined the one you rode, I'm the one who owes you!" she explained.

He watched her take the bicycle in hand and gently boot it's kickstand.

"I've never had such a beautiful bike before!" Allen told her. She was so gracious to him, he thought. Grace was something he knew little about. There wasn't any such thing on Rattler's mountain.

"Do you like it?" Kastanje asked him with excitement in her eyes and voice.

"I love it," Allen exclaimed.

"Okay!" She smiled at him, "Then it's yours!"

After she purchased it, Paul carried it to the car and carefully placed it inside as they watched. Once more, inside of Paul's car, they drove down Foothill Boulevard as they made their way home again. While driving along, they engaged in conversation.

"How do they treat you at the institution?"

Allen heard the Pastor's deep voice inquire of him and he immediately felt put on the spot. The years he'd spent on Mount Gaspar had taught him a lot. How he got along with others was to travel incognito and keep quiet. He hesitated to reveal his own private affairs with anyone, including Harriet's Pastor and his beautiful wife.

"Pretty fair," Allen mumbled. However, he knew he owed them more of an explanation. After all, he and his wife had just purchased for him the Mountain bike in the back seat of their car, so Allen added,

"I've made friends there, all ready."

"This helps a great deal," Pastor Paul said, and he sounded really pleased. "You have a lot in common with the others there, then?"

Allen reflected on how the others at the mental hospital were mainly oddballs who didn't fit in anywhere else in their society. In their own unique ways, they were mavericks, too, just like himself, he thought.

"Yea, what could be better? I'm surrounded by a crowd of off beats." He managed to laugh, although he didn't think it was very funny.

"Sounds to me like a safe, healthy environment," Kastanje commented from her position behind the wheel.

"I guess," he said.

He missed his affiliation with Screech, whom he saw at intervals, but only when he was away from the institution. The raven didn't seem at all attracted to the mental hospital.

They watched a red Mustang speed up from behind them, intending to pass. "What's he doing?" Paul asked, nervously.

The windows were darkly tinted and, therefore, they couldn't see the passengers inside the car. They saw the barrel of an AK-47 which protruded from a crack in the passenger's window, though.

The Mustang sped around them. As it did, a desperado sprayed bullets everywhere. Just ahead of them, a blue Chevrolet Aveo went off the road and into the ditch.

Kas turned the wheel of the car onto the shoulder of the road and slowed to a stop. The Mustang escaped down the road but Paul saw it's license plate number was *DMB636*.

"Dear God, help me!" A woman screamed from inside of the car. "Dear God, won't somebody please help me!"

Paul bolted from the passenger's side of his Navigator and ran to her. The Aveo was covered with bullet holes. He worked to pull the female from the wreckage before the gas-tank might possibly explode.

She was not alone. There were three other people with her inside of the car: two young children in the back seat and an old man in the passenger's side. Paul pulled the driver's door open and the woman, covered with blood, fell into his arms.

"God bless you," she groaned.

He carried her small frame far enough away from the car so she would not be killed in any explosion. When he turned around to go back after the others he realized he wasn't working alone. Allen carried the two children, one in each arm. One of the bodies was entirely limp and the other was conscious enough to have wrapped her arms around Allen's neck. Only seconds after they made it from the wreckage, the gas tank exploded.

"Dad! Dad!" the brunette screamed, and pushed herself to her feet. She started to run toward the carnage but Kas caught her and pulled her back.

"Dad!" she screamed again and fell against Kas, "He was an old man," she told her. "He was just a sweet old man!" she cried.

Seconds later they saw the police car, which was followed by an ambulance. Both vehicles came to a stop at the side of the highway. Meanwhile, other cars drove past them and most of them barely slowed down. Life went on all around them.

When the paramedics came they tried to recessitate the little boy but it was too late for him.

"Gregory," the woman moaned, and then melted to her knees beside her son's lifeless body. "Gregory, my little boy!" she cried.

Paul was sure he would remember his name. The boy had a name, and a life, too, just minutes before. He imagined him riding a bike, playing with a dog, chasing after butterflies in a field of tall grass. All of these things were behind him now.

The little girl put her arms around her Mommy and cried with her. The Paramedics gently put the boy's lifeless body onto a stretcher and then covered him entirely with a blanket. The young woman and her daughter followed after them.

The firemen had arrived now, too, and Allen watched intensely as they worked to put out the fire. A desert fire could spread so easily and quickly by the Santa Ana winds and, therefore, they didn't waste time.

The young man in black cap and uniform recognized the attorney, although the last time he had seen her was under entirely different circumstances. The bloody clothes she wore now were clean and fresh then. He tipped his cap to her out of respect.

"Counselor." He addressed her, "What happened?"

Kas gazed after the people the paramedics had taken away with them and said in a soft voice, barely above a whisper,

"The red Mustang came around from behind us and opened fire with an AK-47."

She was stunned and could hardly fathom the entire ordeal they had just witnessed. "A spray of bullets hit the blue Aveo." She motioned to the wreckage a few yards away, which was in flames now.

Chapter 14

This was not another drive-by shooting amidst the flow of busy, San Bernardino-freeway traffic. This was not just another driver who, while caught up in the gridlock, had lost his patience and, with heated frustration, riddled a car with bullets. Allen knew what had happened but 'mum's the word," he told himself. He mustn't squeal.

He was numbed by what he had just witnessed: the vicious attack and the bloodshed. Jonathan Wright wasn't just another old man. His daughter must have been ignorant of her father's knavish involvement in the occult, the way Jonathan had tried, and failed, to double-cross the cabal, Allen thought to himself, but he clammed up. *Mind your own damn business, it's the safest thing to do*, he told himself.

When they reached the Pastor's home, his children ran out of the house, and his youngest daughter rushed to greet them.

"Daddy and Mommy," little Cadence called out to them. Erin arrested her flight when she saw they were covered with blood, though.

Gage looked wild and unruly. He was in the same suit he had worn earlier in the day when Crystal and Erin saw him from the bedroom window with the red head. Only now the suit was ripped and soiled. Gone were the sunglasses he had been wearing, lost somewhere amidst the bushes where he had lost his boyish innocence, too. He turned to Crystal and urgently begged her,

"Come with me, Crystal!" He grabbed her arm and tried pulling her.

"What do you mean, Gage? There is no place else to go! This is my home! This is your home!" she said as she wrestled away from him.

"There will be trouble," Gage warned her. "There will be even more trouble for everyone unless you come with me right now!" He pleaded with her and Crystal saw the tormented look in his eyes. Gage thought of the diabolical things the mountain people had in store for them, and he knew, unless he could persuade her to go there with him, they were all in grave trouble. In his mind, he heard the sound of Daphne's cruel laughter.

"She is not going any where with you, son!" Paul came forward to inform him. His voice was low, but very firm. There was no way he would allow Crystal to go anywhere with Gage. He didn't even have to think about it. Although, Paul had known Gage the biggest share of his life and, in the past, he'd had no quibbles with him; his appearance now in their front yard, his disheveled look, his forceful way with Crystal, even though she refused to comply, he could not allow Gage to have his way with her.

Allen wanted to take Gage aside and warn him if he said anything about Rattler and his followers on the mountain there would be far more trouble for them than what Gage could anticipate.

They heard the back door to the Petersen's house open and close, and then they saw Jesse make her way to them. She came onto their property and went directly to Gage, firmly taking his arm.

"Please Gage, come home!" she begged him.

On their daily walk through the neighborhood Tim and Chenoa Bailey spotted the assembly and hurried to them.

"What happened to you?" Tim wanted to know. Kas told him. It was the same tragic story she had told the police less than one hour ago. Erin remembered the red Mustang parked outside of Gage's house.

"What were the license plate numbers? Did you get a look at the license plate?"

Paul remembered.

"It was DMB636." He told her.

Erin had read the license plate numbers of the strange automobile she had seen earlier, too.

"The license on the car parked outside of Gage's today were the exact same digits!" She turned to look at Gage.

Jesse had taken Lacy for a doctor's appointment so she wasn't there when the strange Mustang was spotted at her house. She clung to Gage's arm now and wouldn't let go.

Mark Mandarin's '05 blue Cadillac Deville came down the street just then, followed by a police car. Mark had recently arrived in the neighborhood and he went directly to his house, but the other automobile continued until it reached the Petersen's driveway where it stopped and two police officers got out of the car.

They turned to look at the people who were gathered in the neighbor's front yard. The older one, with gray hair protruding from his cap, lead the younger and shorter officer to them.

"Good afternoon," he greeted them as he approached. "We're looking for Gage Archibald Petersen?" he said to them in the form of a question.

Jesse was still holding on to her son when she said,

"This is Gage Archibald Petersen."

Her thoughts turned quickly to the biblical account of how Judas Iscariot betrayed his Lord. It was better this way she told herself. It was much better than to lie and try to hide him from the police. She didn't believe Gage had committed any serious crime and, with time, they would see this, too, she told herself.

The younger, shorter officer came toward Gage with handcuffs. The older gray-haired officer told him,

"Mister Petersen, you're under arrest for the murders of Jonathan and Gregory Wright." He then proceeded to read Gage the rest of his rights as required by the Miranda Law.

Jesse's whole world started spinning around and the ground beneath her feet disappeared. She leaned heavily upon her first-born and whispered a prayer,

"No, God! Not murder, not cold, blooded murder!"

"It's alright, Mom!" Gage told her as he removed himself from her clutches and surrendered to their custody. "This is the best way!"

He knew he'd definitely spoiled things with Crystal. It was too late for them now. He was relieved he would not have to carry out their demands to drag Crystal to the mountain, too.

Inside of a prison Rattler Mackenzie and his followers would have no more sway over him.

Jesse watched the younger officer handcuff Gage. She was appalled at what Archie's religion had caused them.

Paul remembered the woman kneeling beside her little boy on Foothill Boulevard. He remembered she called her son Gregory. Had Gage really slain Gregory and his Grandfather, too?

As the police took Gage away, it was not to Archie Jesse turned. From the front yard her friends and neighbors watched as Jesse made her way all alone to Mark Mandarin's house.

Chapter 15

Kas pulled the burgundy, cotton-terry bathrobe with shawl collar closely around her and tightened the belt around her waist. She pushed strands of wet hair behind her ears, left her bathroom behind and entered her kitchen.

The Native American, Chenoa, was at the kitchen table with Erin. Tim and Chenoa Bailey owned their own wonderful outlet in Althea called Chenoa Sheshoni Toys. Chenoa was busy at the table, teaching Erin how to make cornhusk dolls, when Kas came into the room. They spread old newspapers on the table and on top of those they assembled string, scissors, water and bags of cornhusks. They both glanced up at Kas with concerned faces but said not one word and quickly returned to work.

Crystal was outside in the gazebo with Maurice and his brother, Ariel. Paul and Tim were driving Allen back to the institution. Kas glanced at the clock on the wall. It was ten minutes past ten in the evening and the day seemed pretty much a blur to her. She heard the light tap at the back door and turned to see it was Jesse. Kas always felt fortunate to have close friends like Chenoa and Jesse, but today's events had somehow made Jesse seem different to her.

Chenoa looked at the door. She thought there had been enough agitation for them in one day and it was an excellent idea to avoid any more, but if she knew Jesse Petersen she wasn't about to leave until she accomplished whatever it was she had on her mind. Kas slid the door open and the thin, dark red-head came inside.

"Got something strong to drink, Kas?" Jesse queried her.

"Where's Archie, Jesse?" Chenoa asked her in a crisp voice as she continued working on the dolls. Chenoa had known her more then a decade and she never would have guessed Jesse would cheat on Archie the way she was doing with Mark Mandarin.

Kas glanced at Erin and thought it would be better if she wasn't subjected to their discussion right now.

"Why don't you go see what Crystal is doing, Erin?" Kas said. She worried about Crystal and wondered how she was taking these grim matters. Erin didn't want to leave.

"But Mom, Chenoa is showing me how to turn corn husks into dolls!"

"We can continue with this tomorrow, Sweetie," Chenoa told her. "I want to show you how to paint them, too, and I haven't the paint on hand right now." She said with a frown. Erin hesitated to leave but went any way.

At her Cape Cod kitchen island-bar Kas mixed Vodka with Hazelnut Liqueur and Peach-flavored Schnapps and then added ice.

"Do you want one too, Chen?" She inquired of the woman at the table who felt nervous in Jesse's presence and, therefore, kept her hands busy turning vegetables into dolls. Chenoa nodded.

"I know I won't sleep tonight without some sedative," she answered her, and her dark eyes glared at Jesse. Jesse wondered how some people could be so self-righteous at times.

"Don't make me your scapegoat, Chenoa," Jesse told her. "For crying out loud, you act like Mark and I are sleeping together!" Jesse shrieked.

Kas poured the La Bamba beverage into three glasses and gave it to them.

"Both of you stop it." She reprimanded them. "We're way too close for these shouting matches!"

Chenoa and Jesse knew she was right and they both forced a smile. Jesse lifted her glass in the air and proposed a toast.

"To friendship," she said. "May ours always blossom."

"What a great proposal," Kas smiled, lifted her glass in response, and then tasted her drink.

Jesse drank hers down in one long gulp.

"I could use several more of these," she said, and returned the empty glass to the island's top. "Please refill mine?"

Kas could hardly believe her gluttony.

"Slow down, Jesse," she told her.

"Why?" Jesse shrugged, "What more have I got to lose? You don't fill my glass up, I will get it filled some place else!" she threatened. Kas hesitated, but made her another one and handed it to her.

"You have not because you ask not," Jesse mocked the Bible with a smirk. She had it with her careful plans to lead a virtuous life. She figured it really hadn't brought her anything but heartaches, anyway. Archie belonged to some far out, strange society where they targeted their first-born. It was crazy and upside down, and Jesse felt all of their lives were marked for destruction. She needed several more stiff drinks, she convinced herself.

"How is this going to help Gage?" Kas asked her.

"This isn't going to help Gage, Kas." Jesse admitted, bitterly. "You, my friend, Attorney Scott, are going to help Gage."

Kas was the only one who could help Gage, now, because she and Archie had both miserably failed to help him.

"Please help Gage, Kas!" Jesse begged her. Tears spilled from her eyes and she bit her bottom lip in despair.

Kas would never refuse to help Gage. Jesse would have continued to hound her until she agreed to do something for him. If she even sounded reluctant it would worsen Jesse's frame of mind, she believed.

"I will talk to him," she offered her a ray of hope. "But I want you to seek help too." She told her. She was definite.

"I'm not talking about the kind of intervention you might seek from the bottle, or an extra-marital affair, Jesse." Kas let her know right up front.

She went to the kitchen drawer in which she kept important telephone numbers and addresses and removed one business card which she brought back to Jesse, who leaned against one of the stools at the kitchen island.

"You call this number before you go for a drink or turn anywhere else for comfort. If you help yourself then I will help Gage. Have we got a deal?" Her eyes looked directly at the lovely but distraught woman. Jesse took the card from her.

"I suppose so. If it's the only way." She mumbled. Her eyes examined the card Kas gave her. "Doctor Jaime Kennis?" Jesse squealed. "How is this going to help?" She waved the card in the air as if it was on fire. "I don't need a shrink! I need someone to bail my son out of prison!" she cried. Kas knew better and was ready to convince her otherwise.

"Did you know only minutes before you came to his side, in our front yard, Gage ordered Crystal to go to the mountain with him?" she questioned her.

"No," Jesse shook her head.

Kas swallowed her own terror, remembering the mysterious message she had found in her Viper. The rattlesnake was watching, mind the children.

"So, you never noticed any changes in Gage? None whatsoever?" Kas, the Attorney, drilled her. "Everything was just great until this evening when the police arrested Gage and charged him with murder?" she questioned her, finding this unbelievable. "How do you account for the fact you know so little about your own son, Jesse?" she asked her.

Jesse was tongue-tied and only managed to shake her head, addled by the interrogation.

"They will badger you in the court-room." Kas informed her. "Save yourself humility and seek help." The Counselor advised her.

Chenoa felt embarrassed for Jesse. Kas had blown her right out of the water.

The telephone on the kitchen wall rang, startling the three women who exchanged baffled looks. Who would be calling at this late hour of the night, Kas wondered as she went to the phone. Carefully lifting the receiver, she answered,

"Hello?" her voice filled with alarm.

"Good evening, Mrs. Scott," the low, masculine voice answered her. Without delay, the man continued, "You don't know me, Mrs. Scott, but I'm Peter Wolfe from the State Department of Education."

"This is an unusual time to call, Mister Wolfe," Kas told him as she gazed past her friends' curious faces and focused her attention on the clock on the wall which told her it was eleven pm. already.

"Yes, I know." the stranger said with a nervous laugh. "Mrs. Scott, your daughters demonstrate brilliant aptitudes in academics." The man said, seemingly impressed with this report.

"Thanks, Mister Wolfe, I wish I could tell you their brilliance is inherited." She tried to sound happily nonchalant, even while her heart skipped a beat.

The caller laughed again. This time it was not a nervous laugh, but heartfelt.

"Mrs. Scott, the board of education is determined to give your daughters the amazing opportunity to realize their God-given talents!" Mister Wolfe informed her with enthusiasm. "Could I meet with you tomorrow, say around 3pm at your agency, to discuss these amazing opportunities with you, Attorney Scott?" Mister Wolfe inquired of her very politely.

"Certainly" she said, leading him on, curious over the real reason for Mister Wolfe's strange and misleading call.

Chapter 16

Erin thought Chenoa's boys were cute. Maurice was seventeen and had just graduated from high school the past year. He was tall, dark and handsome, but he barely knew she existed. Ariel knew Erin existed, though, and he liked her a great deal, she thought.

She liked his Native American appearance. He stood in his swimming trunks, with a navy blue towel wrapped around his shoulders. His dark skin was even darker in the summertime. He was somewhat shorter than she was, though. With his hands on his hips, he seemed to be surveying her, she thought. Ariel was fifteen years old; Ten months, fourteen days and eight hours older than Erin, Ariel liked to remind her.

Crystal was perched on the ledge along one wall inside of the gazebo. She stared at the Petersen's house, oblivious to everything else going on. Erin knew why, and she missed seeing Gage and Crystal together. If only she could think of some way to undo all the bad things which had happened to them in one short day. Great mysteries encircled their lives, and it made Erin feel more anxious then she liked.

She watched her Dad's car roll down the street and turn into their driveway. Tim Bailey got out of the car. He carried a couple of DVDs with him, and Maurice and Ariel both followed him home to watch them. Her own Dad went into their house.

Crystal paid no attention but kept her eyes peeled on Gage's house. Erin guessed the long day was pretty much over. Maybe Gage would be home tomorrow, she hoped. She moved quietly toward the blond whose hair beautifully sparkled in the moon's fluorescent light. Erin thought maybe she was unaware of her presence and she didn't want to startle her.

She saw the friendship bracelet Gage had given to Crystal on her seventeenth birthday, two years ago. She still wore it on her left wrist. Erin knew she had very deep feelings for her childhood companion but she didn't think she was ever really in love with him. Crystal had told her as much once. Gage's relentless search for someone who could return his affections had lead him to the red-head in the Mustang they had seen parked outside of his house. Crystal felt Erin's presence and, finally, turned her attention to her.

"If Gage killed two people today, Erin," she said, and Erin saw the worry in Crystal's eyes while waiting patiently for her to finish her thoughts.

"It means I played with, and grew up with, a cold blooded killer!"

Crystal shivered, and thought of the kind of profile which would fit a murderer. Most of the serial killers she had heard about demonstrated cruel tendencies their entire lives long before they ever committed their first murder. Gage was different. She couldn't remember Gage ever really being angry, even. He was serene and sociable.

"Something must have made Gage lose his cool," Crystal continued, expressing her thoughts out loud. "And lose it enough to take down two people he'd never met." Grief-stricken, she shook her head as tears streamed down her cheeks. She couldn't understand it.

"He wasn't on drugs. He couldn't have remained at the university if they'd ever found drugs on him." She told her sister. The recent events made no sense and Crystal longed to unravel the truth of what really happened on Foothill Boulevard that day.

Erin heard a noise on the sidewalk. It was so dark she couldn't see anything, but she heard strange footsteps. Crystal heard the noise, too, and hastened to her feet, staring toward the sidewalk. She grabbed Erin's hand and squeezed it tight. Whoever it was, or whatever it was, kept moving down the sidewalk until it stopped beneath the street lamp, right in front of their house. Erin and Crystal saw the tall, lean man in red baseball cap and yellow windbreaker. The man saw them too. He turned his attention to them, but he didn't say a word. They stood very still, frozen with fear. From beneath his cap two cold, churlish eyes gawked at them.

"What do you want?" Erin finally found her voice and called to him. Crystal felt her own heart leap into her throat. What if the man was armed? What if he pulled a gun on them and shot them right then and there? They might wind up as dead as those two people on Foothill Boulevard had been. She took her kid sister's arm and held onto her.

In total silence, the man raised his right arm and pointed a long, slender finger at them. He said nothing, but he continued pointing at them. His answer to Erin's question? Crystal wondered. They may well have been exactly what he wanted, she told herself.

"Maybe he's aphonic," Crystal whispered to her sister.

"Maybe he's what?" Erin looked at her.

"Mute," Crystal explained. "Maybe he can't talk." She told Erin.

He didn't have to talk. Apparently, the man felt no particular burden to verbally communicate with them. He remained seconds longer, after he'd conveyed his message. Then he continued on his way down the street. Now Crystal was sure, whatever had taken place on Foothill Boulevard, the killer, whoever he was, hadn't operated alone.

Chapter 17

The next morning, on her way to the kitchen, Kas passed Erin's open bedroom door and spotted Erin in her room standing before her bedroom mirror with her pitcher's glove on.

"Another game, Erin" she called to her from the hallway. She wondered what mother wouldn't desire to imagine this ravishing red-head with freckles, excelling in academics.

"No, me and Ariel are going to practice this morning in the ball park." Erin said.

"Ariel and I," Kas corrected her.

She shook her head at Erin's defective grammar and thought of how she demonstrated more talent for sports than for scholastics. If one day Erin's ability to throw a curve-ball awarded her a scholarship to some first-class university, she'd go. Otherwise, she'd probably never qualify.

Erin caught the aroma of pancakes and her stomach made a low growl. She started toward the door and Kas caught her in her arms. Too seldom did she have the opportunity to embrace this animated child who was growing up much too fast. She ran her fingers over the t-shirt Erin wore and Erin laughed and hollered,

"Stop it, Mom! You know how ticklish I am!"

Kas giggled, too. She thought how happy their lives were, and how well-adjusted her daughters seemed to be. Now and then they might stray from the norm but, for the most part, they were content with themselves; pretty satisfied, even though they were not by any stretch of the imagination, geniuses.

She let Erin wrestle out of her arms. Disengaging, the fifteen-year-old inquired of her,

"Do you think I'm pretty?"

"Of course, I think all of my girls are pretty" Kas exclaimed. "Pretty is as pretty does," she added and it seemed to her she had told Crystal and Erin this more than once.

"Ariel says I'm pretty" Erin confided in her as they made their way through the hall, headed for the kitchen where Paul was making their breakfast.

"Ariel Bailey thinks you're pretty?" Kas lifted an eyebrow and gazed at her. Erin wore a red t-shirt with the words, *Go Desert Hawks!* Printed in bold white on the front of it. She also wore her blue jeans. She was a natural beauty, a genuine knockout, Kas thought.

"Yea, when he called this morning to tell me all about the move, *'I, Robot'*, he said some actress in it was nowhere near as pretty as me."

"I wouldn't know, I've never seen *'I, Robot'*." Kas replied. She also wasn't aware of how Ariel Bailey had apparently grown up enough to notice Erin.

"Whatever happened to the little boy who thought all girls had cooties?" she pondered aloud. The world was so much safer then.

"He grew up, Mom and developed a crush on me!" Erin informed her.

When Paul, with skittle in hand and wearing his apron, saw them enter the kitchen he flashed them a smile.

"Here's my two pretty girls now!" he proclaimed. Erin and Kas exchanged looks.

Erin headed for the refrigerator to remove the orange juice from it. Kas sashayed to the stove and kissed the cook. She placed a light, soft kiss upon his cheek.

"Good morning" she smiled.

With skittle in one hand, spatula in the other, and apron around his waist, Paul whispered

"Hi," in a wolfish way.

If they were stuck in routine, Kas deemed it was because they wanted to be. Familiarity was pleasing. Paul added the last pancake to the platter as Kas went to the sliding-glass door to peer out of the window at the Boston Terrier tied to the dog-house. Then she picked up a pen and wrote on the notepaper attached to the refrigerator. On his way to the kitchen table with the pancakes, Paul inquired of her.

"What are you writing?"

"Neva will be here sometime today" Kas told him. "I want to tell her to let Toby inside, out of the heat, this afternoon." She flashed Erin a look and Erin realized then that Toby was well on his way to winning her over.

70

Chapter 18

Allen had risen earlier than usual that morning. He had crucial things to do. As he rode his new two-wheeler, his sleek Mountain bike, in the bicycle lane just off of the highway, he made up his mind what he would do.

Harriet's Pastor had to know about the deadly chemtrails, how the poison was carried aboard military aircraft and sprayed over populated areas, all over the globe. How the toxins weakened their immunity systems, making their bodies susceptible to deadly diseases like cancer. The Delphians had succeeded with their attempts to kill large numbers already. With their evil chemtrails they had murdered Harriet Carter too and now Allen was alone, so agonizingly alone.

Automobiles on the highway breezed by him, ignorant of the toxins in the air. Those who knew about the chemtrails would never tell a soul for they were sworn to secrecy. They would never report the carnage. They flourished for Chimera, their utopia, their new world. But the more Allen was exposed to people's kindness and generosity, the more he realized there was very little wrong with the old world.

This was how it came about: after writing the note for Neva, telling her to let Toby into the house around noon, once more Kas gazed outside the kitchen door and to her dismay, she saw Allen outside, with Toby in his arms. Immediately, she let out a groan,

"Paul," she murmured.

Hearing her groan, Paul spun around and he too saw the visitor who stood just outside their home, at a very curious time of the day; well before nine o'clock in the morning.

Allen did not see their surprised faces, for he was busy gazing into the sky, but this time he wasn't looking for his bird. This time he was looking at the military aircraft, high over his head and the efforts the plane's pilot made to scatter the deadly toxin above the city of Althea, and above their beautiful, adobe home.

Without hesitation, Allen hurried to the door and opened it. He let himself inside, still carrying the dog in his arms. Concerned for their safety, Paul and Kas took several steps in the opposite direction, away from the intruder. Erin did not move from the table. They had no clue as to the kind of trouble they were in, Allen thought.

"Don't breathe the air," Allen told them. It sounded crazy but he was earnest. He firmly believed it was the only way to prevent them from being asphyxiated.

Pastor Paul gave him a half-hearted smile and, with a skeptical look in his eyes, he managed to say,

"We've really no alternatives, Allen. What would we breathe instead?"

Allen groped for words. He hadn't thought that far ahead yet. He had no answers for the problem, other than the one he'd already announced.

"There are more chemtrails above your home this morning," he informed them.

"Chemtrails?" the Pastor repeated him. His voice rose with irritation. "Ridiculous." he uttered. To his ears, Allen sounded just like Roosevelt Schuyler who went on and on about there being something carcinogenic in the air.

"There are no chemtrails," Paul said. Once and for all, he hoped to put an end to such ridiculous reports.

"Then what do you call the filmy stuff left by the military aircraft on the bushes right outside your house?" Allen questioned him, pointing to the door.

"There's nothing there." Paul bickered with him.

"There is, though," Allen disagreed. He tried being polite to Harriet's Pastor, but he seemed so obstinate. "I'll show you," he said and hurrying to the door the Pastor was right behind him.

They went outside and Allen put Toby down. The dog remained close by as Allen pointed the Pastor's attention to the sky and the heavy murkiness left by the plane, which had vanished now.

Looking up, cupping his hands around his eyes to block out the brilliant sunlight, Paul mumbled,

"They're different than most clouds I have seen, but they are still clouds! Just billows of drops of moisture and nothing else." he insisted.

Allen gulped, scared for the Pastor's safety; being subjected to the mysterious weapons Daphne poised against them was unfavorable to their health. He wouldn't dispute Harriet's

Pastor but, being anxious, he blurted out,

"Just to be safe, we should probably go back inside the house!" Daphne wouldn't approve of Allen's decision either. He knew she would have been quick with her rebuttal.

Kas poked her head outside of the house and, with the telephone in her hand, she called to her husband,

"Paul, it's Roosevelt and he says it's urgent." She told him.

"Come back inside," Paul invited Allen. "Have some pancakes with us!" The Pastor said as he hurried off. Allen was right behind him. Then as the Pastor spoke on the phone,

Allen went to the table, eyed the food and took an empty chair. He saw the adorable little girl who drifted into the kitchen carrying her haggard teddy-bear and rubbing sleep from her eyes.

Cadence ran to her Mommy, who was seated in one of the chairs at the table. As she passed Allen, she gave him a puzzled look, as if to say, *What the heck are you doing at my kitchen table at this hour of the morning?*

Kas cuddled the five-year-old on her lap. Allen's presence disquieted her. She felt a mysterious uneasiness, a compelling force, which would draw her to him and, at the same time, the total urge to disengage and remove herself at once, before it was too late. She buried her face in her daughter's clean, yellow hair and closed her eyes, trying to curb the overwhelming distress she felt.

"Pancakes, Allen?" the voice inquired and made her heart flutter. Erin offered the platter of pancakes to Allen. Kas watched his long, slender hands take it from her. His were not the hands of a stranger but hands she may have held at one time, or perhaps she had once caressed them. Maybe hands once caught in the cookie jar, but she had forbidden them to intrude upon her life. Hands which might well change her life forever.

"That was Roosevelt," Paul returned to the kitchen table and informed them. He eyed the young man at his table with the dog on his lap. Allen's appetite for pancakes was obvious. "Rosie said Andrew Martin has been hospitalized with the same illness which killed George Wheaten and Jenny Absalom."

Allen's incredulous proclamation now made him extremely nervous. Andrew was the fourth person from his congregation to be hospitalized this week.

Kas sat Cadence down in her own chair at the table, stood up and hurried to him. She trailed after him on his way to the door as he said,

"Now Joseph Elvio is more determined than ever to be vaccinated with the so-called preventive for it. Roosevelt is practically having convulsions over that, of course!"

In the commotion, he turned at the door to gaze at her. She wanted to reach to out to him, she wanted to tell him about Peter Wolfe and the strange interest he had in their children, how he'd asked to meet with her that day to discuss their children with her. She wanted to beg him to take Allen with him. However, she said nothing.

"It's chemtrails," Allen muttered from the kitchen table before shoving another bite of Pastor Paul's pancakes into his mouth.

"It's not chemtrails!" Paul shouted back at him. "There is no such thing as chemtrails!" he said, and he sounded so very definite.

"Something strange is going on," Kas contended, as she gazed into his eyes with perplexity.

He kissed her cheek,

"I know," he whispered to her, "I know, Kas," he repeated. "I'll call you," he said. Then he turned and left her behind him.

Chapter 19

Very soon Allen and Erin were on their way to the ball park. Allen rode his bike behind Erin's pink Mountain Track bicycle, on their way.

The Pastor's wife had a conniption fit right at first, when Erin invited Allen to join Ariel Bailey and herself, after Allen told her of the way he used to play ball all of the time, whenhe was a boy, when *'times were good'*, he admitted with a tone of regret.

"Allen is too old to spend his time following two kids around in a ball park!" Kas had exclaimed with irritation, being evasive, unwilling to state her real concerns with Allen nearby. However, when Erin explained to her how Mister Bailey would also be there, she finally relented but only after calling Tim Bailey on the phone and speaking with him.

Now Allen followed Erin as they rode down familiar streets lined by ample, affluent houses, wealthy neighborhoods where the people didn't seem to worry about scraping out a living for they bloomed in hog heaven. Or they had, at one time, before chemtrails.

The people Allen saw outside of their homes in this vicinity were older Americans, in their midyears, enjoying the ambiance, ignorant of the blight, so long as breathing. Allen hoped they would keep breathing for a very long time yet.

When they neared the chain-link fence which enveloped the ball park, Erin saw Mister Bailey's SUV on the opposite side of the fence. It was encircled by a cloud of antsy young, want-to-be baseball players. She saw Mister Bailey give a wooden bat to one boy and a pitcher's glove to another. Stopping her bike and dismounting it, she turned to look at

Allen, who was still several feet behind her, peddling toward her. Cadence reached her arms out for Erin, anxious to get off Erin's bicycle.

"Okay, Cadence," Erin said to her. "Are you ready to play ball?" She inquired of her little sister as she pulled her out of her basket and set her feet upon the ground. Cadence looked up at her, her blue eyes filled with enthusiasm, eager to give it a try.

Erin then pulled a chain and lock from the pocket of her blue jeans and secured her bike to the fence. Allen had finally caught up with her and he dismounted from his own bike.

His brown eyes surveyed the ball-field and his attention went to one lone man who sat in the grandstand. He recognized him. It was Wesley Versuch.

Just days ago, Allen had seen Wesley on Mount Gaspar, inside of the dome-shaped building and coming out of Daphne Orion's office, Wesley had stopped to talk to him. Allen was positive Wesley knew of the chemtrails and the new law called, *Universal Health Coverage*. Wesley had to have known all about the military aircraft, strange cirrus clouds called chemtrails, the occult's attempts to destroy the old world in order to build their chimerical civilization.

Allen wondered what he was doing here, in this neighborhood, on this particular day when he should have been at Mercy Hospital. He should have been assisting Robert Costly, the hospital's CPA. This neighborhood was not Wesley's turf. He had no business being here, around this crowd of blameless, law-abiding citizens.

Allen watched Erin cross the field to reach Tim Bailey and the others, with little Cadence following behind her, imitating every move her older sister made and calling to her,

"I want to play ball too, Erin! I want to be the twitcher! Please, Erin, make me your twitcher!"

Allen saw Erin turn around and give Cadence an annoyed look,

"What in the world is a twitcher?" Erin groaned.

Allen contemplated the way Wesley Versuch stared at Erin and Cadence. He appeared frightfully absorbed with them.

Chapter 20

Seated in the grandstand, hunched over and wearing a blue Italian cap, Wesley watched with decisive interest. The Pastor's kids were both engaging girls, he decided.

Erin, who was a rare and seductive fledgling, stood at home-plate, her fingers curled tightly around the bat, her body in position, ready to hit a ball over everyone's heads and into the out-field, hopefully.

The pitcher, Erin's little boyfriend, the half breed, Ariel Bailey, threw her a curve ball but Erin was ready for it. There was a loud crack, the sound of wood striking leather.

"Run, Cadence!" Erin shouted at her little sister. The ball climbed into the sky and floated into center-field.

"Go!" Tim Bailey cheered the five-year-old on.

Wesley, too, couldn't help being swept away by the little girl's attempts to make it to first base before the player in left field retrieved the ball and threw it to the pitcher, who in turn projected it to the first baseman but, by the time it reached him, Cadence had her feet firmly planted on the mound.

Leaping to his feet, Wesley applauded with uproarious noise. At that minute he was oblivious to the attention he attracted. He was so jubilant over the little girl getting to first-base, he couldn't help showing wild enthusiasm for what she had accomplished. Just then it dawned on Wesley, the little girl made him think of his lovely and precious daughter, Caroline, before she died.

A flood of memories came to mind and Wesley wrestled with his feelings, trying to stifle the emotions swelling within him and pouring forth. Tears covered Wesley's face. He returned to his seat a broken man, worse for his soul-wrenching experience. From the core of his being, Wesley's ax to grind had changed.

He'd vowed to kidnap the Pastor's lovely daughters but now he made up his mind not to follow through with the pledge he'd made to Daphne Orion and

Rattler Mackenzie, and to the whole horrible society at the top of Mount Gaspar. Wesley had needs and he would put those needs before everyone else.

He watched the little girl's fellow team-mates gather around, applauding the girl's efforts. It was hard earned recognition and Wesley's eyes swelled with tears as she received their praise. What an adorable child, Wesley thought; she melted his heart and made him feel all cottony inside. He would, indeed, kidnap the blue-eyed blond cherub, but he would not turn her over to Daphne Orion. He would not relinquish her to the occult. He would not part with her for Chimera. All the wealth of Chimera paled in comparison to Wesley's desperate ache to have Caroline, or rather, Cadence, to himself.

Without warning, Wesley felt a cold hand fasten about his shoulder. He heard a bottomless-sounding voice whisper,

"Do you think she's special, Wesley; Do you?"

The man's voice nailed the crux of his being. It was as if he were reading Wesley's mind. Wesley swallowed hard, turned around and found himself looking straight into a dead man's face.

Death had not in any way, shape, or form elevated Rattler's chilling, lightless appearance. Quickly, Wesley turned his eyes away. Turning around again, he focused his attention upon the little girl. He wondered if Rattler appeared out of nowhere in order to caution and dissuade him. He quivered at his thoughts of betraying Rattler Mackenzie. Once more, the deathly voice spoke to him,

"There are billions of children in this world, but there is only one Cadence Scott. Do you know what makes her so special, Wesley?"

Yes, indeed, Wesley knew what made her special. He closed his eyes, inhaled the strong fragrance of recall, encountered the image of his cherished Caroline again.

"This one," Rattler told him, "Is my own flesh and blood. Cadence is my grandchild, Wesley. My own lineage. Bring Cadence and her sisters to the mountain and to me, Wesley. I am waiting there for them."

Wesley wrestled with his feelings; deep within him desire fought fear. He dreaded the thought of what horror he'd encounter if he didn't comply with Rattler's instructions.

Wesley turned in his seat once more.

"What if I don't?'" he questioned, but there was no one there.

Chapter 21

Far away from the excitement of the game, positioned high over the city of Althea, on the grandiose mountain called Gaspar, Daphne Orion strolled through a botanical garden.

Clothed in a caftan of blue and yellow, with a wreath of yellow daffodils and blue forget-me-nots in her hair, Daphne walked among the healthy green-leafed trees and lush shrubs.

Honeysuckle and fox-gloves blossomed everywhere. Sunlight accompanied her as she cheerfully drifted through her private paradise.

Bare-footed and in touch with nature, she followed one particular butterfly, a golden Queen Alexandra. The queen fluttered about as though playing with the sorceress.

Humming a melody, a song by Billy Preston, *With You I'm Born Again* Daphne let the butterfly direct her to one particular apple tree with dense leaves and white flowers. Regarding the tree with fascination, Daphne found hidden amidst it's leaves, enticing plump, red apples.

The tiny butterfly floated near one of its limbs, dancing about one beautiful apple as though tempting Daphne to pluck it. She groaned as she reached for the apple situated in a branch over her head. Finally, she was able to reach it.

Bothered by the twinge of guilt she felt for taking the apple, she turned her back upon the tree and, holding the apple with both hands, she gazed at it, wishing she'd had the strength to resist. As she looked it over, to her dismay, she found the choice fruit had already been claimed by one small, green worm, though.

The diminutive creature lifted itself to gaze back at her. Suddenly, being acutely aware of its arduous situation it slithered back into the hole it had made in the apple. Daphne watched with curiosity, amazed by it's stubborn claim on the fruit.

"Daphne," a breath or small breeze signaled her. "Daphne," once more, the faint breeze called to her.

The butterfly had already flown away, the timid worm was hidden inside the apple and certainly neither one of them had called to her.

"I am here." She whispered softly and then she heard the fluid lisp and turned around to eye the rattle snake, concealed in a sprig of leafs and coiled around a branch. They exchanged glances. The rattler's cold green eyes looked directly at her.

"Rattler?" Daphne said, concerned for his welfare. After all, she was the one who had given him an afterlife. She had recreated him. He was a shape shifter, capable of altering his image. There was no end to his expertise. Nothing hampered him, nothing except the God-fearing Pastor griped him.

She wondered if, in the valley below them, Rattler had encountered the Pastor. She dare not ask him. If he had, the confrontation might have made him cross and she dreaded to uncover his foul frame of mind then.

She wondered at her own amazing ability to inspire something more powerful than herself. Her ability to bring him back from the dead made her feel almost immortal.

She reached out to touch him but he slithered back through the branches, crawling higher; he didn't wish to be so bothered by her. She supposed he had something on his mind because he seemed contemplative.

"What is it?" She lifted her eyes to gaze at him. "Please, Rattler, what is it?" she urged him.

"They say it's a statutory offense," he hissed. "What do they know and what do I care?" he clamored.

"It's not her again," Daphne shook her head at the Reptilian's fixation with his daughter.

"Why does it always have something to do with Kastanje?" she lamented. "Why is it you cannot feel the same depth of passion for me as you demonstrate toward her?" Daphne felt bitter tears swell in her eyes.

"I share your ambitions!" she explained."I comprehend your aspirations! I, and not Kastanje, restored life to you, Rattler Mackenzie!" she admonished him. In spite of her lofty position as high priestess of their extensive esoteric society, she carried on just like a jealous woman.

The snake felt some compassion for her. A twinge of sympathy for her brought him down from the tree. Coiling, winding around her, his velvety form slipped down, around her neck. Cheerfully, he slithered beneath her caftan, over vulnerable parts of her body. He knew she enjoyed this as much as he did, if not more. He heard her softly groan with ecstasy. He was totally beguiling. Eventually, he returned to the tree. His cold, green eyes examined her beautiful face, made all the more so by the total satisfaction he'd brought to her.

"Daphne, when you bear seed of your own, then you will understand what I feel for Kastanje." he illuminated her.

"Am I pregnant, Rattler?" She found her voice and questioned him. Her heart beat joyously at the thought of being so.

"Yes," he hissed. "Yes, you are indeed," he assured her. "You bear the boy's seed," he informed her. He lifted his head and smiled. It was not within his power to impregnate her. The dead could not produce life. "Go, ensnare him even further, to the point of despair." He urged her as he slithered and curled around a limb. "I am exhausted," he told her as he yawned and added, "I think I shall take a long nap. Remember, my darling, I love you, and will continue loving you throughout an eternity in hell." The snake laughed lazily before finally, closing his eyes and falling into deep slumber.

Chapter 22

Kastanje arrived at the 12th precinct, sharply, at nine o'clock in the morning. She was smartly dressed in a navy blue, pinstriped business suit. Beneath her jacket she wore a fuscia silk blouse. Her long hair was in a French braid, pulled together and lifted off of her neck with a barrette made of Black Forest gold. She was stunning. With black leather briefcase in hand she climbed the sixteen stairs to the building. The navy blue pumps she wore hadn't been broken in yet and caused her some irritation.

She'd petitioned Doctor Jaime Kennis to speak with Gage Petersen and report to her on his mental condition. Jaime agreed to do it and drove from Pomona to Althea. She assumed Jaime had left her report in her small office at the precinct.

She reached the building's towering double doors and opening one of them, she entered the building. Beneath the large beams and very high ceiling were gold-veined marble walls. Several feet away from her and to her right was a black marble statue of Harold H. Burton who was the Associate Justice of the United States Supreme Court from nineteen forty-five to nineteen fifty eight. Burton had vigorously pressed for U.S. participation in the United Nations.

Beside the statue, leaning against one wall, she spotted the detective, Lieutenant Cody Baldwyn. Wearing a long, gray trench-coat, and holding a cigarette, he appeared no more happy to see her than she was to see him. He brushed a hand through his tangled mass of blond hair, then, once more, he eyed her.

She considered the reason he might emerge out of nowhere, from no place else but the dark, chilling past. The very fact he was there meant situations had suddenly turned sorely esoteric. Somehow, subconsciously, she had suspected it. She was just too scared to admit it to herself.

Swallowing hard, she started toward him, acutely aware of every step she took, and the loud click-clack of her high-heels over the tough, linoleum floor was almost deafening to her ears. With every move she made in his direction, her body stiffened. When she finally reached him she was a bundle of nerves, and on the edge of upheaval. He fastened his gaze on the floor and didn't look up when he said,

"Attorney Scott."

"Detective Baldwyn," she replied.

Their exchange of formal greetings carefully concealed the fact they shared any relationship beyond that of merely acquaintance.

"It's been a long time", she told him, although, not long enough.

He nodded his head and took a deep, long drag from his cigarette, before snuffing it out in the ashtray beside him.

"Ten years", he acceded, looking distressed. He had aged a lot over those ten years, Kas decided. His sad-looking dark green eyes inspected her.

"You look good", he said, and he attempted to smile at her but it was a very poor effort. She understood why. He was a desolate man in his middle thirties, drift less, left with very little purpose except to hunt down and destroy dangerous men like Rattler Mackenzie, who single-handedly had destroyed the happiness he once knew.

She saw the pistol under his trench coat which he wore in the holster on his belt. His pistol had secured their safety once, but not before it was too late and Rattler had taken down both the Detective's wife and ten-year-old little boy.

"Let's cut through all of the smoke," he stipulated as he squinted at her. "We both know why I'm here."

She firmly shook her head at him. It was the last thing in the world she wanted to dwell upon. If she denied it, would it make it go away? she silently questioned. No, it wouldn't, she decided, and she nodded to him. She knew what Detective Cody Baldwyn was doing here again.

Suddenly, there was noise as Jesse saw Kas and called to her from still some distance away. The attorney and detective exchanged glances, grateful for the invasion.

Jesse hurried down the hall and Archie followed her, he looked extremely ill at ease. In a v-neck wine colored dress Jesse approached Kas and the man who was with her.

No slouch, the Detective thought, as he studied the woman. She was very attractive, although a bit too lean and probably much too fragile as well. Jesse wore sunglasses to hide her swollen tear-filled eyes. The sunglasses drew more attention to her troubled state of mind, though.

"Gage won't even see us!" she told Kas, and wiped at her nose with a wrinkled hanky.

It wasn't good news, Kas thought. It made it sound like Gage was hiding something, but what, she wondered. She lead them to her office. It was just a little hole in the wall with a sign above the door which read: Defense Attorney K. Scott. Inside there were several folding metal chairs gathered around a metal desk, and one small metal filing-cabinet beside the desk. The only personal touch was a photograph of Paul and their girls, placed on top of the desk beside the telephone. After they entered the room Kas motioned for Jesse and Archie to sit down in one of the four chairs strewn about.

Kas saw the white notepaper with black ink writing laying on top of the desk. She picked it up and quickly went over Jaime's message:

"Kas; I have talked with your client and he seemed disconcerted to me. He is isolated and reclusive so I strongly advise he should be removed from these premises and placed in a mental hospital. I am concerned, in his present state of mind, he is a real danger to himself. I believe he should be administered to by a Psychiatrist, treated for depression, and possibly schizophrenia as well. He stated he hears voices and has hallucinations. He requires medical intervention, i.e. drugs. Call me, Jaime."

Bugged by the note which made it only more clear this was no normal case, she gave Gage's mother a fleeting glance.

"This is not the kind of thing I wanted to hear." She murmured, then sighed and sat down in a chair beside Jesse. She looked at the woman beside her, who seemed to be on pins and needles, and then at the man who towered over them. His face was peaked and he chewed at his bottom lip. She wanted their permission to relocate Gage.

"I've had a psychiatrist examine Gage," she told his parents. "Her written advice is to transfer him to a mental hospital." she said, and waited for their reaction.

Jesse groaned and rubbed at her nose with her hanky. One look at the soiled Kleenex made Kas wish she had a box of them on hand. Jesse still hadn't removed her sunglasses.

Archie placed his left hand upon his injured wife's shoulder. Kas saw the gold wedding band on his finger. Archie and Jesse had been married longer then she and Paul, even. Archie must have put on several pounds through the years because the band was tight on his finger. Kas had the fleeting thought he should have it re-sized. Archie shook his head.

"Gage isn't nuts," he informed her. "No matter how many psychiatrists claim otherwise, Gage is neither insane or homicidal," he asserted.

Jesse saw through her husband's bluster, though. He always had covered up the truth, and he would continue to cover it up, no matter how steep the price became.

"Gage complained to me not long ago of having a headache. I suggested he take a couple of extra-strength Tylenols. I remember how he held his head in pain and complained of hearing voices. At the time I thought very little of it."

"And now?" Kas questioned her.

"Now I believe I was wrong to make light of it." Jesse suspected she had been wrong about a lot of things.

The door opened and Detective Baldwyn stuck his head in the room. His green eyes scanned Archie and Jesse and he gave Kas a concerned look.

"Might I speak with you for a minute, Counselor, outside?" he asked. He gave the two people in the room with her an anxious look and then cocked his head at her.

Kas excused herself, got to her feet and followed after the detective. He closed the door to make sure they couldn't hear what was said. Once more, she felt ill at ease in his presence and she thought of the letter and the Psychiatrist's reference to schizophrenia. Absurdity coincided well with the uncertainty of this case.

"I just talked with the officer who interrogated Gage when he was brought in." the Detective told her softly enough so he couldn't be over-heard.

She stood against the gold-colored wall to stabilize herself and listened carefully.

"The kid is in way over his head and apparently, he was in the car when the shooting took place. However," the Detective drew a long breath and continued, "he was not alone; there were two others in the car with him, but he won't tell them who those other people were." He put his hands in his pockets, "If they even were people," he added.

She nodded as if she understood, but she didn't, not really. The high priest of the occult was dead; the Lieutenant had shot and killed him ten years ago. He couldn't return to haunt them, or, could he? She gave him the paper with the Psychiatrist's writing on it and he quickly read it.

"That's another thing, Counselor," he lowered his voice even more, "he tried to kill himself last night!"

"What?" She gasped and he nodded at her.

"He tied a sheet to the light fixture and tried to hang himself, which is the way the warden found him this morning, passed out with the sheet twisted around his neck."

When Kas returned to Archie and Jesse, they noticed the troubled expression on her face.

"We've had time to think about the doctor's suggestion to put Gage into a mental hospital," Jesse told her.

"It's too late." Kas glanced at her. "The decision has already been made." she explained to her. "It's no longer up to us." she told them as she crossed the room and lifted the telephone receiver from its cradle. She dialed Saint Regis Mental Hospital.

"Gage tried to kill himself last night." she informed them and saw their disheveled looks.

Chapter 23

Once again she had failed to come through for Gage. She'd missed all of the warning signs. In fact, the decision for his personal safety was being taken from her and given to a

Psychiatrist at a mental hospital. She felt even more like a miserable failure. They couldn't allow her the privilege of caring for her own son any more.

Jesse glanced at the heavy-set, balding man who towered over her chair and she rose to her feet to move away from him. It was impossible to put up with his doctrine and ethics any longer.

As soon as Kas left the room to interrogate Gage, Archie sighed, loosened his tie and muttered underneath his breath,

"I hope Gage has learned to keep his mouth shut."

"I don't," she told him as she slid out of the chair and moved away from him. "I hope he spills the beans and tells them everything!" she said with her back to him. Archie had sold his own son to the devil and there was no limit to the lengths he would go now. She saw the small, empty trash can in one corner of the room and tossed her wet, mutilated hanky into it. She had no more tears to cry. Just like the container, she felt empty, and she threw her tears into the garbage can.

"The truth might set him free." She remembered the Bible verse and quoted it now.

She decided quite sometime ago the truth hadn't made her free. Maybe it wasn't the truth which had failed to loosen the chains which bound her. Maybe it was her failure to respond to the truth in any appropriate manner. Maybe it would be different for Gage; maybe Gage would find a way, at last, to loosen his chains, and break free from his dad and from the trap he had set for him. The snare which had snapped shut on his bright, youthful life and was threatening to end it now.

Archie did not reply. He slipped his hands around the back of the chair and squeezed. It was safer than fastening them around her neck. He had visions of doing so sometimes, but he didn't want her dead. He wanted her love and respect. He just couldn't make her see how they owed the society something.

She thought the sacrifice for their livelihood was much too steep. They weren't like others in their neighborhood. Others in their community were gifted enough to succeed very well on their own. Archie was not so gifted and he needed the society to provide for his rich life style.

"Did you hear me, Archie?" She raised her voice and turned to look at him. His humorless face was nothing new. She couldn't recall the last time they had smiled at each other.

"Yes, I heard you. You muttered something about truth." Archie thought of her as being extremely thick-headed. "But what do you, or any of these people, know about truth, Jesse?" he grilled her.

She stared into his cold blue eyes and listened to him continue.

"You lead your sweet little lives, relying upon your sweet little religion you've heard all about from your sweet little pastor who has blissfully blinded you to the truth!" He was civil to Pastor Paul Scott because the society wanted him and his entire family, and it was all a part of their charade.

"You're wrong Archie!" She told him. He thought she relished telling him he was wrong. She managed to do so at least a couple dozen times everyday now.

"I haven't lead a sweet little life for a very long time!" She said and she thought by now he should realize this fact but he was so ignorant to her agony. He could see no further than his desire for money and prestige. "My God has given me enough truth to see into your heart, Archie, and it's as black as coal!"

She felt the room swirl around her and the hard, linoleum, hunter-green floor was soft as silk beneath her feet. She felt her growing desire to escape his controlling influence. It was a slow miserable death he fashioned for her.

He pulled his pants up by his belt, straightened his posture and attempted to explain the facts of life to her.

"I hope so, my darling!" he said with a confident smile. "Because the only way for you and I to make it in this world is by attaching ourselves to infinite powers most human beings have very little knowledge of."

"That's so damned foolish, Archie!" She said and she refused anymore to put up with his dangerous indoctrinations and raced to the door in a mad dash to leave him behind her.

"Jesse," he called to her, and turned to gaze at her as she stood at the door with her hand on the knob. "Where are you going?" he inquired of her. He was quite sure where she was going and he felt somewhat relieved because of it. At least, for a little while, she would be flexible with him until the booze put her to sleep again.

Chapter 24

Kas was thirsty and her feet hurt. As she made her way down the long hall to detention where Gage was, she paused for a drink at the water fountain, but she couldn't do a thing about her new shoes which made blisters on her feet.

"It's strange!" Detective Baldwyn, who walked beside her said as they continued on. "They've impounded the red Mustang driven yesterday but the DMV has no record of the license plate number so they can't say who the car belongs to."

"I'm sure they've checked the glove compartment for registration and anything else inside of the car which would identify the owner?" Kas asked, trying to be helpful but still

feeling strained by the Detective's company. It wasn't so much she didn't like him, but she couldn't accept what he symbolized to her.

She stopped at the closed door and thought of the person behind it. She was undecided whether or not he was responsible for the double homicides. He might have been, but she highly doubted it now.

She entered the room alone and found him facing the furthest wall from her. He stood beneath the steel-barred window, with his back to her.

"Mrs. Scott," he addressed her, and turned around to face her. "I almost achieved my goal last night." he told her. "I want so much to end it all." he sadly said. He was dressed in an orange jump-suit the prison had required him to wear and he was haggard-looking. He watched her go the table to set her briefcase down.

"I don't think it will happen, Gage." She told him and motioned him to join her at the table.

"The banshees care very little how I wind up and, I'm as good as dead, anyway."

She found it particularly difficult to hear such statements proceed from the boy next door. She had heard awful things many times before in this room, but those poor, pathetic people hadn't grown up with Crystal. She hated to think of how Crystal would respond when she discovered Gage had tried to take his life last night.

"They're going to transfer you to a hospital in Pomona." she informed him.

He laughed but it wasn't a cheerful noise, and certainly not the kind of laughter Gage and Crystal had shared not long ago, before all of the bloodshed.

"It doesn't matter where I'm at." He leaned dog-tiredly against the table and looked at her. "I can't get away from them." he groaned.

She couldn't understand his thoughts and she very much wanted to. He was obsessed over something, something other than his present foul situation. Before the tears spilled from his eyes again, he stood and rushed once more to the furthest wall from the table. She turned in her chair to observe him better and gave him time to attempt to collect his thoughts. She wondered with frustration what in the world had happened to change him so much in one short summer.

"Do you know why I tried to kill myself last night?" He was so quiet she had to strain to hear him.

"No, I don't. I wish you would try to explain it to me." she urged him. She watched his shoulders shake as he sniffed. Once more she wished she carried a box of Kleenex with her.

"She came to my window last night and she told me I knocked her up and she is pregnant with my kid! The witch is carrying my child!" His voice grew louder with distress. He turned to look at her and there was pure terror on his face. "I am the soon-to-be father of a bouncing baby demon!" he proclaimed with horror.

He blamed himself for the inability to keep his pants zipped up. But Daphne came to him last night, to announce how she was pregnant with his seed.

"She was outside of my cell." He trembled, and his teeth chattered when he wasn't using his mouth to articulate his thoughts. "Daphne Orion was! I have no privacy!"

She felt helpless and she couldn't imagine any way to provide him security.

"At first all I saw was an owl who hooted at me, and the next thing I knew, the owl lunged down from its tree and attached itself to my window. Then it was no longer there, but Daphne was inside of my cell."

He knew he sounded ridiculous to her. He moved away from the woman who could only stare at him because she had no comfort or guidance to give him. No one did.

"I thought if I cooperated with you, you would protect me from the mountain people."

He had left his Mother and Crystal behind for the cold confinement of a prison cell because he truly believed he would be safe there from the ghouls who were after him. Daphne knew right where he was, though, and she came to call on him.

"It's why she took me to the mountain. She wanted my child!" he shouted. "She's an evil witch!" he exclaimd, "What does this make my offspring? You know, you're one of them?" he shouted at her.

Kas turned her eyes away from him. An arctic chill pierced through her. He knew Rattler Mackenzie was the man who had brought her into the world. Daphne apparently had told him so. His next door neighbor, Crystal's mother had grown up in Hades.

"I'm glad you've taken my case, Mrs. Scott," he told her, and he meant it. Her first-hand experience with his insane dilemma gave him what little bit of solace he knew. It wasn't enough to keep him together, though. Trying to regain her balance, she said to him,

"What you're telling me, Gage, is you experienced intimacy with someone called Daphne Orion and last night she came to your cell and announced she was pregnant by you, which is why you tried to kill yourself?" She appealed to whatever logic, even some smidgeon of coherence.

She watched him slide down the wall and drop to the floor, where he sat with his arms tightly around himself and rocking back and forth, he wept. When the two men from the mental hospital rapped on the door and she let them in, this was how they found Gage Peterson.

After the men helped Gage to his feet and escorted him from the room, Kas closed the door. She needed privacy. Once more, she thought back to the day when she discovered the odd note in her Viper. *The rattlesnake has long been watching. Guard your treasures and, in particular, take great care of the children.* The rattlesnake, she thought, the words had to have been written in reference to her father. Rattler Mackenzie was the rattlesnake and her dearest treasures were her children.

She sat down in the chair and attempted to think. The occult had crushed Gage, turning him into little resemblance of his former self, but how had their neighbor's son become so entangled with the occult? She couldn't comprehend. Archie and Jesse had to have known something, anything, which might be helpful in solving this enigma. They couldn't possibly be as dumbfounded as they appeared to be.

She stood up and retrieved her briefcase, determined to speak with Gage's parents. Then she heard the loud knock on the door.

"Come in." Aware of her mournful greeting, she cleared her throat and tried again.

"Come in." she said.

The door opened and the Detective stepped into the room.

"Are you all right?"

She appreciated his concern and nodded her head, but she wasn't all right. If Rattler Mackenzie had returned from his cold grave, no one was all right.

"I'm okay," she told him, but it didn't ring true. She sat down once more, "Excuse me, Detective, but these shoes are killing me," she said, removing her shoes. She rubbed at her aching feet. The shoes made painful sores on both feet, but it wasn't the shoes which threatened to end her life.

"Gage told me he wasn't alone in his cell last night." She told the Detective, and hurled a glance at him, a cold, hard look.

She saw Lieutenant Baldwyn take the seat across the table from her and then nod knowingly at her and she resented it. He seemed so damned certain and, yet, he could have been wrong. They both could have been way off track.

"You shot him, Lieutenant. You shot him through the heart, remember?"

"Yes", he agreed,"And there's no way he could have lived…ordinarily," he assured her, "but we're not dealing with the ordinary when it comes to the occult."He sighed, staring at the floor for a minute, and then added, "The dead often don't remain dead in their league. Isn't this correct?"

They exchanged a long glance. She offered no comment. He studied her and thought her gorgeous blue eyes appeared to be a little misty. He also thought he saw her blush before returning her attention to her feet.

"Counselor, it seems to me you had much more to gain than anyone else by your father's death. After all, the fact your father was dead meant you would be made the high priestess.

That's a lofty position, some might conclude."

"I'm not going to dignify your statement with a remark," she sharply informed him. She'd had the mistaken impression the Detective, Cody Baldwyn, somehow knew her. He was familiar with her story, Rattler

Mackenzie had jeopardized both of their lives. Her father had stolen something precious, something they could never retrieve, from both of them but he certainly did not know her, she decided. Changing her mind, annoyed by his innuendo, she gave him her full attention now.

"You know, detective, a little girl once drew digits on the wall of her bedroom after each and every time her father raped her. I can't tell you how many digits I made on the wall; I lost count."

Her words were sharp, hard to digest, but there was a time when she believed the Detective had understood her. He could hang his hat on the fact she was grateful to him Rattler Mackenzie was dead. Staying dead was an altogether different thing and, yet, something she had counted on, of course.

"I was relieved you killed the pervert," she said. "Hell, I was euphoric!" she told him.

"You wouldn't have carried out a little hocus pocus and awakened him again, then?" He raised one eyebrow and studied her.

"Hocus pocus," she shook her head. "That's hardly the way it's done, Lieutenant. No, absolutely not!" she told him.

"Counselor…"

"Kastanje," she reminded him, "but if it's too difficult to commit to memory, most call me Kas."

"Kas, the occult is worldwide, it's a global community. You didn't fulfill the position of high priestess, so, by now, some one probably has the job and we can't be a hundred percent sure Rattler Mackenzie is even involved."

"Or, if it's even the occult," she said.

"No," he said with such determination it chilled her to the the bone. "No, it is the occult."

"How do you know?"

"The old man who was killed on Foothill Boulevard was a defector, he'd blown the whistle on the occult's activities and they killed him because of it."

"Who killed him?" She asked him, it was all so bewildering to her.

"Who knows," he shrugged. "I think the shape shifter, or, who ever made their way into Gage Petersen's cell, without being spotted by the warden last night, may know a lot about it, though."

There was a heavy silence between them during which she recalled the note. She'd brought it with her. She opened her briefcase, removed it and handed it to him. He read it.

"This leads you to think it could be Rattler Mackenzie?" he asked her.

"Yes, and it might be in his mind to cause trouble for his grandchildren, too." She admitted to him, feeling anxious.

"I suggest you take your girls on a vacation." He advised her, folding the note exactly the way it was when she handed it to him. Then he stuck it in the pocket of his coat.

"Do you still have the chateau at Huntington Beach?" he asked, but he didn't give her a chance to reply. "You could do a little fishing for tom cod in Surf City, right on the pier, there. It could be a real nice get-away!"

The Detective sounded like he was selling a vacation package. She got to her feet and he followed her lead.

"Do you really think there is any place on earth we could go where the occult would not find us?"

She knew the Detective would not have made such an error, he was also aware the occult was supernatural and it possessed enormous power. It could track down anyone in the world, on any spot on the globe, if it so desired. She turned to leave and heard him call to her.

"Kas," he said.

"Yes, Detective?" She turned to looked at him.

"Call me Cody," he told her.

"Okay, Cody," she said, and in spite of their perplexity, she managed a tight smile.

Chapter 25

Jesse Petersen came through the opened doorway and they turned their attention to her. Cody knew when he looked at her she was several sheets to the wind and he wondered how she found something to drink at this dry depot.

"Where's Gage?" she questioned them and, gazing around the room, she stumbled over her own feet.

Kas ignored her, grabbed her briefcase and left the room in a mad dash with Jesse following along behind her.

"Did you hear me, Kas?" She stood in the hallway and called after her as she watched her stride through the hall. "Kas, don't you ignore me!" Jesse scolded her. "I have every right to know where my son is!" Try as they might, they couldn't split them apart. They couldn't just rend them asunder, Jesse told herself.

She was far too rowdy, she knew, and she glanced around to see if anyone had heard her. No one had except for the aristocratic-looking detective who lingered in the doorway behind her.

Kas reached the closed door to her office and opened it. Once inside the room she slammed the door shut on the well-oiled woman who pursued her. Were it not for Archie, who was still sitting in her office, she might have bolted it too.

"Archie," she turned to Jesse's husband, "They've taken Gage to Saint Regis Mental Hospital in Pomona. Do you need me to draw you a map or can you find it yourself?" She was anxious, but civilized, which was more than she could say about Archie's wife right now. Archie lumbered to his feet.

"I can find it," he said.

She grimaced and gritted her teeth. It wasn't the way she'd imagined it. When she questioned Archie, his wife was supposed to be there at the same time. However, the woman had to take control of her own life before she could do anything for her son. While Jesse dawdled, Kas asked Archie,

"Do you know if your son had connections to the occult?" She watched Archie shift his weight from one foot to the other.

"Really," he returned her question. "Did Gage tell you this?"

"Not in so many words", she admitted. "But he claims there was a woman inside of his cell last night. He said her name is Daphne Orion. Do you know of any one by this name?"

"How did she get past the warden, Kas?" he questioned her.

"I don't know," she answered him, truthfully.

They heard Jesse's heels in the hallway and then the noise stopped and the door opened.

"Kas, do you intend to keep me in the dark?" Jesse shouted at her. "What, do you think I'm going to abandon my responsibility and let you do the same?"

In her foul, drunken state of mind Jesse thought she made a great deal of sense. Kas continued to ignore her and collected her things. She saw the picture frame and the altruistic look in Paul's eyes. What an omen, Kas thought. It was impossible to become outraged with their pastor staring at her.

"You just hold everything a minute, Kas!" Jesse shouted and hurried across the room to her. Kas could smell the wretched stench of alcohol on her breath and it turned her stomach.

"I don't like your silence, Kas!" Jesse kept at her and Kas bolted away from her.

"I don't like your drinking, Jesse, but, nevertheless, here you are, in your foul drunken state!" she replied, feeling trapped by a dear friend who had traversed the boundaries of friendship. Glaring at Jesse she said, "We had a deal and you reneged!"

Archie was upset by Jesse's irrational behavior, too. If he had been a man of prayer, he would have prayed she wouldn't also spill the beans about the cabal.

"Try to wear my shoes," Jesse pleaded with her, hoping for her sympathy. "Before you drop his case and desert Gage, consider how you would feel if the tables were turned and it was your child, heaven forbid!"

Finally Kas had it with Jesse's disorderly conduct and she outright told her,

"If the occult had anything to do with the murders on Foothill Boulevard then Gage isn't the only one who's in danger, Jesse. Everyone is threatened!"

Jesse suddenly froze and turned to look at Archie. She wasn't so drunk she didn't realize Archie and his whole evil coalition was on the verge of being found out.

Chapter 26

"I guess this is it, Loraine. I'm going to check out, Sweetheart." Andrew labored with every breath to tell his wife, the confidant with whom he had shared fifty-six years.

Loraine squeezed his hand and gently kissed his feverish brow,

"No," she begged him, "I'm not ready to let you go, Andrew!"

"You'll do fine," he struggled to comfort her. She felt Andrew's hand grip hers. The poor man gathered every bit of strength he could muster together just to grip her hand.

"Don't let them end your life, too, my angel, my darling Loraine," he pleaded with her.

Andrew gave both Loraine and Roosevelt a tortured look. "Find out who did this," he urged them.

Roosevelt nodded to him; he would find out. He wouldn't quit snooping around, or asking questions, until someone came clean and confessed, or until he and Loraine somehow stumbled upon the answers they needed. More than anything, Roosevelt wanted the names of all of those who were guilty, and a clear, definite reason behind their insanity, the cold-blooded murders of his friends.

Roosevelt and Andrew exchanged looks. Roosevelt was going to miss his old crony whom he had known much longer than he'd known the others. They met when they were young men, and both had hopped a boxcar on a train bound for California.

"I love you, Andrew Martin," Loraine told him with so much fervency.

"Me too you," Andrew said with a wink. "See you up yonder, Angel," Andrew managed to tell her, just before the angel of death swept down and collected Andrew Martin's soul.

Loraine turned to Roosevelt. She walked right into him, forcing him to cradle her in his arms, something he was always averse to doing. After all, Loraine was Andrew's guardian angel; his better self.

It was a long time ago, shortly after Abbey's death, when Roosevelt discovered he had complicated, difficult feelings for Loraine. She was a lodestar, a fragile, shimmering beacon of light in Roosevelt's dark world and now, all of a sudden, she was in his arms, too. He held her gently and while holding her, he felt his massive ache and dire loneliness abate. She leaned upon him, heavily as he guided her out of the room.

"We will find out who killed my Andy, won't we, Rosie," he heard her difficult inquiry.

"Yes," Roosevelt responded and once more pledged himself to the task. "We will learn what criminals killed Andy and the others too. We surely won't let them get away with this,

Loraine," Roosevelt promised her.

He led her down the hall and into a side room and then he watched Pastor Paul take Loraine's hand and seat her in one of the chairs in the small room. There were other chairs scattered about and Pastor Barry Guire and his wife, Lena, sat in a couple of the chairs. The deserted room afforded them much needed privacy. Who the hell had done this to them, Roosevelt wondered, fearful and too uptight to sit down.

Even while the Senior Pastor and his wife watched, Roosevelt paced back and forth across the light blue carpet. He was sure it had something to do with the mountain, Mount Gaspar. Some type of imminently foul crisis lurked up there. Harriet had written it down in her diary. There was something, or someone, on the mountain eager to crush them, and the barrage had already started.

He glanced at Andrew's beloved widow. She looked pale as she dabbed at her eyes with white tissue. He hoped Loraine wasn't also becoming ill. He didn't think he could take it if she too grew feverish, choked and coughed. The virus attacked their lungs, debilitating them.

"No, God," Roosevelt said a silent prayer. "No, spare us! Please, God, spare us from the despair and debilitation!"

"Calm down," Senior Pastor Barry Guire said to Roosevelt from his easy chair where he seemed at total peace with himself. His lively, pretty wife sat right next to him, sipping Pepsi from a can as if it was a barbiturate. "The doctor will be here soon, and then he will explain everything to us." Pastor Guire assured him.

"Yeah, right!" Roosevelt laughed, shaking his head in disbelief. It was ridiculous how trusting the Senior Pastor seemed to be; perfectly happy with whatever fabrication the doctor and his staff wished to communicate to them.

'What do you mean?" Pastor Guire crooked his head and eyed Roosevelt suspiciously. He seemed to have no idea of how Roosevelt was feeling as he clicked his size thirteen shiny black shoes together. A man obviously unmoved by adversity, Roosevelt concluded.

He was sure some beast, some human being, or perhaps, some alien life form beyond anything Roosevelt had known in the seventy-six years he'd been alive, existed on the mountain. It wasn't satisfied to reign there alone but it claimed the valley, too. Not just the mountain and this valley, but it coveted the entire globe as if it had some legal right to it.

"What I mean is there's something in our midst which is killing us and we haven't any clue as to what this something is," he asserted.

He was disgusted, and he needed answers and soon too, if he was going to survive it and keep Loraine alive as well.

"That's crazy," Pastor Guire uttered. "That's outright bizarre!" His eyes went from

Andrew Martin's grieving widow to the indignant old man, Roosevelt, and then he turned to his wife. "Did you hear him, Dear?" the Pastor pointed his finger at Roosevelt. "Did you hear the ludicrous statement Mister Shuyler just made?"

"Absurd," Lena stated, and rolled her eyes.

"Is it?" Pastor Paul questioned them. All morning long he'd been thinking about Allen's bizarre allegations he'd made in his kitchen earlier. Allen had seemed so sure there were chemtrails above their house. He'd taken him outside and tried to show him. Paul wondered about it now. If he was truly honest, the clouds he saw outside his house that morning could well have been made by an airplane. Allen said it was a military aircraft.

"There's something fishy in the air," Paul admitted, to his own surprise. "Loraine, did Andrew have any problems with his lungs only months, weeks ago; you know, asthma, bronchitis?"

Loraine sniffed at her tears and replied, "Well, yes but Andy had only a slight case of asthma. It wasn't anything which would have killed him." she told her Pastor.

Right at that moment Doctor Foster, looking haggard, entered the room. He was a tall, middle-aged man in a white coat and with a stethoscope dangling from his neck. They hurried to greet him. Pastor Guire shook the doctor's hand.

"I'm sorry," the doctor began slowly, a look of genuine compassion in his eyes, "I'm afraid Mister Martin has died."

Loraine wept harder and Roosevelt put his arm about her as he swallowed his own tears. Although they had been there when Andrew drew his last breath, the mere mention of his death produced more tears and anguish. It was now official. Andrew Martin had died at ten twenty-five am, on a Wednesday morning in August, of something Doctor Foster explained was very similar to Chronic Obstructive Pulmonary Disease. Only this was a new virus.

The doctor told them there had been an unusual number of senior citizens afflicted by the new strain. He told them of a recent vaccine on the market and he urged them to be vaccinated against the virus immediately.

It was a fiasco, Roosevelt thought. The Doctor had no real explanation for their dilemma and he appeared to be one more parcel of their deceptive community. After the doctor left

Roosevelt grumbled, "So, we know very little more now, after listening to the good doctor, than we did before."

He put heavy emphasis on the word 'good.' Roosevelt wasn't sure the doctor was good. Maybe he was as crooked as the day was long, he thought. He turned to gaze down at Loraine who stood so close to him, almost pressing her head against his chest. She gave his life far more meaning. His concern now was not just to survive, but to also diligently watch over Loraine.

She was a charming woman. Some may have even said she was beautiful before the wrinkles lined her face and her hair turned silver. Loraine's eyes were still radiant, though and her mind was still sharp as ever.

"If they knew anything, I doubt they'd tell us, Rosie," she whispered to him, loud enough so the others heard her too.

Pastor Guire immediately glanced angrily at Loraine, then he shook his head and snickered, "I would be willing to bet the doctor doesn't believe in flying saucers and aliens from outer space either." Just the thought of anyone being so gullible as to fall for such idiocy made Lena laugh.

The Senior Pastor and his wife were mocking them, Roosevelt deduced, and for one split second he wanted very much to bash the minister's teeth out. What good would it do though? It would solve nothing and, being a Christian as well as a gentleman, he restrained the temptation.

Paul shrugged his shoulders; He'd been thinking and now he replied,

"'Love not the world', because it is in opposition to the Word of God. I suppose," he added, "at some point in time, this might also include the medical field."

Surprise appeared upon the Senior Pastor's face and he blasted the subordinate minister with,

"Where did this cynicism come from, Paul? You're beginning to sound like a fanatic."

"Similar opinion wiped out the world trade center several years ago," Lena reminded them.

"There's a big difference, I think," Paul disagreed. "I simply quoted the Bible," he said.

"Well, you're way out of line," Barry informed him. He glanced at the gold watch on his arm and gave Paul another serious look. "I have time to speak with you alone, Paul. Let's go get a cup of coffee," he suggested. "You stay here and keep an eye on those two," he turned to his wife and motioned to Roosevelt and Loraine, "Don't let them out of your sight, even for a minute," he said, and gave them all an ample smile, seemingly amicable.

Leaving the others behind them, both clergymen walked side by side down the long corridor until they encountered a Nurse pushing some kind of heavy hospital equipment cart. They made way for her to angle around them. An older man confined to a wheel-chair appeared to be following the Nurse with a frenzied look on his unshaven face. He could have been lost, or at least, temporarily adrift.

"Do you have some beef with me, Paul?" Barry asked him. He didn't return Paul's gaze, either, but kept his eyes directed straight ahead as they made their way through the corridor.

"Definitely not," Paul said, shaking his head and exhaling a sigh. "I think it's odd how over the last week, we've lost five seniors of our congregation and, except for Harriet, they've died of the same mysterious illness, too." Paul thought Barry should have found this extraordinary as well. "Not only so," Paul continued, "but the very same bacterium has inflicted the whole country."

Barry said nothing and Paul had the fleeting thought he just didn't care. Barry actually appeared unfazed by any news of the disease and it's adverse affects on them. The only thing which seemed to bug Barry was the investigation of it. This surely wasn't conventional, and extremely unlike a clergyman, he told himself. Then, when Paul brought up the Bible, Barry claimed he was the one who was out of line.

"Besides," Paul added, feeling upset by the Senior Pastor's erratic behavior. "You said you had a bone to pick with me."

"Where should I start?" Barry murmured.

"Really!" Paul exclaimed. He was astonished by Barry's admission. They had been co-pastors of their church for more than twenty years now and Barry had never found fault with him before.

They rounded the corner and entered a small coffee shop called *Café Mélange*. The aroma of coffee, a variety of flavors, brewed to perfection, wafted through the air. Paul ordered a special blend and Barry, oddly enough, ordered a cup of plain black coffee. Then they went to a booth toward the back. Paul slid in opposite his colleague and proceeded to savor his coffee, which was a unique fruit and nut flavor, before he enquired, "You have a problem with me?"

Others who spotted them there would have correctly concluded they were pastors because they both wore clerical collars and didn't try to hide this fact. No one, least of all, Paul, could anticipate the direction their conversation would proceed, though. Barry had a frown on his face and a hard-boiled look in his gray eyes as he began,

"Mind you, I'm a pretty closed-mouth guy much of the time, an introvert and a bookworm," he stated, "But I'm honest, and I don't't find the need to use cloaks, such as the Bible."

The Bible was no cloak and Paul had never held it up as a front for a devious lifestyle. He couldn't imagine ever doing so.

"In my personal opinion, there's nothing worse," Barry continued. "Then a charlatan."

Paul took note of Barry's accusative tone of voice.

"Whoa! Wait a minute, Barry!" Paul motioned for him to stop. "Neither one of us is a charlatan!" he told him, astonished by Barry's words.

"I've known about your affiliation with the occult for awhile now," Barry told him with a deadpan look on his face.

"My affiliation with what?" Paul questioned the minister.

"You heard me!" Barry snarled. "Correct me if I am wrong, but I understand your wife fell heir to the profession of high priestess in the occult after her father was murdered."

Barry lowered his voice and looked around, as though he wanted to make very sure no one had heard him. Paul was flabberghasted.

"Kastanje?" he gasped, "The high priestess of the occult?" It blew him away to imagine Kas in this abnormal context. He knew her father had been the bishop of the occult at one time. However, Kas hadn't emulated her father. She had fallen in love with a Christian minister and married him which was why her family would have nothing more to do with her. He possessed no knowledge, none whatsoever, of her father and his questionable homicide, or of her debatable heritage and he was totally shocked.

"Your occult is worldwide and fatal," Barry said, criticizing the organization.

"My occult?" Paul objected. "Where do you get these outlandish ideas, Barry?"

"The Bible says to depart from evil! The Bible ostracizes all those with ties to the occult!" the minister continued.

"I've no association with the occult," Paul protested.

"You attached yourself to them when you married one of them," Barry informed him."Now you bewail any repercussions? You want to buddy up to the adversary but then grumble when he bites you! Are you out of your mind, Paul?"

When they'd returned to the same area where Barry had told the others to wait for them, Barry's wife was with an athlete Paul thought he recognized from last summer's Olympic games. The good-looking man spoke with a heavy French accent.

"Look who I bumped into," Lena said, flashing a dazzling smile. Her blue eyes sparkled with delight.

"Bonjour," the Frenchman greeted them as he shook their hands.

Roosevelt and Loraine were nowhere around and when Barry asked Lena what had happened to them, she shrugged and replied, "They mentioned something about getting to the bottom of things and then they just took off." She told them before she turned to give the Frenchman one more come-hither look.

Chapter 27

When Kas reached her kitchen sliding door, she heard the loud vroom of the vacuum cleaner and assumed Neva was busy cleaning the carpet. She breathed a sigh of relief as she entered, dropped her car keys down on the kitchen counter and slipped out of her uncomfortable shoes. She picked them up and carried them across the kitchen, relishing the luxury of being barefooted.

The shoes would be discarded. She would give them to the women's refuge which she passed almost daily on her way to the law firm.

As she headed for the living room, the direction from which the loud noise proceeded, she thought of the women at the Refuge. Most of them were flat broke and would appreciate her small but pricy donation, the shoes which did not fit her feet.

She went to the living room and her eyes canvassed her beige shag carpet. It was spotless and, yet, the vacuum cleaner continued to roar. On closer observation she realized it was unattended, just standing in the middle of the living-room floor making loud noise. Where was Neva Paloma?

Surely, Neva would have turned off the vacuum before she left the house, Kas thought. She knew precious little about the machine and fumbled around, trying to locate the switch which turned the thing off. Finally, she found it and succeeded in shutting the machine down.

She looked around her and gasped. The door was wide open. It appeared to her Neva had left the house in a hurry, leaving the door opened and the vacuum running. What in the world had called her away so abruptly, she wondered. She raced across the room and peered outside, but she saw no sign of Neva.

Beginning to worry now, she hastened through the hallway toward Crystal's bedroom. Crystal must be awake by now, she thought, and she might know Neva's whereabouts, she told herself. She knocked on her bedroom door.

"Crystal!" she called, "Crystal!" but there was no answer. She'd seen Crystal's Eldorado in the driveway, though, so she couldn't have gone far without her vehicle unless…. She shuddered to even think of it. Not unless Crystal and Neva had both been abducted.

A piercing scream mobilized her and sent her flying from Crystal's bedroom down the hallway and into the kitchen again.

"Mom!" she heard the shrilling cry for help. It was Crystal who called to her. She imagined Crystal helpless, the way she had been with Gage when he goaded her to ascend the mountain with him. Crystal's father had intervened then. *Guard your treasures and, in particular, take great care of the children.*

She flew outside and sped around the swimming pool, hastening to the gazebo. Crystal was inside of it, frightened and helplessly threatened by the monstrous serpent.

The reptile coiled around the wooden beam and the crossbar just above Crystal's head. It was the rattler, the very same snake the note alluded to. The rattle snake which for quite sometime had watched them from a distance, and now threatened to attack.

"Stay still, Crystal!" Kas instructed her.

She knew Crystal's despair emboldened the snake. He'd already cornered her, backed her against one side of the gazebo. Crystal was dressed in skimpy shorts and white t-shirt, and the snake seemed to revel in her anxiety. Kas paid no attention to the crowd now drawn to the calamity.

"Reptilian," she murmured. Reptilian, chimera, serpent; the occult's very own mascot.

The snake, with tail coiled around the beam, whipped back and forth in the air; dangling, fluctuating, then turning around, he centered his attention on Kas. His cold green eyes, mean and nasty looking. His long, black tonque vibrated with horrible dread. With hissing contempt the serpent spoke to her,

"You failed to care for the children and your employee, too. Now Neva is somewhere amidst the ensnared. Not quite up to par are you, Kastanje?" the fearsome reptile questioned her. "Nothing compared to what you once were, Witch!"

Kas knew the dragon empowered the serpent, and it possessed the dragon's infinite power. The ancient manuscript said so. The Book of Revelation explained the arcane event.

She refused to communicate with the snake. Standing beside her was the odd young man. Allen had Cadence balanced upon his shoulders. Frightened for her safety, repelled by what she perceived to be imminent danger, she reached up to take Cadence. Sunlight burned her eyes as she pulled her daughter away from him. It wasn't Allen's insanity which scared her half as much as the fact he may have had something to do with the evil all around them. She sensed this. She knew it.

In the sky she saw the bird, a mysterious raven. Again, the reptile spoke to her.

"Not much your God. Where has He disappeared to, Kastanje? Is He asleep? Who will wake Him for you?" the snake kept badgering her.

Then, at breakneck speed, the raven swooped down. His long, sharp talons took hold of the reptile and, with a screeching noise, he carried him away. Ascending the mountain, the huge black predator flapped its strong black wings, the awful snake dangled in the air.

Chapter 28

"What I want to know is why the rattlesnake called my Mom a witch?" Crystal inquired.

It seemed like a sensible question to her. She looked at the dumbfounded faces of the others now present in the room with her. She had so many questions and this seemed to her like a good place to start. Sitting on the couch, several spaces away from her Mom, she examined the older woman's face,

"It's not like he knows you, you've never been formally introduced, not to my knowledge," she said softly, analytically.

Kas regarded her inquisitive gaze. Maybe she should have shared the story of her esoteric childhood with her girls sometime ago, before Rattler Mackenzie paid them a social call.

How could she have known? How could she have had any idea these damnable exploits would occur?

She had read in the Bible how, in the last days, kingdom would wrestle against kingdom. Once upon a time, no more than twenty years ago, she had poured over the Bible. She'd studied it with avid devotion and had committed many of the amazing passages to heart.

According to what she had read, the kingdom of antichrist would contend against God's kingdom until, for a brief period of time, God permitted the devil dictatorship. Was this what was happening to them now, she wondered, and glanced at the deacon of their church who was seated in the chair facing the sofa where she and Crystal sat.

Tim Bailey was hunched over with the Bible he'd taken from the small table beside him, in his lap. He held the sacred book carefully, as though aware of it's monumental importance. God alone could sustain their faith now.

Her eyes traveled from Tim to the young man who stood at the end of the room, apart from the others. Only a day or so ago she could identify him as being Harriet Carter's adopted son.

They were neither friends nor strangers. She'd bought him a bicycle because she wrecked the one he rode, but she was far from trusting him. He was a sad young man who had suffered the loss of both of his parents and she felt sorry for him. His mental problems certainly warranted the recognition of a Psychiatrist. Now, in this strange light of events, his aura frightened her. Even more so than Detective Baldwyn frightened her. The Detective resumed pacing their living-room carpet.

Cadence, worn out, left her sister Erin's side and hurried to Kas, placing her curly head on her Mommy's knee. Kas lifted her onto her lap and cradled the child in her arms, giving them both more a sense of security.

The Detective came to an abrupt stop and looked down at the young woman who reclined on the couch beside her Mother and little sister. Kas scowled. Surely Baldwyn could see the credulous look on Crystal's face. She couldn't tell him anything more then what she'd already told him.

Apparently, according to Crystal, she had awakened, arisen from her bed and ventured down the hallway where she saw a man in a yellow jacket and wearing a red baseball cap leave the house with Neva Paloma. It appeared to her that Neva must have agreed to go with the man, and she wondered why on earth Neva would drop what she was doing to leave with the unattractive man.

Therefore, when they left the house, Crystal had slipped to the window to spy on them.

The black Bentley Arnage was parked at the curb right outside their house. Crystal saw Neva and the stranger both get into the back seat of the car and then the man behind the wheel sped off down the road.

"What puzzles me," the Detective said. He held his note-pad and pencil as though ready to write everything down, "Why did the cleaning lady accommodate this villain? Why wasn't there a dispute? According to what you've told me, there was no struggle. Why was she so compliant?"

Crystal shrugged. She didn't know why, and the fact she didn't know made her fidget. She wished she had paid more attention so she could be more helpful.

"Then there was the bizarre episode with the rattlesnake which you say crept up on you and twisted himself around the beam in your gazebo?" Baldwyn said as he squinted at her.

"The snake told your Mother," he continued, pointing his pencil toward the woman beside her, "Neva is somewhere enslaved?"

Both women nodded their heads. This was the snake's exact words. They saw Baldwyn turn and gaze around the room before he challenged them, "Would this place be in or out of our universe?'"he asked them.

Chapter 29

Gage opened his eyes to find himself flat on his back and staring up into Daphne Orion's face.

"Yell and I'll shove these narcotics into your veins!" she admonished him in no uncertain terms. She applied her attention to the needle and syringe she held with steady hands.

"What are your veins like, anyway? I hope they are big ones, unlike other parts of your anatomy. It's no wonder to me you remained a virgin so long; probably embarrassed by your equipment. It sure did the trick, though, didn't it?" Daphne was being a real chatterbox.

"How did you ever wind up so profane?" He couldn't fight her. All he could do at the time was lie there and endure her abuse.

"Some people say it was luck, although I suspect it had something to do with genes." She giggled as she jabbed him with the needle.

She wore a nurse's cap and uniform, and where she swiped them from was anyone's guess. He saw her large round breasts and noticed the top button of her dress was hanging by one lone thread.

"Now you should sleep quite nicely so Rattler and I can relax this evening and not have to worry about you saying things you ought not."

She lifted his head and propped his pillows up for him. She wanted to make sure he was comfortable for the evening. A major fault, Daphne thought, was her easy-going, charitable disposition.

"We wouldn't want to spoil things for our new baby now, would we?"

She smiled at him and leaned over to plant a wet kiss on his lips but he turned his head away from her. She laughed.

"Oh, well, what the hell, they say you are as crazy as a loon, any way. It looks like you're not completely to blame. It would be nice, though, if our baby would inherit your eyes and my superior intelligence."

She slipped her hand into the pocket of the uniform she wore as tight as a leopard wears its skin.

"Look what I acquired!" She held before him his mother's wedding ring. "I guess mommy won't be wearing this any more because her hand is disfigured." She glanced down at him and explained,

"Well, I couldn't take the ring without the finger, too. By the time we're married mommy probably won't be around to miss her ring any more."

He tried to object, but the strong sedative made it impossible for him to do or say anything. What on earth was Daphne doing to his mother, he anxiously wondered. Before the darkness invaded and he went to sleep, he heard her evil roar of laughter.

The Doctor removed the chart, clipped to the end of Gage Petersen's bed, and quickly glanced through it.

"What's this, sedatives every eight hours? I didn't order sedatives for this patient!" She told the psych technician standing over her patient, who was out cold.

The tall Black man in uniform looked at her.

"The R.N. who was here about an hour ago told us you personally ordered him a sedative every eight hours."

"Why would I ever issue such an order? What good is it going to do anyone to keep him asleep day and night? I'm telling you, I did not issue those orders!"

"Then you want us to ignore them?"

"At once!" She charged him and ripped the page from the chart. Some unqualified person was obviously trying to play doctor with her patient.

"Mom!" She heard the young man call for his mother. With the help of her cane she made her way to his bedside and stared down at him with concern. Unfortunately, he would sleep through the entire evening now.

"No! Mom! Don't! Mom! Don't!" Deep in rem his eyes made rapid movement, his limbs convulsed as some phantom prankster troubled him.

She would eventually get inside of his brain and discover what, or who, caused his suffering, but she needed him to be awake to do anything of this nature.

"Ben," she said, "I want you to keep a close eye on him for me." She told the young technician at the other side of Gage's bed. "I suspect there is someone with easy access to this room who intends to destroy his mind."

The technician recognized the seriousness in those green eyes and heard the urgent timbre in her voice. Doctor Kennis was the best and responded to her calling passionately.

"Watch him like a hawk…around the clock. I don't want other nurses and technicians hanging around his room. Before anyone comes into this room, find out what their intentions are, and if anyone seems to be particularly interested in him, call me."

He nodded to her.

"This is Gage Petersen, Ben. He has witnessed two horrendous homicides, and in order to apprehend their murderer we need to keep him alive and coherent." Doctor Kennis clearly outlined their goals.

Chapter 30

Kas was not one minute late for her appointment with Mister Peter Wolfe. Exactly at 3pm she drove her Viper close beside the curve, outside of the cooperative which comprised her law firm.

The corner of 5th and Vine was crowded with traffic. This was a busy division of Althea, monopolized mainly by large, lucrative cartels.

When there was a breach in traffic, on the opposite side of the boulevard, facing her direction, she saw the expensive black Porsche and at once imagined the man inside of the car had to be Peter Wolfe. The man who had telephoned her late the night before and introduced himself to her as being with the state department of education.

His hands still curled around the wheel, Wolfe lifted three fingers and accorded her a skimpy wave. He made it obvious he also recognized her.

She noticed he was a man of distinguishable and striking characteristics and she was profoundly curious as to his genuine identity.

It took her seconds longer to undo her seatbelt, open her door and get out of her car.

She peered across the busy boulevard, trying to keep a watchful eye on Mister Wolfe through the flow of passing traffic. She saw him climb out of his posh sports car with a brown leather briefcase in his hand. He was very much the way she had imagined him; administrative-looking.

He took long, brisk steps as he proceeded to the crosswalk. As Wolfe narrowed the chasm between them, she felt a growing rush of excitement. She was quite positive this man held firm grasp of the mysteries which now beset them. He may have known of Neva's whereabouts too.

Upon reaching her, he extended his right hand and she accepted his friendly gesture. He was a tall man, thin, with a neatly-trimmed beard and mustache. Quite good looking, she thought. This didn't surprise her because being physically attractive was an edge and might make the difference in their desired outcome. Therefore, the majority of Rattler's agents were so endowed.

He had a firm grip of her hand when with great enthusiasm, he said, "Counselor, you must be proud of your daughters!"

Kas regarded his wide grin and eyes which sparkled like the bulbs on a Pine tree on Christmas Eve.

She turned and examined the fountain just outside of the stately five-story building they were about to enter. The circular fountain with the bronze statue of three angels was a dazzling work of art. Some architect, unknown to her, had sculptured three angels above the sand-stone fountain.

The Artist had distanced one above the other so each of them appeared to enable the other to reach its goal. It was quite effective, this assemblage of angels in busy, downtown Althea.

There was the angel of enterprise, the angel of justice and the angel of prosperity. The Artist called his magnum opus, *Justice in Industry Empowers Good Fortune*. Integrity in any enterprise would bring about similar affects, Kas thought. To Mister Wolfe she responded,

"The girls are very close to their father. He has even more influence upon them than I do. I think you should speak to him about whatever extraordinary talent they display, Mister Wolfe."

She reckoned she saw a blemish in eloquent Mister Wolfe's suit of armor. He exhibited some discomfort with this idea. His gaze quickly left her face and he seemed to prefer looking at the ground rather than making eye contact. Of course, Peter Wolfe would not agree to speak with Pastor Paul Scott about anything. The devout Pastor filled Mister Wolfe and his entire organization with huge terror. She didn't intend to frighten Wolfe away though. His knowledge of Rattler's activities and, perhaps, Neva's whereabouts was crucial to them.

"My husband is one of the minister's of His Holiness Church." she told him. If by some outside chance she was wrong and Peter Wolfe was not affiliated with the occult, he still would have to have known of His Holiness Church because it comprised such a large number of followers. There were twenty-two hundred active members who met there every Sunday morning.

Like waving a Christian cross before a vampire, Paul's occupation seemed to have a similar effect upon Mister Wolfe. He skirted around the subject and said,

"I believe you'd be better able than I to talk to your husband, Mrs. Scott."

"Yes, of course", she said as they made their way down the sidewalk together toward the building, "The same thought crossed my mind, too," she answered him. She made no effort to conceal a telltale smile.

The automatic doors opened and they entered the building. There was a long, dark hallway ahead through which they had to walk in order to reach the elevator doors. Located off to their left was a sales area for Panorama Landscaping. There was a sign over this department as well as the sign outside of the building, both directing clientele to their location.

Despite the fluorescent lights on the ceiling, the hallway always seemed dark and isolated to Kas. Rather spookish too, she thought, but never more so then today. Peter Wolfe and his addiction to the occult set her on edge, although she did her best to hide it.

At the end of the hallway they turned to the right and Kas pressed the button on the elevator. They didn't have to wait long before it's doors opened and they stepped inside.

Alone in the elevator with Wolfe and caged in the compact box, she wondered if he was also a Reptilian. He was evidently a master of Black Magic or, at least, a practitioner. Rattler would have been out of his mind to send anyone on a mission if he lacked the ability to defend himself with wizardry.

She wondered if Wolfe possessed knowledge of her background as well. How she was Rattler's sole descendant and, therefore, after his death she would have inherited his lofty position. She'd refused to accept his scepter and now the art she had once practiced, that of witchcraft, was taboo. She saw Wolfe reach into his shirt pocket for his pipe.

"Do you mind if I smoke this?" he asked her when they reached the 5th floor and were on their way out of the elevator.

"No, not at all", she replied, as she guided him through the spacious lobby; the foyer decorated in black and white with pictures of zebras and primates on the walls, and a desk and counter for the receptionist who worked for *Scott and Spencer's Law Firm*. He was not there now, though.

"My partner is in court today," she said. Cameron Spencer was in the midst of a case involving domestic abuse. The devil's work. Satan mixed the ingredients of anger and discord together until he'd created one hell of a broth.

Wolfe followed her to her office, which was a lavish room, adorned in rich colors of pink, turquoise and sandy mauve.

"Have a seat," she called to him over her shoulder, on her way to the large picture windows. She pulled open the pink drapes and the windows offered them a bird's-eye-view of the city of Althea, a city set on the southern California desert. It's buildings, citadels and sky-scrapers were surrounded by awesome mountains.

When she glanced in his direction, she saw he had wasted no time. He had taken a chair, pushed it to her desk and he had then spread out.

With pipe in mouth, he was sprawled over some diagram he'd pulled from his briefcase. He appeared to be engrossed in it, and eager to hoodwink her into thinking he'd actually come from the State Board of Education to talk with her about her brilliant daughters. It was a downward spiral for the Board of Education, she thought.

"Mrs. Scott," he addressed her, "What I have here is a chart."

His brown eyes glanced up and she noticed the unusual length of his eyelashes. He loosened the black tie he wore, which rather matched the hair on his head as well as his beard. Mister Wolfe was probably of Latin descent, she decided. He was completely absorbed with his chart.

"My chart is an accepted standard of grade levels and curriculum geared for average California students. It's really very simple," he explained to her "Come here and have a look-see!"

Wolfe puffed on his pipe and invited her to survey his handiwork. The aroma of sweet cherry tobacco flooded her office. She was cautious about being near him, fearful of what he might do, especially if he had any clue of how leery she was of him.

She moved across the room until she stood directly behind him and then she peered over his shoulder at the chart he was huddled over. It looked credible, an authentic logo and the diagram included a copyright at the bottom of it. While she stood behind him, he pulled yet one more diagram from his briefcase.

"This is a diagram of the capacities at which your daughters normally operate. Of course, everyone has their bad days," he laughed, and pointed to the places on the chart where the lines dropped but not below the apparent standards set by the Board of Education. She wagered to disagree with him.

"According to the grades they've received so far, throughout their education, the girls prove to be somewhat above average but far from exceptional", she said.

Wolfe leaped from his chair and in doing so he startled her.

"It's the curriculum, Mrs. Scott! Can't you see, it's the curriculum!" he shouted with wild enthusiasm. He was quick to blame the school's standards. Had the girls been there to witness Wolfe's exhibition they would have fervently agreed with him.

Somewhere, though, there was a catch…. *"Would this be in or out of our universe?"* It was a question Detective Baldwyn had put to her the day Neva was found missing.

Although Rattler was out of their universe, the members of his cult weren't. They were beings who appeared to be just like every one else. Several cuts above everyone else, in fact. They blended with society, climbing the corporate ladder until they reached prominent positions of great influence in society. They were able to bend and mold the world, and the dragon gave them their power.

She returned to staring out the window. In this rough, yet beautiful, region where life blossomed like a desert cactus, how many legions of them were there, she wondered.

"If indeed my daughters are geniuses, what's next, what plans have been made for them?" She asked quietly while turning her back on the city she had been gazing at through the window and giving him her full attention.

"Not if," he corrected her. "We believe they are clairvoyant, Mrs. Scott," he said with certainty. "Therefore, your daughters will be trained at facilities of special education," he promised her. "By agents and representatives of the new empire. They will be on the cutting edge of advanced technology and information. One day, too, they will be leaders of the fresh and exciting global alliance called Chimera!" Caught up in the possibilities, Wolfe's face seemed to shine like a beacon in the night.

So, this was it, she thought. This was the catch. If she gave her consent then Crystal, Erin and Cadence, Paul's daughters, their daughters, would be prepared to take their place in the new world order, to reign as Rattler Mackenzie's own descendents.

"Over my dead body!" she said.

"That can be arranged," he informed her.

"This conversation is over." she told him clearly and firmly.

Wolfe held her gaze for what seemed like a long time. He said nothing but his eyes urged her to reconsider. She was adamant. The thought of polishing up Rattler Mackenzie so Crystal, Erin and Cadence might be partners in his degenerate social order was repulsive to her. She watched as Wolfe finally put out his pipe, returned his charts to his briefcase, and collected himself.

"I hope you will reconsider this, Counselor." he urged her again.

"I won't." she told him, and watched him turn around and leave her office.

Wolfe was angry and disappointed as he marched through the foyer toward the elevator. It wasn't supposed to happen this way, he thought, as he pressed the button for the elevator. He was supposed to win her over, persuade her to entrust her daughters to them. The doors opened and Wolfe entered the elevator.

Kastanje Scott's daughters were, in truth, telepathic; they had no doubt inherited their Grandfather's bent for the cryptic. Crystal, Erin, and even little Cadence, surely were not run-of-the-mill, ordinary children, Peter thought, as he pressed the button for the main floor. As an educator, he knew Kastanje Scott was dead wrong. Instead of being flexible and willing to listen to him, the woman was obstinate and narrow-minded.

Alone in the elevator, he felt an overwhelming shame at the way he'd conducted himself. He hadn't intended to threaten her. When she flat-out rejected his ideas, he had responded by telling her that her death could be arranged. This was a big mistake and it disturbed him deeply the way he'd blown any opportunity to convince her of the advantages of being a part of the new world, of being a part of Chimera.

Peter was lost in thought when, suddenly, he felt the elevator bounce and fall several feet in midair and then, just as abruptly, stop. He was agitated at being jounced around and nervously tugged at his tie, switched his briefcase from one hand to the other, and wondered if there was some kink in the mechanism. When the elevator started moving again he breathed a sigh of relief. Accidents occurred all of the time, for no apparent reason, but usually he managed to take them in stride.

The lights above Peter's head flickered and the elevator breezed to a brisk stop again. He wondered if he'd be stuck there today. If the thing broke down, sooner or later some janitor would spot the trouble and repair it. Meanwhile, he could be stuck for a very long time.

After Mister Wolfe left her office, Kas closed the door and then crossed the room and pulled her drapes shut too. She sat at her desk, the dark shadows deepening as she calculated the chance of surviving this chilling ordeal. Rattler had somehow escaped his coffin and his dismal end. The bottom line: Rattler

Mackenzie's ghost was hovering around them, raising hell. She was startled when the telephone, like a loud siren, sounded. She picked it up on the second ring.

"Hello?" she questioned her caller.

"Kas!" It was Paul's endearing voice. "Something is very wrong! Things just don't add up…"

The lights in the elevator vacillated and Peter also heard a voice. He recognized the grisly timbre; it made his blood curdle and his heart pound.

"Rattler?" he whispered. "God," he blubbered, "It's you, Rattler! What do you want with me?" Peter dared to question the phantom, frantically disturbed by the insane evil which now flooded the elevator cage he was in.

"You are a failure, Peter," the phantom said. "A failure, and an idiot, too." The cold-blooded voice sounded through the four dense walls confining Peter. If not for the walls which imprisoned him, the container from which there was no escape, Peter would have ran so fast not even hell its self could have caught up with him.

"You threatened to kill my daughter whom I created solely to inherit my position as archbishop." Rattler raged at him.

"She doesn't want your position!" Peter cried, sweat pouring from him; the type of dreadful sweat which gave the Reptilian an appetite for blood. "She doesn't want anything to do with you!" he shouted. "I tried my damnedest to explain the advantages of being submissive to you!" He howled like a baby, falling on his knees in order to to beg Rattler for his life.

"Now she will have nothing more to do with me." Rattler pinned the blame for this on him too.

Peter grasped the change and direction of the shape shifter's voice. Now it emanated from the floor and scaled the walls. The snake's hiss ascended from the abyss, its fangs lacerated

Peter's neck, its deadly toxin brought Peter's life to an excruciating end.

"Please, Kas," Paul begged her, "Take the girls and leave for Huntington as soon as you can!"

Chapter 31

Archie Petersen was behind the wheel of the Honda Odyssey minivan and Jesse was in the passenger's seat as they drove home from the Althea police station. Jesse gazed down at her hands and she saw her nail polish was somewhat worn off.

She also realized she had lost her wedding ring. The one symbol of love she kept with her was gone. Maybe she had misplaced it, though. She grew tense as she tried to retrace the day's events, though in her present frame of mind the day was nothing but a blur to her.

"I want to see my son!" she told Archie.

No one could stand in her way. Poor Gage needed his mother to nurture him back to health, she thought.

"We would be in the way." Archie said, trying to be tactful. He didn't want to hurt her by pointing out the truth. The truth was, the last thing Gage needed around him was his boozed-up mother.

"If you won't take me to see him I will go there by myself!" she informed him.

He saw her put her hand on the door and try to open it with her shoulder and he grabbed her other arm to pull her back. Then he slapped her hard. So hard he left his handprint on her face. She was going to get herself killed if she didn't quit it, he thought.

She felt the pain but it was only a dull sting. It was why she drank. Although he had never hit her before, she drank to dull the pain of living with his insanity.

She was humiliated. Archie had slapped her and Kas had called her a drunk. They could go straight to hell. She wanted nothing more to do with either one of them.

"Stop the car," she told him. "Stop the damned car!" she shouted at him.

He decided to do anything to keep her quiet and slowed to a stop. They were on the highway less than a quarter of their way home when he brought the vehicle to a complete stop at the side of the road and then watched her open her door.

"It's a long walk home, Jesse," he warned her.

"I don't care! I'm going to Saint Regis to see Gage," she told him.

She didn't know where Saint Regis was but she could find it. The hospital probably wouldn't be too difficult to find.

Archie looked into her deep brown eyes and tried to reason with her.

"You won't find it this way!" He didn't raise his voice, or yell. He wasn't the kind of man who wasted his time carrying on so. She was simple and uneducated. Those qualities had drawn him to her twenty-two years ago. It made him feel like a bigger man to be so needed. He wished she could see everything he did was for them.

The society promised to take care of all of their needs in return for Gage's generous donation and he had signed their contract. He had written both of their names down on the dotted lines. This bought them a ticket to hell, but they could sure live well on their way there.

"What alternative have you given me?" she persisted. "To sit here while you beat the crap out of me?" She stumbled from the minivan. "No thanks! I'd rather look for Saint Francis, or, I mean Saint Regis! Well, damn it, one of the saints!" she told him as she slammed the door shut.

She was surprised, though, when Archie started down the road without her. She stood and watched the vehicle roll down the highway until it disappeared from sight.

Feeling completely alone now, Jesse looked around and saw the flashing sign of a bar on the corner. Her feet were tired and she was thirsty. She told herself she would drop in for just one drink before she continued on her way. By this time the drinks she'd had were wearing off and Jesse convinced herself she needed more alcohol to numb the pain.

The bar's parking lot was not empty. There were several cars there and already a good-sized crowd inside, apparently. Jesse had seldom seen the inside of a bar. She always drank some place else and most of the time by herself. She labored to convince herself she drank for medicinal purposes only. The fact she drank alone helped her justify her drinking.

There was a Motel 8 right next door to the bar. Jesse put on the big sunglasses she carried in her handbag and hoped they would hide her identity. In her wine-colored dress she knew she would look out of place. She really didn't intend to waste her time inside of this dive, anyway. She would have one drink and then continue on her way. Her goals were clear to her when she went inside.

When Jesse entered the bar-room she was stingingly aware most of the men turned their heads to gaze at her and it made her feel even more fidgety about being there. She marched to the counter like a woman on a mission and forced herself to smile at the big, blond man with a mustache who inquired what she wanted to drink.

Jesse liked being asked for her opinion on things. It so seldom happened to her anymore. Even her children turned to their dad rather than to her these days.

"Vodka, on the rocks." she told him.

It was nice to have some one wait on her. There were other people at the counter. The bartender had been talking to one of them when she entered the place. Now, though, he focused all of his attention on her.

"So, what's your story?" he asked her.

"Story?" she questioned him, and thanked him for her drink.

"Everyone here," he motioned to the people around them, "has a story!" he told her. "What's yours?"

When he moved closer to get a good look at her she was fearful but found some relief in the barrier between them. She placed her empty glass down on top of the counter. He took it and promptly brought her another drink. Her hands shook but she managed to get the next drink down, too. She didn't ask him for another one. She planned to leave after the first drink but he seemed to feel obligated to talk to her.

"What brought you to my bar?" he asked her.

"I am trying to find Saint Regis." she told him and thought maybe he might direct her. She heard him laugh and say,

"I think he's been gone for a long while now, and he never visited my bar when he was around." His eyes glistened and she saw the dimples around his mouth. "I'm not disappointed he never dropped in. I think he probably preferred the privacy of his cloister." he told her. He made her laugh the way Archie used to a long time ago.

"What a great gift you've got there!" he cheered her on. "Would you mind repeating it?"

She drank down the second shot of vodka.

"Repeat what?" she asked him.

The vodka began to numb the pain in her tired body, to erase her frustrations with the world around her and the awful way things were. The vodka was her friend. She wondered if it was okay with Christ and imagined it was, since He turned the water into wine at the wedding in Cana.

"You know," he said, and leaned even further in her direction. "The cute little giggle!"

He wasn't so bad, she told herself as she removed her sunglasses. He saw her large, brown eyes and thought she resembled a fawn; a fawn caught in the brushes of this world; a timid animal which came to his pub looking for Saint Regis. He didn't see a wedding ring on her finger. Obviously, she was not married. He never dreamed of running into anyone like her; not here at this joint. She was someone he very much wanted to know better. He reached out and offered her his hand,

"Hi, I'm Hank, and you are?...."

"Jesse." she told him.

It was okay not to exchange last names, addresses or telephone numbers. After all, she was only passing through. She gave him her hand.

"Hey, Hank," A pie-eyed and objectionable bloke down the counter from them vied for his attention. "What does a person have to do to get a drink around here?"

Hank didn't take his eyes off of her when he answered the guzzler.

"You've had enough already, Stu. You drink anything more and we'll have to peel you off of the floor."

The others at the counter thought Hank had drawn an appropriate picture of Stuart Mackenzie. His remark made them laugh.

Jesse and Hank were preoccupied. They gazed long and hard into each other's eyes. She thought Hank was charming. Archie was once so charming. She couldn't get Archie out of her head. Archie was irresistible once.

It was a long time ago and he was just a kid then, still wet behind the ears, they said. She lost Archie somewhere along the way. Somehow Archie had even lost himself. She had tried desperately hard to recover him but she gave up and made up her mind to survive their marriage for Archie's sake, for Gage and Lacey's sake, for everyone's sake but her own. There was no way she would ever wash away the stains with liquor, but it helped.

"Hey, I'm buying this damned whiskey!" Stuart yelled at Hank, "You don't get over here now, real pronto like, and I will take my money some place else. Some place where I get a little less sarcasm and a lot more service!"

Jesse thought Stuart sounded serious.

"I think you will lose Stu if you don't wait on him now, Hank." She didn't want Hank to lose business because of her.

"The world is filled with clodhoppers and all of them have been here at one time or another. On the other hand," Hank gave her another one of his dimpled smiles, "I can't recall the last time someone came to my bar in search of a real saint."

Sadly, he knew she was right. He had a business to manage and yet he worried she might disappear into the night as mysteriously as she had appeared to him.

"Will you wait right here for me?" he asked her. "Sit right there and don't move, not even if Saint Regis himself comes through the door?" Hank had a smile which illuminated his whole countenance.

She fixed herself to the stool and looked around. Jesse had learned something already about the atmosphere. It invited all kinds of troublemakers, from Stu, who was drunk and set on getting drunker, to the couple at a table in the far corner of the room who, as the night wore on, went from being quiet and friendly to loud and aggressive. She overheard one of them warn the other guy if he didn't stifle himself he would do it for him. She was pretty sure it was the booze talking.

After waiting on Stuart, Hank crossed the room to their table and told them to be civil to each other or he would put them both out on their cans. Jesse thought a place like this put

Hank in jeopardy and she worried a bit for him. He had been nice to her. He set himself up to be let down, though, because she wasn't there to start a fire. In fact, she wouldn't have been there at all if Archie had just taken her to see their son the way she had asked him to.

By the time Jesse finished her forth drink she doubted she could even move from the bar-stool without major difficulties. Suddenly she heard music and then she also saw Hank. He appeared behind her with his arms out-stretched, inviting her to dance with him.

"Could I have this dance?" he asked her.

The song she heard playing on the jukebox was, *Could I Have This Dance for the Rest of My Life* by Anne Murray. It was always one of her favorites. Hank's arms were inviting.

"Oh, why not?" she giggled. It had been a long time since anything other then liquor had swept her off of her feet.

"I'm not so sure I can do this right now!" She warned him as she staggered to her feet.

"Just follow my lead," Hank told her.

He lead her onto the dance floor and gently glided her around the same way Gage had done only days ago when she was so confident nothing in his life could ever go wrong. She was grateful to Hank for making her remember the joyful occasion.

It was the way Hank dreamed it would be if he ever came across the right woman. If he ever really fell in love with anyone then he would waltz with her to Anne Murray's popular tune. He enjoyed the way her tanned and slender hand felt in his. It felt so right and good to hold her.

"Is there any one else beside Saint Regis?" he whispered into her ear.

"Yes," she answered him," There's Gage Petersen."

She wanted to tell him all about Gage and she hoped he was someone who would listen to her, and respond, too.

"Is Gage one more saint, or is he someone from the here and now?"

"Gage is my son." she told Hank. Gazing up into his eyes, she saw, to her pleasant surprise, genuine concern for what she said. Had he ever met any one inside of this place who could fill those shoes, he wondered.

"Are all bartenders good listeners, too?" she wanted to know and saw him nod.

"The good ones are," he answered her. "People have a story, and they want someone who cares enough to really listen to their woes. I guess I'm somewhat of a shrink as well." he explained.

Kas had tried to coerce and manipulate her into seeking professional help. She was dead set against it. Jesse didn't like people prying into her business, and she didn't like psychiatrists either, and she told Hank so.

"They ought to mind their own businesses and find a real job!" she said and he wondered why she disliked them so much. It didn't really matter to Hank for everybody was crazy over something. For instance, at the moment he found he was growing crazy over her. He pulled her tighter to him and she didn't resist. They clung to each other like two lost people until Stuart Mackenzie couldn't stomach it anymore so he got to his feet and made one quick telephone call.

Chapter 32

They laughed at something Hank said as they approached the motel next to the bar. It was dark and the glow of a door-light nearby, together with the brightness of the stars, was their only illumination.

They stopped before they entered the room. Hank thought he should carry Jesse over the threshold. There wasn't time to purchase a marriage license and call a chapel but at least he could carry her across the threshold.

He unlocked the door and gave her the bottle of vodka and she laughed as he picked her up and carried her in his arms. Hank was a cavalier and there weren't many of them left anymore.

He put her down and closed the door, then he gave her a gentle, passionate kiss. She was slipping away and far past the point of caring. All she wanted was to be truly cherished and treasured. She pulled away from him and gave him a measured look. He did indeed treasure her. She sensed it. She could hardly recall what it was like to be so adored.

"Do you believe in love at first sight?" he wanted to know. At long last Hank had fallen head over heels. He was a forty-five year old bachelor who had never truly been in love and now he discovered he couldn't keep his hands off her. He longed to touch every part of her body, to fondle and caress every inch of her. Never in his life had he wanted anything so badly.

Yes, she did believe in love at first sight. She'd had such feelings for Archie the first time she saw him in his Navy uniform.

He reached for her but she escaped him and grabbed for the doorknob. She couldn't go through with it. No matter how much she drank, she could never bring herself to be unfaithful to Archie.

"I have to go." she told him, and he saw the sorrow in her beautiful eyes. "You made me feel like something other then a lush and for a little while I forgot all about the turmoil of my life." She would always be grateful to Hank for the way he made her feel but she had to leave him now; an even stronger purpose gave her direction.

"Go?" he asked her. "Go where? We just got here! No, Jesse, please stay!" He pleaded with her and reached out to hold her one more time but she resisted him.

"I have to find Saint Regis mental hospital." she said, trying to explain her reasons to him.

"Why?" he asked her. "It's after midnight!"

"Because Gage is there!" she answered him. There was no more time for small, selfish pleasure, she told herself as she pulled the door open. She leaned forward and kissed his cheek.

"I'm sorry, Hank," she apologized to him.

She turned to go but found she couldn't move. She ran straight-way into an immoveable object. Archie was blocking the doorway.

"Archie!" she shrieked, and he threw her aside like a bag of potatoes. She landed against the hard cement pavement outside of the motel room, tearing her dress and skinning her knees. From the ground she heard the loud, crashing noise inside and staggered to her feet. Archie was like a bull.

"Stop Archie," she shouted at him, "Stop it!"

He wouldn't listen to her but plunged into Hank, driving him all the way across the room and into the wall. Hank never fought back. Archie slapped, struck, hit and beat him and poor Hank never fought back.

She was sure Hank could have got in some pretty good slugs if he had only tried. He was the same size as Archie and a couple of years younger, too. But he either couldn't, or wouldn't, defend himself.

Jesse didn't know if Hank was alive or dead. He was a puddle of blood. Once he was down, Archie's steel-toed boots kicked at his face and stomach.

"You're going to kill him!" she told him.

Archie would have done so, too, if he hadn't heard Jesse's heels scrambling away from him. Sweat poured down his face as he turned away from Jesse's lover and listened to the sound. Then it came to him what she was doing. She was running away from him.

He raced to the door and saw her in the midst of dozens of headlights on the highway, scurrying across the busy road while motorists blew their noisy horns at her.

She escaped the traffic and then fled down the sidewalk, past newsstands, a café and liquor store, and past Stuart Mackenzie who watched her with grave concentration from the shadows.

She ran into a telephone booth and overcome with fear, she opened her handbag and searched through its contents for the proper change. She didn't know what else to do so she removed the card she had thrown into her purse days ago. She deposited the money and dialed the number on the card.

"Hello? I want to speak with Doctor Kennis!" Out of breath, she managed somehow to make her request known to the person who had answered her call.

"This is she. I am Doctor Kennis." Jaime was working late.

"Hello Doctor Kennis," she said, "My name is Jesse and my husband Archie just killed Hank because I drink too much!

Chapter 33

Neva Paloma had been chained to the cold sheet of metal, the table which had been stolen from the hospital.

Daphne strolled over and gazed down at her hostage. The fearful look on the woman's face, the horror in those cocoa-colored eyes, brought her sheer enjoyment.

They had actually entered Kastanje's home and abducted her employee. They'd been so close to the woman who enraged Daphne and filled her with seething jealousy and, yet, still so far away. She hungered to have Kastanje's head in a noose, her attractive body upon this table. It would have been so much nicer. To Neva she said,

"Your disappearance should make the wench squirm a bit, don't you think?"

Neva did not respond for she was frightened beyond words. None of this made any sense to her. She had been inside Pastor's house, busy with her work when, all of a sudden, somebody had broken into their home and threatened to destroy the Pastor's house if she didn't cooperate and go quietly along with him.

Neva knew the Pastor's oldest daughter was asleep in her bedroom and she was more anxious for the young woman's safety. She felt obligated to protect the Pastor's daughter from the brute in the yellow jacket and red baseball cap. Therefore, Neva dropped what she was doing and obeyed. It could have been worse, she told herself. It could have been

Crystal Scott imprisoned here on this icy cold table. Neva didn't even try to answer the woman; instead, she silently petitioned God.

It didn't seem to bother the woman when Neva refused to answer her question, though, because she went on without a reply,

"I think we should consider Kastanje's feelings. How depressing it must be to find the woman who cleans your house has vanished." She shook her head at the sad ordeal.

"We might send her a little piece of you. What do you think?" Daphne yammered on as she studied the woman. She brushed Neva's black hair away from her tawny neck to examine closer one of her earrings. It wasn't Neva's garments or jewelry she had in mind, though.

"We could send her your ear, with the earring intact," she suggested. She actually seemed to think this would be a generous offer and she added, "We could send it C.O.D. and she'd have to sign for it. Do you think Kastanje would recognize your ear?"

Neva squeezed her eyes shut, horrified at the idea. The red-head who hovered over her was out of her mind.

"Por va vore, Seniorita, por va vore," she begged mournfully.

Daphne's eyes moved from Neva's face to the scalpel which lay on the cart beside her, amongst other instruments a surgeon would find useful. She picked it up and held it over the woman as she determined the appropriate incisions she'd make to remove her ear.

Chapter 34

"I feel like Bonnie and Clyde must have felt after they'd robbed a bank!" Lorraine said, as she rummaged through her purse for one specific photograph. They were speeding down the road in a stolen car.

"You better slow down, Rosie. We surely don't want to attract the police," she told him as she glanced at the speedometer on the deluxe dashboard of the Lexus.

Roosevelt had hot-wired and stolen Pastor Guire's automobile from the hospital's parking lot. They had no other mode of transportation, though, and they were in a huge hurry. It was only a matter of time before the Pastor learned they'd sneaked away from the hospital in his car, in pursuit of the truth to Andrew's, as well as the others, untimely death.

Roosevelt was going much faster than the posted speed limit. From the corner of his eye, he gazed at Lorraine as he let up on the gas pedal. He saw the photograph in her lap. It was an old black and white photograph, probably taken of them at a Church picnic, he supposed. He knew Charlie and Harriet, Andrew and Lorraine, Abbey and himself and, of course, Joseph Elvio, too were in the picture.

"Those were happy times," he commented, feeling their misfortune and massive loss.

He remembered thinking, at the time, how he and Abbey would have the wonderful pleasure of their friendships, for the rest of their natural lives. Now, most of the people in the photograph were no longer around. They had died as a result of the virus decreed for them.

"This photo prompts me to reconsider my purpose," Lorraine told Rosie, in a heartsick tone. "To apprehend the ghouls responsible for their horrible end."

Conversation proved much too painful; therefore, they drove on in silence. They felt comforted by their mutual friendship, though. Finally, Rosie told her.

"We're going to stop at Joseph's," he said, making a sharp right turn. "Joseph was vaccinated with the antidote, too. Remember how Doctor Foster urged us to be vaccinated?"

"Yes," Lorraine replied.

"Let's see how he is doing. According to the wise Doctor, Joseph should be well on his way to recovery by now." Roosevelt said with skepticism.

Lorraine then leaned forward to turn the radio on. Cruising along in a stolen vehicle made her very nervous. She turned the knob but heard only static. She continued turning the dial until she finally found a station.

Although the reception was poor, Lorraine and Roosevelt heard the deep, masculine voice on the radio, say, "Meanwhile, the virus which baffles medical science advances through out north America, crippling and killing thousands of the aged, and others, too, who have less than perfect health. The figures are staggering!" The Commentator went on explaining to his listeners,

"I don't know about you, but I have several health issues and I'm not in perfect health."

Lorraine thought it may well have been the first time the Commentator had ever admitted to his audience there was anything less than perfect about him.

There must have been someone else present in his sound-proofed studio because, next, he posed the question,

"Could this possibly be bio-warfare, Jack?"

"Yes, indeed, Buster!" Jack answered him. "Terrorists could well have manufactured this virus to bring about even more anarchy!"

Lorraine was almost positive when terrorists were mentioned, many of Buster's listeners envisioned hell-raising Muslims in New York City, hidden underground and being lead by Osama bin Laden.

"Those terrorists have a hideaway on Mount Gaspar," Roosevelt grumbled.

Amazed at this tidbit, Lorraine turned to him,

"They do, Rosie? How do you know?"

"You might say Harriet told me so; Or, I discovered it in her diary. She wrote how her son, Allen, is a member of whatever organization thrives up there on Mount Gaspar!"

"Well, if this is so," Lorraine gulped, "Shouldn't the police be notified so they can investigate and, maybe, detain the people who brought about the deadly virus?"

This made sense to her because she had never really accepted the theory Muslims, somehow, were behind every phenomenon which fell upon the United States.

"We can't know whose involved; the police may already have a pretty good idea, Lorraine," Roosevelt said. "The police, just like the doctor, and probably Pastor Guire, too, may very well be allies with those who are responsible," Roosevelt told her. He realized, though, how preposterous this probably sounded, so he elaborated,

"These are troubled days, Lorraine. I wouldn't be at all surprised if these are the last days of this earth age."

This was unsettling to her. As her eyes swelled with tears, she turned her back on Roosevelt. Through the passenger window she saw the desert's tangerine sand which stretched on for miles around them. She recalled the documentary she'd seen once on hieroglyphics. According to the documentary, an ancient race of beings had made obscure scribbles on many of the rocks in this area. Probably they had intended to document their early civilization. A curious world, a diverse society, one so alien to their present-day world.

"A demonic entity has mapped out our destruction?" Lorraine questioned and was surprised she had actually verbalized her thoughts.

"Pretty much, Lorraine." Roosevelt replied. "A demonic invasion was foretold eons ago."

"Yes," she murmured and wished so much Andrew could be here now, so he could hold her hand and calm her fears.

By the time Roosevelt and Lorraine had reached Joseph Elvio's home, they had so upset themselves they were braced for almost anything, except for what they encountered.

They found Joseph on his front porch with an iron kettle in one hand and a dipper in the other. Joseph lived in a mobile home, alone and completely isolated, surrounded by miles of rich, dry desert scenery. He'd never married, preferring solitude over what he called, *a frenzied life-style*.

The handsome Italian man had a black beard which covered his chin and flowed to his chest. They watched as he struck the kettle with the cast-iron dipper and shouted,

"Geronimo!"

Roosevelt turned to see if Geronimo would appear and come running at Joseph's command.

Lorraine, who was still sitting in the vehicle they'd stolen from Pastor Guire, got out and closed the door behind her. She stood stock-still and gazed around her at the barren landscape. She thought she heard an animal's deep growl.

She was aware Joseph had a pit-bull named *Geronimo*, although they weren't close friends because she half believed the stories she had heard concerning pit-bulls, how they were usually bred to be fierce attack dogs.

A distant roar set her even more on edge. She was more uptight now than she'd been when Roosevelt shared with her his beliefs in a present-day demonic invasion. She turned to look at Roosevelt; he had to have heard the ferocious growl as well.

A desert wind picked up. It seemed to develop from nowhere, and Lorraine held onto the straw hat she was wearing. She stretched an arm and pointed, calling

"Over there, Roosevelt!"

Beyond the rough terrain about the space of a baseball field away from them and from behind a crag, the frightful sound emanated over the moan of the wind.

Lorraine spotted the aircraft over their heads as it sprayed the earth with a flurry of white stuff, similar to clouds, only clouds had never appeared in this peculiar formation, leaving an intertwine of contrails behind.

Joseph must have heard another sound because he took off running faster than either Lorraine or Roosevelt had ever dreamed he could run; faster than a man half his age.

"Go after him!" Lorraine shouted to Roosevelt. It was ridiculous to think she could catch up with Joseph, and there wasn't much chance Roosevelt could snag him either.

Roosevelt started out, but he was a great deal slower than Joseph. Lorraine followed them. She hurried, holding onto her hat because the wind had become even worse.

Joseph halted on the opposite side of a boulder. His dark eyes gaped at the ground. What was it he had found, Lorraine wondered, frightened for her friend's safety.

Roosevelt reached Joseph and he, too, gazed down with a terror-stricken face. A human skeleton lay against the boulder.

On closer scrutiny, Roosevelt saw not just one human skeleton, but three of them settled around the boulder where Geronimo had been when Joseph called him.

Now the dog licked at his master's hand and then his coal black nose sniffed at the strange formations. Roosevelt turned to Joseph,

"What on earth is this?" he questioned, disturbed by the mystery Geronimo had uncovered.

Roosevelt was quite sure Joseph was also surprised by the pit-bull's find.

"Could the virus have killed them?" Lorraine asked. Once more she turned her eyes upward to view the plane which was making the queer compositions in the sky.

"They should have been vaccinated like I was," Joseph said, more to the dog at his side then to Roosevelt and Lorraine. The dog jumped up on him, knocking Joseph to the ground where he lay...dead.

Chapter 35

Kas and her daughters packed their bags and left Victoria Street just as both Paul and Detective Baldwyn had advised her to do.

Paul wasn't around as they hurriedly left to escape the fury of Rattler Mackenzie, though, so she left him a note. Just as she had done the previous day for Neva, she posted this one to Paul on the refrigerator, too.

She turned around to gaze at her kitchen once more, before leaving it behind. It had never meant more to her than it did at this moment. This kitchen, in shades of green, where with her husband and daughters she had spent so many happy hours. Now she was forced to desert it, as if it was hazardous, or as though some danger lurked in every nook and cranny.

Crystal appeared from the hallway, struggling to carry a large suitcase. The tall, lean young man, Allen, took it from her and carried it for her. The heavy weight seemed to be no trouble for him. He may have been dense but, Kas noticed, he was stalwart; possibly a deadly combination, she suspected.

"I wish you didn't have to leave," he confessed with a sad face.

Allen had quickly become pals with Erin and this troubled her, too. Erin seemed to share a great deal in common with the peculiar young man and Cadence seemed really taken by him, also.

Kas was deeply troubled by his presence and sensed he had something to do with the esoteric twister which was unsettling their lives. She'd decided for safety's sake not to discuss her fears with her girls but, instead, to get away from Allen and all the disasters they had encountered ever since they'd taken in Harriet's dog and Allen had started hanging around their house to visit the Terrier. Kas figured it was anything but a coincidence, this was the exact time all of their trouble started.

Poor Mister Wolfe had died on the elevator. Kas shook her head as she remembered his awful demise. Allen could have had nothing to do with his death, though, because he'd been bitten by a rattlesnake while stuck on the elevator.

She was sure this was Rattler's own doing because it had his teeth-marks all over it. Allen, though, was more informed than he let on. He was associated in some way with the occult and she was acutely aware of this.

"What are we going to do with Toby?" Erin asked her.

"We're going to leave him here with your dad," Kas replied. "He's going to need Toby to keep him company." she gently explained to her.

Erin lifted the dog off the floor and gave him a firm embrace. Toby licked her face and wagged his tail.

"We'll leave him inside of the house for now," Kas told her. The thought of Toby being anywhere around the reptile which had threatened them just yesterday worried Kas now. It surprised her she had grown so fond of the little dog.

"I hope dad will be okay here, all by himself." Crystal said, expressing anxiety over her father's well-being.

"Me too!" Kas said. "I've left him a note and asked him to call us this evening," she told Crystal.

She ushered her daughters to the door while Allen followed them. Kas opened the sliding glass door, thinking of Neva and how she had probably disappeared with the two men from the occult. She wondered where on earth they had taken her.

After the others filed out, Kas once more turned around at the door, to survey her kitchen. Toby stood in the middle of the ceramic tiled floor and barked at her. She suspected he very much wanted to come with and Kas didn't blame him a bit. This was no longer the kind of place where she would want to be left all alone, either.

In a hidey hole where nobody would ever think to look for him, and camouflaged if they did look, the spectator watched. It brought him a great amount of pleasure to be a silent observer, which is why he spent so much of the time engrossed in the activity.

How was it, he wondered, not one of them realized they were being watched? He watched them exit their house. He watched them hurry to the garage, and he especially watched her. He watched her open the garage door with the remote control. Did she think she was being clever? There was no way she could ever be as clever as he was.

It intrigued him the way they were so swift to leave the Pastor behind, never realizing how much safer they'd be if they managed to remain together. It was the Pastor, though, who had encouraged her to leave. His gross mistake would cost him dearly.

The spectator watched her walk Allen to his bicycle. He heard Allen promise her once they had left he would swiftly return to the mental hospital. He knew the young man had no intention of keeping his promise for Allen wasn't quite the blockhead they mistook him for being.

It amused him the way Allen showed her the new horn he'd bought for his brand new bicycle. Like the imbecile she believed him to be, Allen grabbed the horn and squeezed, producing the sort of noise which rattled her nerves and made her jump. The very same way her own mother had responded to her on various occasions when she was a child.

The observer watched her return to her garage where she embraced her daughters. Oh! She was so very proud and happy with her daughters, wasn't she? They brought her so much delight, he noticed. It was going to bring him even greater enjoyment to separate them now. Although Peter Wolfe had failed at his mission, there was no reason for dismay. He could easily abduct each of the girls at any time.

They had left their little pet behind them. Not a very wise decision for he was privy to their dog now, too. At any time at all he had access to their home. Locked windows and bolted doors could not stop him. The righteous Pastor could prevent his intrusion but the Pastor was not available, was he? No, he was tied up some place else. What a pity.

He watched them then as they exited their driveway in two different vehicles. Her daughter, Crystal, drove the Eldorado, and she positioned herself at the wheel of her sports car. They were off, headed for a vacation, or at least, they were hoping for a reprieve from the snarls which plagued them. They were not about to experience what they were counting on, though. The spectator laughed at their brainless attempts to dodge him.

As Kas drove away, she thought she heard an oddly eerie noise which sounded to her a whole lot like maniacal laughter.

Chapter 36

The doctor was nowhere about when Jesse entered the room but she marveled at the space the woman worked in. It was homey.

She moved around the room as her eyes probed every inch of it with curiosity. The walls were peach tempera and dark apricot carpet overlay the floor. The peach and plush chenille curtains at the window were opened and sunlight poured into the room.

High above her head she saw the inverted honey glass Chandelier and underneath it was a square solid birch coffee table with inset glass fold down doors. A clay sculpture of an object she couldn't quite make out set on the table. It looked to her like something a child might have made. Grouped together around the coffee table were a dark brown leather recliner and Caldwell sofa in cream with matching chair.

The left side of the room was decorated somewhat differently then the other areas. The wall was almost an entire birch wood bookcase with a library of books there. There was a built in wooden bench covered by a nut brown cushion and several throw pillows of cream were tossed about upon the bench.

Above it on the wall was a large wooden framed picture some one had drawn of a playful little boy with blond hair and whose brown eyes were filled with mirth. His red lips were separated by laughter as the little boy in a blue shirt, surrounded by lighter blue sky, gazed into a tree where a parrot was perched on one leafy green branch. He reminded Jesse of Gage when he was around seven or eight. Little boys grew up much too fast, she thought.

"That is Daniel, my son!"

Jesse heard a friendly voice behind her and when she turned around she was surprised at Doctor Kennis. It astonished her how petite the woman was. She just assumed the doctor would be much taller and some how more authoritative looking too. The small, dark, curly-headed woman crossed the floor and, as she did, Jesse noticed the significant lameness of her gait. The doctor was clearly crippled.

"Hi, I'm Jaime," she reached forth a hand to greet her.

"As you already know, I'm Jesse Petersen." Jesse's voice was cold and obscure and the doctor took note of it. Doctor Kennis stood beside the woman and focused her attention on the picture as she explained it to her.

"That was done one year ago on Daniel's eighth birthday. A dear friend of mine painted it with his oils and canvas. It's quite good, isn't it?"

Jesse saw the doctor's green eyes dance with glee. She towered over the short, handicapped woman. She was stronger and healthier than she was.

"Do you collect canes as well?"

She went to the huge wooden hutch with large glass windows and peered at the canes inside. There was a collection of five of them on display there.

"Yes, I do." the doctor answered her with a nervous laugh. She did not try to cross the room after her but instead went to the sofa's matching chair and sat down. From there she studied the restless woman while they engaged in small talk.

"Those are made from twisted and knarled tree branches which captured my attention. Some I've carved from drift-wood I found on the beach when I went to visit Kastanje Scott and her family at their home in Huntington."

The fact they both knew the Scott family was something they shared in common and so Jaime brought it up to her. She saw Jesse turn and face her now.

"Pastor Scott and Kas are my neighbors." she informed her but imagined she was probably all ready aware of it.

"You live right next door to your Pastor?" Jaime laughed. "That's got to be a grind. I wouldn't want to live next door to my priest!"

"You are Catholic?" Jesse questioned her and then felt somewhat sheepish. She noticed the large crucifix on one of the walls when she entered the doctor's office. She pointed to it now.

"Of course, you are Catholic!"

Jaime nodded and turned her head to gaze at the crucifix. "Gage Petersen has made a lot of interesting comments on this religious artifact," the doctor said.

Jesse was excited to learn how Gage had been there and the doctor saw how the news changed her. It lifted her countenance.

Jesse hurried across the room and, in her maroon shell and stone-tinted Capri pants, settled down at one end of the sofa, near Jaime.

"When I saw the address of Saint Regis Mental Health Clinic on the front of your building, I hoped I would discover Gage here!" she said.

"You mean you haven't seen him yet?" Jaime inquired.

"I tried to but I couldn't find him!" she said and thought it must have sounded very silly to the doctor. "I'm not very bright." She quickly turned her eyes away and focused on the carpet. "Archie says I couldn't find my way out of a paper bag." She tried to laugh at his ridicule of her but imagined it wasn't really very funny.

Low self esteem helped make alcoholics. It was a pattern Jaime witnessed many times before. People who felt inferior to other people drank to feel better, at least until their first sober breath when they had to face themselves. Jaime smelled the liquor on Jesse's breath when she shook hands with her but Jesse chose not to mention it.

"Archie is your husband?" Doctor Kennis inquired. She knew he was because she recalled Jesse's urgent telephone call last Friday night and she remembered her exact words to her then.

"Poor Gage," Jesse sighed and frowned.

"Why do you say that?"

"His mother is a drunk and his dad is a Satanist," Jesse shrugged, "I can't really call him a lucky kid now, can I?"

At least she was bright enough to know this. She leaped to her feet and hurried to the one thing in the doctor's office which warranted further attention. It was the crucifix. The Man fastened to the wooden beams wore nothing else but a flesh colored loincloth. She was intrigued by His image. His naked humiliation.

"How long have you drank, Jesse?"

"Too long, long enough so I have black-outs and can't recall what day it is. I've missed birthday parties and school plays and programs because of my drinking. Many, many times Gage and Lacy have come home to find me passed out on the couch or floor. I don't recognize my reflection in the mirror any more."

Jesse thought she was nothing at all like the One on the cross. She admired His virtue. However much she extolled Him she found it impossible to be anything like Him. She was weak-minded and powerless. The liquor was one more thing which had her by the throat and wouldn't let go.

"Life's a vicious circle, twisting and whirling. I've tried to place my confidence in my God. But dear God, would you look at Him!" Jesse reeled around to the doctor and from the crucifix she raised her voice, "Look at Him!" she repeated. "He is dieing and what is the advantage of it?"

She felt the same way she did the day Gage was arrested and, then, later at the police station when he refused to see her. She argued with Archie and then went to his car to retrieve her bottle of vodka in his glove compartment and drank what was left of it. Later, when she tried to talk with Kas about Gage, Kas refused to listen to her.

That day Archie refused to take her to see Gage and, instead, he opted to use her as his punching bag. The whole world was against her and yet Pastor Paul insisted the Man on the cross had given His life for them. She didn't know why. The whole bunch of them weren't worth the dynamite to blow them to hell, she thought.

She finally moved away from the crucifix. She advanced across the room and tried to put enough distance between herself and the image. She couldn't identify with Him and, instead, she went to the window to stare out at a frigid world.

"Are you angry, Jesse?" the doctor asked.

It finally dawned on her why she drank. She became addicted to the bottle to overcome her annoyance at the world around her, the same world which had nailed the Gentle Stranger to a cross. She didn't answer Doctor Kennis.

"Last Friday evening when you contacted me you said your husband, Archie, killed Hank. Who was Hank?"

"Did I say he killed him? I don't recall telling you he killed him." She was plagued with excruciating guilt. The doctor saw her face grow ashen.

"Yes," Jaime attested."You told me then Archie killed Hank because you drink too much. I wrote it down. Would you like me to get it and show it to you?" Jaime struggled from her chair to cross the room to one cabinet of drawers.

"It isn't necessary," Jesse told her.

She didn't want to see what the doctor recorded of her telephone call. She had vivid memories of the night and didn't wish to see the doctor's written account.

"Archie beat the hell out of Hank! Archie descended upon Hank like a fierce ape, bloodthirsty and murderous. Poor Hank never knew what hit him. I don't know if he killed him, though!" Jesse told her in tears. She wanted to let her know right up front she didn't have proof Hank was dead, although he may well have been. "Hank was a great guy whose only fault was his feelings for me!"

Jesse was filled with indignation and her dangling hands folded into fists, clenched fists she hungered to use upon herself. She knew she hadn't merited God's forgiveness. Her pastor was wrong. The Man on the cross hadn't died for her. He was far too intelligent and He would not have given her the time of day even.

"I can't even take care of my son! This is why they've placed him in your care!"

Doctor Kennis could talk with Gage and apparently even help him. She could nurture him while Jesse hadn't even been able to find him. While she was away, and behind her back, they had developed the type of relationship she wanted with him but didn't know how to achieve.

"If you would put yourself in Saint Regis for two weeks I believe we could help you." Jaime told her. She marveled at the way Jesse had so bravely confronted her alcoholism. "It wouldn't be so hard because it's where Gage is, too! What a family reunion!" Jaime laughed with delight. She enjoyed the idea of reuniting them once more.

The color returned to Jesse's cheeks and she brushed the tears from her eyes.

"Come," Jaime motioned to her, "and I will show you where we are keeping your son!" She put heavy emphasis on the words, *your son*.

On their way outside Jesse saw Doctor Kennis remove from the coat hangar beside the door the blackthorn derby-handled cane. It was a beautiful piece of burled wood. The doctor was mobile with her cane. In fact, so mobile, Jesse had to hurry to keep up with her.

"The reason you couldn't find Saint Regis before is because it lies hidden by an arboretum!" she clued her in.

They made their way through the hallway where Jesse saw three other rooms with names of other doctors on the doors.

They went through an archway to the waiting room where Doctor Kennis paused to inform the Receptionist she would be away from her office for an hour and to hold her appointments until she returned.

They walked together through the blue foyer where other clients waited for their doctors and the heavy automatic doors opened to them as they made their way outside.

Jesse was nervous about seeing Gage. He refused to see them at the police station in Althea and then, when Kas told them Gage tried to kill himself, she almost came undone.

She thought about his present state of mind and wondered at this stage of the agenda what she could expect from him. He would probably be frightened and depressed, although she imagined being with Doctor Kennis should have elevated him some. It was difficult to picture Gage, the happy, normal youngster, in a mental hospital. If only Archie hadn't subjected him to the cabal, she thought, but then retracted her thoughts. It took two to tango and two to screw up their children's lives, and kill innocent bystanders too. She was as much to blame for their afflictions as he was.

Following along behind the doctor, she found herself in a lovely grove. They proceeded down a narrow cobble-stone pathway which wound around the building and through an arboretum. Jesse saw green Chinese Pistachio trees she never knew existed. A ground squirrel hurried across their path and Jaime giggled.

"Around here we have to watch out for the squirrels and other animals who've made their homes in our arboretum." Jaime told her.

It was a picnic when Jesse compared it to the world she was from. She imagined she could grow quite accustomed to watching out for squirrels. Several yellow canaries in a walnut tree sang to them.

"There is a convent here too," Jaime told her. "Last Sunday evening Gage, Daniel and I ate dinner with the sisters there! They make the most wonderful chocolate pistachio pies!" she said with a smile.

They reached the freshly painted brick building and positioned at one side of the entrance was a huge statue.

"This is Saint Regis," Jaime gestured to it. "Well, at least an image of Saint John Francis Regis. His valuable contributions are better demonstrated by the people and activities inside of the building."

She was a devout Catholic, and while it caused some difficulties for Jesse who was a Protestant, she thought maybe in this case she would make exceptions. It pleased her how Doctor Kennis displayed an interest in her son. She invited Gage to eat with them at the convent and Jesse thought it probably was not her habit to ask her patients to have dinner with her too.

Finally, Doctor Kennis opened the door and they entered the building. Jesse felt her heart leap into her throat when her eyes surveyed the place where her son had been locked away all of this time.

She stopped to gaze into a dimly lit room to her left. As she peered inside she saw the space was filled with empty pews and a small crucifix was fastened to one wall, above a dish of holy water.

There were two statues around the altar. One of them was an image of His Sacred Heart and the other was the Madonna with the Holy Infant in her arms. There was only one person in the church and he was dressed in a knee length brown robe; over his head he wore the robe's hood.

He carried a matchbook in his hand and with his other hand he struck one of the matches to light one of the candles which were grouped together in red containers several feet away from the statue of Sacred Heart. His actions were deliberate and she was moved by the intensity he demonstrated in the things he did. His activities made very little sense to her though.

Jaime saw how Jesse was pulled to the chapel and curious over the activities she witnessed there. Upon investigation Jaime recognized the young man and smiled at his mother.

"That's Gage." she whispered.

As they watched him from the door he was unmindful of them. He pulled something from the pocket of the heavy flannel robe he wore. It looked to her like a beaded chain. With meticulous care he held it in his hands. She saw him kneel before the statue of Sacred Heart. Once upon his knees he kissed the chain and lowered his head in prayer. He was her own flesh and blood and yet she could hardly recognize him and no longer understood him.

"Is he a murderer?" she whispered to the doctor who stood beside her.

Jaime's eyes turned to Gage. The sisters had given him the rosary he prized. Although Gage found great consolation in the Catholic religion, it was probably only a stepping-stone for him, Jaime thought. He was a Protestant and she didn't mean to proselyte or to steal sheep from Pastor Scott's fold.

"I'm ready to testify in court for him." she said. "I'm more curious about what you think, Jesse. Do you think your son held an AK-47 in his hands and coldly murdered two people in a drive-by shooting?"

Jaime saw the frail woman lean her weight against the archway and saw her brown eyes blink back tears, then in a low voice she whispered,

"Although, Archie and I may well have made such a monster." Jesse shook her head. "I know Gage would never kill any one! He could never do such an evil thing! He's a compassionate individual", she said.

"Then why don't you share your feelings with him?" Jaime suggested, nodding toward the young man on his knees in the chapel.

Chapter 37

She tried to be silent but she was too heavy on her feet and he heard her behind him. Gage jumped up from where he was knelt and turned around to face her.

"I guess I could never keep a vow of silence," she apologized to him.

"Mothers are not meant to take a vow of silence," he informed her with a grin.

Seeing now how he invited her to him she followed her heart. He still wore the hood over his blond head and his hands held the rosary.

Jaime watched them from a distance and Gage waved to her.

"Thank you," he called to her.

She nodded and lingered only a minute longer before, with cane in hand, she rushed away down the hall and off to visit other patients.

Gage imagined his mother probably thought he was nuts if she had watched him for any length of time. She could not understand these procedures. He returned the rosary to his pocket and looked at the candle he had lit. The flame danced inside of the red vase.

"I lit the candle for you, never thinking my prayers would bring you to me!" The day Daphne visited him and showed him the ring she'd swiped from his mother he worried about her. Whether or not it was just another of his insane dreams he didn't know but it unnerved him.

"We pray because we anticipate an answer." She said as she made her way to him. She taught him to pray with faith when he he was a little boy. When she was finally within reach he stretched forth an arm to take her hand with his and pulled her to him. She pressed her slender hand against his rosy cheek.

"You will have company, my dear. Your nice doctor-friend has warmly invited me to Saint Regis to recuperate from my addiction here." She shared with him and thought he should be quite happy to hear, since her hellish addiction was the major reason they were both there.

"We're going to be room mates," he happily smiled at her.

She nodded and wondered how big of an issue it would be to abstain from alcohol, to end all craving and become drug free. She would have to make other provisions for Lacy while she was away. She could not leave her with Archie to endure his madness all by herself. There was probably no safer place on earth then with Tim and Chenoa Bailey. She needed a place to sit and think and she found a perch on the altar's steps.

"So, what do you do around here to keep yourself busy besides pray with your rosary and wear your bathrobe hood over your head?" She should not have said this. It was insulting and hurtful. Such words easily escaped her lips. It was the productive, scholarly thoughts which were always most difficult to disclose.

He forgot he was still wearing his hood and pulled it off his head. She saw his tousled mop of blond hair and he was even dearer to her for it, if it was possible. He was on pins and needles and couldn't really sit, but he did kneel on his knees beside her.

"They have an extensive library here!" he told her.

"I'm an avid reader and at this minute I am engrossed in a book all about Saint Gregory the Great who was the son of a wealthy Roman senator and was educated by the finest teachers in Rome. Finally, turning his back upon all of his wealth, he turned his home into a Benedictine monastery." Gage was enthusiastic.

She spotted the excitement in his blue eyes and she thought he couldn't very well be insane if he was still so absorbed with life. She cradled her knees with her hands as she listened with admiration to him. He saw how she wasn't wearing her wedding ring and it bothered him so he asked her about it.

She remembered the day she found it missing. How odd Archie hadn't noticed it. He would have asked her about it if he had noticed. He would have inquired if she took it off when she met the troublemaker, Hank, at the bar. Hank wasn't a troublemaker, though. Hank didn't have a clue she was married.

"I misplaced it somewhere," she said. It was odd she hadn't lost the other rings she wore. It was just her wedding ring she misplaced and it might have been on purpose she thought, although she couldn't recall it. There were lots of events and even entire days she couldn't remember now. It was as if someone or something had reached into her brain and stolen from her many of the details she was supposed to file away and remember.

"Daphne did take your ring!" He jumped to his feet and began to pace back and forth. Jesse watched him with growing concern. "Daphne drifts in and out of rooms and stations, laying waste and lifting other people's property! Some one has to stop her!" he babbled, and his torment flashed in his eyes.

"Who is Daphne," she inquired and struggled to understand his impetuous thoughts but it made no sense to her.

He hurried away from her. He had to put distance between them for her safety.

She got to her feet but didn't go after him. Alarmed for him but unable to fix things, fearful she would make things worse, she maintained her distance and refused to invade his privacy. She turned to see Doctor Kennis just outside of the chapel. That minute she was engaged in conversation with someone else but she hoped for Gage's sake she would hasten to intervene. Until then Jesse didn't know what to do and found she was quickly becoming unglued too.

"For Pete's sake, I'm your mother, Gage, and you can tell me anything! Who is Daphne and what does she have to do with the murders on Foothill Boulevard?"

He turned around to face her and she saw the tears in his eyes as he yelled,

"Daphne Orion was driving the car the day Gregory and Jonathan Wright were shot and killed!"

Jaime heard him, too and immediately reacted to the disturbance.

"I didn't do it!" He didn't know whether she believed him or not. With all of his heart he wanted her to.

"I know you didn't do it, Honey! Nothing in this rotten world would ever make me think you were the one who killed them!" Blinding tears streamed down her cheeks. He was her first-born and she wanted to cradle him the way she did when he was a little boy and fell down and skinned his knees.

There was more to it though. It was something he was unable to tell anyone before. No one could have pried it from him. It was something so horrible he couldn't keep it to himself any longer.

"Dad was the one with the AK-47! He was the one who murdered the old man and his grandson!"

He was delirious, Jesse thought.

Jaime made her way down the isle to stand behind him. She gripped his arm.

"It's all right, Gage" she endeavored to calm him. In Jaime's estimation Daphne Orion was capable of anything. She knew what Gage told them was the truth although it scared the living daylights out of her.

149

"He's irrational," Jesse protested. Archie was a wretched sinner, who in a jealous rage had beaten a man half to death but he wasn't a murderer.

"He isn't irrational and he's not schizophrenic, either. Gage has been traumatized and we owe it to ourselves to listen to him!" Jaime told her.

"You've bought into his insanity and now he's become worse!" Jesse shouted at her. To think she ever entertained the idea of being involved with all of this absurdity. She disapproved of this bedlam and bughouse mumbo-jumbo and this only convinced her she was right to abhor psychiatry. "Well, count me out! I am not going to allow you turn me into a lunatic too!" Jesse would defend her husband right up until her last breath, as they witnessed when she marched away from them.

"Mom!" Gage called after her and lunged forward to stop her but Doctor Kennis clung to him. He was under arrest and confined to his present environment until the law of California decided otherwise.

"Let her go, Gage!" Jaime directed him. "Sometimes, no matter how difficult, we have to let go and pray the Author of our lives will intervene!" she told him.

He knew she was right. In solitary confinement he had discovered redemption. He would stay there at Saint Regis' with Doctor Jaime and with his thoughts of Saint Gregory and with the statue of Sacred Heart.

"What should I do?" It was unclear to him what action he should take and destitute, he turned to her for guidance.

"Pray, Gage! Pray like you've never prayed before!" she urged him. Then she left the chapel to try and track down Jesse.

Chapter 38

Their home should have been the center of their lives, Jesse thought. It was the way she was brought up and she had tried without help to make their lives comfortable and pleasing. She surveyed their yellow brick home from her coronet blue 1999 Volkswagen Passat parked beside the curb. She was painfully aware their lives had become a living hell. After twenty-two years of trying to find happiness with Archibald Petersen it was finally time to call it quits. It was the only safe and healthy thing to do. Archie would not put Lacy through the same insanity he inflicted upon her older brother. She would see to it.

Archie hadn't killed those poor people on Foothill Boulevard, though. He hadn't gunned down anyone with an AK-47. He didn't even have an AK-47.

Jesse undid her seat belt and slowly proceeded from her car, turning to carefully close the door behind her. She had no intentions now of staying. She was going to announce her decision to divorce him, collect her things, ask Tim and Chenoa to keep Lacy just until she found suitable lodging elsewhere and then she would walk away from Archie for good.

Those were her plans as, in her maroon heels, she made her way down the sidewalk and up the steps which lead to their front door. She turned the handle but found the door was locked.

Archie was inside, reclusive and detached. She knocked and rang the doorbell and then waited for him to answer her. As the minutes passed she tried to ignore the feelings she had of impending danger.

Lacey was with the Bailey's at their store. She wonderd what would happen to Archie and their house once she and Lacey left it behind them. She had visions of it being condemned. It was only a house she told herself. The people forced to reside there with a Satanist were all that really mattered to her.

The door opened and she found herself looking into Archie's cold, dilated eyes. He looked like an iceberg to her; an iceberg clothed in the oriental red robe he wore. The one with the picture of a dragon stitched on the back of the cloth. She wasn't as much afraid of the robe or of Archie or his insanity as she was petrified of the dragon and his presence inside of their home.

"Jesse!" He seemed surprised to see her there.

Gone were the blinders from her eyes. At long last she saw through him, his true colors. He was a child lost in his dreams for power and wealth and sympathy was all she felt for him now.

"Hello Archie," pity dripped from her voice. She knew he despised pity and especially from his wife and children. Now when she looked at him the anger which consumed her for the way he had behaved disappeared. There was little she could expect from one so miserable.

The curtains were drawn and the room was dark and dank, lit only by the candles which burned everywhere in their living room. She was confronted with the heavy scent of burning myrrh and she knew what he was up to. He was engaged in another séance.

The demons failed to deliver to him the goods he requested from them and so he sought their attention again. It was an endless charade and the fat, greedy man miserably failed to comprehend how the more he begged from them the less they gave to him. They ensnared him even as they smothered the life out of him.

He looked around them. There was no way he could explain these things to her. The spirit he conjured up, the one who called himself Cadmar, or Dragon's Teeth, was a valiant warrior who had just promised him prosperity. It was something he could bank on.

Then, when Cadmar heard the knock at the door he evaporated before they could seal their contract. Archie displayed very little patience now for whatever problems she might have or her reasons for being there. When she interrupted him he was right on the verge of turning all of their turmoil around and making them filthy rich for the rest of their entire lives.

He was so zealous in his pursuits for wealth and prestige he was determined to stop at nothing to obtain these things. He subjugated his son to his demons and sold him into bondage to them. Nothing was sacred and precious to him now.

Cadmar had disappeared only for a moment but now he returned to him again. His voice stretched from everywhere, from behind the drawn curtains, through the walls and even from their sofa and chairs.

"She cannot help you, Archie. She will only interfere and turn you over to the police, too. Destroy her now while you can. Kill…Kill…Kill!" Cadmar, the warrior, encouraged him.

In the quiet chapel at Saint Regis' Hospital Gage lit more candles and dropped on his knees to pray so much harder for her.

Jesse saw how the devil held Archie's neck in his noose and was about ready to pull on the rope. She told herself she had the responsibility to dissuade the man she once loved from his inevitable demise and she reached out to him but he pulled away from her.

"The groveling witch wants your life's blood! She and her ungrateful youngsters have made you the pauper you are today! All right, here is my contract with you: I will grant you nothing until her cold, dead body lies on the floor!" Cadmar assured him.

She didn't appreciate being pushed away when she was trying to rescue him. She never saw Archie so carried away with the devil.

"Did you kill someone, Archie?" she questioned him.

Archie felt her cold accusations and he didn't know where to turn. Cadmar refused to give him a cent unless he killed the woman he loved. Love was something which escaped him. He lost all understanding of love. What he could wrap his mind around was Cadmar's promise to him of riches, insurmountable.

"I'm going to divorce you, Archie!" she let him know.

"She is going to divorce you for the lowly scoundrel, Hank! Apparently she fancies stinking failures!" Cadmar informed him. "Kill her and I will make you a king among men!"

Enticed by lofty promises and enraged by jealousy, Archie doubled his fists and delivered his first blow to her stomach. Jesse lost her balance and staggered. She was a rag doll to him and as fragile as one in his hands.

Spurred on by Cadmar he delivered another blow to her left shoulder and then one blow to her face and even when she lay on the ground in a fetal position trying to protect herself, he continued to beat on her until, just like Cadmar demanded of him, he assumed she was dead and the sight of her lifeless body on the floor, at his feet, moved him with agony at what he had done to her and doubled over, he loudly groaned.

"Jesse!"

It was one more sacrifice he made for wealth and power. Now the devil was indebted to him. He fled the scene and ran outside. Jesse heard the door slam behind him. On the porch he fell upon his knees and cried,

"Oh! God! What have I done? What have I done?"

Cadmar was dissatisfied, though, when she weakly pulled herself up on to her feet. In intense pain she made her way to the thin screen door and by then Archie was inside of her car.

She should have pocketed her keys, she thought, when she heard him start the vehicle and squeal the tires as he raced away. Archie was gone and only the red, oriental robe which he had stripped off lay on the ground.

As he stood at Pastor Scott's front door the visitor turned to see someone lying on the ground across the preacher's driveway and in his neighbor's yard. It was a female's body he saw, lifeless and immobile. Was it a transient, he wondered, a bum or bag lady passed out there.

The neighborhood appeared to be an affluent area; too upscale for even a small time pastor let alone a bum. Upon closer examination he saw the woman was covered with blood. Being a humane and tender-hearted man he was compelled to help if he could, so he left the preacher's porch and dashed across the driveway to the body which lay broken on the bloodstained grass.

It was Jesse. She was unconscious and appeared to have been battered and then discarded. There were cuts and abrasions on her face, the clothing she wore was ripped at her left shoulder and her long auburn hair was soaked in blood. He knelt over her,

"Jesse," he gasped with remorse. He heard her groan and saw her open her eyes.

"Hank! What are you doing here?" Hank was dead, she had thought. He shouldn't have been there. He shouldn't have been anywhere in this morbid world. "I'm not in hell so this must be heaven." she said, and coughed up more crimson fluid.

"Lie still," he told her. Unable to ascertain the extent of damage done to her, he couldn't move her. He had to find a telephone and call for help, he agonized. He didn't have a cell phone with him; he didn't carry one.

"Archie will pay for his crimes," she whispered.

Hank imagine the same brute who had mercilessly wounded him had beaten Jesse to a bloody pulp and now he had to rescue her. He had to find emergency help for Jesse.

"Stay there, don't move!" He ordered her and this time he managed to convince her. Jesse lost consciousness.

He couldn't get inside the pastor's house because his door was locked so he hastened and ran to the front door of the house adjacent to the yard on which Jesse lay, unconscious and possibly bleeding to death, he surmised.

He didn't know what he would find inside of the house, or who it belonged to, or where its owners were right then but he thought he could find a telephone somewhere if the doors were not locked.

He threw open the screen door and shuffled into a grim room lit only by smoldering candles standing everywhere. Hank knew something about séances, channeling up ghosts and calling on the dead. He once had a roommate who did this type of thing. They had parted and gone their own separate ways a long time ago.

Finally, he spotted a telephone on top of the fireplace mantle and raced to it, picked up the receiver and dialed 911.

Chapter 39

Kas drove her car onto the Hesperia off-ramp and at the intersection she waited for the light to turn green before proceeding. She saw Crystal not even a block away on the right hand side of the highway. At a Texaco gas station Crystal stood between her car and the gas pumps as she filled her tank.

Kas didn't need gas so she drove from the highway onto the station's cement lot and came to a stop on a twisted spot of land right beside a field of cut green grass. She got out of her car to stretch her legs and see how the girls were doing.

Through her sunglasses she could see a raven circle above them and thought it was strange. An omen? she wondered.

Crystal saw her stroll toward her and smiled. Kas called to her over the noise of a particularly loud motorcycle.

"We've still got a long way to go but it's a nice day to drive." she shared with her.

Crystal nodded to indicate she had heard her despite the noisy motorcycle engine.

Kas examined the bike and its rider. He was stationed at the end of one line of gas pumps and only feet away from Crystal. It was a big Harley Davidson and its rider was a middle-aged man in dirty blue jeans, turquoise muscle shirt and a red bandana around his head. One silver earring shaped like a cross hung from his left ear close to the snaggle of beard and mustache he wore. His stringy blond hair was dirty and he had a large tattoo on his thick upper arm. It was a serpent coiled around a bottle of whiskey. He revved the engine of his bike.

The raven circled in the sky above them and she moved closer to the car and gazed inside of it at the light upholstery. The car was empty and she immediately became frightened.

"Where are Erin and Cadence," she called to Crystal who was still busy with the pump.

"Erin took Cadence to the bathroom," she shouted back at her.

There were crazy fiends on the loose and they were stalking her children.

"Crystal," Kas yelled, "How could you?" She thought Crystal had far more sense then to allow two little girls to wander off all by themselves.

The guy on the bike eyed them closely. She didn't know what to do. Someone should stay with Crystal and make sure the rider didn't come any closer. The raven encompassed them. Finally, she decided to leave Crystal with the bird and hurried away to find her two little girls.

The bathroom was on the same side of the building where she had parked her car. She had seen the sign before leaving her vehicle and she raced there now. It was a big white metal door which badly needed new paint.

"Are you in there?" she rapped against it and waited for an answer. When none came she called out again, "I'm going to get the attendant to unlock this door unless you answer me right now!" She waited for one of them, either Erin or Cadence to answer her. "What's the matter with you? Why don't you answer me?" she was panicky.

The door slowly opened and Kas saw a blond woman in denims and halter-top step out from behind it.

"What's wrong with you lady? Why can't you just get in line and wait your turn?" the young woman inquired of her.

"I'm terribly sorry," Kas apologized, feeling quite sheepish, "Have you seen my daughters?" The look in her eyes begged for an answer. "One is five years old and wearing pink shorts and a flowered top. The other is fifteen and has on blue jeans. Have you seen either one of them?" she inquired.

The blond shook her head and stumbled on her feet. On closer scrutiny Kas saw the pupils of her eyes were dialated. The blond was stoned out of her mind. Crystal came from around the building and approached her.

"Should we check the convenience store?" She was helpful.

Kas nodded and saw the blond weave her way to her car and thought someone should arrest her before she got behind the wheel and caused a major accident on the highway. She couldn't right now. She had more pressing matters to attend to.

Crystal followed her mom into the small store and at the counter she paid the man for her tank of gas while her mother combed the isles.

"Have you seen my sisters? One is an adorable little girl and the other is older and taller, a thin, red headed kid?" Crystal asked the heavy-set man in a white button down, long sleeve -shirt.

"Yea," he mumbled as he took her money. "They came in here about ten minutes ago and bought some licorice."

"Mom," Crystal called to Kas and saw her dash to the front of the store. "He says he saw them. They were in here about ten minutes ago and bought some candy. They couldn't have gotten too far away yet. Should we call the police?" she wanted to know.

"Not yet," Kas shook her head. They might have to but not until they searched the location.

"What's with the raven?" the man asked as he gazed from their faces to the window behind him. "He's been here circling my place ever since she got here." He pointed his thick finger at Crystal as if he blamed her for the bird's mysterious behavior. "My customers think something around here has died."

"I know nothing about the bird," Kas told him. They didn't own the raven and they had no jurisdiction over which way he flew. They couldn't call him off even if they wanted to.

"The bird flies where he chooses," she said. There was nothing else she could tell him about the raven and she wasn't going to stand around and try to make sense of it. She had to find her daughters.

Crystal thanked him and followed her mother out of the store and saw the raven still hadn't left them but squawked and screeched just over their heads and then flew over the building and made a grand circle in the sky there. They went where the bird led them.

"Horsie," the curly headed blond exclaimed to her red-headed sister. They were just behind the gas station. Cadence stuck her red licorce through the fence and offered it to the speckled pony.

She ran to them and lifted Cadence in her arms. As she pressed her small daughter against her she softened and reached for Erin's hand.

"Oh! Thank God, you are alright!" The ugliness of this affair made her realize now they were in big trouble. "I want you girls to stay together from now on!" She turned her attention to Crystal. " I don't want you to let either one of them out of your sight again, Crystal!" she ordered her.

Crystal nodded her head and then directed her attention to the raven perched on the building's roof-top. He cocked his head as he eyed them.

"He knew where they were and he led us to them." Crystal whispered. He was truly an abnormal bird, she thought and she stared at him and he stared back.

"Thank you." Kas said to him.

"You are welcome, Kastanje," he answered her as plain as day.

They would take Cottonwood to Atlanta and they had three hours of driving ahead of them before they finally reached their destination in Huntington Beach. She put Cadence down and took her hand.

The mysterious bird left them. The gas station's owner would probably have said they were in thick with the bird if he knew they shared words with him.

They didn't see him again but went right to Crystal's car. Kas gave them each a hug before she tucked them inside of the car. Huntington never seemed so far away to her before.

"Okay," she forced a smile and told Crystal, "I'm going to follow your Eldorado every mile of the way."

Crystal gripped her hand and didn't want to let her go. She was apprehensive. Through her sunglasses Kas gazed down into her blue eyes. From behind the wheel of the car Crystal managed to return her smile.

"You'd better," she answered her. "I will keep my eyes on you."

"You keep your eyes on the road," Kas admonished her. She gave them another tender look before she, finally, turned away from them and marched across the hard cement ground to her car. She was inside of it before Crystal started her engine, shifted gears and proceeded forward.

Chapter 40

Roosevelt felt they were fortunate Lorraine had been their church's Secretary up until a couple of months ago when she retired.

"All those years you spent employed at the church will come in handy now," he told her, as Lorraine sat down at the computer in Harriet's den.

She nodded in reply as she went right to work with dexterity and, once online, she typed *chemtrails* into search. She'd told Rosie about seeing the curious clouds above them at Joseph Elvio's place, before they learned what kept Joseph's dog at bay and unresponsive to his master's voice, those frightful human skeletons the dog had dug up.

Roosevelt wandered from the den, going into the living room as though he were directionless. There had to be more of a lead somewhere in the house, he thought; more than just the mysterious words he'd uncovered in Harriet's personal diary. Harriet's very brief description of how she would not blame the mountain for the virus she and Charlie confronted. This sole admission led Roosevelt to think Harriet must have possessed some understanding of their dire situation.

Poor Joseph; Roosevelt deplored what had happened to Joseph. Hours earlier, before his sudden and unexpected death, Roosevelt had struggled to advise their friend against being vaccinated. He wouldn't listen to him, though, and now Joseph was gone too.

Roosevelt leaned against one wall in Harriet's living room and brushed his hand over his eyes. He wasn't about to let the enemy steal his golden years, too, or cheat him of the opportunity to explore his deep feelings for Lorraine. When he opened his eyes again, in the heavy shadows of deepening darkness, he noticed Harriet's book-shelf stacked with books. Maybe there was something there, a clue as to their plight.

He crossed the floor and began to thumb through the books. Among them he saw 'Pilgrims Progress,' by John Bunyan, and 'Facing Your Giants,' by

Max Lucado. Both very fine books and still in excellent condition, too. As he handled John Bunyan's inspirational book, Roosevelt was overwhelmed with rich memories of Harriet. Holding it carefully in his hands, he gazed through more books and titles on the shelf. '90 Minutes In Heaven,' by Don Piper and Cecil Murphy, and 'Ever After,' by Karen Kingsbury, 'Casting Out Demons,' by H.A. Maxwell Whyte.

Casting out what? Roosevelt blinked twice, in disbelief, and looked at the title of the book beside it, "Demonology Past and Present," by Kurt E. Koch, and beside this one he found another one of similar nature. The book was called "Demons And Deliverance" by H.A. Maxwell Whyte. It was a very strange collection of books, indeed, he thought. The books on Harriet's shelves proved they were up against something with enormous power; demons from the abyss.

"Rosie?"

He heard someone softly call to him and he turned in surprise. He had been lost in thought and the sudden voice startled him. In the dim light, he saw Lorraine standing in the doorway. Before he could answer her, she went on,

"There's a lengthy amount of information online about chemtrails. There's something else here I want you to see too." She pointed to the room from which she had just emerged.

Roosevelt followed Lorraine into Harriet's den, which was dark except for the light from the computer screen, which made it an eerie setting, he thought.

Lorraine's eyes were adjusted to the darkness. She didn't even seem to notice it as she raced to the computer and sat down. Then, with excitement, she said to Roosevelt,

"This website which is called, *'Prince of the Power of the Air'* has lots of info on chemtrails!"

He moved closer to her until he was standing right behind her. From there he could get a good look at what she was referring to.

"The military has been spraying the skies in North America for several years now." she told him in a soft tone. "The government denies having any knowledge of chemical sprayings." She looked up into his face and thought he looked rather tired in this light. She went on, "This would explain Pastor Barry Guire's refusal to admit anything erratic is happening. Wouldn't it, Rosie?" Lorraine questioned him and he nodded at her.

"Yes, it sure would", was all he managed to get out. He found all the information mind-boggling. Roosevelt suspected the host must have some knowledge of ancient manuscripts for the ancient Scriptures called Satan, '*The Prince of the Air.*'

The information Lorraine shared with him was in line with what he'd discovered in Harriet's living room, too; those bizarre books on demonology he had found there. All of this pointed to the fact the devil had a hand in what was taking place. Lorraine studied the screen and read aloud to him,

"Biological warfare has turned the pharmaceutical industry into a multi-million dollar enterprise. Because of chemtrails, multitudes of people are sickened and poisoned to death." Once more, Lorraine turned to Roosevelt and said, "Biological warfare, Rosie? America is hostile to its own people, innocent, plain folks who have no idea as to what their government is doing to them, none whatsoever!"

Roosevelt glanced at her and saw the mist in her blue eyes, Lorraine's grief because of what she had learned. To whom would they turn if their respected officials were pitted against them? They'd seen the deadly result of the vaccination medical doctors were prescribing for them. Their doctors, administrators and clergymen were all involved in a cold-blooded assault against their own fellow citizens, Roosevelt suspected.

"What made them turn against their own countrymen?" Roosevelt inquired.

Lorraine shook her head. She didn't know, but she had an idea and she had to share this with Roosevelt too. She left the website and typed into the search engine the word, chimera. It was something she'd discovered before by accident. She'd meant to type *chemtrails* but, instead, had entered *chimera*. Before long she'd downloaded what seemed to her to offer a possible and terrible explanation for the chemtrails.

She read the strange, thought-provoking page to Rosie even as he paced Harriet's carpet, back and forth, just behind her chair in the darkened room. The thumping noise of his feet accompanied her reading.

"Years ago," Lorraine began, "a part of the world was extremely affected by a man called Darragh James Mackenzie. The burly Mackenzie ruled as Bishop over an arcane society known as the *Delphians*. The Delphians realized a large following in the decade of the 80s and the early 90s. Their aim was to destroy the system in order to create a global empire which they would call 'Chimera'.

"The new empire would be composed of only what the *Delphians* believed to be the most astute and zealous. The rest of the debilitated population would be eliminated, leaving only the most able-bodied who would plan and execute the affairs of Chimera."

"Within Bishop Darragh Mackenzie's lifetime the Delphians never achieved their ambition. A lone Detective, by the name of Cody Baldwyn, interceded and prevented their revolution from ever taking place. Detective Cody Baldwyn shot and killed the Delphian's evil mastermind. "

"However, Bishop Mackenzie left behind him one daughter and his grandson who was conceived through Mackenzie's own devious affair with his daughter. Occult members cherish the hope somehow Mackenzie's daughter will one day succeed to establish their longed for Chimera, a modern Garden of Eden."

After reading the first page of the website, it had become so gruesomely quiet, she hurried to the light switch on the wall just as fast as her legs would carry her.

The last time she'd seen Rosie's face, he'd looked so tired. Perhaps he was really ill, she thought, however, she couldn't determine this in the darkness which surrounded her. She flipped on the light switch and the bright fluorescent light over her head illuminated the room. Roosevelt stood completely still and looked at her but, thank heaven, he appeared to be alright.

"Rosie, there's more!", she announced. On her return to the computer she added, "The website's author says the evil society's headquarters has always been located on Mount Gaspar!"

"Mount Gaspar", he grumbled. He had been right all along. He wasn't demented, or a kook, as others seemed to think but now he had to go to Mount Gaspar. He had to put a stop to the occult's activities. He had to for the sake of his friends. For Harriet's sake, and for Andrew's and Joseph's sake too.

He would go and reason with them, demand they stop their pursuits. It would have been nice had they been able to trust the Althea Police Department but they couldn't. They couldn't trust another living soul. It was up to him to bring their senanigans to an end, Rosie told himself.

"This may sound sacra religious," he heard Lorraine say, "but Kastanje Scott's maiden name was Mackenzie." she reminded him.

At the same time the light over their heads suddenly flickered and then went out, leaving them in complete darkness, meaning the computer had crashed, too. Yet, they were amazed to see on the black screen in red letters,

"You were not authorized to view the predated website. Dreadful consequences will ensue."

Lorraine moved away from the computer as if it was possessed and raced to Roosevelt's side.

"I think we're in deep trouble now, Rosie!" she whispered to him.

When he pulled Lorraine to him he wasn't at all surprised to discover she was trembling.

"What more can they do to us?" he inquired as he stared at the mysterious message on the screen. They heard someone bang loudly upon Harriet's front door.

"Roosevelt, let me in! This is Pastor Paul! I know you're in there!" They heard him call. "You're in a world of trouble, Roosevelt! Let me in!"

"It's possible Pastor Paul is involved in all of this, Rosie," Lorraine said in a hushed tone. "Pastor Paul's wife may even be the occult's ring leader, their high priestess," she told him.

Within moments, Roosevelt was at the door and immediately opened it to see the Pastor standing there, his face a map of anger.

"What the h-e-double hockey sticks are you up to now, old man?" the Pastor, in his white, clerical collar, roared as he burst through the doorway.

Roosevelt didn't reply but he did move out of the Pastor's way as he barged into the house. Lorraine contemplated the Pastor's abrupt appearance. His thick brown hair was rumpled, his chestnut-colored eyes were fierce-looking. She dared not say a word but followed Roosevelt's lead and remained silent. She wished they hadn't taken Pastor Guire's car but how else would they have arrived at Harriet's to access the information they'd collected? Lorraine kept quiet as Pastor Paul Scott marched around the room.

He turned to one of the lamp stands in Harriet's living-room and fumbled with the switch. When he found the knob and turned it, the light went on and the room lit up. However, just minutes ago, the electricity had failed and they faced a complete black-out. She wondered what part Pastor Scott might have played in their dire situation.

"I wasted the biggest share of the day with Pastor Guire at the police department!" Pastor Paul complained to them, enraged by their lawlessness. "He accused you of stealing his vehicle from Mercy Hospital's parking lot!" Pastor Paul turned around and gave Roosevelt a direct look. "What's wrong with you, Rosie? Are you eager to be locked away?", he questioned him in disgust. The elderly man set his jaw.

"Do you really need to ask what's wrong with me, Paul?" He held back his anger but wouldn't call the other man by his proper title. "Joseph Elvio died this afternoon and he was vaccinated with the supposed prevention Doctor Foster prescribed. You apparently don't believe many in our society are being victimized. You and the Senior Pastor of His Holiness Church seem to disapprove of my meddling in these affairs."

Roosevelt's voice rose by decibels. "I don't know what your trouble is and I can't say I trust your motives but Lorraine and I refuse to be more sheep for the slaughter and we are determined to learn who's behind all of this corruption." Rosie saw the other man roll his eyes at him.

"You have a strange way of going about being such an humanitarian, Rosie; embezzlement and infringement? I won't applaud your efforts." Paul told him and heard Roosevelt snap at him in response.

"The truth is all we are after and I will go to any length I deem necessary to prevent Lorraine's and my own extinction!" He gave Lorraine a fleeting look and saw her nod at him. She agreed and understood his reasons. No one else might ever understand what drove him but Lorraine was smart enough to comprehend it. The bottom line was: he wasn't about to let them be killed. Rosie turned his back on Paul to speak to Lorraine. He gave her a tender look and said,

"I'm going to take you home, Lorraine and then I'm going to Mount Gaspar." He'd made up his mind. It was the only thing he could think of doing to stop the devilish culprits on the mountain. She moved toward him, looked him in the eye and firmly told him,

"Not without me you aren't, Rosie!" Lorraine despised the thought of being left alone, or of facing the world without Andrew and without Roosevelt, now, too.

"Mount Gaspar?" The Pastor groaned. He dropped down on Harriet's brown, leather sofa. He felt so weary. "Would someone please tell me what's going on?", he begged them.

Lorraine glanced at him and thought he looked like a total wreck. She sympathized with him. She crossed the floor and sat down on the sofa beside him, wondering how she'd ever explain these things to him. She took a deep breath and began.

"It seems sometime ago, there was a man called Darragh Mackenzie. Mackenzie became the Bishop of a group of Satan worshippers whose goal was to create an empire, an ideal world. Darragh Mackenzie and his advocates planned to destroy everything which wasn't perfect. This is their reason for chemtrails and biowarfare, Pastor," she told him.

He turned as white as a ghost and shook his head in disbelief.

"How pathetic," he groaned.

"Yes, I know," she agreed with him. "They couldn't ever pull such a thing off, could they?" she wondered aloud. "In this whole world there's no such thing as perfection."

"This society will never be perfect," Rosie gingerly added as he sat down in the chair close by them.

This wasn't at all what Paul had on his mind, though. He leaned forward and covered his face with his hands.

"Don't tell me, Darragh Mackenzie was killed and his daughter was supposed to replace him as high priestess?" he mumbled.

"Yes, I'm afraid so," Lorraine answered him. "This is your wife, Kastanje Scott, we're talking about, isn't it, Paul?"

"Yes," he answered her with tears in his eyes.

Lorraine saw his big shoulders shake and heard him weep. Her own eyes were wet with tears, too, as she reached forth and touched his shoulder.

"Darragh Mackenzie's daughter has a son who was conceived through an incestuous affair with her father." Lorraine told him. "I'm so sorry, Paul!" she said.

"No," Paul groaned, "Good God, no!"

Chapter 41

There were many lovely condominiums in this small Spanish-looking village; this choice community where Wesley Versuch dwelt when he wasn't at Mount Gaspar, or at Mercy Hospital.

It was nine o'clock at night and the stars over Isleta Village sparkled like jewels in Ferdinand's and Isadora's crowns had, at one time. Wesley Versuch was walking his girlfriend's small Tibetan Spaniel, just as he did almost every night. Cinnamon, on her gemstone adorned leash, strolled proudly ahead of him.

"Good dog," Wesley assured her.

The black-top pavement they followed wound around clean, freshly-painted adobe-like condominiums in a circular loop. Wesley noticed the glimmer of lights through many of the apartment windows; the bustle of neighbors who were out and about, busy with various household chores.

Wesley had only recently moved to the neighborhood in Isleta Village from a much less wealthy locality. After he'd landed the job as the hospital's CPA's assistant, he had the good fortune of meeting Carla Ciprano, a Registered Nurse who also worked at the hospital.

Carla was drawn to Wesley's darkly handsome appearance. She said she found him *mysterious* but *in a nice way.* After two weeks of charming the pants off Carla, she invited him to move in with her. He knew it was an advantageous move for him so he eagerly concurred. Now, if he had to walk the dog every night, take out the garbage and do up the dishes, it was well worth it, he decided.

Cinnamon pulled on her leash and Wesley stopped to let the dog sniff at something in the sand. He felt the weight of the world on his shoulders when he remembered the request Daphne Orion had made of him. How she'd finagled him into promising her he would kidnap Pastor Paul Scott's daughters and transport them to the mountain.

When he considered his obligation to the occult, he was plagued with mixed feelings for the Delphians. Thinking of Cadence Scott, he was destroyed by memories of Caroline.

Caroline Versuch was a curly, blond-headed little girl, a crackerjack comedian, and with a soft heart which made her want to care for all of the forlorn creatures of the world, including Wesley Versuch.

She was up very early every morning and Mister and Mrs. Versuch could rely on Caroline to disturb their sleep long before they thought it was time to arise. They would awaken to see her blue eyes staring at them and then they would pull her into bed with them, where she would giggle and talk non-stop.

Caroline was four years and four months old when she became sick and Wesley and his wife took her to see a physician. Maybe the doctor would prescribe the appropriate medication which would then make her as good as new.

They were horrified at the doctor's diagnosis when he determined Caroline had leukemia. The doctor explained leukemia to them as being a children's form of cancer. He held out little hope to them for Caroline's recovery.

They took their daughter home with them and nursed her through eight heart-wrenching months, through the high fevers, the loss of her beautiful blond hair after chemotherapy, the gradual loss of her appetite, until she was nothing more than skin and bones. Finally, her body so worn out by the disease, Caroline cuddled up in her daddy's arms and died. From then on, Wesley's marriage went down-hill and months later Mister and Mrs. Versuch parted and went their own separate ways. Daphne swore it was not the chemtrails which had killed Caroline but Wesley always harbored suspicion.

Wesley couldn't forget Caroline, or her mother, and the happy life he once knew, and his memories ate away at him until they finally devoured his soul.

Cinnamon was excited as they neared home, anxious to return to her beloved owner so Wesley, with the dog at his side bounded up the stairs to the front door and entered the apartment. Accosted by the strong pungency of marijuana, he heard Carla's sister's voice in the living-room and he sped to that area.

"This place smells like a marijuana plantation!" he yelled, as he opened a window. "What if our landlord happened to walk in and discover what you're up to?" he questioned Carla. Carla was addicted to marijuana, a real weed-head, he surmised.

"Our landlord wouldn't be able to detect weed if he stood in a field of it and somebody dropped a match", Carla laughed and her sister, too, thought this was real funny. However, when Carla's sister laughed the noise she made reminded Wesley of a croaking frog.

"Marijuana is still illegal", he reminded them.

"If there wasn't the risk of getting caught, I doubt very much we'd smoke it", Carla told him, from her place on the sofa as she took another toke of the joint and then handed it back to her sister. "Not only is it an adventure, Sweetheart", she told Wesley, "but we're in the midst of a joyous celebration here!"

"Yea, I moved out of my boyfriend's house today", her sister told him. "I just packed up all of my things and left", she added with her head held high in self-dignity; more croaking.

"So, you see, Wesley, we're burning bridges", Carla explained to him as she lifted the joint to salute her sister.

Wesley decided he'd better disappear before Carla got the idea of booting him out too. He drifted from the living-room and into their bedroom. Before falling down across their bed, he lifted the picture of Caroline from his nightstand and clenched it to his chest as he lay there, tears trickling down his cheeks.

He stared at the photograph of his precious daughter. Blue eyes beamed back at him. *Daddy's girl*, he called her and it always made her smile. Caroline was supposed to grow-up being 'Daddy's girl'; she should have experienced a full life and lived to a ripe old age.

How tragic things never turned out the way they were supposed to be.

Wesley pressed Caroline's picture to his chest. Feeling desolate, he closed his eyes and fell into a deep, dream-filled sleep. Wesley seldom had dreams any more. He didn't dream the way he did as a child, or even as a young man. Now he was plagued with nightmares; Nightmares which seemed so real he often couldn't tell the difference between what he'd dreamed and what he'd actually lived.

He opened his eyes and was immediately repulsed by the dark-haired woman on top of him. Her laughter was much too loud, her actions much too wild for the bleak atmosphere around him and he suspected she was up to something.

"I'm stoned out of my mind and horny as hell", Carla told him.

Bending over him, she pulled the picture out of his hands and flung it into the air. It went flying and smashed against the lamp on the night stand; pieces of broken glass flew every where. This upheaval didn't stop her, or even slow her down. She pulled persistently on the leather belt around his waist.

Bewildered and with visions of Caroline's picture in pieces on the floor, Wesley repelled her advances. Before she grasped her peril and could respond, he had his belt wrapped around her slender neck.

He pulled her down upon the bed and she lay there in shock, her hands clutching at his belt. She kicked her feet and struggled to break free but she couldn't escape him. He was much too strong for her. Her dark eyes were brimming with fear. Only seconds later, though, those expressive eyes were mere, empty containers.

He ascended from the bed and dropped to his knees. In the dim light which proceeded from the adjacent room, he tried without success to put the broken pieces of Caroline's picture back together again.

Chapter 42

Peach spotted Kas the moment she arrived at their beach house in Huntington and with great excitement she rushed out of the house next door, clapped her hands together and exclaimed with enthusiasm,

"You must have lunch with us, Kas! I simply will not take no for an answer!"

Kas made up her mind to make the most of their time at Huntington Beach and she responded warmly to her neighbor's invitation. It didn't take them long to put on their swimming suits and then join Peach and her family at their poolside barbeque.

Peach was a sixty-year-old short, plump woman of Spanish descent. Her real name was Imelda but people called her Peach because it fit her.

Her husband, Ketil, was an astute-looking man who covered his balding gray head with a sea captain's hat which read SS Harpoon after the yacht he owned. He was a professional Fisherman and the founder of the marketing cooperation known as Ketil's Kettle of Fish.

Ketil and his grandson, Geoffrey, managed Ketil's Kettle although, as of yet, Geoffrey took no real active position in the business and he was slow to catch on. Geoffrey was most comfortable in the water, diving below its surface or racing through the waves on his cutter.

Kas was seated at the round, sea-green patio table in one of the hardwood outdoor chairs. She was famished and the hot-dog in bun was delicious. Cole slaw, potato salad and a pickle filled the plate in front of her.

Crystal helped Ketil at the barbeque while Cadence played with two of Peach and Ketil's grandchildren.

Erin was mainly interested in Geoffrey's underwater camera. For this reason she stuck close by him. They were at the edge of the pool, side-by-side on the turquoise and white tiled floor where Geoffrey explained to her his camera.

"Erin," he said to the sizzling red head. Geoffrey had known Erin since she was a toddler but he was amazed at how much she'd grown over the past year. She was stunning, he thought. "If you go diving with me later I will let you handle the camera and take underwater pictures too!" he promised her.

Erin turned to her mother for her permission and Kas nodded her head. She thought Geoffrey was somewhat eccentric but trustworthy.

Erin had never been diving before and she was excited about it. Geoffrey had another wet-suit which would fit her so she was dressed appropriately before leaving Peach's house. They left Ketil alone, by himself as they rode with Peach in her SUV Dodge Durango to the beach where Geoffrey docked his cutter.

Kas watched with some concern as the two divers in their wet suits untied the cutter which was roped to the wooden dock. It was a thirty-foot utility boat and often used to carry skin-divers into deep waters where they dove into the vast ocean.

Geoffrey almost lived on the water and she knew Erin was safe with him. Still, she was a little apprehensive as she watched the two of them set out in his fiberglass boat. She made them promise her they would not sail out of sight but stay where she could see them. She felt safe as long as she could see the boat. She watched them steer the craft across the water. It clipped over the waves at about 35 miles per hour and she couldn't actually see them as they steered the boat from underneath the canopy but around two miles out she saw them cut the engine and drop anchor.

"They will be fine, Kas," Peach told her as she wrestled with a beach blanket she had brought with her.

Kas grabbed a corner and helped her spread it on the sand so they could sit on it. Meanwhile, she also watched the sensuous young man in blue swimming trunks who flirted with Crystal. They were several feet away from her. Two teenage girls were more than a handful, she thought.

From deep within her beach-bag, Beethoven's 5th called to her before she even sat down. She kept a close eye on Crystal and also the boat Erin was in, as she withdrew her cell-phone from her bag and answered it.

"You've reached Defense Attorney Scott. How can I help you?" she inquired of her caller.

"Hello," the man answered her and he sounded disoriented. "I'm Wesley Versuch. The police say I strangled my girlfriend."

"Did you?" Kas asked.

"Did I what?"

"Strangle your girlfriend?"

"If I'd killed my girlfriend, I wouldn't be calling you, would I?"

"You might". she said, and turned to gaze at the boat. It was still there, and by now Erin and Geoffrey should have been somewhere in the Pacific.

The man in the yellow windbreaker and red cap found an easy entrance to the Anderson's home. He only had to open the door; it was not locked.

The stranger was quiet as a mouse when he entered Ketil's home. He looked around him and saw the richly extravagant way Ketil and his family lived. At one time he had been surrounded by costly precious items, too. When he was a general practitioner he'd had everything he wanted, but had lost it all, and now he depended on Daphne Orion as well as his brother, Rattler Mackenzie, to support him.

He had another task to perform and this was to persuade the witch who stubbornly resisted them. It was for her own good, as well as the good of Rattler Mackenzie's granddaughters. Kastanje would comply with them. They would force her to do so.

Ketil stood beside his desk and returned the telephone's receiver to its cradle. He was still wearing his captain's cap as he adjusted the pipe in his mouth and turned to peer out of the window to see the sun was already setting in the sky. The day was drawing to a close. Always the diplomat, he had wrangled a real deal with some fishermen in Anchorage, Alaska, who promised him several tons of salmon for a reasonable price.

He thought now of how he and a couple of his salesmen from Ketil's Kettle would fly up to Anchorage on Monday to pick it up. He would go along with them because he appreciated the rugged environment of Anchorage. Heck, he thought, just for kicks he might even take Geoffrey along with him and they would do some sight-seeing at Denali National Park. Once they were there they were bound to spot a grizzly and maybe some caribou and moose, too.

He inhaled the sweet cherry smoke from his pipe and brushed a couple of white specks from the shoulder of his navy blue Sailor's jacket. He was indeed very neat and meticulous. The picture on his desk of his own personal yacht gave him a deep sense of satisfaction.

Those were the last happy thoughts Ketil ever had. Stuart Mackenzie thrust his weapon into Ketil's back and the old man gasped from shock and misery.

He heard the brutal sound the knife made when it punctured his own frame and he spun around to see the vicious look in the villian's eyes.

Ketil worried for his family, where they had gone, what kept them away and if the brutal beast with his knife had injured them too. Ketil didn't worry for long, though, because under the Dragon's direction, Stuart pressed the jagged edge of his knife into Ketil's heart and the old man fell down dead.

Chapter 43

That night the mountain burst into celebration. It was a very prosperous day in the valley. They crowded into the pagoda like a band of bandits after a clean sweep.

In the subterranean level, beneath the pantheon, a fortification had been built at one time to provide an avenue of escape for the Delphians should the valley ever retaliate for all of the destruction heaped upon them.

The Delphians had never found it necessary to burrow deeply underground, though, for the valley had never threatened to retaliate. The valley people seemed ignorant of, and oblivious to, the evil the Delphians carried out against them.

The excavation was massive, well-constructed and able to sustain their members for a long time if the need ever arose. It was being used for other purposes now. Within the manmade cave, through a long, narrow channel which lead to a broad area of underground quagmire and bedrock, the Delphians concealed their prisoners. Hanging from particular places in the cave were lanterns and the flame from each lantern cast a darkish flicker of light throughout the cavern.

Roosevelt Shuyler felt it wasn't for their sakes the Delphians kept the lanterns aglow. No, they would never be so kind, he told himself. The Delphians kept the lanterns glowing so they could easily find their way to them. Bound by heavy chains around their wrists and ankles and then fastened to the walls, there was no escape.

The glasses Roosevelt wore had been broken when he tried to get away. It was when they first brought them here and he had struck the big, burly men cloaked in black robes. His fists didn't seem to phase them one bit but his glasses had fallen off and one of them had stepped on them.

After they had left, Lorraine found his eye-glasses buried in the dirt and she gave them to Roosevelt. He put them on but could see very little through the broken lenses. He could hear better then he could see and he heard the distant celebration and the applause for their adversaries who'd imprisoned them there in their underground compound.

Roosevelt could hear another human being sobbing nearby, too. Lorraine told him, barely above a whisper, what shape the poor, deranged woman was in and how she was missing an ear, an arm and a foot. Lorraine said it looked like someone had made a game of cutting off parts of the woman's anatomy.

Their adversaries were insane! A bunch of lunatics set upon ruling the world; the sort of world Roosevelt and Lorraine despised the thought of being any part of. While they were far from ecstatic over their present lot, they agreed they could never be entangled with chimera.

It was hopeless to think anyone would look for them there, hidden in a remote underground cave. No one would ever find them. Roosevelt turned to Lorraine. She leaned against the solid wall and when he looked at her, she tried her damnedest to smile for Rosie's sake.

He took off his broken glasses because it made no sense to wear them. He moved closer to her so he could at least get a glimpse of her face.

"I made a promise to take care of you" he whispered to her and she thought the look of disappointment on his aged face was heartbreaking.

"You did, too," she encouraged him. "We took care of each other until we discovered what we were looking for. Here it is, Rosie," she groaned. "These are the monsters who poisoned our world without one ounce of remorse."

She listened to the poor Spanish woman whose crumpled body lay in a corner of the cave. The woman groaned and jabbered in her native language. Perhaps she was praying, Lorraine thought. Perhaps she prayed for death to come.

"Can you imagine the world they will build?" she asked and because her hands and feet were chained to the wall so she couldn't use them, she motioned with her head to the long, narrow tunnel at the end of which they could faintly catch the celebration which took place in the pagoda above them.

"I'm thankful we have so many warm and happy memories of the old world," Roosevelt replied. Even as blind as a bat, he could still find his way to her lips. For the first time ever their lips met and it was unforgettable.

From far away Roosevelt and Lorraine could hear heavy footsteps coming down the long tunnel, undoubtedly the noise of their adversaries as they advanced.

Lorraine squeezed Roosevelt's hand because she knew they were coming for them. It was time again to face their adversaries. They had cold, piercing eyes; eyes which cut to her very soul.

She wondered at their purpose now. The last time two of them had called on them, she and Rosie were ill prepared for their hostile looks and their malicious swearing. One of them had spit on the ground and then described to her how his spit meant considerably more to him then the lives of outsiders, from the valley.

Lorraine had mustered the courage to ask him the reason for their chemtrails, why they had poisoned Andrew and so many others. He looked her in the eye and had the nerve to tell her Andrew's life was only a small donation to Chimera. She didn't know how she could tolerate another visit from them now.

"Rosie, what are they and what makes them tick?" she whispered. "We can't identify them in their black robes, which is probably why they wear them." Anxious and terror-stricken, she went on, "I've seen their eyes, though, and they don't look human. No human's eyes were ever so devoid of feeling!"

"Maybe they're our escorts for this evening's celebration," Rosie said.

"Are you inclined to sarcastic humor when you're trapped underground?" she asked him.

"I've never been trapped underground before," Roosevelt answered her.

He wanted to see Lorraine smile just one last time. Her smile would assure him they would meet again, after death, where murderers do not reign over the meek.

The heavy pounding of feet drew nearer. In the desolate subterranean cave, the sound their feet made was magnified. They could see them now. They were both dressed in their black robes but only one of them had draped the robe's hood over his head. The other, stouter one, did not wear a hood and they could plainly see his face.

Lorraine gasped with horror when she recognized Pastor Barry Guire. The Senior Pastor of His Holiness Church, the man whose car they had stolen from the hospital's parking lot.

"Didn't I tell you he was in on it?" Roosevelt said in a hushed voice.

"What a charlatan," Lorraine murmured.

When the ghouls reached them, the Pastor shouted at them, "Thieves!" Enraged, he continued shouting, "Thieves! Did you really think you'd get away with it?" He approached Roosevelt, towering over the elderly man while casting his fiery gaze upon him. "There's a special place in hell reserved for car thieves! Did you know this?" Barry taunted him.

"There's an inferno for swindlers, too," Roosevelt answered him.

Barry's countenance reddened as he shook his finger in Roosevelt's face.

"The devil and I are intimate friends. On the other hand, you, Mister, have no friends here!"

"I expected this," Roosevelt countered, "and I would accept no charity from you!"

"Quiet!" the other one hollered at them. He took his hood off and Lorraine and Roosevelt saw Harriet's son, Allen Carter. "Just do as I say," Allen ordered them. Unlike Barry, there was some spark of compassion in his eyes.

While Allen watched, Barry went to work loosening the chains which had bound them. It seemed to them Allen was the one in control. He seemed to command Barry's respect and obedience. Hardly the type of thing one would expect from a young man whom every one thought was retarded. Once he'd freed them, Barry pushed the old man forward.

"You asked for no charity," Barry mocked him.

However, when he moved to assault Roosevelt again, his hand clashed with Allen's.

"Don't touch him, Barry!" Allen warned him with a threatening look.

Allen and Barry led them back through the tunnel and up a cement stairway to the domicile's entryway.

Lorraine could hear her heart racing. She was terror-stricken as she pondered hers and Roosevelt's demise.

Through the portal and inside the dark coliseum, Lorraine saw innumerable tiny lights. Each devotee there was cloaked in a black robe and held before him a lighted candle. The light from the candles sparkled and illuminated the darkness.

The many adherents stood in rows before their dignitary upon her pedestal. The red-headed woman, decked out for the evening, wore a black and golden tiara upon her head. Clouds of smoke floated in the air and arose over the podium. The whole arena smelled of sweet herbs and bitter potions.

Lorraine wondered at the reason for their celebration. She had the dreadful feeling, somehow, she and Roosevelt would be forced to play a significant role in the evening's agenda.

As she listened at the door, she heard someone's voice, a deep, male voice which commanded the attention of its audience. She strained to hear every word he said, hoping to discern the reason she and Roosevelt had been brought to this ghastly affair.

"This will please you, Daphne, two more offerings made to Chimera upon this sacred night. Oh! This night," he intoned. "This night of terror when the bells tolled for almost three thousand souls who lost their lives!"

Lorraine could now see the apostle in his black robe who moved about in the shadows, around and through the crowd, as he delivered his dissertation.

"The humans who have been detained, who will be sacrificed on this glorious night, may well be old but they are far from being debilitated," the orator droned, complementing them. It was a complement Lorraine knew she could have lived without.

Through the darkly burnished arena she saw it then. On the stage was a silver cart with wheels, almost unrecognizable because of the black cloth draped over it, but it looked to her like a hospital bed. Was it the occult's makeshift altar, she wondered, and both hers and Rosie's deathbed? The speaker droned on.

"Both Lorraine Martin and Roosevelt Shuyler outlasted the poisoned skies. Although they breathed the toxins from our chemtrails, yet they survived." He pointed the crowd's attention to the couple, Lorraine and Roosevelt collared by the two men: the Pastor and Allen. "They surely aren't body-builders but, nevertheless, they are extremely healthy specimen," the orator reveled. "After surviving our chemtrails, they came to us. We did not go to them. They are eager, maybe even grateful, to offer their lives for Chimera. Our beautiful and honored high priestess has told us to offer our praise to the dragon." His voice was filled with emotion.

"To the dragon!" the red-head on the raised platform, the occult's high priestess shouted.

"Extol Abaddon!" the audience uproariously proclaimed.

At this time, even as the crowd loudly chanted the dragon's praise, Allen leaned forward to whisper to the prisoners "Move forward and do not stop until you have reached the altar." He spoke loudly enough for Barry to hear him, too.

As Barry followed Lorraine and Roosevelt down the aisle to the designated altar, Allen turned and pushed on the big door next to him, opening it enough so he could stick his head out and see it was evening and the sun was setting. It was eerily quiet, the way it often gets before a twister touches down. Then a breeze began to pick up, a breeze which threatened to grow even more blustery.

"Any time now, Screech," Allen whispered.

He didn't see Screech but he knew he was nearby. Allen left the door ajar rather than closing it completely.

As the two prisoners made their way to the altar, Lorraine reached out for Rosie's hand and he clasped her hand in his.

"I love you, Rosie," she whispered.

He was her dearest friend in all the world and she wanted him to know how much she appreciated him. She didn't hear him reply and perhaps he hadn't, she thought. It was okay; under these circumstances, she was willing to overlook it. He had kissed her though. Confronted with death, all she could think about was Rosie's kiss.

The high priestess waited for them. With every step they took, she grew thirstier for their blood. It was the occult's ritual to drink the blood of the sacrifices they received. There had been many such sacrifices.

At that moment the huge door blew open as though by divine intervention. Like a tale straight from ancient Scriptures, dozens of vultures flew into the stadium. Screech was leading a magnificent army, a battalion of birds who attacked the villains.

Blasphemous maledictions were heard as the devil's hirelings endeavored to dodge, trying to escape the birds whose talons clawed at their heads, while their sharp beaks tore at their flesh.

Now in complete chaos, the robed worshippers dropped their candles and the flames leaped from the containers and onto the walls and licked along the floor. Fire and smoke quickly billowed and spread throughout the building.

"Go!" Allen called to Roosevelt and Lorraine. "Get out of here!" he urged them, giving them a gentle shove toward an alcove doorway.

Still clinging to each other's hands, Lorraine and Roosevelt hastened through the doorway and sped down the aisle the same way they had entered just a few minutes ago. Allen followed behind them and Screech accompanied him, flying over his shoulder.

"I told him to end his friendship with that horrible bird," Daphne wailed.

Everywhere around her malefactors were either burned alive or pecked to death by the birds. In the midst of total anarchy, Daphne hurried to the makeshift altar. She crawled beneath it, trying to hide from the birds and the several small explosions the fire was still causing.

Meanwhile, Lorraine and Roosevelt struggled to make their way out of the coliseum, dodging figures, many of them on fire.

The casualties stumbled about in a frenzy, trying to escape from the birds and to quench the flames, too, as the fire broiled their flesh.

Lorraine felt the evil blade as it punctured her skin and dug into her back. She halted and swiveled around to glance at the con man, the one whom she had called her Pastor. The calloused look on his face, the brutal smile on his lips, as he grunted,

"Bulls eye!".

Lorraine lost her balance and fell into Roosevelt's arms. She gazed into Rosie's crinkled face and saw the tears flow down his cheeks. Rosie said,

"I meant to tell you, I love you too, Lorraine," he sobbed.

She clutched at his collar,

"This is but a brief victory in an ageless war and I'd rather die a martyr," she whispered valiantly.

Allen turned around to see the elderly people whom he'd risked his life and jeopardized his position in the occult to save.

Their sagging frames on the floor were a picture of misery. The man held his injured friend in his arms. He glanced up at Allen with a destitute look on his face.

"Help us," he desperately begged, but it was too late.

One of the walls, gutted with fire, fell on Rosie and he was instantly wrapped in flames which spread and enveloped both beings, two more victims of Chimera.

Chapter 44

Allen ran all the way to Victoria Street, and didn't stop until he reached Pastor Paul's house. His legs felt cramped and he was out of breath but, he was alive and this fact astounded him.

He banged on the Pastor's door. Surely, Harriet's Pastor would have to believe him when he told him what he had witnessed in the night, the conflagration and the many people who were killed in the inferno.

It was a dark night, darker than he could ever remember, and there seemed to be no light from the moon and stars. Allen worried this was caused by the thickly heavy layers of polymer toxin the military planes had been spraying.

He thought about God's mercy and grace, something Harriet had tried to explain to him many times. She had referred to God's divine charity for every living thing He had created. Yet, he didn't recognize God's grace in the chemtrails, the poison which had killed so many people.

He couldn't detect God's grace this evening, either, when the older couple were burned alive in the inferno on the mountain. What had happened to Harriet's God? Allen wondered. Had God withdrawn His grace? If indeed He had, such a thing could have caused a total eclipse.

Finally, he saw the Pastor moving about in the kitchen, then turning on a light as he made his way to the door, dressed in a green bathrobe. When he opened it, Allen charged into the house and anxiously exclaimed,

"Either the chemtrails have obscured the stars or God has forsaken us!" he announced. He lifted the little dog from the floor and hugged him, burying his face in the dog's fur. This brought him some solace.

Paul imagined, had he not spent the biggest share of the night with similar thoughts, he might have believed Allen was talking nonsense, but he could comprehend Allen's gibberish. All night long, feeling restless and unable to sleep, he repeatedly asked himself if he hadn't forsaken God because God felt so far away from him.

"Calm down, Allen!" he attempted to console the young man. "Would you like a cup of hot cocoa? We can drink our cocoa at the kitchen table while we talk," he suggested. He knew he also was in need of conversation. As he went to the kitchen sink to fill the tea-pot with water, Allen was trying to compose himself.

"There used to be stars; you know, like the North Star, Eunice Minor and Polaris…" he said, holding Toby close in his arms.

"Yes, I know the stars, Allen," Paul told him, "Although, it sounds to me like you have a great deal more knowledge of them than I do. Do they teach you about the stars at the institution?"

Allen was upset at his own lack of ability to describe the catastrophe he'd witnessed on the mountain. Once more, he was awkward and clumsy instead of being direct and informative. He took a deep breath and tried again.

"No, they don't teach us about the stars at the institution. I haven't been at the institution." he explained. "There are still stars, too, only we can't see them the way we once did."

"I haven't been outside," Paul replied, as he went to the cupboard to fetch mugs for them. "But do you suppose, this is the way things are with God at the moment, too? He's still there only we can't see Him? Something has obstructed our view of Him?" This made sense to Paul and the thought brought him some relief, only he wasn't sure what this obstruction could be. He remembered what Barry had told him,

"You want to buddy up to the adversary but then grumble when he bites you!"

Paul opened the can of Hershey's Chocolate and, as he spooned it into the mugs on the counter top, he remorsefully told Allen,

"Son, I've made a big mistake, one which has proven to have horrendous consequences."

"That's all right, I didn't want hot cocoa, anyway," Allen told him, trying to sound understanding as well as convincing. Then he added, "I'd rather have coffee. I take mine black."

"There's instant coffee in the cupboard," Paul said, and pointed to the cupboard just above his head.

Allen preferred hot cocoa to instant coffee but, he didn't want the Pastor to think he was unable to make up his mind too. It was time to come clean with him, Allen decided as he moved closer and reached for the jar of Maxwell House instant coffee.

"Sir, there was a rattle snake here earlier today," Allen told him. "He spoke to Mrs.

Scott. As a matter-of-fact, he called her a witch." he said, and saw the Pastor frown and shake his head.

"First chemtrails and now talking rattlesnakes, what's next?" Paul asked, stirring the liquid in his mug. Finally, he took a sip, turned around and gazed at his kitchen. There was a different aura to it, something he'd never felt before. The room seemed somehow treacherous to him.

Earlier in the evening, at Harriet Carter's, Roosevelt and Lorraine had told him about the occult on Mount Gaspar and about Darragh Mackenzie too. How they needed Mackenzie's offspring to fulfill the position of leader of their empire. He was beginning to feel like some character caught in the middle of a spine-tingling, Grimms fairy-tale.

The telephone's loud shrill made Paul jump. He glanced at Allen, who returned his look, and then he went to answer it. Picking the receiver up before the third ring, he said,

"Pastor Paul Scott of His Holiness Church." as he eyed the wall clock, the one which read *Kastanje's Kitchen*. The fact it was late in the evening lead him to consider the nature of the call. It had to be a crucial matter which prompted a caller at this hour of the night, he imagined, and he tried to prepare himself for whatever disturbing news it might be.

"This is Barry, Paul. I saw you brought my car home so I assume you must have seen Roosevelt and Lorraine. Why didn't you drop in and let me know you'd seen those two car thieves?" Barry asked him, sounding fittingly suspicious.

"Roosevelt and Lorraine are extremely upset, Barry. It seems Joseph Elvio as well as Andrew Martin died sometime today. They didn't intend any harm, Barry. As a favor to you, and to them, I returned your car and hoped you might overlook the wrong they committed. Do you know what I'm saying, Barry? Could you manage to overlook things, just this once?" He sounded to his ears like he was pleading. Well, it was exactly what he was doing, though. He was begging the Senior Pastor of His Holiness Church to forgive those who had wronged him; in this case, not only to forgive Rosie and Lorraine but, also, to try and place himself in their shoes.

"So, you talked with them? What did they say?" Barry asked. He remembered the startled look on Lorraine's face after the knife he threw entered her body. Roosevelt and Lorraine were dead and they could not bring him any more trouble now.

"They believe the occult is behind the chemtrails. Lorraine discovered loads of information on the computer about the cabal." Paul carefully weighed what he said to Barry; how much he told him about Darragh Mackenzie, his illicit affair with his daughter, the Delphians and their objectives.

"It's as I suspected," Barry said. "The Delphians are a huge and dangerous organization."

"Yes, this is the knowledge Lorraine and Roosevelt acquired, too," Paul agreed.

"I have learned their high priestess has a lot to do with the chemtrails and the curious death of a large number of people; small people, the common people, those whom we swore to defend and protect." Barry said, and he thought he sounded suitably concerned.

Paul braced himself; leaning against the wall, he covered his eyes with his hand and wondered how Kastanje had managed to murder so many innocent people. How she had betrayed him. She was always reluctant to commit herself to their church, now he remembered.

"Barry," Paul murmured into the receiver. "Kastanje…?"

"Yes, Paul," Barry said, and he seemed to be reading his mind. "I'm afraid she is the high priestess of the occult, and she's been working against you all of these years, scheming to thwart you on every hand. She and her son, Allen Carter, too." Barry said, and he smiled to himself. He was really quite good at this, he thought. He could deceive others so well, he told himself, and he praised his own endeavors.

Chapter 45

Their entire domicile lay in shambles. The inferno had turned the modern, state-of-the-art building into ashes. Daphne stood in the shambles and gazed around her.

The diviners, what was left of their numbers, still worked feverishly to douse every last ember. They labored with their fire extinguishers even while the smoke permeated everything around them, thick layers of smoke.

As Daphne scrutinized the calamity the birds had brought upon them, she was enraged by the scene.

"All of the flames are out now!" one of the soothsayers called to her through the heavy, blinding smoke.

She waved her hand, attempting to fan the air so she could see the one who had spoken to her, one of the lucky ones who'd survived the horrible fire.

Burned bodies were strewed everywhere, filling the air with a putrid odor. She recognized the bedraggled, although still handsome form of one of her servants.

"What horrible destruction," Daphne lamented. Her voice sounded hoarse and her throat burned. "It will take weeks, months, years to rebuild," she groaned, thinking of her computer and the priceless documents and other information stored on it, all destroyed in the inferno.

She stumbled around the clutter as the small band of devotees watched their high priestess. Most were still dressed in their black robes while standing in the blue mist of daybreak, the smoke of their once leading-edge domain swirling around them.

Daphne went to find Rattler. Archie Petersen and Barry Guire followed a ways behind her, concerned for their queen's well-being.

She entered the forbidden room, forbidden to everyone else except those to whom she'd granted access. Archie and Barry were two who had been given special privileges. Their loyalties to Chimera had been tested and they'd proven to be unyielding, unlike Allen Carter, who'd brought all of this devastation upon them when he'd befriended the bird.

Daphne felt nothing but cold animosity toward Rattler's son. He was a backstabber and a fraud. Under her breath she cursed his companion, the raven whom he called Screech.

In this room, the first light of day shone through a window, but in the thick shadows Daphne saw where she'd detained the Latino woman while she mangled her body with the scalpel. Things had seemed so much merrier to her then.

Here, too, was the secret passageway to their subterranean level. Daphne found the wooden door over the opening had been burned in the fire, so now it was only a gaping hole. She paused to view more damage the fire had made. It infuriated her.

Finally, she began her descent down the spiral staircase. Their private hideaway appeared to be untouched. All of the lanterns were still attached to the walls and tiny flames flickered in their containers. While the air was a bit chilly and humid, there was at least a quality of safety here. She moved through the tunnel, searching for Rattler Mackenzie.

In the distance, at one end of the underpass, she heard the hiss of the Western Diamond Back Rattlesnake. She had exceptional hearing and she listened closely to the noise.

Something, or someone, occupied his attention and she was quiet as she moved closer to see what it was and to eavesdrop on Rattler's conversation.

"Hush, Neva, I am not going to kill you, although you may well wish you were dead," the rattlesnake whispered to the woman who was terror-stricken and wept with fear. He balanced his six foot long slippery frame on a ledge beside her and eyed her intently. "Yours is a fate worse than death and you owe every bit of it to Kastanje," he informed her. "The red-head, Daphne is a witch with a heart of stone." he hissed, as he lifted his thorax in pride. Then, with a wide grin upon his atrocious face, he continued, "I taught her everything she knows. Yes, it was me who instructed her in the fine art of black magic; but she is not my daughter, Kastanje."

He glided up her leg even as she lay there on the hard ground, shivering in the cold and sweating in distress. The rattlesnake's elongated body slithered over her body until he reached the woman's stomach, his tail still twisted around her tennis shoe.

He slinked to her chest, and was directly connected with every breath she took. He was not about to end her morbid life. It would have been too easy. Neglected, without food and liquid, it would take days for her to die. The time would crawl by for her and hours would seem like years. She'd have plenty of time to think.

He lowered his head and stared at her face, watching the tears fall from her eyes.

"You think about this as you lie here dying, Neva," he whispered to her. "My daughter will one day rule the society which has brought you so much misery. Kastanje will rule over

Chimera one day, very soon!" He proclaimed with utter certainty.

Daphne was appalled by the conversation she heard. Rattler had admitted she had done a pretty fair job of running things but he was determined to position Kastanje on his throne instead of her. She made up her mind to follow through with the action he'd forced her to take. Daphne turned around to face her loyal subjects, Archie Petersen and Barry Guire, who were following her.

"What are the others saying?" She questioned them in a frustrated and angry tone of voice, agitated because they too had heard the rattlesnake's treasonous declaration.

Archie and Barry quickly glanced at each other before Barry replied,

"They've said they will go elsewhere. Most of them have abandoned their allegiance to our high priestess". He risked the penalty of being so candid because he hoped even now the she-devil would turn matters around. She would have the authority to prove them in error, to put an end to their decision to so swiftly desert her.

"Doing so will avail them nothing and it's certainly no remedy to the crisis we face," Daphne said in a low, contemplative tone.

The threat of losing control of her domain and of her adherents made her eager to confront Rattler's daughter, the woman whom the rattlesnake preferred above her.

She lowered her head and strolled past them. It seemed to them she might even abdicate her throne. Without a fuss the she-devil might cave in to pressure and relinquish her desire to rule Chimera.

Once more, Archie and Barry glanced at each other and shook their heads. Feeling dejected, their sad eyes stared after her. They watched her until, in the flicker of fire light, she seemed to just vanish from their sight.

"Where did she go?" Archie asked.

"God only knows where she went," Barry answered him.

Chapter 46

Kas wrung her hands together as she paced the carpet in her den. The girls had gone to bed hours ago. She knew she should be in bed, too, but even if she lay down to sleep, rest would evade her. The world which encompassed her forbade her any such luxuries.

One more person had wound up dead today and she was pretty sure the killer had meant to convey a message to her by stabbing Ketil. She suspected Ketil's murderer was mixed up with the occult too, intent on establishing her in Rattler's vacant position as archbishop over the occult. He probably wanted to impress upon her how easily they could wreck havoc if she continued to resist them and their designs for her life.

Her new client, who'd contacted her just hours ago, called himself Wesley Versuch. Kas wasn't about to trust any newcomers right now. She had begun to suspect every outsider who caught her attention.

Eager to learn Wesley's real identity, she sat down at her computer and clicked online. Then she entered her new client's name into the search engine. To her surprise, she saw there were more than fifteen hundred websites which mentioned Wesley Versuch. He was said to be the great-great nephew of a particular Leopold Versuch. The internet explained Leopold was a soothsayer, an alleged wizard. He was also the headmaster over the largest subdivision of the occult, the Delphians. He was listed as being an ambitious visionary and *otherworldly*.

One specific website explained how Wesley had lived with his uncle at his mansion in Salzburg, Austria, until seven years ago when he left for America. Wesley was brought up in the occult.

Kas shook her head at the incredible knowledge she had just acquired. Still, there were things which were not clear to her. She thought the account of Leopold's date of birth was a misprint. Yet, as she searched the Net, she felt even more baffled. Every search revealed the same dumbfounded information. Leopold Versuch was born in 1789.

He couldn't have accomplished all he did in this present century if he had been born in the late 1700s. Leopold Versuch couldn't tour their contemporary world as an Orator if he'd been born almost three hundred years ago unless, of course, Leopold Versuch was something similar in nature to Rattler Mackenzie, and someone had raised Versuch from the dead, too. Kas was so engrossed by what she read, when her doorbell rang she leaped out of her chair.

Wondering who would be calling on them this hour of the night, she left her den and walked through the hall on her way to the door. It wouldn't be Paul because he had the keys to their beach home and he wouldn't be ringing the doorbell. It rang once more before she finally answered it.

When she saw Detective Cody Baldwyn standing there next a backdrop of darkness, her gut reaction was to gulp with fear and take several steps backward.

"What brings you to Huntington this hour of the night, Detective?" she inquired of him.

He read the alarm in her voice and saw it in her gorgeous blue eyes, too. He wished she wasn't afraid of him, although he completely understood the reason for her fear. It seemed he never turned up unless it had something to do with the occult, and usually the message he brought her was anything but optimistic.

Like ten years ago in Nevada, when he'd knocked upon the door of the motel room she was staying in and, when she opened the door, he'd greeted her with,

"Kastanje Scott, your father just killed two people!" Those two people had been especially significant to Cody for they had been his wife and little boy.

That was their first brief encounter, but he couldn't remember, now, her exact words to him that night. He remembered, though, how he'd entered her motel room with a gun in his hand, and then he'd proceeded to search her room, under the bed, behind every closed door, until, finally, he was satisfied she wasn't hiding the archbishop of the occult.

"May I come in?"

She stepped aside and held the door open for him to enter, then once more she asked,

"What brings you all the way to Huntington from Althea?"

He looked around the room, taking in her beautiful, expansive beach house. It was a very pleasant abode, he thought.

190

"I've good news to share with you this evening", he said. "We arrested Daphne Orion today, the woman who paid your client a visit when they first apprehended him and charged him with double-homicide."

"How?" she questioned him with surprise as she lead him further into her house. She moved gracefully over the eggshell-beige, shag carpet and into the living room where she directed him to a comfy chair. He noticed she was very good at this sort of thing, moving people about.

He scratched at his blond head and smiled in satisfaction over his planning and maneuvers.

"We stationed a team outside of Saint Regis'. The particular interest the high priestess has in your client lead me to believe she'd return for him. Today, when she did, we nabbed her. It was all pretty simple, really." He sat down.

Yes, simple, he thought, but it required being there twenty-four, seven. It took plenty of patience, and patience was something the detective had in small storage. He watched her move across the floor in the spacious room with an alpine ceiling. She moved to the maple wood bar and reached into one of the cupboards as she asked him,

"Would you care for a drink, Detective?".

"I thought Christians never touched liquor?" he replied, fascinated over how someone from her background ever wound up married to a Pastor.

"Some don't," she confessed, "However, even the Founder of our order drank on occasions. What can I get you?" she added.

She was easy going, and answered his questions, aware of his suspicions but friendly any way. While her graciousness brought him some gratification, it also made things much harder. He stood up and crossed the room to the bar where she was busy making a Pina Colada for herself. He shook his head at her and refused her offer of a drink. He couldn't imagine celebrating at a time like this.

"Kastanje, you and your whole family are in grave danger and I don't really know how to protect you from these monsters." he confessed to her. These criminals made him feel so much less than invincible.

"C'mon," she appealed to him, "You mean to say, all of the peace officers and military in our country couldn't put an end to these spooks?" She shook her head, gave him a half smile and sipped her drink. She knew they couldn't.

He leaned against one of the stools at her bar and gazed at her.

"Even if they could, would they? These days it's hard to tell who's a part of the cabal and who isn't." he said angrily.

She felt his criticism of her and she responded,

"You have a problem with me? You think because I was a Mackenzie, witchcraft is in my blood? I will return to my former estate? Or good god," she laughed, "Perhaps, I never left it?"

He got up and moved away from the bar. She watched him saunter over to a collage of pictures on the wall; photographs of her and Paul, other pictures of Crystal, Erin and Cadence.

"See, Detective, this sort of thing puts a real wrinkle in there ever being a friendship between us," she told him.

He turned around to look at her once more, standing there at the bar with her Pina Colada in hand as she objected to his suspicions because it put a crimp in their friendship.

It might have been a touching scene, he thought, however conventional it was. On the other hand, it may have been the best bamboozlement he'd ever witnessed.

"You're an attorney, and we both know the majority of lawyers are crooked. Trying to find one honest attorney in the bunch is a lot like hunting for a pearl at the bottom of the Pacific."

"Yes, but, we know pearls do exist," she defended herself. "Besides," she said, "Your major problem with me has nothing to do with me being an attorney. It has more to do with me being the daughter of Rattler Mackenzie, the man who destroyed your family."

He turned his eyes away from her and glanced through the doorway to the foyer. He had visions of the blatant hell raiser; blurbs in magazines and news papers about how a certain segment of their society found his highness appealing, charming even. An unusual amount of people hoped he would run for the Presidential Office. At one point, in his miserable life, he was made Governor of Nevada.

The archbishop of the occult had made the cover of the Times magazine more than once. It was quite a lot of notoriety for the slimy snake, the devil's servant. For these reasons, like she said, there might always exist some level of skepticism between them, he supposed, and he changed the subject.

"This afternoon someone broke into your neighbor's house and stabbed the owner, a Mister Ketil Andersen, I believe?"

He watched her set her drink down upon the bar and then lower her eyes to frown at the half-empty glass,

"Yes," she sighed, "It was brutal."

"I have been thinking a lot about Neva Paloma, the woman they abducted from your home in Althea." he told her as he reached into his suit coat pocket, removed his note-book and gazed at it. "Yes, according to your daughter they kidnapped your employee, escorted her to a black Bently Arnage and then sped away." They exchanged glances. She didn't protest this statement so he went on.

"They were inside of your home but apparently they didn't search it because it wasn't ransacked. They didn't disturb your daughter. It would seem they came only for your employee. Why? What possible value would a simple, Hispanic woman who cleans houses for a living be to them?" He stopped pacing and wound his way back to the bar, standing on the opposite side of it and concentrating on her response.

"You're implying they killed Ketil for the same reason they kidnapped Neva?" she answered him, speaking with extreme difficulty, and he saw the tears in her eyes. The same thought had been on her mind too. However, he was the one to bring it up. "They planned to bully me into submission, to agree to accept his position as archbishop of the cabal." She shook her head and added with fervor, "I'm not the only one they're after, Detective. They also want my daughers and my illegitimate son too. They're supposed to have a significant role in Rattler's immoral kingdom, as well" she said. She knew they would stop at nothing in order to attain their goals for their empire.

"I would venture to imagine, they already have your son." he told her.

For some unknown reason she could hardly fathom, a vision of Allen Carter raced through her mind. She was quite positive he was wrapped up in the occult. There was a familiar aura about him, something she could relate to, something she'd known far more about years ago when she, too, was absorbed in the occult.

"I'm going to Mount Gaspar tomorrow to search for Neva there," he confided in her. "I may not find her, and then again, who knows what I might come across while on the mountain," he said. He picked up her unfinished drink and sipped it. She noticed his hand shook.

"I want to go with you," she told him, as she wiped at the tears on her cheeks. "I think you would find my experience with the occult beneficial."

He finished her drink and nodded his head.

"Yes, I'm sure your experience would be useful," he agreed with her. "There is only one condition," he added.

"Yes?"

"You call me Cody and not Detective, Kas," he scolded her.

At the door, before leaving, he told her how Daphne Orion had asked to speak with her.

"No way in hell would I defend her, if that's what she wants to talk about!" she said, and she was almost believable. He liked to think they might actually be on the same side.

Chapter 47

She didn't like the thought of leaving the girls behind. It wasn't completely safe, even with Geoffrey there to look out for them. She stood in the kitchen facing Crystal and trying to reason with her.

"I will be gone most of the day. I'm holding all three of you responsible for Cadence's safety while I'm gone!" She included Geoffrey, who wore a white sailor's cap, making him look a lot like the Captain's little buddy and first mate on old reruns of Gilligan's Island.

Erin rubbed the sleep out of her eyes and took a sip from the glass of milk she held, leaving a white mustache behind. Their safety was foremost in importance and she struggled to impress this upon them now.

"If dad should call do you want me to tell him you went with the Detective to Mount Gaspar?" Crystal questioned her. "How safe are you going to be, up there on the mountain with those ghouls from hell?" It was apparent it frightened Crystal to envision her mother in such horrific circumstances.

"I will be far more safe with the Detective," Kas replied, and then, remembering the one condition he made for her going along with him, she continued, "with Detective Cody Baldwyn than Neva is right this minute; supposing she's still alive, even!"

She gave Crystal a direct look.

"This is something I have to do, Crystal," she tried to explain to her, "Neva's my employee and she was abducted from my house."

She saw Cody's car outside, and she also noticed, at six o'clock in the morning, he was all ready to go. He hadn't ventured back to Althea last night, but he'd been scouting the beach for signs of the trespasser who'd murdered Ketil Anderson. She embraced both Crystal and Erin.

"Now remember, entertain yourselves indoors today, with the doors locked," she charged them, and gave Geoffrey a harsh look, too.

Cody drove a red Dodge Wagon, and when she opened the passenger door and slid into the front seat, she said,

"Good Morning, Detective. It still feels strange and I'm not used to it yet, but I'm trying to remember to call you Cody," she reprimanded herself.

As she buckled her seat belt, he reached across her to the glove compartment and removed a plastic bag to show her what he'd found on the beach sometime late last night. In the bag she saw a desert ironwood burl-handled, blue steel-edge knife stained with blood. Ketil's blood, she suspected.

"Why would the person who murdered your neighbor carelessly discard his knife where others could stumble on it and discover the murder weapon and crime he committed?" Cody questioned her.

"Was it a careless accident?" she wondered aloud.

Perhaps Ketil's killer still roamed the beach, she thought, and prayed the girls would mind what she'd told them and stay inside with the doors locked.

"Or, did he count on someone like you or me, finding it, thereby making one more statement?" Cody questioned.

He returned the bowie knife to his glove compartment, then fastened his seat belt, turned the ignition key and she heard the car's engine roar.

It was a long drive from Huntington Beach to the San Bernardino desert. Cody retraced the miles she and Crystal had driven just a day ago, before Ketil's cruel demise. Ketil would still be alive today had she stayed away and gone someplace else. Now she was like a bad omen and everywhere she went, trouble followed.

Cody took his eyes off of the road and gazed at her. Dressed in blue jeans and matching sweater, she appeared to have inherited her father's nerve as well as his good looks. She might also have been an innocent and injured victim. Although mixed up in his evilly deceitful affairs, perhaps she'd somehow managed to rise above her father's degradation.

"I've thought about something you said last night," Cody told her.

"Really?" she asked. He sparked her curiosity.

"The creep who murdered my family was made the Governor of Nevada." he shook his head, "Unbelievable," he sighed. "He killed dozens of people, including his own grandmother when he was a boy, and yet he was even nominated to run for president." Once upon a time, he'd demonstrated far more faith in the American people. Now he realized the majority of his fellow countrymen were absorbed in football, or competed for the world's money and position, jeopardizing their own souls. "America is an indoctrinated and easily manipulated nation of people," Cody told her.

They made a stop before they reached Althea. Cody was hungry, famished really, and he saw a little café just off the highway, so he stopped for a bite to eat.

There were others inside of the restaurant, but the waitress had no trouble finding them a table. After they were seated, the waitress handed them a menu and promised, with a smile, to return to their table. They watched her in her green uniform race away.

Kas was surprised Cody didn't read his menu. Instead, he set it aside, sipped from his glass of water and gazed at the people around him.

"Aren't you going to look at your menu?" she asked him.

"I already know what I want," he told her with an air of confidence as he continued watching the crowd inside of the *French Beagle* at this time of the morning.

"What if they don't have what you want?" she asked him.

"Then we'll leave and go someplace where they do," he said.

"Oh," she replied, reaching into her carryall to find her glasses so she could read her menu. As she put them on she murmured, "My father was a popular icon which is why I never seemed to be able to convince the police he was also a homicidal maniac." She wanted Cody to know now, she had tried her damnedest to convince the police of Rattler Mackenzie's abhorrent behavior.

Kas decided what she wanted to eat and then laid the menu aside and gazed around at the restaurant's interior decor. There were framed pictures of beagles on the moss-green walls, each inscribed with canine footprints. Then she noticed the man in the far corner of the room, wearing a red cap and yellow jacket, and staring directly at her.

His face was coarse and he had a depraved look in his eyes. He saw her regarding him and accorded her a dingy, teeth-stained smile. He was ugly and she turned her eyes away.

The waitress returned to their table and took their orders. Cody asked for two eggs, over easy, hash browns and sausage. Kas ordered one wheat bagel with cream cheese, and orange juice. After giving the waitress her order, she glanced at the man again, he was still staring at her.

"We've drawn attention from someone." she whispered to Cody as she leaned against the table.

"Ignore him. He's either just a casual observer, or he's a villain involved with murder." he said.

"And if he is?" she asked him, finding it difficult to ignore the ugly man.

"He will probably make a move…" Cody answered her. "He may even come over, and he may be armed, too, although I doubt he will attempt anything with so many people around."

"There's safety in numbers?" she asked.

"Right," he answered.

The waitress returned with their orders. They thanked her and watched her walk away. Cody thought of asking the waitress about the guy, maybe his name and if he was a regular customer, but then thought it safer if he didn't involve others.

Kas turned her attention away from the stranger and spread cream cheese on her bagel. Before she had finished, she saw the man had wandered to their table and, without being asked, he sat down on the bench next to Cody and continued to stare at her. He smelled of alcohole, tobacco, and cheap aftershave.

"I seem to have lost my appetite. Would you like a bagel?"

She pushed the plate toward the stranger who had the coldest-looking eyes she'd ever seen.

He ignored her breakfast and looking at her, he asked,

"You're on your way to Mount Gaspar, aren't you?"

"We're headed in that direction. Do you want a ride?" she asked politely, hoping to disguise her awful feelings about him. He was repulsive.

"What business is it of yours?" Cody asked in a confrontational tone.

One of them was sure to get his response, Kas thought, and she wasn't surprised when he answered Cody first.

"Who said anything to you?" Pointing to Cody's plate, he said, "Eat your runny eggs." Then, turning his attention to her again, he said, "You will find who you're looking for there. Give me your hand," he requested of her.

"What are you?" Cody protested, "Some nut-case fortune teller?"

"Think of the poor people in Ethiopia and eat your food" the man reprimanded him. "You have something in the glove compartment of your car which belongs to me." he told Cody.

"I have a lot of things in my glove compartment," Cody replied. "If you want it back, you're going to have to be more specific." he said, thinking of the bowie knife covered with Ketil's blood.

"It would be brainless of me to try to deceive or hurt you" the stranger told Kas, attempting to persuade her to give him her hand. "Rattler would not allow it" he said. Then, "You've stashed the item which belongs to me in a plastic bag." he informed Cody.

"I put a lot of things in plastic bags," Cody said. He wanted an outright confession.

Finally, Kas reached across the table and gave him her hand. Cody gazed at her. She had a lot of nerve, he thought. She could be holding hands with the man who murdered her neighbor and yet she never batted an eye.

Her skin crawled, but she was too curious not to comply with him. She saw the way he held her hand, gently, as though he were holding something of great value to him. He examined the lines in the palm of her hand the way a real palm-reader would do.

"You could rule an empire. You've been given an extensive global federation. You've been chosen, but if you stubbornly decline you will die." He said, wrapping his hand around hers, he squeezed, "Count on it" he told her.

She took her hand away from him. Their kingdom would topple down around their feet before she would rule it. She saw him turn his attention to Cody.

"The knife" he said, "Is mine." There was really very little the youthful-looking detective could do about it.

"You're under arrest for the murder of Ketil Anderson," Cody informed him.

The man stood up and, gazing down at the detective who thought he had control of things, he said,

"The knife is not yours. It's mine and I will take back what belongs to me." Once more he gazed at Kas. "Take seriously what I've said. If you do not take the kingdom, we will take your life." he told her very convincingly.

"I don't think so," Cody told him as he slid out of the booth. However, the man continued on his way, paying no attention to him. "Hello? Are you listening at all to me?" Cody inquired as he followed the man. "You're under arrest!" he repeated. He didn't know what kingdom on what planet the man intended Kas to rule over, but he thought he should understand a simple command. He didn't. "You can't leave here! I won't let you leave!" Cody told the ugly guy, pulling his pistol from his holster.

The man stopped at the door, his hand around the door knob. Cody thought he was either hard of hearing or very dense. The gun should have convinced him, he thought.

The stranger said nothing but lifted one hand, as if there were more power in his hand than the detective ever dreamed he might possess. The man pointed his finger and an alien force overtook Cody and sent him flying backward, slamming him hard against the wall.

People watched in amazement. It was unbelievable. The ugly guy hadn't even touched the detective. The man stood on the opposite side of the room from the detective, in fact. The cop's pistol was pointed straight at him when he lifted his hand and sent the cop flying into the wall. Then the villain addressed the crowd.

"I hope I haven't destroyed your appetites for a good day," he said, tipped his cap and left the café.

Chapter 48

Hank saw Jesse glow. She was wearing a sheer, black lace dress with lace bodice and square neck-line. He thought she was absolutely stunning. She moved so effortlessly around the table, pouring grape juice into the empty wine glasses while maintaining a brilliant smile. Gage was home and this was a special occasion.

Lacey stood beside her brother. The candlelight reflected in her dark eyes as she gazed at him. He was her hero and she adored him. Her mother had come to mean a great deal to her also.

She saw the woman move around the table, finally stopping beside Lacey to fill her glass with grape juice. Once more, she observed how much she resembled the woman. There was no better person on earth to pattern herself after than her Mother. After all, she was a tower of strength, Lacy thought.

Her Mother had escaped her father's demonic cult and evil influence. She'd done everything in her power to raise him out of the muck and mire which eventually swallowed him. Her many efforts proved impossible and she had to escape him in order to survive, which she had managed to do, but only narrowly.

Jesse stood beside the brawny black man at their dinner table and poured juice into his wine glass, too. He was the Psyche Technician, Benjamin Jabari, who had brought her son to her apartment, and his appearance added depth to the feelings at her dinner table on this very special night.

She wound up beside Hank again. This was more than all right with Hank. He lifted his glass so she could pour the grape juice into it. As she did, he smiled at her, thinking to himself, he was fortunate to have her in his life and to be one of her guests on this special occasion. This was a new beginning for Jesse, and for all of them seated at the dinner table. Except for the black guy. It was probably just a good time and a delicious dinner for him. Jesse was exquisite, Hank thought, as he gazed at her; her long, auburn hair and olive complexion, the silver cross necklace suspended from her lovely neck. She giggled as she labored to fill his glass.

"I'm a bit nervous," she admitted, and he saw her hands tremble.

"No!" he mocked her teasingly.

It was plain to see how very carefully she'd planned everything out, paying extreme attention to the evening's most minute details. The cucumber soup, Brussels Sprouts and stuffed chicken breasts had all been scrumptious. After dinner, Lacey followed her into the kitchen and when they returned, Jesse carried a Chocolate Mousse heart-shaped cake she'd made for the occasion. She was really good at this sort of thing Hank perceived, and he credited her for being a wonderful Homemaker.

Once she was beside Hank again, Jesse gazed at the others around her. These divine souls had inspired her to live...truly live...free from all addictions, and to become self-sufficient. She loved this small apartment where she and Lacey had managed to carve out a comfortable life-style, thanks to her job at Pet Emporium. She had escaped death and, because of her experience, life was much more dear to her now. Jesse raised her glass in a toast:

"To new beginnings" she said.

"To Jesse" Hank joined in "our incredible hostess!"

Grand expectations filled their hearts as felicity flooded the room.

"To the priesthood!" Gage said with excitement.

"Yes, to the priesthood!" Hank lifted his grape juice.

"To what?" Jesse choked on her drink. Oh, no, she thought, Doctor Jaime Kennis, what have you done to my son?

Chapter 49

Wesley Versuch, with his fist doubled, banged upon the battered old door and shouted,

"Naomi, it's me, Wesley! Let me in! Please, let me come in!"

Wesley could hear the noise his ex-wife was making behind the paper-thin walls of the dingy apartment. He heard the sound of her feet, probably wearing the pink slippers he'd bought her two years ago for her birthday.

Naomi lived in this decrepit apartment building, one floor above her nosey, unfriendly landlord who would most likely complain about Wesley's noisy visit at this hour of the night. To prevent this ruckus, Naomi would hustle to the door and let him in; at least he hoped she would.

He saw the door knob turn and then heard the door open only as far as the safety chain would allow. Naomi stared at him through the space and, rubbing the sleep from her eyes, she asked,

"Do you realize what time it is, Wes? How come you've shown up at this godforsaken hour?"

The truth was, Wesley had no place else to go.

"I need help, Naomi," he pleaded with her. "Let me in and I'll explain everything to you!"

He watched her grapple with the door and then she opened it, standing to one side while yawning and scratching the disheveled mop of hair on her head.

"You'd better have a damned good explanation because I've got to be at work in a couple of hours!" she grumbled.

Naomi wore an old, pink chenille bathrobe and her face was covered with some kind of green, plaster-like cream, but beneath her half smile and behind the sleepy look she gave him, he thought he saw Caroline, and for this reason alone he inched closer to her and kissed her on the cheek.

Then he wiped the green stuff off his mouth and gazed around him at the hell-hole Naomi lived in; the creaky water pipes, the old, marred and stained walls. Things should have turned out better for Naomi, he told himself. Things would have turned out better, too, if Caroline hadn't died. He blamed her death on the occult. The despicable chemtrails had ruined their lives.

From the door, Wesley could see everything in Naomi's small, dingy apartment. Through the open hallway he could even see into her bedroom and the unmade bed. He saw the old black and white TV set in one corner of the room and a second-hand sofa which she'd picked up at a Salvation Army store. Across from those was Naomi's beat-up white, refrigerator with the door which didn't shut right. All of these things were bleak indications of Naomi's gut-wrenching misfortune: Caroline's horrible death.

He watched her close the door, fold her arms in front of her, and then inquire,

"Well, what's your problem, Wesley, and how come it couldn't wait until tomorrow?"

He paced the creaky old floor in her living room and then replied,

"I killed someone this evening, Naomi! I killed someone with my own hands!"

"Oh, shit!" she sighed. "How?" she asked him.

"I wrapped my belt around her neck and strangled her to death," he uttered.

He remembered the terrifying look on Carla's face as he ended her life.

Naomi sat down on her sofa and shook her head at Wesley's words. In tears she questioned him,

"Why, Wesley? Why did you kill her?"

Wesley looked at his ex-wife, whom he adored for so many reasons. Naomi didn't even know the woman he'd killed and, yet, she was in tears over her death. Wesley knew she wouldn't have liked Carla, had she known her. They were as different as night and day. Carla had a lot of money but very little sense, and Naomi had nothing but human compassion. He dropped on his knees before her and struggled to explain his actions.

"I went to sleep in the bedroom we shared and, when I woke up, she was on top of me! Carla was aggressive! She ripped Caroline's picture out of my hands and threw it, hitting the lamp and busting the picture into pieces! At the time, half asleep, I thought I was being mugged by a wild boar!"

"It wasn't premeditated, then. You didn't set out to kill her, Wesley!" Naomi gave him a concentrated look and attempted to persuade him. "If you turn youself in now the police probably won't do anything to you!"

The tenderness he felt for her flooded his being and he smiled at her. Naomi was the most righteous person he'd ever known. They were so different, yet, they had many things in common. He wanted a safe, sinless life, but he'd been brought up in the occult. He was a full-fledged member of a hateful organization, one he couldn't escape. He'd never escape it alive, anyway. He raised himself off the floor and sat down beside her. Taking her hands in his, he assured her,

"I've called the best defense lawyer in California and have an appointment with her tomorrow. The thing is, I don't know how I will ever pay for it."

She watched as he shook his head sadly. She knew he couldn't afford appropriate representation, and this bothered her, too. She stood up and moved away from him.

"Be sure to correct me if I'm out of line here, Wesley," she said, as she went to the stove for the kettle of water. "You've been living with someone called Carla for who knows how long, humping her regularly, and when you accidentally kill her you discover, whoops, you haven't the sufficient means to defend yourself, so then you turn to me?"

"Don't do this, Naomi. It cheapens you!" he told her.

"Don't do what?" she asked him.

"Don't sound like a jilted woman..." he said, as he left the sofa and started on his way into her kitchen and to where she stood at the stove, lighting it with a match.

"You mean, it makes you feel like a guilty double-crosser?" she snapped at him.

"We both know I'm no good for you" he attempted to explain to her.

They'd had this conversation thousands of times before. It broke his heart to have to admit it again, but he couldn't stay with her. They couldn't live a normal life, married to each other. The occult would not allow it. He stopped only feet away from her. Feeling the familiar ache of wanting her in his arms, he continued,

"I should never have involved you and Caroline in all of this, Naomi! We should have stayed together long enough to have Caroline, and then I should have left you both and never returned!"

She looked into his despairing eyes and she felt an overwhelming desire to lift his sorrow.

"We did do something right together, didn't we, Wesley?"

"Yes, we sure did," he said, and he tried his damnedest to to choke back his tears but they overcame him and spilled from his eyes. "She was flawless!" he exclaimed.

Chapter 50

When Cody and Kas left the *'French Beagle'*, they went straight to his wagon. Cody opened the passenger door and searched through the glove compartment. The knife was gone. Obviously, the greasy guy in the red cap had taken it. The fact it was the murder weapon made it police property and swiping it was a serious crime. The thief now had possession of the knife. The same knife which was stained with his victim's blood.

Kas, as though thinking aloud, said,

"He took from you what was his all along."

"You sound just like him!" Cody told her.

She leaned against the car. It was in these particular circumstances he grew most wary of her intentions.

"Well, maybe there's a logical explanation for it. He's my uncle." she informed him. "He's Stuart Mackenzie, Rattler's little brother...."

"Well, evidently, he's no ghost. Everyone in the café saw him."

"No, he's flesh and blood, and a master of black magic." she told him.

Cody rubbed at his aching neck. He'd slammed against the wall of the cafe and for several minutes he wondered if he'd broken something, like maybe a couple of ribs. He recalled the loud *splat* when his body hit against the bricks, knocking the wind out of him. What hurt him most of all, though, was his injured pride.

"Are you all right?" she questioned him. "Do you want me to drive?"

"I'm fine" he growled. "He seems to think we will find who we're looking for on Mount Gaspar." he added. Walking around his Dodge and giving it a once-over, just to make sure the knife was the only thing the con man had taken, or messed with. "How much of what he said can we take for fact?"

"What reason would he have to make things up?" She answered him with a question, as she opened the the van's door and slid into the front seat. Anyone with the kind of power Stuart Mackenzie possessed had very little need to make things up, she thought.

"Maybe he wants us to go to the mountain" Cody replied, as he got into his car.

"Maybe" she said. "Actually, I think he was pretty easy on you, Cody. I mean, after all, you did kill his brother, didn't you?"

Cody caught the point the blond coolly made. He saw the sign on the roadside which said, *'Welcome to Althea-population: 6,000.'* and he felt a chill on the back of his neck. The felon in the yellow jacket and red cap could very well have intended to lure him to the mountain.

He tried to take his mind off the hazards which might lie in store for him and, instead, concentrate upon Neva Paloma, the woman whose body was probably somewhere at the top of Mount Gaspar. He imagined her still alive and paralyzed with fear, hoping someone would rescue her.

As they started up the mountain, Cody wondered aloud,

"Will we find Neva Paloma alive?" He was antsy, and his voice revealed his uneasiness as they ascended the mountain in his Dodge.

As they rounded a sharp turn, they saw a man on the shoulder of the road, or maybe an apparition, decked out in black tuxedo and top hat. The image which finally emerged was that of an old man with white hair flowing from under his top hat down to his neck line, and a bushy white mustache. His azure-blue eyes stared at them…empty eyes. Unable to turn his gaze away from the ghostly figure, Cody whispered to his passenger,

"You see him, right?"

"As clear as day," Kas whispered.

"Have you any clue as to why he's here? What his appearance is meant to convey?"

"None, but I have the feeling he's not the only ghost in this vicinity." she sighed.

"Have we entered a parallel world, one where the paranormal is routine?" he asked her as he sped past the apparition. He turned his head to look at her. She slid down in her seat, gripped the arm-rest and returned his glance.

"We were conditioned to see elusions. I've a hunch this is why Stuart Mackenzie appeared to us at the French Beagle. It was his purpose to fix our minds on the transcendental."

She could see a flurry of smoke, or maybe it was fog, as thick as pea-soup roll down from the mountain and threaten to envelop them. The occult at the top of Mount Gaspar was not about to spare them, she surmised.

"The best advice I can give you, Cody, is to try not to take any of what you think you see as being factual. They are masters at trickery."

He brought the Dodge to a screeching stop. There, in the middle of the road, appeared another apparition which looked amazingly real. This one was a carbon copy of his beloved son. The sandy, blonde-headed boy was dressed in a dark suit and tie, and looked to be the same age Kevin was when the sadistic Rattler Mackenzie killed him. Cody opened his door and hastened from the van as Kas raced after him.

"It's a hologram, Cody!", she called to him, but she knew he wasn't listening.

Cody stood only a few feet away from the chimera, or illusion, afraid if he stepped any closer the phantom would disappear. He felt the familiar ache deep inside and complete desolation washed over him. The deception, that of a ten-year-old boy, every hair in place, looking so angelic bore a visible resemblance of his mother. With clear voice the thing addressed him,

"Dad." Cody's strong desire to reach out to his son almost overpowered him, yet he maintained his distance. Then, once more, the apparition called to him, "Dad!"

This time, Cody answered it.

"Son?" He saw the boy's expressive eyes turn stormy, and Cody heard his accusation,

"You are a dangerous and violent man, Dad and you will never occupy a place in Chimera!"

"Some one on the mountain doesn't like you, Cody, and for a clear and coherent reason, too."

He heard the voice behind him and turned to see Kas. He wondered if she was of the same mind-set, but then told himself she wasn't. He glanced upward. The fog rushed in around them and Cody knew they couldn't drive in this thick soup. They'd have to trek the rest of the way on foot.

"Give me your hand," Cody coaxed her. She gave him a nervous look.

"Why?" she asked him.

It seemed to him she was pretty cautious for someone who'd seemed more than willing to offer her hand to a suspected murderer a while back, at the French Beagle. Of course, the ugly guy wasn't being hounded by a madman at the time, either, he told himself.

"We're going to proceed through this fog on foot and it's safest if we stay together," he told her. There was no way they'd manage to keep track of each other unless they clung together, he figured.

Finally, she reached her hand out to him and he took it. They turned toward the steep incline, braced themselves and headed into the fog. There were more holograms, three dimensional images and more bizarre emanations too. Someone on the mountain definitely intended to scare him.

The massive amount of ooze which enveloped them hampered his ability to see very much around him. The further they trekked, the thicker the fog became and the less he could see. He could barely recognize Kas, let alone see anything else. Yet the holograms were extraordinarily clear, and the voices which accompanied them were discernable.

They hadn't ventured very far before Cody saw, straight ahead of them, a three dimensional image of a woman with an injured child in her lap. The boy's wounds were bleeding, blood flowing from deep gashes the child had sustained. Chilled to the bone, Cody identified the familiar voice because it was so similar to his wife's when she sobbed,

"Look what they've done to our son! How could they do this to us, Cody? Do you really think you are any competition for them?"

He stifled his emotions, telling himself it wasn't real and, clenching Kas's hand with his own, he proceeded through the hologram until he'd reached the other side. Then turning around he grumbled,

"This is unfair!"

"They've gone for your emotions," she said with frustration.

Cody shook his head and admitted,

"There's no way to defend myself against these familiar images".

Alone, he could not have fought the frightening facsimiles which bore close proximity to his nightmares, ghosts and head trips which had kept him awake countless nights. Someone had liberal knowledge of his internal turmoil. Far more knowledge than Cody had ever shared with anyone.

Now, though, because of the gut-wrenching images, the woman beside him was aware of his intimate thoughts, too. Since she had already been subjected to his misery, Cody felt it only appropriate to level with her now.

"According to the Coroner," he said, "Kevin's body was repeatedly slashed with a knife." He struggled to explain it unemotionally as he choked back his impulse to explode.

He set his jaw and determined to control his anger. He had the premonition this is what they wanted from him, this was the reason for their three-dimensional images.

"I'm sorry, Cody," she said, "I never knew exactly what happened to your little boy."

The image disappeared and only the fluorescence of colors:red, blue, purple and green, lingered. Someone succeeded in flashing before them one more lifelike illustration. This one, followed by a loud clap of thunder, was the dreadful image of the high priest adorned with a gold crown and black scepter, seated on a throne, settling on the horizon.

Cody shivered, still holding Kas's hand, and she trembled, swallowed hard and told herself this one was worse than all of the others put together. It was so real, she struggled to convince herself it was nothing but counterfeit, some fool's attempt to confound them. More explosive thunder and lightening streaked through the dense fog. Rattler laughed with ghoulish pleasure.

"I have already deceived you, and you remain unaware of what I have done", the ghoul, apparently on an ego trip, exclaimed. "Nothing now is as it was, nor will it ever be again. By coming here as I directed you, you have defiled yourselves," he said.

"We came here to rescue Neva Paloma," Cody countered.

"I don't feel defiled; do you feel defiled, Cody?" Kas coolly asked the detective. Rather than to address the image, she sought to poke fun at it and the fiend behind it too. She had a feeling it may well have been her uncle toying with them now, and she refused to let him manipulate them. Cody gave her a quizzical look but said nothing.

"Just tell us where Neva is and we'll leave you to your folly," she insisted, speaking to the image. "Or," she said, pausing to think their predicament through, "We might hang around and uncover the beggarly fool behind these pathetic tricks." she threatened.

"Silence!" the voice roared, and lightening nearly struck Cody, splitting the ground beneath their feet. The image raised itself from it's lofty position and stood up, expanding several stories high as they stretched their necks to observe it.

"She-devil, you dare to provoke me when I could easily crush you and your little companion too?"

Kas swallowed hard and had second thoughts. Cody imagined the thing quite possibly would deliver some type of punishment, so when the black Bentley Arnage broke through the axles of light and headed straight for them, he leaped and fell upon Kas, knocking them both to the ground. They rolled several feet over rough terrain and out of the vehicle's way, narrowly escaping death.

Cody crouched on top of her and gazed into her alluring eyes. Had she lost her senses? He wondered. They were nothing compared to the enigmatic powers on the mountain, he reasoned. She made no effort to wrestle out from beneath him, but lay totally still, a befuddled look on her face.

"Maybe we shouldn't provoke it?" he suggested to her.

"Get off of me" she grumbled, and he quickly clambered to a sitting position. He had a feeling she might be capable of causing him great injury if he didn't comply with her. He knew, somehow, she was harnessed to this enormously obscure power.

She sat up.

"It called me a she-devil!" She gave him a troubled look, massaged her elbow and groaned. He stood up and turning around, he pulled her from the ground.

"Are you all right?" She saw the concern in his eyes and nodded.

"I'll live", she sighed, as she brushed herself off. But nothing will ever be the same, she thought but didn't share this with Cody.

"That was the Bentley Arnage your daughter saw parked outside your house, the one Neva got into. She can't be far now" he said, and he seemed, somehow, fitter for the fall, sharper and more lighthearted. He was a cop, she told herself, and cops thrived on calamity.

He turned and saw the Bentley, without a driver, barreling toward them. Some invisible force intended to either terrorize them or use the car to massacre them. He wasn't about to stick around to find out which course they'd take. He noticed again the thick, soupy fog, the obstacle which blocked their way to rescuing Neva. The road ahead was the only course open to them now, and they could barely see it. He noticed the fearful look on her face when she returned his gaze. Cody took her hand again and they scampered away, running as fast as they could, trying to outrun the Bentley.

Cody felt like a helpless animal in danger of being cornered only this was worse because an animal, under normal circumstances, could have seen the path ahead and what barriers and booby traps might exist. They could see nothing but dense fog wrapping around them like dirty cotton.

They followed no visible passage, directionless, counting on sheer instincts to avoid veering too much to the left or to the right and possibly falling over the embankment. The Bentley revved its powerful engine and continued to advance.

They ran until they were out of breath, chased by a crazy ghost who apparently could see much better then they could. They swore they couldn't run any further and then told themselves they had to keep running to get away from the demonic automobile.

Finally, the ground beneath them disappeared and they were falling….falling….into complete and utter darkness, their bodies slapping against the cold, hard earthen walls like bags of discarded rubbish.

Chapter 51

Cody opened his eyes and saw nothing but deep, enveloping darkness. He seemed to be lying against hard earth, but where he was, or even what dimension he was in, he didn't know. The air was putrid, an odor so foul it burned his nostrils to breathe.

As he lay considering his situation, he heard a dreadful spine-chilling noise like the deadly rattle of a Western Diamond Back Rattlesnake. Cody reacted instinctively, rolling away from the direction of the noise and rapidly getting to his feet, knowing his life depended upon the actions he took.

Still dazed, he staggered about, bumping his head on some metal object which seemed to protrude from the wall. He grabbed the thing and found, to his amazement, it was a hot-blast lamp, the type of lantern the British Army had used fifty years ago, and he hoped there was still fuel in it.

He reached for the cigarette lighter in his pocket. Lucky for him he smoked, he thought, or he wouldn't have a lighter on hand to even try to light the old lantern, of course, he wasn't at all sure the lantern would light.

He fumbled around with it before, finally, he was able to ignite the wick and adjust it. He saw there was fuel in it, as though someone had used it recently.

Once more, he was made chillingly aware of the snake when it made a loud rattle. He grabbed for his gun, circled around, and spied the reptile in the lamp's light. It was mean-looking, and coiled as if ready to strike.

Cody fired at it and knew the bullet had hit it, but it failed to even phase the creature. The bullet had left no hole, or even a dent in the snake's flesh, yet Cody knew ordinary snakes were no match for a deadly slug fired from a 9-millimeter gun. The snake was still coiled in attack mode.

Cody could see the reptile's forked tongue and poisonous fangs. It was extremely real, he told himself, and not a hologram, or optical illusion, but then, why didn't it die?

He fired another bullet when the reptile's rattle grew louder, but his shots still made no impression on the snake. The snake had been angry before he fired, and now it was furious with him. Its green eyes were livid with rage.

"The banshee is my progenitor," a voice whispered in his ear. "You can't kill something which is already dead," Kas informed him.

"Kastanje?" the monster groaned in anguish, lowered its head and took on an altogether different carriage. It uncoiled and seemed ashamed of its actions.

"The thing recognizes you!" Cody uttered, and turned to face her.

He didn't think of how the shocked look on his face might make her feel. He stared at her with malediction. She was a part of all of the chimera taking place around them, indigenous to it.

He saw the large rattlesnake, or rather, the demon with venomous fangs, slink back and away from her as though she had an enormous amount of persuasion over it.

"Yea, we go way back" she concurred, giving him a quick glance and then looking away.

Her eyes followed the snake which slithered past them and oozed into the darkness.

"I bet Rattler has some knowledge as to Neva's whereabouts, too" she said. "Maybe he's even headed in her direction now."

"Rattler Mackenzie?" Cody gasped in amazement. He found the thought incredible. The archbishop, who at one time possessed enormous clout over their society, was now reduced to a lowly snake, much like the devil in the Garden of Eden had been reduced to a serpent, he thought. "Seems like a suitable fate for him," Cody commented, shining his light to follow after the reptile.

"It's just one of the costumes he wears," she said, as she trailed close behind him. "He's a shape shifter," she told him, wanting to clue him in.

"Much like the shape-shifter who made it past the warden and showed up in Gage Petersen's prison cell?" he asked.

"Very much like her." she answered as, bewildered, she spotted something in the dirt which flashed beneath the puny light of Cody's lamp. "Wait!" she called to him.

He turned his head to see her stooped over, reaching for something on the ground.

She removed from the dirt a pair of gold, wire-rimmed eyeglasses and thought she recognized them. The frame was twisted and the lenses broken, but they looked somewhat familiar to her. She looked them over, trying to place them, but she couldn't. Finally, she handed them to Cody. The precinct in Althea could do a test and determine who they belonged to, she decided.

"Neva doesn't wear eye glasses," she said with disappointment, wondering if they'd ever find her employee and friend.

Cody pocketed the glasses and they continued picking their way through the dismal underground cavern. The subterranean passageway seemed to go on forever, this underground shelter which the Delphians probably used as a secret hideout. The further they walked, the stronger the odor became; a sooty smell, charcoal mixed heavily with the stench of ruin, perhaps fleshly decay, he thought, and his stomach felt queasy.

Kas was startled when Cody suddenly stopped and pointed toward something lying on the ground. Approaching closer, they could see it was a body and she knew, immediately, who it was. She recognized Neva Paloma and she prayed the woman was still alive. In the dim light, she hurried over the rugged earth and dropped on her knees beside the body of her friend.

Staring down at Neva, she was afraid she'd make the situation even worse if she moved her. Then Cody shed his light to the woman's deathly gray face, with eyes staring up at them. Neva was still alive but only barely.

There had to be something she could do for her, some way to elevate her pain, Kas thought in frustration. Neva Poloma was dying, and Kas couldn't think of any way to comfort her. She shot Cody an anxious look and he saw the desperation in her eyes. He moved closer until the light from his lantern shone directly over them.

He was appalled at what he saw. The woman's poor mangled body, and someone had severed her arm, leg and ear from the rest of her torso. Blood oozed from these amputations and permeated the ground. The smell, as she lay in her own feces and urine, was detestable.

"What sort of fiends would do this to her?" Cody exclaimed.

"Demons" Kas answered him. "Demons like the one you have behind bars at Althea's prison! " she reminded him, thinking of the hellion. There were no bars which could confine malignant spirits.

Finally, moved by her uneasy flood of emotions toward the woman, she threw caution to the wind and reached for Neva's broken body, pulling her close into her arms.

"Neva?", she called to her, in a soft voice.

"Quiero que mi hijo!" Neva groaned. Then she deliriously cried, "Larenzo!" out into the darkness, but to no avail.

"What is she saying?" Cody softly questioned Kas.

"She wants her son," Kas answered as she wept. "She is calling for her son, Larenzo!"

Neva Poloma breathed her last weak breath, and died cradled in her employer's arms. The woman had given more to her employer than ever required, or expected of her Cody thought with remorse.

Kastanje bent over her and sobbed.

"No, Neva, no hazer die!" she cried.

It was one more incident in which Cody felt completely defenseless. Helpless against the invincible forces which labored to destroy them inside of this dark, dank cavern, this loathsome place, he thought to himself. Someone like Neva should never have possessed knowledge of such inhuman conditions. God knows how many hours Neva had spent helplessly imprisoned in this cave, debilitated, pining away, and hoping someone would discover her. Kas lifted her head,

"Son of a bitch," she murmured angrily, pushing at the filthy ground with the heels of her boots, propelling herself away from Neva's sad, mangled body. Sliding across the terrain on the seat of her pants, she positioned herself in a corner of the cave, drawing her knees in front of her, "Son of a bitch!" she repeated with bitter anger.

Cody moved the lantern so he could see her better, but she turned away from the light to face the barricade and waved her hand at him.

"No!" she shouted, "Please, No!"

Understanding her despair, he fell on his knees beside her.

"All of your misspent blame won't bring Neva back, Kas," he whispered. He spoke as much to himself as he did to her, for Cody had spent a great deal of his time blaming himself for what had happened to his wife and son, and their barbaric end. He propped himself against the firm blockade, stared straight ahead into the darkness and shared with her,

"Rattler made Belle watch him when he mutilated Kevin with his knife. Only afterward, after he'd finished with his fun, did he kill her too."

Cody repeated the same insane story he'd told his shrink years ago. He was a real head-case then, saturated with anger, enraged by the ogre who'd butchered his family. He was driven by seething anger and hatred, but self-condemnation too. His anger got the best of him until, finally, he was let go, told to take a very long intermission. His intermission lasted three years in which he drifted about, without direction, until he finally sought the help of an excellent psychiatrist.

"They want me, Cody" she said, turning her head to look at him, and he could see the animosity in her tear-filled eyes. "This had nothing to do with Neva!" she said, and she sounded convinced of it. "Their beef is with me," she insisted.

"Rattler's beef was with the reporter, Belle Baldwyn, ten years ago and he slaughtered an innocent ten-year-old boy to crush and destroy her, too" Cody fumed.

Conversation was stifled when they heard the distinct sound of footsteps in the darkness, somewhere in the tunnel toward the opposite end of the cavern. The footsteps grew louder. Someone was approaching, and Cody had the strong feeling they should flee, although there seemed to be no where to hide. He thought about extinguishing the light from the lantern, but then the idea of being impaired by blindness, unable to see their opponent, made him feel a good deal more nervous. They were like fish in a bowl and would make easy captives. He held onto his gun, for all the good it might might do him, Cody thought with frustration.

The figure finally emerged from the darkness, wearing a red cap and yellow jacket.

"There's a familiar sight" Cody said. "He's real, right?" he added, unwilling to make any more snap decisions concerning the ghouls who inhabited the mountain.

"Real as concrete" Kas answered him.

The ugly man waved his hand in the air and Cody gripped his gun, hoping there would be no more tricks, or apparitions called up by degenerates. He'd barely recovered from his last encounter with the weird magician, he thought, as he kept his gun trained on the man.

"I see you've uncovered your friend," the pariah taunted. "Poor Neva Paloma, left to bleed to death in the clay while her employer slogged miles away in a useless attempt to find her in time." The ugly man clicked his tonque and shook his head, saying, "Why, you can see how troubling it must have been for her, can't you?"

He sounded pleased with the Society's efforts to cause so much agony for the helpless woman. Kas squelched the desire to vent her rage. Cody tried to think up some method of retaliation. This degenerate had killed Ketil Anderson and he was in some way responsible for Neva's death too.

"Neva's ear, leg and arm were all amputated and our present high priestess anticipated sending her body parts to you, special delivery." His ugly lips curled as he smiled at Kas. Shrugging, he then added, "I don't know what happened to this idea, or why it was abandoned. Oh, well, I suppose it doesn't matter now, seeing as how Neva is quite dead."

"You killed her, thinking you'd thrust me into claiming the position of high priestess over you esoteric clique?" Kas said abruptly, hardly believing her voice when she heard it. Neva's dead body was lying between her and her uncle and, by the light of Cody's lantern, she could see Stuart Mackenzie shake his head before he answered her.

"When we nabbed her at your house, Rattler and I, both of us, thought the fact your cleaning lady was missing might pressure you into assuming the position," he admitted, as he took a step in their direction. With a smile on his ugly face he continued. "However, it was solely Daphne's idea to sever Neva's body parts with her scalpel. Needless to report, Daphne enjoyed the operation very much. You cannot appreciate how it feels to inflict upon another human being, intense pain and misery." Once, a long time ago, Stuart Mackenzie was a doctor, one who delighted in his ability to inflict colossal pain. He didn't wait for her response, but turned his attention to the detective with the shot-gun in his hand.

"Your performance is so moronic, Detective." he said, and his voice rose in volume but he stopped short of shouting. "I can understand how, at first, you had the mistaken idea your gun gave you some edge over us. However, now you must accept your inability to solve every problem with hardware," Stuart said with a laugh. "Put your gun away, detective, for it will do you no good here."

Cody, though, had a lot of affection for his gun. In difficult spots, his gun had come through for him, more than once. He refused to part with it now.

"Even if you succeeded to kill me, your woes would not vanish," Stuart assured him. "There are thousands of us, all over the world, and we have enormous persuasion over everyone in the universe."

He seemed to relish his dialogue with those he considered to be less brainy than himself.

He fancied the role of a teacher, an elegant scholar, he thought. In truth, there was nothing elegant about Stuart Mackenzie, and he didn't resemble either a doctor or a scholar. He looked to be just what he was, a homicidal maniac.

Kas considered Cody and his gun, which looked threatening in the light from Cody's lantern. She disliked guns; she disapproved of bloodshed, too. Those were two conditions which made her a poor candidate for archbishop of the cabal.

"So, what makes you think I'll ever consent to your request?" she enquired of him.

Stuart straddled the ground, folded his arms in front of him, he propped his chin with one hand, as though he were contemplating a nice way of telling her what her fate would be if she didn't cooperate with them.

He wasn't about to make the same mistake which had cost Peter Wolfe his life. He'd not threaten to end her existence. He was reluctant to agitate his brother, Rattler, whose spirit he could sense in their midst, attending to every word and passing judgment upon them.

"Imagine all of the poor, pathetic souls, and the transactions they've made to purchase a lowly spot in the world to come. How lost they would be without an attorney, an advocate to negotiate on their behalf. Why, without your life-saving diplomacy, many of them might wind up no better off than Neva is right now."

Yes, he contemplated, this was the kind of manipulation which would win Rattler's approval, he confidently decided and strolled toward them, around the dead body, edging closer to Rattler's lineage.

Cody grew nervous, bothered when the vulgar man advanced. Fearful about Kas's safety, he held the gun, and made up his mind he'd use it if necessary.

"The cabal is millions of years old", Stuart continued, like a doctor explaining to a patient the cure for her dilemma. "The cabal has always existed….and always will…exist. Whereas, there was one, now the one has gathered a throng of followers and it's up to you to decide whether to unite with this merry multitude, or to align yourself against this magnificent movement and suffer the horrendous consequences of your actions." Stuart took a great deal of effort to explain to her in detail. Reading Cody's mind, weighing the fatality of the detective's actions and preparing to put a stop to those actions, he turned to Cody and said,

"I told you to put your gun away!"

Cody considered the possibility the magician might well send him flying into the rocks, he still objected to the way the lunatic stood so close to Kas, and when the maniac reached out to touch her, he eased the gun to his shoulder and pulled the trigger.

A loud bang echoed through the cavern and, in a second, Stuart Mackenzie turned to face the detective who had shot him.

"My brother has struck out at me!" he groaned. "Why? How could what I have said displeased him so?" Stuart murmured, seemingly more upset over his brother's rejection of him then with the fact he was dying.

When Stuart Mackenzie's dead body hit the ground with a rumble, Cody was pretty sure his bullet hadn't killed the magician but, somehow, his brother's disapproval had ended his miserable life.

Chapter 52

Wesley Versuch sat down at Naomi's table with the newspaper in his hand. The old, oak table was stained and an assortment of pen marks had been etched into the wood. It might have been beautiful at one time but was now showing it's age, and the legs were uneven, which caused it to wobble a bit. Nevertheless, Wesley held the newspaper and set the cup of hot coffee, which Naomi had brewed for him, down on the worn surface.

Wesley hadn't expected to see the crime he'd committed making front page headlines all ready. There were plenty of crimes committed every day in the San Bernardino desert and very few of them made the front page headlines. He saw what had made the front page, though.

There was a picture of his Attorney, the woman he had contacted to represent him in the court-room when he was accused of Carla's murder. Defense Attorney Kastanje Scott, a gorgeous blond appeared on the front page. She was bent over, her hands cupped around the face of the adorable little girl who reminded him so much of his very own daughter. The caption read:

The Woman Nominated To Run For Senator of California.

The article revealed how Kastanje Scott was a decent, hard-working, conservative-type of person, an extraordinary role-model who, in spite of horrendous difficulties, had become an iron-hard, unyielding representative for the people of California.

Kastanje had first-hand experience of the adversities the people encountered with government bureaucracy, the journalist wrote. She was the daughter of Darragh Mackenzie, who was once Governor of Nevada. He served Nevada with dedication for eight years before he was nominated for president of the United States. Although, he lost this specific race, his outstanding influence over the hearts and minds of the American people had helped mold and shape the country.

Now, apparently, it was time for Darragh Mackenzie's daughter to step up to the plate in the race for Senator of California. Could she do it? Wesley wondered. Yes, of course, with the cabal's patronage and support, she could ascend to any position she set her mind to, Wesley imagined, for the occult was more popular then it had ever been.

Wesley felt Naomi's presence as she leaned over his chair while closely examining the picture on the front page. He glanced up at Naomi and saw her cleavage exposed beneath her v-neck blouse. Naomi had perfect cleavage, he thought.

"She's the lawyer I contacted to represent me," Wesley told her.

His eyes scanned the picture in front of him. The picture of mother and daughter, the type of setting which brought to Wesley's mind a hoard of memories of Naomi and Caroline. He had one particular memory, a favorite one of Naomi holding Caroline's chin with her hand as she asked her if she'd taken the very last chocolate chip cookie. Caroline had confessed,

"Yes, Mommy, I took it! Teddy and I shared it with our cups of tea at breakfast this morning".

Wesley swallowed hard as he considered the small child in the picture whom Rattler claimed was his granddaughter. The article lead Wesley to believe Rattler's daughter had finally sunk to his level and had taken help from the cabal. He felt great anxiety for the little girl. What fate awaited the child now that her Mommy had succumbed and consented to being a part of the cabal's evil plans for world domination?

"Look at her!" Wesley insisted, and Naomi shivered.

"Look at who?", she asked, trying to remain aloof, hoping Wesley wouldn't go into another tangent. Wesley was sometimes far less than reasonable, she thought. In fact, when he became zealous over something, Wesley could be overbearing.

"Are you obsessed over her?" Naomi questioned, staring down at the blond woman who could just as easily have been a model or a movie star. She knew Wesley was attracted to beautiful women.

"Not her!" Wesley raised his voice, "The little girl, who does she remind you of?" He asked, and Naomi felt put on the spot, thinking she had to come up with the answer he wanted.

Wesley was so distraught, he jumped up from his seat, knocking the chair over in his determination to show her the picture.

Naomi ignored the chair as she closely inspected the picture of the child who bore such a close resemblance to Caroline, although she knew many blond-haired and blue-eyed little girls did.

Wesley didn't wait for her to answer but, consumed by his fixation, he continued,

"Why she looks exactly like Caroline, Naomi! Our Caroline, and there she is, in this morning's headlines!" He sounded outraged and shouted, "They're making merchandise from her!"

Naomi stood up, picked up Wesley's empty coffee cup, carried it to the kitchen sink, set it down gently and ran tap water into it. Then she went to the table and picked up the chair which Wesley had knocked over.

"She's not our problem, Wesley" she said. "We have enough problems. We don't need to create more" Naomi said, sounding like the small voice of common sense.

According to Wesley, he had killed someone the night before. He claimed it was a mistake and, while in a state of utter confusion, he'd strangled a woman with his bear hands. This created a huge problem for Wesley. A problem which wouldn't disappear until it was somehow resolved. Meanwhile, the last thing Wesley needed was to take responsibility for this little girl.

At the table, she gazed at the two people in the picture again. It didn't appear to her the little girl suffered any particular dilemma. It seemed her Mommy was very wealthy and the little girl was probably accustomed to the very finest things in life.

Naomi thought of how there had never been a time when she'd suffered the same sort of problem. She looked around at her makeshift apartment, and knew she probably would never know what it was like to have money, or expensive items. What a plight, she thought with sarcasm, and she had no sympathy for the little girl in the picture.

"Naomi, the girl is Rattler Mackenzie's granddaughter and Daphne Orion ordered me to kidnap her." Wesley admitted in a worried voice. He went to the table and stood over the newspaper, looking grief-stricken as he gazed down at the picture. "Her Mommy is supposed to become the high priestess of the cabal. If this happens, this beautiful child will suffer the same deplorable situation I have known throughout my life," he groaned. "The cabal will control every minute of her existence."

Naomi shook her head at him. Things hadn't changed, she thought. Wesley was still entangled with kidnappers, child abductors and murderers. Heartless

224

people, without a conscience. People who had a completely different agenda than others aspired to attain. They were the same demons Wesley had fought his entire life. The demons who'd destroyed their marriage, the ones who had killed Caroline.

"You're going to save her?", Naomi questioned him. "You're going to save her when you can't even save yourself? When you couldn't even save Caroline? How, Wesley? How do you imagine you're going to do this?" She was almost moved to tears as she questioned him. She saw him shake his blond head, sadly, bewilderedly, and her own heart almost broke over his dilemma.

Then, suddenly, Wesley removed the newspaper from the table.

"I'm the only hope she has," he told her, giving her a wild-eyed glance. "No one else knows what it's like to grow up in the occult! No one but me and this little girl, so I have to do something, Naomi!" Wesley insisted.

She watched him march out of the kitchen. Seconds later she heard the door slam shut too.

Chapter 53

Paul was in his den, working on his resignation, when he heard the doorbell ring. The sound made him recall his peculiar dream, the dream in which he could remember having no idea what he was doing at his desk. This incident was an alarming reproduction of what he'd dreamed, a living nightmare. Before he left his chair, he muttered underneath his breath,

"For whom the bell tolls."

His red, swollen eyes gazed at the photograph on his desk, a favorite picture of them together. He had thought he'd known the woman in the photo. Her smiling blue eyes sparkled at him and made him bitterly resent the way she'd deceived him. He wondered if everything they'd ever shared was also counterfeit, a mere delusion.

With these morbid thoughts, he went to answer the doorbell. Barry stood alone at Paul's door and pressed the bell again as he weighed the actions he was about to take. A cowardly man would not have opted to pit himself against Rattler Mackenzie. Rattler had invaded their arena once more from his dark domain, and had made obvious whom he had decided should ascend his lofty throne.

Through his thick eyeglasses, Barry again studied the caption in the newspaper he was holding. It was so unfair and he deplored Rattler's traitorous decision. Daphne might never go against him. She had raised him from the dead and felt obligated to him. However, the serpent had betrayed her.

Barry's keen mind had already devised a way to accomplish the results Rattler craved, and without turning against their reigning high priestess either. Daphne could keep her elevated position and they could still convert Rattler's beloved daughter, as well as her family, too. Barry would see to it and, in the end, Rattler would be grateful for his wise meddling.

The thick wood door opened and, through the screen, their eyes met. Barry held the newspaper so Paul could see the picture of his wife and his youngest daughter in the photograph and read the words, *'The Woman Nominated To Run For Senator of California.'*

"Did you know about this, Paul?" Barry asked suspiciously.

Paul read the caption and shook his head. What an idiot he had been. This was further proof she had another agenda. He pulled the screen door open and Barry sped through it like a cockroach. Paul had no idea the evil he was courting.

"I didn't think you had any idea regarding her activity! How she's determined to turn the whole country into the cabal!" Barry growled, and pushed the newspaper at him.

Paul didn't read past the caption but, instead, he studied the picture. The alien to whom he had been married cupped her hands around his daughter's face as Cadence gazed at her with trust. Cadence displayed the same type of profound trust he had at one time felt for her.

"Where are the girls, Paul?" Barry questioned him, unable to hide his fury.

"They're with her in Huntington Beach", Paul stammered.

"Good god! Do you realize the fix they are in? It's the least safe environment for your daughters!" he roared.

Crystal, Erin and Cadence, at this very moment, were in this deadly woman's care. Now Paul began to believe this, indeed, was a crisis, and wondered if he was too late to rescue them. Had she already brainwashed them into knowing participants in the cabal?

They were only children, his children! Even if she had succeeded in conditioning them, altering them to her crazy, immoral designs, they were his daughters, and they were in danger and needed his intervention.

Chapter 54

After Kas and Cody descended the mountain, they went to the precinct in Althea. Daphne was still being interrogated so they edged into the glass-walled interval next to the room she was in.

Gazing through the one-way window, Kas swallowed nervously, even though knowing Daphne couldn't see her. This was the woman who had fulfilled her father's last wishes and had succeeded to raise his miserable form from the dead. Daphne Orion had created the occult up on Mount Gaspar, and she also bore the responsibility for Neva Paloma's heinous death. This witch had dismembered Neva's body. Standing with Cody at the window, she studied the devilish woman.

Daphne's face was very white, like she had spent too much time with the dead inside the coven. There was not a blemish on the visible parts of Daphne's body, but Kas knew her heart was totally corrupt. Her posture was straight, her body tense, and her hands folded, but her green eyes were filled with anger. She was frowning and Kas could almost feel how furious she was with her present situation.

As Kas watched, she was overcome with thoughts of the relationship which she suspected existed between Rattler Mackenzie and Daphne Orion. No person with even an ounce of dignity would ever have conspired with him. His ways were brutal, and his ideas were insane.

"As long as she allows us to confine her here, our world is safer" Kas whispered, as if the walls had ears, and she gazed at Cody, who didn't take his eyes off of the hellion behind the window.

She wondered what Cody must be feeling as he stared at the woman who had accomplished such a dreadful feat by bringing his worst enemy to life again, giving him animation and empowering him.

Once more, Kas turned her eyes to Rattler's willing servant and shuddered to think what alien forces possessed and motivated her.

"We do not control things here, Cody." she cautioned him in a low voice. "She's toying with us; maybe she finds our reaction to her amusing. Like a wild animal with his prey, he plays with it before he devours it."

The two police officers in the room with Daphne kept a close watch on her but it would hardly help matters if she was determined to create havoc. Thus far, with her arrest, and in their endeavors to restrain her, things had gone too easy for them. There was something she wanted from them, something she sought to gain from her present situation, Kas suspected.

She would comply and visit her, as Daphne had asked. Walking around the detective, she made her way to the door. It was now or never, she told herself. It was either confront her now or turn and flee.

Courageously, she put her hand on the door knob and turned it to enter the room and knew Cody was right behind her.

Immediately, she recognized the gross change in climate, as if confronted by ghostly currents, or like a flood disturbing their peace, while sapping their energy. Daphne gazed into the eyes of her antagonist and sneered.

"Finally, you drop in. What kept you away so long?"' She seemed to demand an answer and expected some smart ass remark from Rattler's posterity and her rival.

"Oh, you know how it is, Daphne" Kas responded, taking a seat across the table from her, aware Cody was standing by the door and there was a gun in his holster. "Other important contacts kept me busy, like trying to find a new employee to replace the one I lost." Kas said.

Daphne expected some pungent reply and she was not disappointed. She simply nodded as though she understood her plight.

"It looked to me as though I wasn't the only one who lost something valuable. Neva lost parts of her anatomy." Kas continued, sarcastically.

"You've been to the mountain then?" "Daphne enquired, with enthusiasm. Kas nodded toward Cody,

"The detective and I" she said. "We just returned from there. By the way, while we there I came across someone's eye glasses," she continued, as Daphne watched the detective move toward the table. He waved the eye-glasses before her as Kas asked, "Do you recognize those? Could you tell me who they belonged to?"

Daphne looked closely at them.

"May I?" she asked, reaching for the spectacles. Cody handed them to her. Turning them every which way, she finally answered, "These belong to an old man who was on the mountain just the the other night, before the birds invaded and the whole place caught on fire. Unfortunately, the old man and his female friend were killed in the inferno."

Daphne handed the eye-glasses back to Cody and watched as he pocketed them again.

"Was the old guy a friend of yours?" she asked, angling about in her chair, turning her attention to Kas once more."It wasn't my fault, exactly" Daphne continued. "I had altogether different designs for the aged couple, but then Allen Carter took it upon himself to invite his raven to our celebration and from then on everything went downhill."

Daphne seemed to enjoy her conversation with them. She could see how the slightest mention of Allen Carter seemed to discombobulate her opponent, so she persisted for the pure fun of it.

"I see you know him, too. It looks like we travel in the same circles. Or we did, before the detective collared me the other day while I was visiting the father of my baby." She smiled with pleasure and added, "He was your neighbor on Victoria street, wasn't he?"

Kas leaned back in her chair.

"Your point is…?" she enquired, feeling hostile toward this evil woman who had caused so much heartache and unhappiness.

"I'm simply making conversation," Daphne fibbed. "It's bizarre how we move about in the same circles and yet we've never had the pleasure of meeting before."

"Pleasure of meeting before?" Kas asked, rolling her eyes. "Are you for real?" she groaned.

"Maybe more pragmatic than you, even." Daphne leaned across the table in the other woman's direction, tightening her invisible grip. "We're absorbed with every facet of your life, and in every relationship. We're in contact with every shred of your existence and yet, you've been unaware of our presence." Daphne lifted her chin and continued with amusement.

"You don't see the serious influence we have over every person around you, including your friend here, Detective Cody Baldwyn, who's alone…so miserably alone."

Kas looked at Cody, who returned her glance. She remembered the holograms on the mountain, the images created to cause Cody so much turmoil.

"I've heard just about enough!" Cody interrupted, but Daphne ignored him and continued.

"Allen Carter came to the mountain looking for his biological roots and he found them, too, didn't he?" Daphne questioned her, incited by the way she appeared so blown away with this revelation.

Kas left her chair and, turning her back on Daphne, she hurried over to the wall, putting distance between them. Daphne hoped it was in mortification.

"Allen found his Mother and now everyone has a family," Daphne said with pretended glee. "Every one except the poor detective, that is," she giggled.

Daphne saw the woman's shoulders quiver and heard her sniff and supposed she was crying. She glanced at the detective and saw him staring at her with a frigid, piercing look in his eyes, and his hand caressing the gun on his hip. Finally, she thought, things around her had really brightened up.

"Just for kicks" she went on with enjoyment, "imagine the way your husband, the Pastor, feels now that he's learned the person he trusted most has completely deceived him. It's a pity, I suppose, but then, he shouldn't have become entangled with a she-devil. He has only himself to blame." She voiced her twisted opinion.

Kas was incapacitated by her guile, the crushing enormity of it. However, when Daphne brought up the Pastor, she spun around and snapped at her,

"What have they done to Paul?"

"Nothing, nothing they have'nt done to millions of other people just like him." Daphne looked at her, smiled and shrugged. "They destroy with deceit and, if you will recall, they're exceptionally skillful at it too. I suppose it's something you will have to practice before you're ready to control the new world." Daphne said, but she had no intention of abandoning her position without a vicious fight.

"I don't want to control the new world!" Kas hurled at her. "I want you and the occult to stop meddling with our lives!"

"That's impossible" Daphne answered her. Her voice grew louder and rang with certitude. "You know as well as I do the devil isn't going to throw in the towel now. He's been at this for eons and he's not going to give up his grip just because you want him to, or desire it."

One of the police officers came to the table and nudged Daphne.

"Time is up" he told her. "The time for visitation is over."

Daphne nodded and, leaving her chair, decided to consent to him, at least temporarily, while it pleased her to do so. She beamed at her visitors.

"I hope we'll do this again, soon." She smiled at them and thought of leaving something of herself behind, perhaps a spirit or two, to entertain them until their next joyous encounter. She changed her mind, though, and escorted by the cop, she simply waved her hand. But before disappearing through the doorway, she turned to them, "I assure you, the pleasure has been mine." she said with a giggle.

As the door closed shut, Kas immediately thought of the click of a closing casket. She lowered her head and pressed her hand to the nape of her neck. She felt like the whole world was mindful of her. As if a throng of people were watching her through the one way window. The Watchers stared at her while pointing accusative fingers, judging her unmercifully.

She felt such utter destitution, she couldn't even lift her eyes to look at Cody. She told herself she truly was a she-devil simply because Rattler Mackenzie's blood flowed through her veins. Perhaps she really was evil, and so was her son, Allen Carter.

"Let's get out of here" Cody whispered. He went to the door and opened it. She heard him say, "Kas, you're my friend. Are you coming with me?"

He offered her a way out of the abyss and she took it, proceeding to follow him out of this blackened expanse. Once outside of the room, they walked through the long bleak hallway which seemed to have no end. She thought of Paul and worried over his frame of mind and what he'd discovered, who had revealed what to him.

How would she ever explain these things to Paul now? The dreadful hologram on the mountain had warned her, 'Nothing will ever be the same', and she was beginning to believe it.

"I'm going to investigate everything Daphne Orion just told us, including Allen Carter's background," she heard Cody tell her.

"Charlie and Harriet Carter adopted him," Kas replied, and knew she sounded vague. Allen Carter was indeed hers, and she'd had the overwhelming premonition all along. A

A mother knew these things, instinctively. "He was on the mountain" she said. There on Mount Gaspar, the godforsaken bluff where Neva's leg, arm and ear had been brutally amputated; there where the older couple had been burned alive. "He was on the mountain looking for me." she laughed weakly. "Good god, he was looking for me!"

Chapter 55

"The temperature today will reach into the triple digits, and the air quality will remain poor. We advise you, if possible, to remain indoors and out of the heat and smog." The nice-looking weather-forecaster on the News told Jesse.

They never said what caused the smog, but last night she had watched some sort of documentary concerning something called *chemtrails* with Hank and Lacy. The investigative reporter lead them to believe chemtrails hadn't been proven and was probably nothing more than a lot of back-fence talk. Those who swore to their authenticity maintained the government was spraying its own citizens with poison which eventually made people sick, or killed them, especially if they had defective immune systems.

"Why would they do such a thing," from her position on the floor, Lacy questioned both Hank and Jesse. "Wouldn't it be a lot like genocide?" she shrieked.

Hank and Jesse couldn't tell her why the government might commit such an atrocity, and they had to believe it wouldn't. It was just a lot of hype and there were other matters far more pressing to them, like the high cost of living and Lacy's education.

Jesse, wearing light-blue culottes and navy t-shirt with *Pet Emporium* in bold white letters stitched on the back, stood in place as she cupped her hands around her calf and lifted her leg until it was touching her hip, a feat she couldn't have done three months ago while she was still drinking. There was nothing wrong with her immune system now, she firmly told herself. She felt good, and looked at least five years younger, too, according to Hank.

From the corner of her eye she saw Lacy come into the living room wearing blue jeans and yellow t-shirt, with Hank following behind her. Lacy marched over to her and kissed her cheek.

"Where's your car keys, Mom? " she wanted to know.

Lacy had her permit and, in his spare time, Hank took her driving. Two weeks from this very day, Lacy would turn sixteen-years-old. A cold, hard fact which Jesse still hadn't accepted, but she couldn't prevent it either.

The first event on Lacy's agenda, after she blew out all of the candles on her birthday cake, was to acquire her driver's license. Jesse swallowed her anxiety and answered Lacy,

"Where they usually are, on the hangar by the front door."

While Lacy went to retrieve them, Jesse turned to Hank.

"There will be busy motorists on the highway this morning. Please don't drive the highway, Hank," she pleaded with him.

"I understand, Jesse." Hank closed the space between them, put an arm around her shoulders and kissed the tip of her nose. "There's little reason to worry, though. Lacy is cautious and she's going to be an excellent driver, too," he said, and smiled at her reassuringly.

She was about to answer him when they saw the picture of Kas on TV, with the paid for commercial. She was climbing the stairs to the precinct in downtown Althea and the announcer sang her praises. Surprised, they heard him declare.

"She's the smart Attorney who stays a step ahead of every one else, plus being the caring mother of three growing daughters. She's the faithful wife of a Christian Minister and the daughter of the one-time Governor of Nevada. Kastanje Scott is a Defense Attorney, a Homemaker, and a strong advocate of justice, fairness and truth. Do the right thing, stay a step ahead and vote Kastanje Scott to the Senate in November!"

"Wow" Jesse gushed, "I didn't even know she was running" she admitted to Hank.

"This is the first I've heard about it, too." he answered her.

"Well" Jesse sighed, "She's more than qualified and she's got my vote!"

"You sound so sure," he said, taken back a bit. There was a time when Jesse wouldn't even speak to this woman and now she was ready to rally behind her.

Jesse crossed the floor, feeling anxious and pressed for time. She was going to work this morning and she wasn't going to drive there either. She was going to jog, and let Hank and Lacy use her car. She bent over the maple-wood coffee table and lifted her cup of coffee from the coaster.

"Her opposition is a colleague of Archie's," Jesse responded flatly. "I've met Mister Papers before; he's a full-fledged member of the occult and I can't stand him! He's immersed California in the occult!"

"Well, then, why would they appoint him to run for senate?" Hank mused, and Jesse smiled at him.

234

She sometimes found his naivety so refreshing. Hank owned a bar and motel and both were in the process now of being sold. Hank would walk away from these ventures, where they had met, well over a quarter million dollars wealthier. He was a clever business man but he was retrograde concerning the populace, or the cabal. Actually, the populace was, in many ways, the cabal, Jesse thought.

Society was attracted to, and held captive by, the occult. She was a rebel, and the occult was unfavorable to those who revolted against their association. Jesse had tried to explain this to Hank. She had warned him he'd be smarter to walk away from their relationship and never turn around.

However, Hank refused to listen to her because he was in love and his special type of love, Jesse told him, was more than just blind, but it was the strongest bond she had ever known.

Now Jesse pushed the strands of dark copper hair, which had fallen loose from her head-band, behind her ear and answered him,

"For the same reason you'd hire a bartender to serve drinks."

"But I didn't" Hank protested. "I always took care of the bar all by myself," he reminded her.

"Before you met me, I know" Jesse countered.

With the empty coffee cup in hand, she came to him and, standing beside him, she gave him the look, the look he claimed was beyond his ability to contest.

"Are you sure you want to sell the bar? You don't have to, you know; no one's asking you to sell it" she told him.

Jesse witnessed his attractive grin, the same grin he had sprung upon her months ago when he asked her to dance.

"I'm far too preoccupied these days" he said, and gently cupped his hand beneath her chin. "I'm having far more fun courting the girl who was looking for Saint Regis!"

She laughed and Hank gave her a long loving kiss.

"Hey, Hank" Lacy called to him from the doorway. She was on her way to the car and stood with the door opened. "C'mon, you can woo my Mom anytime" she complained, anxious to be on the road again.

Hank tore himself away from Jesse and, with a laugh, he encountered Lacy.

"Can I?" he asked her.

"Sure" Lacy promised him, "and with my blessings too!" she said on their way out.

"Be careful!" Jesse called after them.

Shortly after they left, Jesse grabbed her back pack and opened the door. She proceeded outside, being sure to lock the door behind her. She stood on the steps to the cooperative where she lived. She had no idea someone was watching her and alert to everything she did.

She pulled the navy straps of the yellow backpack around her. The backpack held pet grooming equipment: brush, comb, a breaker, nail clipper, stripping knife. It also held library books which were due and her wallet. As she wrestled with it, she realized what a perfect day it had become.

It mattered very little to her how hot it might get in the afternoon, or the quality of air. Even the chemtrails were secondary compared to the fact she was alive. She was a survivor. She'd survived the worst of conditions and, therefore, it was only natural to assume she'd probably survive everything else life might throw at her. Feeling as though she could climb Mount Everest, Jesse started running in place with an exuberance she hadn't felt for a long time.

Her landlord, who lived right next door to her, came out of his apartment, waved a hand at her and shouted,

"Hi Jesse! Made any more apple pies, lately?"

"Not yet!" she called back, breathing heavily, "I have more than enough apples on hand though, so who knows?"

"Well, don't forget the Mrs. and me" he called to her.

She nodded at him. Ted Klinger and his wife, Rachel, loved her apple pies. She did far more baking these days, too, which was a great motivation for working out. She'd gained five pounds since being released from the hospital, but with daily exercise the weight she'd gained had been redistributed to her fanny and other places where she'd needed a little more cushioning.

"It's going to be another hot one and I just heard the quality of air will be poor too. Better stay indoors this afternoon, Jesse," Ted advised her.

The man made her think of a big teddy bear.

"I'm on my way to work now" she told him, "Then I will be inside, grooming dogs much of the afternoon."

He was so kind and thoughtful, and she didn't want him worrying over her needlessly.

When Ted retrieved his newspaper and went back indoors, Jesse gazed again at the bright, sunny morning and started on her way down the flagstone footpath to the sidewalk.

So, how about that? she thought, as she ran. Her old bosom buddy was competing for the senate. Maybe life actually did begin sometime after forty. She was pushing forty now and it relieved her some to think it might.

The onlooker had other designs for her, though. Designs which wouldn't have pleased Jesse at all had she only known. She was unaware of the vigilant watcher who followed her with a camera in his hands and snapped one picture after another.

Jesse stopped at the corner to wait for the traffic before she proceeded, and the watcher hung back and snapped more pictures of her.

He was overweight, dumpy-looking and unaccustomed to this sort of diversion. He struggled for oxygen, feeling rather light-headed. His job would have been much easier had Jesse still been a drunk. He liked her much better before she became sober, he concluded. They'd been a match made in hell.

After the traffic cleared, Jesse started out again, feeling refreshed with the brief stop. Her pursuer wiped the sweat from his brow and, staggering a bit, proceeded after her.

Jesse briskly climbed the steps to the library and her follower rested beside a street lamp, once more pointing his camera at her. He had nothing but a harmless camera, although he wrestled to hide it beneath his shirt when the patrolman in the crosswalk eyed him. He pocketed one more photograph he had snapped of Jesse and wondered if he wasn't being too concerned. After all, there was no law which prohibited picture-taking.

Jesse entered the library and immediately she saw Reuben Neely. There was a time she might have ignored Reuben, but now she called out to him. Reuben was a thirty-two year old mentally encumbered man Jesse had met when he brought his Labrador in to be groomed. Reuben insisted upon staying with his dog the entire time. He explained to her rather awkwardly,

"It's his first time, although, I imagine later, he'll bring me in on a leash."

"I don't see why not" Jesse bantered, unsure of just what to say, or if he was serious.

Now he waved a '*Hi*' back to her from his position on the floor holding a big picture book in his lap. He wore a cap with the words, '*Ask me about my dog!*' sprawled in red letters across the front of it. So Jesse did.

"How's Lion?"

"Real good" he answered her. "Only he brought home a female in heat, the other day!" Reuben confided in her.

"It's okay" Jesse said, as she made her way to him. "Lion's been fixed." she reminded him.

Reuben's grey eyes looked at her with a blank stare. It was so apparent he didn't comprehend what *being fixed* meant. She leaned over him, lowered her voice, and said directly to him,

"Lion will never be a father because he can't reproduce."

He pulled the cap off of his head, wiped his brow with his arm and answered her.

"Well, then, somebody should probably tell him this!"

The watcher snapped another picture, this one of Jesse and Reuben together.

Chapter 56

Cody Baldwyn was on his way to see the D.A. and Kas was following right along behind him.

The DA's office was elaborate. The door was open and Cody walked in unannounced, with Kas right on his heels. Netherton was seated behind his imposing desk complete with computer and fax machine. When Netherton saw them he stood up.

"Detective Baldwyn and Attorney Scott, I wasn't expecting to see either one of you," he said with a surprised smile.

"You're going to send the witch, Daphne Orion, up the creek, aren't you, Warren?" Cody stood on the opposite side of the desk, his anger in check, but his eyes locked with Netherton's as he asked him.

Netherton tried to ignore him and extended his hand toward Kas instead.

"Congratulations," he said to her, with a twinkle in his eyes. Perplexed, Kas refused to offer her hand. "I'm sure you will make a very fine Senator," Netherton added, warmly.

"I'm not running for Senator," Kas answered him. Surely the D.A. didn't have his facts straight, Kas thought, although it was very unlike him to make any statement without facts to back him up.

Netherton seemed surprised. He bent over his desk and opened a drawer to retrieve the newspaper he'd put in it. Laying the paper on his desk so she could see it, he said,

"It's in this morning's news!"

She saw the picture and groaned with discomfort,

"I had no knowledge of this," she told Netherton, and glanced at Cody who returned her look as he removed the newspaper from Netherton's desk. He scanned the article and said,

"You certainly haven't had time to make any statement of this sort. You've been far too busy running for your life!"

239

She nodded at him, a look of consternation on her face. Daphne Orion might very well have alluded to this, as well as Stuart Mackenzie, though, she thought, as she recalled the strange statement Stuart made,

"You've been given an extensive global federation."

It was in the newspaper and, therefore, Paul had to have seen it, too, she told herself as she quickly retrieved her cell phone from the bottom of her handbag. She had to call Paul and explain to him how this was a shock to her, too. She dialed her home phone and heard it ring. It was answered on the second ring.

"Hello?" She heard the doleful voice which sounded to her like a very unhappy Crystal. How strange, she thought, knowing she'd left them early this morning in Huntington with Geoffrey.

"Hi, what are you doing there?" she asked.

"I'm sorry" the dejected voice answered her. "I can't talk with you right now."

"Crystal, this is Mom," she called to her, but to her utter amazement, she heard the cold click of the receiver in her ear.

"Tell me you're going to put the high priestess of this despicable organization away, Netherton! Just tell me this!" She heard Cody yell and saw Netherton go to the door to close it.

"It's not so simple" Netherton informed him. He returned to his desk and motioned to them. "Have a seat," he said, buoyantly.

Kas sat down and Cody eyed her. He saw the pale look on her face and worried over her well-being.

"What do you mean, it's not so simple" Cody inquired. "Are you one of them, Warren, old friend? Have you joined forces with the enemy? Have they bought you, too?"

"Of course not" Netherton answered sharply. "As far as I know, no one has bought me! Hell, I'm not for sale! It just isn't a simple matter" he insisted.

"Why isn't it a simple matter? It certainly should be a simple matter!" Cody challenged him.

Netherton gazed at the pretty Attorney in the chair, and then again turned his eyes on the Detective who was too busy being rambunctious to sit down.

"No one yet has come forward to make any statements concerning Miss Daphne's guilt, or even her association with the occult. My guess is, no one is going to."

240

"When she was on the mountain she lead the assemblage and managed all of their affairs. No blood was spilt, no boulder overturned, until she said so" Cody argued.

"Well, mums the word on the streets" Warren informed him. "People have learned it's smart not to take sides against the occult."

"We just returned from Mount Gaspar where we found the Attorney's employee mangled, her body sliced into pieces!" Cody told him bitterly. "You can't let her walk, Warren! You just can't turn your back on this one!"

"I could get killed! Do you want my death on your conscience too, Lieutenant?"

Kas rested her elbow on the arm of Netherton's chair and held her head in her hand, closing her eyes. She wondered how in the world her daughters had made it all the way back to Althea, and why they'd ever left Huntington Beach. She also wondered if Paul had anything to do with their relocation. She could only hope he was home with Crystal, Erin and Cadence now, they were all together, and everyone was okay. She wanted more than anything to be home with them too, and not here in this room with Cody and the D.A. who was obviously, too yellow belly to go against the occult.

"Oh, I see!" Cody turned on Netherton like a penned bull, "You're chicken liver" Cody accused him. "Let the occult have at it; let them take over the world if this is what they want! More violence, more bestiality, just as long as you protect your own sweet ass!"

Kas saw Netherton turn beet red and she wasn't sure if he was angry at Cody, or just embarrassed by Cody's accusations.

Cody crossed the floor and stood over the desk, leaning in on the D.A.

"So, what are you going to do about this, Warren?"

Netherton didn't answer. He looked to be thinking it over, and finally drew a long breath and exhaled slowly

"I'm going to play the hand I've been dealt. I'm going to prosecute Miss. Daphne Orion. I'm going to be very likeable and hope like hell the defense wins this case so we can all get on with things."

"What things," Cody quizzed him. "Things like iniquity, oppression and death? You mean, you want to get on with these sort of things, Warren?"

They were now pretty sure what the D.A. would do, and how he intended to handle the situation. He'd try the she-devil and contest the occult's bloodthirsty criminal activity like the real pushover he was.

The thought of how soft the D.A. would be on them disturbed Cody and he left the D.A.'s office angrily perturbed. Kas turned at the door and thanked Netherton for his time, though. Then she followed Cody down the length of the hall and all the way to the precinct's exit.

"For crying-out-loud, Cody, he's scared, and for good reason, too!" Kas called after him as she tried to catch up with him.

"I expected more from him, Kas!" Over his shoulder, Cody grumbled at her, "No way did I expect Warren to turn and run!"

She knew he felt let down. In Cody's mind, this was Warren's big break, the opportunity to bust the biggest and worst alliance ever but, this would mean risking his own life and the lives of family members and friends too and Kas understood better than anyone how much this scared Warren.

Cody stopped at the door and, turning around, he waited for her to catch up with him before he proceeded outside. She saw the disappointment in his deep-set eyes and was stirred by his dedication to justice. She approached him and lowered her voice,

"You can't change archaic habits in one day, Cody. It takes time, and dedication, too." She said with a sympathetic smile. "They've been frightened by the occult since almost the beginning of time." she said, thinking of the holy manuscripts once more. "People are really just lost souls drifting in a sea of lethal corruption" she said.

Cody looked at her. In her blue jeans and matching sweater, her blond hair tussled about, and the compassion which flooded her gorgeous blue eyes, Cody felt quickened by an ancient fire within. The inferno he'd pretty much disregarded the biggest share of the day, or at least, since their experience together on Mount Gaspar.

He remembered something her uncle said. It was just before Cody shot him and was astounded at how he'd fallen for Cody was positive it was not the bullet from his gun which had taken down Stuart Mackenzie. No, it was something else, something cryptic which killed the sinister magician.

He thought of how Kas appeared on the front page of their local newspaper. It was made very clear some strange and powerful entity had planned to run Kas for Senator of California.

She also had an obligation to fulfill and Cody had no clue as to whether she planned to accomplish the task. He thought he knew, though, what she should do. What, without a doubt, he would have done had he worn her shoes. It was within her grasp to turn the tables and bring their calamity down upon their own satanic heads.

Kas caught the twinkle in his eyes and the look of triumph on his face. It was unbelievable the way he was smiling at her.

"You're going to turn their designs around and use them to smash them, aren't you?" he whispered.

She shook her head, resisting his admiration, and attempted to explain to him,

"I'm not up to this, Cody."

Up until now it had been a clear matter of staying alive, keeping abreast, and even several steps ahead, of the occult. She'd been weakened, though, and had lost any grand vision to challenge the occult. She explained to him,

"Cody, I just called my house a few minutes ago and my own daughter hung the phone up on me. It may have been a simple misunderstanding. On the other hand, if I discover I've lost the support of my family, how could I ever hope to win favor from the state?" She tried to choke back her tears.

"It's a mistake!" he exclaimed. "It probably was an error, or even a bad connection" he assured her. "Probably your daughter couldn't hear you so she hung up. I've had the same thing happen to me before, plenty of times" he said, struggling to convince her. He realized, though, before she could accomplish anything else of value, she had to repair things in her personal life, and he opened the door to let her proceed.

Once outside, they were immediately surrounded by a horde of reporters. Cameras flashed while microphones were pushed in their faces. One of the newspersons, a male standing next to her, questioned her,

"Mz. Scott, what issues inspired you to run for the California Senate?"

Light bulbs flashed in her eyes and, overwhelmed by the chaos on the steps outside of Althea's police station, she grasped for safety and her fingers folded around Cody's. He moved closer to her and whispered

"What a parade of blood suckers!" He was opposed to the media and considered them nothing but parasites. Cody watched her timidly respond to the the clamorous press.

"I'm shocked by this major response to the item in this morning's newspaper!" she said, and had no clue as to what else to say.

There was nothing else she could say except that she had no aspiration to run for the Senate, but she didn't tell them this.

"Then, Attorney Scott, you haven't seen the commercial yet, paid for by those who support you?" A woman pushed through the crowd until she reached her and then extended another microphone toward her.

Kas shook her head. She was not even aware she had supporters, and imagined the occult couldn't very well whip them up out of thin air.

Something forced her to move. She was compelled by some impulse which she could not resist. The crowd of reporters, the *parasites* as Cody had called them, moved right along with her. Down the thirteen steps she proceeded and onto the sidewalk, through the crowd of onlookers, even while the television cameras zoomed in on her.

Once, on the sidewalk, Cody shouted,

"Taxi!" and managed to flag one down. The yellow cab came to a stop beside them. She was in the detective's arms and she felt his breath on her face when he told her,

"I have work to do but I'm going to send you home and make sure you arrive there in one piece!"

She nodded at him to let him know she understood the decision he'd made on the spur of the moment. She was grateful to him, and glad he'd acted on her behalf. Her mind in a whirl, she fought to ignore the attention being lavished upon her, and was determined to keep her eyes focused on his to avoid the camera. She also heard him say,

"Call me!" Then he opened the door of the cab and gently tucked her inside. Closing the door, she heard him give instructions to the driver and watched as he paid him to take her home.

Chapter 57

"Look!" Barry exclaimed with disgust, as he pointed the crumpled man's attention to the t.v. set which Paul was watching with a sour look on his face.

Barry knew this image of Paul's wife with the detective, amidst the crowd of reporters in busy downtown Althea, would cause Paul more grief. The man was already doing a slow burn. The woman's foolish shenanigans enabled Barry to most handidly deceive her husband.

"Do you know him?" he asked, as he pointed to the man whose arms were around Paul's wife.

From his position on the sofa, Paul felt Crystal squeeze his hand.

"Oh! Dad!" she groaned, and she was beginning to believe Pastor Guire's slanderous comments concerning her mother. "He's the detective, Cody Baldwyn, I believe!" she told them. "I can't imagine he'd be a part of the occult too," she said. She didn't want to buy into the idea either her mother, or the detective, had anything to do with the occult but Pastor Guire was so sure of it. Crystal remembered, too, how the snake had called her mother a *'witch'*.

Erin was angered with Pastor Guire's endless expose and she felt personally insulted by him. Crossing the room, headed toward him, she finally let go of a few insolent comments of her own.

"How come you want to lambast my Mom? What's in it for you?" she chided him.

Mrs. Guire hurried to embrace her and, as she did, she told her,

"No one wants to lambaste your Mother, Honey, least of all Pastor Guire."

Chenoa stepped quickly toward them. She didn't trust this woman and didn't know how Kas could ever be involved in criminal activities, but the woman who berated her best friend should not attempt to comfort her daughter, too. It wasn't right or fair, Chenoa thought.

"I should probably handle this." She told Lena as she fastened her arm around Erin and pulled her away from the woman.

Erin, though, wrestled away from Chenoa, too, and admonished both women.

"This is my Mom's house and we're her family! " she fiercely scolded them. "As soon as she returns, she'll know what to do. She'll take control of things then!"

"Of course, she will, Erin," Chenoa agreed with her.

"I don't know about this" Lena answered her. "Your Mom's in pretty deep trouble!" she warned her.

Crystal thought better of telling Erin how their Mother had called only a half hour ago and she'd hung up on her. She hadn't shared this with any of them yet, not even her dad. Crystal was angry at her mother, though.It irritated her how her mother allowed her dear husband and daughters to become entangled in this bloody mess. When she saw her mother in the detective's arms, on the t.v., she felt even more betrayed by her.

Paul paid close attention to the answers Kas gave the reporters. He expected to hear a long spiel about why she'd decided to run for office, but when she nervously answered them, and seemed threatened by the chaos, he felt some compassion for her swell within him. With the difficult situation she was in, he put himself in the detective's shoes and knew he would have done the same had he been there with her. Then for the umpteenth time, he reprimanded himself for being such a pushover when it came to Kastanje.

He knew he was weak-kneed, nothing but a lump of clay, when just looking at her. Irritated by the way he allowed her to manipulate him, he arose from the sofa and crossed the room toward the kitchen, passing his senior associate on his way and seeing the fiery look in his eyes. Images on the t.v.News reflected in Barry's glasses. This huge man who towered over everyone else. His very presence commanded the respect of others, but now made Paul feel inadequate.

Paul drifted into the kitchen and saw his neighbor, Tim Bailey, who was also an elder of their church, sitting at the table with Cadence. They appeared to be involved in a serious conversation. Tim gazed into Cadence's eyes, while holding Toby in his arms. The dog had never been at the kitchen table before and Paul was positive Kas would have protested. She was never as easy-going as he was, Paul thought, and was far more set in her ways. That, at least, was what he had believed at one time. Now he was quite positive she was nothing but a rebel-rouser.

Paul neared the table and stood behind his daughter's chair. Tim's blue eyes gazed up at him.

"Cadence asked me if dogs, like snakes, can be possessed by the devil." he said.

Paul shook his head with regret at the five-year-old's question. Cadence had been subjected to the cabal as well, her young mind exposed to such harmful knowledge. She had been there when the snake called her mommy a witch.

Paul dropped on his knees on the floor beside Cadence, crushed by the thought of the evil his little girl had so viciously been made aware of, and he couldn't fathom why her mother had ever subjected her to such hurtful situations.

He took the dog from Tim and, holding him in his lap, he ran a hand over his short coat. Then, with tears in his eyes, he told Cadence,

"Toby is filled with God's Spirit, Honey, and this is why he loves us so much!"

The smile on Cadence's face melted his heart and he was determined to never let any one, their mother included, attempt to corrupt and damage his daughters again.

"Most snakes aren't possessed by the devil, Cadence," Tim offered her even more insight, unwilling to let snakes take such a bad rap for the evil misbehavior of one serpent. He saw Paul shake his head at him, though and he clammed up.

Paul stood up, reached down to Cadence and said,

"Now give your Daddy a hug!"

He opened his arms to her and Cadence threw herself at him with relieved laughter. He lifted her out of the chair and pressed her small body to him and felt uplifted by the exchange.

"Cadence, it's time for your nap."

From behind him Paul heard the Native American, Chenoa, and he turned to look at her. She was sweet to offer him assistance, he thought, and he gave Cadence to her. The little girl wrapped her arms around Chenoa's neck and they left the kitchen, disappearing into the hallway.

Just then, there was a loud bang on the kitchen door and Paul anxiously turned around to see who or what it was, imagining it could be anything, cryptic or otherwise.

He saw Archie Petersen bobbing around in a furious flutter and, once again, he pounded with his chubby fist against Paul's sliding glass door.

"Just a minute!" Paul shouted at him, as he hurried across the room.

He figured by now Archie must have learned of Kastanje's rash decision to run for senate, and maybe he suspected some major commotion would result. Paul opened the door and Archie barged into the house. Looking around him and seeing the others, Archie wailed,

"What the hell, Paul! Kas is on t.v., on every channel, and all over the news!"

"Yes," Paul groaned. "Yes, she is, Archie." Archie's own wife had left him months ago, and, as far as Paul knew, Archie still had no idea where she had gone.

Chapter 58

The gigantic sign, with rainbow-colored printing, spelled out PET EMPORIUM above the front entrance of the huge outlet. Inside of the orange brick building, displayed on numerous shelves and occupying spaces on the floors, were a wide variety of pet essentials. Among the colorful collars and leashes, the latest pet shampoos and conditioners, and tons of toys, there were also saddles with popular designer names, blankets, barley, oats and feed for almost every domesticated creature.

Jesse had been put in charge of personnal and it was among her many duties to make sure the seventeen employees who worked at Pet Emporium did their job well and maintained a fairly happy, stressfree morale. Therefore, she was agreeable when later in the day, during their lunch break in the employee's lounge, one of the employee's had expressed her desires to her.

Diana Reese, a middle-aged woman with brown hair, pulled back in a ponytail left the table and went to the coffee-maker.

"I think it would be a great idea if the store ran ads in support of Kastanje Scott's crusade to the California Senate! Of course, we'd need to take it up with the boss first, I imagine?"

Diana poured coffee into a Styrofoam cup. There was a radio beside the coffee-maker, tuned into an *oldies but goodies* radio station. Paul Mc Cartney sang about how some people wanted to fill the world with silly love songs. It was always one of her favorites.

She brought her coffee cup back to the table and, as she took a chair across the table from Jesse, she said,

"This morning at breakfast my kids and I talked about how we hope Kastanje Scott wins the race. You once lived right next door to her, didn't you, Jesse?"

Jesse nodded.

"She was on the t.v. today, too!" she said with enthusiasm. "Most people are fed up with Desmond Papers!" Jesse said, displaying her strong feelings for their current Senator. "I think we could do some window displays for her campaign. I'll check with Campbell to see if it's okay," she told Diana.

Paul MacCartney ended his song and then some newscaster with a strong baritone voice announced,

"A small bomb at the home of Mister Reuben Neely exploded today and killed the owner's beloved dog, a Laborador. Mister Neely resided at 2016 Grand Avenue in Althea, California, but he was not at home when the bomb exploded, killed his dog and destroyed his home."

A robust man with a thick silver beard, wearing denim bibs and an apron, came into the lunch room.

"Jesse, there's a telephone call for you!" Keith Campbell, announced, even while the door he'd just come through swung behind him. "It's that kid whose dog was killed in the explosion today!"

His words attracted the attention of the other employees in the room and they suddenly became an intrinsic part of the tragedy they'd just heard about on the radio. The room began buzzing with conversation as all eyes stared at Jesse.

She followed her boss out of the room and through the brightly decorated depot where customers, with their pets in tow, strolled the isles. Jesse heard several barks, and one hiss from an highly insulted cat offended by the incessant racket the dogs made.

Jesse wondered how Reuben Neely had come to think of her at all at a time like this, when his dog and home had been destroyed by some mini-bomb powerful enough to do major damage.

She followed Keith Campbell into his cluttered office, empty cardboard boxes strewn about and old discarded newspapers scattered all over the hard linoleum-covered floor. Keith pointed Jesse's attention to the phone on the wall, the receiver placed on top of a pile of empty boxes.

"Thanks" she murmured nervously as she picked up the phone and spoke into it, "Reuben, is this you?"

"Jesse! My home was broken into, Lion was killed and the whole place set on fire! Oh, god, Jesse, Lion is dead!" Reuben shouted, and she could tell he was devastated.

"I heard about it on the radio" Jesse told him. "Where are you now, Reuben?" she questioned the shattered man.

She had a crystal-clear memory of the night she ran from Archie after he'd slapped the shit out of Hank, and how she'd wound up in a telephone booth, hysterical and not knowing exactly what actions to take. She had dialed Doctor Jaime Kennis who, as it turned out, was Gage's Psychiatrist.

"Lion never had a chance, not even a small chance, of dodging the explosion!" Reuben shouted into her ear.

"I know, Reuben!" Jesse answered him. She had to do something, had to go to Reuben, but where on earth was he? Once more, she asked, "Where are you now, Reuben?"

She thought of the honey-colored Labrador she had bathed and trimmed, and she remembered the way Reuben had smiled at him all the while, standing right beside her through the long tedious process, unwilling to leave Lion's side.

"It's the jail, I think" Reuben replied. "The one in Althea. The cops wanted to know if I'd put the bomb in the kitchen cupboard and then left the house. Why would they think I'd ever do this, Jesse? What would make them think I would ever kill Lion?"

"They don't know the special bond you shared with Lion, Reuben. Hold on" she told him. "I'll be right there!"

She turned to look at her boss and saw the way he gaped at her, the agonized expression on his face. *Oh, please, Keith, let me leave work to help Reuben,* she thought and, as though he could read her mind, he nodded his head.

She remembered, though, she hadn't driven her car to work this morning; Hank and Lacy had it. She couldn't scamper away to rescue Reuben from his present plight. In a frenzy, she tried to think of what she could do to reach out to the poor man and help him. Suddenly it occurred to her.

"Reuben, tell the police you want to see Attorney Scott. Tell them you won't say anything until you've talked to Attorney Scott! Will you do this, Reuben?"

"Attorney Scott?" Reuben repeated her.

"Yes, that's right, Attorney K. Scott!" Jesse told him.

Chapter 59

The taxi came to a stop right in front of Paul's and Kas's beige flat-roofed adobe home. The uniformed driver had said very little to Kas as he drove, but she'd noticed in his rear-view mirror he'd kept one eye cocked on her almost since they'd left the precinct. He probably thought he recognized her from the newspaper and the t.v. commercial, she imagined.

She didn't want recognition now. She wanted to be home with Paul and their girls now, although she couldn't imagine how she was ever going to explain these esoteric activities to them. Most lawyers were great actors and could camouflage the truth quite easily, but there was no way to hide the occult and their horrendous enterprise.

At least, Kas couldn't figure any way to do so. It was time now to come clean and to tell them everything. In fact, it way past time, she thought, and she trembled at the possible outcome.

"This is your destination, and it looks to be an elegant one, too," the Black cab-driver remarked.

She eyed her house, the way it looked in the late afternoon with the hacienda accentuated by beautiful Mount Gaspar rising behind it like some elegant, yet atrocious, giant threatening to devour it.

She'd been on the mountain just hours ago, where they'd discovered Neva, her body so mangled she was hardly recognizable. Neva had been abducted from this location, this place the driver described as being *elegant*. He didn't know, he couldn't tell by looking at it, what mysteries surrounded it.

"Do you want me to come around and open your door for you?" the driver asked her politely, when she didn't get out of the cab right away. Once more he eyed her through the rear-view mirror.

"No, thank you" Kas answered, and she tried to smile at his image in the mirror. "I can handle it" she told him. "Thanks" she said as she got out and firmly closed the door behind her.

"Any time," he called, waving his hand, and she watched him drive away.

She saw more than one car parked on their wide cement driveway. Pastor Barry Guire's Lexus was parked right behind her Viper. She envisioned the reverend inside their house, busy consoling his bereaved associate.

It occurred to her, they must have driven the Senoir Pastor's vehicle to Huntington, picked up Crystal, Erin and Cadence, and then one of them had driven her Viper home.

She suspected they had been very annoyed at the way she'd left the girls behind when she'd headed for the mountain. They probably thought her actions were negligent at best.

All she'd wanted then was to find Neva alive, bring her safely back from the mountain and restore her to her son, Lorenzo. However, Neva was almost dead when they stumbled upon her body in the underground tunnel.

The house next door appeared to be empty. She hadn't seen either Archie or Jesse in weeks, not since she'd seen them at the police station where she'd questioned Gage.

It seemed so long ago to her, now, and so much had happened since then; ghosts and goblins had appeared out of nowhere, and one specific snake had crossed her path, a dangerous venomous Western Diamond Back Rattlesnake, Rattler Mackenzie, whose objective was to make her a Senator.

Kas slowly made her way up the flagstone walkway to the kitchen door, which was locked. She wondered if it was locked as an attempt to prevent the entrance of malignant spirits, or if it was locked in order to block her own access. She knocked, and seconds later Crystal slid open the glass door. With a frown on her face and fury in her eyes, she said,

"Mom, I'm so angry at you right now, I'm not even going to talk to you!"

"I understand your disappointment, Crystal" Kas softly assured her. "However, would you please let me come inside?" she requested with a nervous laugh.

"I've no alternative. I mean, after all, this is your place, not mine, isn't it?" Crystal grumbled, moving to one side so she could enter the house.

"I could have barged in, had the door not been locked" Kas replied, "although I am trying to be considerate and kind, under the circumstances, and I hope you would expect this of me."

"I expected a lot of you" Crystal answered, and Kas saw the tears spill from her eyes. "I expected you to stay with us at the beach house. When you left, I expected you to return soon, too." Crystal said, and tears flowed freely down her cheeks. "I expected you to actually try to help Gage, and not to hinder him! I totally did not expect you to be a part of his problem!" Crystal struggled to communicate to her even as she wept.

Kas had no idea what Crystal had heard about her, or from whom, or in what tone of voice, but she suspected she'd been subjected to a lot of negative criticism and half-truths concerning her mother.

"Don't believe everything you hear, Crystal" Kas told her, and affectionately reached to comfort her, but Crystal moved abruptly away. In the background she heard a voice saying,

"I won't tell Kas, she can't run for Senator when she's already been nominated, Barry. It's a free country, remember? I suspect Kas can do pretty much whatever she wants to do."

Apparently Paul was talking to Pastor Guire as both men entered the kitchen from the living-room. He came to a sudden stop when he saw her, still standing at the door next to Crystal.

He felt torn apart and overwhelmed by the parental instinct to defend his offspring, like a mother bear would fend off a vicious attack. He thought of her apostasy, as all along she had beguiled him and pretended to be something she could never be. Damn, she was good at it!

"You can't stay here, Kas" he told her, finally finding his voice. "It's not safe for the children. You have the detective guarding you, like a bulwark, but Crystal, Erin and Cadence have no one else but me to defend them." he told her, and he was inflexible. There was no way he would provide safety for her now. She'd left the shelter he had once attempted to provide.

Kas saw Barry standing silently behind Paul, and it was clear to her, he supported him. Barry's posture was so rigidly straight, his jaw set, and his lips tightened into a thin line of disapproval. He restrained himself and allowed Paul to handle things, though.

Crystal pressed herself against the kitchen counter, her arms wrapped around her waist, her head lowered as she squeezed her eyes closed and continued to sob. It about destroyed Kas to see her so distraught and she reached her hand out to touch her, but then withdrew it, remembering how Crystal had responded to her before.

"Who's behind all of this mud-slinging?" Kas questioned Paul, trying to maintain some civil approach.

"Need you ask?" She heard a loud, raspy voice and saw Archie burst through the doorway and push Barry and Paul aside.

"You are behind this!" he shouted, and pointed a thick finger at her as he bounced around, yelling and pulling his drooping blue jeans up over his big belly. "After all, you, and not someone called Daphne Orion, as you falsely implied at one time, are queen of the cabal!" Archie accused her.

She recalled, now, the conversation they'd had behind closed doors, at the precinct, only weeks ago, before Archie's wife barged in on them in a drunken stupor. She had asked him then if he knew someone called Daphne Orion, the woman his son insinuated was behind the shooting on Foothill Boulivarde.

"Daphne is up to her skinny little neck in this, Archie.Right now she's behind bars, confined to the Althea prison." Kas informed him. "Check it out!" she insisted. Then she turned her eyes to Paul, appealing to him, "If you don't believe me, call the precinct!" She pointed to the telephone on the wall.

"You're Darragh Mackenzie's offspring" Barry finally piped up as though he were telling her something she didn't know. "He was the archbishop of the cabal, the man who once took the country by storm. Your father possessed colossal appeal," Barry continued in a smooth, even-toned voice. "The same way you do now." Barry tilted his head and gave her an accursed look, "You do not, in any way, shape, or form, belong here among the righteous constituents of our Christian congregation!"

"Why, she's nothing else than another Judas Iscariot!" Lena Guire said as she stepped forward and took her place beside her husband.

Kas examined their faces, looked into their eyes, their stony eyes and she wondered what Paul ever saw in them, why he surrounded himself with such hostile people.

"Is there no mercy in your hearts for another sinner?" Kas inquired of them.

"I reserve any charity for the truly repentant. If you were of this nature you would not persist in advancing your father's evil agenda of promoting the occult and attempting to convert the world!" Barry told her.

"Stop it!" Crystal shouted at them. "Stop it now!" she hollered, raising her hands to cover her ears. "I've heard enough!"

Convinced of the harm all of this was doing to Crystal, Paul intervened.

"If you've any feelings for our family, Kas, you will leave!" he pleaded with her, as he put his arms about Crystal.

Kas had sought an alliance with them, but they were immovable. She left the kitchen to collect her things, leaving them to stare after her and shake their heads as if she was their archenemy and some higher power had granted to them the strength to prevail against her. For now, they could bask in their accomplishment, but she had a strong sense their triumph might be short-lived and they'd meet with disaster eventually.

As she moved through the house on her way to her bedroom, she saw Tim and Chenoa sitting on the living room sofa with Cadence and Erin. It was a gold-tone Ernest Hemingway sofa, very pricey, Kas recalled. Behind them and near the wall was the matching Ernest Hemingway Savoy China which they'd bought at the very same time they'd purchased the sofa. Chenoa held the sleeping child in her lap and Erin sat beside them.

"You too, my old friends, my soul mates?" she softly questioned them.

Tim gestured as though saying what else could he do under these difficult circumstances, and Chenoa shook her head at her. Kas wondered what they meant by their actions. She guessed it really mattered very little now because, for the time being, she was on her way out and there was nothing they could do or say to change this fact.

She looked directly at Erin and, amazingly, she saw Erin return her look. They exchanged weak, yet, fond smiles. Kas's heart leaped into her throat for maybe Erin, unlike the others, was not against her. Maybe she could find some compassion in her heart for her mother. If she'd been staying she would have shown more attention to the dog Erin held in her lap, too. Harriet's dog, Toby, gave Erin unconditional love. She would need this now, and so would Cadence when she woke up from her nap.

Kas continued toward her bedroom, but stopped when she reached the open door. Lingering in the doorway, her eyes became misty when she gazed at their bed. The antique cheery-wood bed where she had snuggled beside Paul on so many nights. She'd never seen it in this sad light before, and she had never cherished it more. Now, it seemed, her whole world had been stripped from her and she felt as if she was being tossed out with the daily trash.

There were still so many things Paul didn't know. Things she'd never had the courage to tell him. As she proceeded to fill the large duffle bag with items she'd need while away, she considered how she had deceived him, but not the way Archie, Barry and Lena Guire claimed she'd deceived him. She'd done so by being so much less than honest with him. She should have told Paul how her father had raped her, how she'd born his child, and also, how Cody had killed her father. Hell, she hadn't even let Paul in on the fact her father was dead.

"Why didn't you tell me? She heard Paul's low voice from the doorway, now. "Why did you lead me on? Why make me think you're something you aren't, something you can never be? The woman I have loved never existed." She heard his bitter laugh. "Talk about 'Sleeping with the Enemy'!" he exclaimed.

She didn't look at him but continued removing her clothes from the cherry wood dresser drawer and carrying them to the bag she had placed in the middle of their bed.

"You're right, I should have told you. I should have told you of my father's incessant attacks and of how I had borne his child."

"Allen Carter!" Paul raised his voice. "He has a name, Kas. No matter how many times you deny it, Allen does exist!" he insisted.

"I never saw him in the hospital, after they took him from me. I could never have guessed someone in Althea, someone from your church, Charlie and Harriet Carter, would adopt him. I wasn't sure Allen was my son until earlier today when Daphne Orion told me." she confessed to him.

"The fact of the matter is, you and your son are supposed to reign over some perfect utopia called Chimera." Once more, Paul laughed bitterly. "We've really got a corner on spirituality, haven't we? Only we seem to be working for agents who are totally opposed to each other."

She bent over the bag and zipped it up. Standing there beside their bed, Paul thought she looked every bit like herself, the woman he had fallen in love with. He imagined that in his arms she would feel every bit like Kastanje, too, but he couldn't allow himself the enjoyment of holding her because she wasn't who she pretended to be and Kastanje had never existed.

The others surrounded Kas in the kitchen as she stood there with her duffle bag in hand. They had anticipated she would make an humble and contrite retreat, and had expected to see a conscience-stricken woman accept defeat and leave. They'd never anticipated such a dramatic exit.

"Marriage is based on trust and fidelity" Kas said, as she took off her wedding band and laid it on the couner. "There is neither of these virtues left in our marriage now." she conceded.

There was a downcast look on Paul's face as his eyes went from her to the couner. He looked nauseous.

"Hogwash!" Barry grumbled. "Don't you fall for her theatrics, Paul" He put his arm around Paul's shoulder, fully intending to steal this moment from her, too.

"Your car is right in my way, Barry, and you're going to have to move it before I can leave" Kas told him with a frigid look.

"Of course" he agreed, "Nothing would please me more!"

Turning to Erin who stood beside her, she smiled and reached out with her left hand, ringless now, her fingers curled into a fist, and she gently punched her shoulder,

"Chin up, kiddo", she said, "You haven't seen the last of me!"

She turned to Crystal and said,

"This is what happens, Honey, when you're put in the middle of a quarrel, and I'm sorry you were!" She meant to convey to her she'd not hold this against her. "Take care of my girls, okey?"

"Okay" Crystal answered, turning her eyes away from hers, and gazing at the floor, feeling small and helpless.

Once more, Kas looked around her kitchen; at her solid wood square kitchen table, her bakers rack with slatted shelves, Nantucket Buffet Hutch. She treasured her kitchen more than any other room. Her family often gathered in the kitchen. They'd gather there without her, too, at least for now.

Toby stood between Crystal and Erin and whimpered and she felt she could relate to the dog's sentiments. Kas glanced at Paul.

"So long, for now" she told him, and swallowed hard, determined to hold back her tears. He was speechless. She thought of giving him a quick hug good-bye, but decided he would not accept it. He strongly believed he was doing what was right for their daughters.

With no further delay, she turned and followed Barry out the door.

She encountered him outside, before getting into his car, and he was ruthless with her. He grabbed her arm, physically hurting her, and he told her in a menacing tone of voice,

"I will personally make sure you are never able to return here again, and you will lose the race for Senator too!"

She was shocked, and she couldn't think of any come-back for she hadn't expected such hostile behavior from a preacher-man.

He proudly turned and walked to his car. She watched him open the driver's door of his Lexus, get inside, and then he slammed the door shut.

As Barry shifted into reverse he felt something move around his feet. He turned his head to look behind him as he backed out of the driveway. Once his car was on the street he shifted gears and then stepped on the gas pedal. He heard the doors lock automatically about the same time he became aware he was not alone.

There was something, or someone, in the car with him and he felt a little twinge of fear. He turned his gaze from the road and looked at his right leg. A slimy-looking creature, adorned with white diamond shapes along its back, was slithering up his leg, just above his knee, and Barry saw it was a deadly Western Diamond Back Rattle Snake!

The viper made its way across his leg and onto the car seat beside him. Barry panicked, his hands left the steering wheel and he threw his upper torso against the door, hoping it would open. It didn't, and Barry found himself trapped inside his car with the reptile known for it's vulgar disposition.

As Kas watched, she saw the pastor's vehicle veer recklessly over the road and, concerned with Barry's well-being, she hurried to her car, got behind the wheel and rolled from the driveway. She had the awful hunch Barry's disasterous driving resulted from her father's animation, but she couldn't see the rattlesnake in the car with Barry. She followed his Lexus as it careened around the corner.

The rattlesnake on the beige leather seat coiled himself into a corkscrew, lifted his head and frowned at the big man behind the wheel. Big men shrunk and became so pitifully small when he confronted them. The reptile had the reputation of being the most dangerous rattlesnake in the world. There was only one thing worse then a Western Diamond Back Rattlesnake, and this thing was staring right at him. It was the spirit of Rattler Mackenzie.

"You are such a very silly man" the snake taunted him with devilish jesting.

Forced to defend his actions, Barry exclaimed, "Rattler, I can explain everything to you!"

"Then say it…", the snake told him. "Say it, Barry!"

"Say what?" Barry clamored. "Anything! I'll say anything! What is it you wish to hear me say?" He was anxious to appease him, wondering if he'd be let off if he managed to satisfy Rattler.

"Say, 'I am a very silly man," the snake commanded, as he edged even closer until he was only inches away from Barry.

"Yes, of course, I am a very silly man!" Barry agreed, and took one hand from the wheel to wipe the perspiration from his face. He had small hope Rattler would be so easily appeased.

"It loses its appeal when you say it." the snake complained. "After all, everyone knows what a silly man you are, Barry, so saying it sounds so dull. Don't you see?"

"Of course, I see!" Barry wasn't about to disagree with Rattler's heckling at this point.

"But do you agree, Barry, everyone recognizes you are a laughingstock?"

The snake looked around its hideous self at their environment, the road with houses and busy people on both sides of the street. "The whole world is aware you are nothing more than an ignoramous!" the snake said with far too much conviction, Barry thought.

"Yes, yes" Barry concurred. "The whole world thinks I am an ignoramous, a crude and emptyheaded fool." He was intent on pleasing the reptile to avoid being bitten by him.

"Then say it," Rattler ordered him.

The windows appeared to roll down without assistance, but Barry knew Rattler had done this. With the window open, Barry felt the hot wind whip against his skin and ruffle his hair.

"Tell the world what you are, Barry." the Western Diamond Back charged him. "Shout aloud and tell the world you are an ignormous!"

"You said they already know it, Rattler" Barry contended. He didn't really relish the idea of shouting castigations at himself, not out his opened window. He didn't like even being the subject of nasty comments. No, he prefered to wear his clerical collar and be thought of by others as pious, and so much better and smarter than they were.

"You know how I become when I am provoked!" The snake reminded him, and Barry heard the trademark rattle begin. It started almost softly, and then grew louder, a fearsome sound, and Barry knew he had no other option but to yell out his opened window.

"I am an ignoramous!"

"I am a wolf in sheep's clothing" the snake egged him on.

"A what?" Barry inquired of the snake, and turned his head to look into two fiery eyes which glimmered with wily certitude.

"A wolf in sheep's clothing." the snake repeated. "Say it NOW, Barry!" he admonished him, showing the sharp fangs at both sides of his mouth, stained with yellow venom.

"I am a wolf in sheep's clothing!" Barry cried, and prayed to whomever, and no one in particular, the rattlesnake would not puncture his flesh with those sharp fangs.

Trailing behind Barry, Kas had a difficult time believing she was hearing Barry yell out such a profound confession. She wondered if this was for her

260

benefit, or for his own, or if it was similar to the last rites and final confession Catholics benefited from just before their souls departed.

She looked around her at Barry's audience. A man who stood on a ladder and polished his boat shafted him. A woman who held her baby in one arm while holding her dog by its leash shook her head with disapproval as Barry drove by. Two young lovers beside a Juniper tree waved their hands at him, finding it easier because they were in love to indulge him. The old man on the street corner, though, frowned, raised his fist and shouted back,

"Damn you! Damn you, you evil bastard!"

Kas worried over their welfare and thought about calling to them out of her own opened window, urging them to flee into the safety of their houses before the crazy man, whose driving was so impaired, struck and injured them, or killed them. Still, Barry continued.

The serpent enjoyed these adventures and thought he could come up with even more adjectives to describe Barry Guire, so he said,

"I am a Pharisee and a hypocrite!"

Barry heard the rattle and saw the snake's deadly fangs and he shouted out of his window,

"I am a Pharisee and a hypocrite!"

Barry heard the serpent's demented laughter as he forged ahead, saying "I am taking you all to hell with me!"

"I am taking you all to hell with me!" Barry repeated the snake.

Kas saw Barry's Lexus careen around the corner and right out into traffic.

"Oh, shit!" the man inside of the 18-wheeler groaned, for he knew he was too close to the car to avoid barreling right into the side of it and, as he did, Barry was thrown out his side door and his head came in contact with the hard pavement, killing him instantly.

Chapter 60

The fly crawling along the window brushed its legs together, preening itself before it engaged in whatever goal it intended to accomplish. Kas watched it, and thought its efforts to meet its ambition would prove futile because she held the fly swatter.

She crept up on it quietly and, in a flash, she clobbered the window, missing the fly. Aggravated with the fly's successful escape, and dismayed at her own vain attempt, she watched it soar to another location, taunting her with it's bothersome buzz. The scavenger possessed some contrary spirit which gave it an edge in evading her, but Kas accepted the challenge and thought, sooner or later, she'd ambush the fly and squash it.

When the fly landed on a leaf of the Lithop plant which grew in the pink vase on top of the white bookcase, opposite the window, Kas went after it with the agility of a bloodhound.

If not for the knock at the door just then, which arrested her mad pursuit, she knew she would have brought the fly swatter down on the unsuspecting plant, capsizing the Lithop and destroying the blameless bloom right along with the felonious fly. Conscience-stricken, and alarmed at what catastrophe she had narrowly avoided, she called out,

"Come in!" as she watched the bedeviled fly circle again.

The door opened and a petitely youthful, attractive woman slipped into her agency.

"Is Wesley Versuch here?" the small female inquired with a soft girlish voice.

Kas, so intent on killing the fly, had almost forgotten her reason for being there.

"As far as I'm aware, just me and this pesky fly are here at the moment." Kas said.

Looking at the wall clock, she realized now Wesley Versuch was late for his appointment with her. However, his pretty, young ally might be able to fill her in on the mystery which surrounded Wesley, the nephew of Leopold

Versuch, the man who, according to what she had gleamed from the computer, was the ring leader of the organization known as the Delphians.

"Your name would be?" Kas questioned her young visitor, who was dressed in faded blue-jeans and a gray t-shirt.

"Naomi…" she replied, and this was the only information she gave her, no last name.

Kas went to her computer desk, pulled out the bottom drawer and tossed the fly swatter into it, then pushed it closed with her foot.

"My name is Kastanje Scott," she told her.

"I know." the young woman replied, and she seemed rather anxious as she closed the door behind her, and then advanced across the room until she stood opposite Kas, on the other side of her desk.

"Look," she sputtered, "You may as well know right now, Wesley isn't going to show up. Don't take it personally," she continued, "but it's not the first time he's been in trouble and it won't be the last, although it is the first time he's been wanted for murder."

"But by no means is he lily white?" Kas questioned.

"No, not by any stretch of the imagination." Naomi replied.

"So, then, why don't you take a seat?" Kas motioned toward the empty chair, "Tell me what other misdeeds Wesley has been wanted for?"

Naomi followed her advice and sat down. She crossed her legs in front of her and Kas saw the beat-up tennis shoes she wore. Naomi made her think of the women at the refuge where Kas had left the high heels which hadn't properly fit. Naomi looked almost as destitute as they were.

"Know anything about the occult?" Naomi probed, tapping her foot and looking around her at the well-appointed office.

Kas sat down at her desk.

"I've heard of it," she fibbed, desiring to hear what Naomi knew, and how she knew about the cabal. "Is Wesley absorbed with the occult?" She was pretty sure he was since this was the knowledge she'd gathered when she'd searched the computer.

"Did Bill Clinton screw Monica Lewinsky?" Naomi queried. "Yeah, Wesley is up to his neck in the occult. In fact, poor Wesley is submerged in it!" Naomi was candid with the Attorney.

"You're running for Senator?" she inquired, and then added, "You going to put a stop to the trouble Desmond Papers has heaped upon us?" She looked right at Kas, her blue eyes piercing her. Kas found the woman compelling.

"I don't seem to have any choice," she answered straightforwardly. "The occult has decided the matter for me."

She wondered if Naomi knew enough about the cabal to understand her dilemma.

"Wesley has often said the same thing." Naomi jiggled her foot, wrung her hands together and answered, "He's often stated how the occult dictates every detail of his life."

Naomi seemed to be familiar with the occult, and its esoteric activities. Kas saw the dirty scavenger fly settle on her desk and made a conscious effort to ignore it.

"How long has Wesley been a part of the occult?" she asked.

Naomi shook her head, frowned, and then once more turned her piercing eyes at her.

"He was born in it" she said.

"And how old is he now?"

"He's thirty-six…" Naomi answered her. "He's thirty-six and going on one-hundred."

After all of the headaches the occult had caused her over the last several weeks, Kas felt she could relate well to Wesley's distress. She leaned forward, lowered her voice and asked pointedly,

"Naomi, exactly what is your relationship to Wesley Versuch?"

Naomi scrunched down in her chair, wrapped her arms around her skinny frame and, with a trembling voice, she answered her.

"We were married to each other for a little over five years. We had a baby girl together, Caroline." Her lips quivered and tears started to fall. She wiped at them and complained, "Damn it, I do this all of the time!"

Kas pushed the box of Kleenex on her desk toward the troubled woman and then sat back in her chair, resolved to give Naomi all of the time she needed.

"Take your time." she told the young woman sympathetically.

Naomi removed a tissue from the box. She crumbled it in her hand, bit her lip and struggled to keep back more tears. By this time, Naomi's mascara had streaked down her cheeks. Gazing around the room, absent-mindedly, Naomi continued.

"You know, when I was a kid," she stated awkwardly, "I remember feeling very much alone. We didn't have much, and what we did have Dad usually blew on booze and prostitutes." Naomi made a choking sound as she strived not to fall apart completely. "I remember a little black dog, a Cairn Terrier." Naomi glanced at Kas and saw her nod as she recognized the breed.

"He wandered onto our property. I guess he was hungry. I know he was dirty, sickly-looking, and he desperately needed immediate care." Naomi laughed miserably. "Of course, I was just a kid then. What did I know?" she asked, but she didn't expect an answer to her question and Kas didn't give her one.

She listened to the young woman, absorbed in Naomi's account. Childhood was seldom a picnic, she thought, but added to this had been her father's abominable behavior. It was a genuine tragedy.

"I didn't have the money to buy Rudy any dog food. I gave him a bath, brushed and combed his hair, and then, I fed him a handful of lunch meat from our refridgerator. I had Rudy…I named him Rudy….for two days, and then dad came home drunk and kicked the shit out of him. For no reason, just because he was there, taking up space. I tried to nurse Rudy back to health, but he never recovered from the trauma, and a little more than a week later the dog died in my arms," Naomi sobbed.

"Oh, Naomi," Kas whispered, as she thought of Toby and the way Erin loved the dog. How much she missed the little pig-faced Boston Terrier now. "I am so…."

"Wait!" Naomi interrupted her, as she struggled to gain control of her emotions. She wiped at her face with the wrinkled Kleenex and said, "There's more! You haven't heard the worst of it, yet!"

Kas braced herself as Naomi continued.

"Wesley and our daughter, Caroline, were so close! He honestly was a very caring father and Caroline loved him to pieces, too" Naomi explained. "They followed after each other like" Naomi shrugged,"Like, I don't know, best buddies, I think?" She glanced at Kas, who nodded at her again.

"To tell you the truth, I was somewhat jealous of their relationship. I know it was wrong of me, but I had always been alone, and Wesley and Caroline had each other and I felt so left out. Mind you, I'm not making excuses for the way I felt…".

"I know," Kas tried to assure her and listened as she trudged on through the muddy waters of her personal life.

"Caroline was a little over four-years-old when she was diagnosed with leukemia. Despite the way Wesley took care of her…he did everything for her and I was so proud of him…but in spite of it all, nine months later, on Caroline's fifth birthday, she died in his arms! The same way Rudy had died in mine!" Again, Naomi made the sad little sound in her throat, almost a very poor impression of laughter. "Caroline was so much like that poor pup who'd been kicked around and was so sickly! Even now, I try telling myself Caroline and Rudy were fortunate. They both died in the arms of someone who cherished them more than all this sad and sin-sick world!"

Naomi took a deep breath and exhaled. There were no more tears. The brave young woman stood up, pushed the pink tissue into a pocket of her tight-fitting blue jeans and then sat down again, as though determined not to shed one more tear. Pushing a strand of her long dark hair over her shoulder, she gave Kas a blank stare. Her silence was odd, Kas thought.

Kas wrestled in her chair, pulled herself together and couldn't resist the desire to ask her,

"Naomi, why did you feel it necessary to tell me all of this now?"

The troubled woman answered her,

"Because I wanted you to know, I don't believe Wesley would ever hurt anyone, not intentionally."

"So, you don't think he killed Carla Ciprano?"

"Oh, no, he killed her, but it was an accident. He told me he was asleep on the bed and woke up to find Carla on top of him. She took the picture of Caroline he was holding and threw it across the room. The picture frame broke into pieces. Still half asleep, Wesley didn't know what was happening and he strangled her with his belt but it was an accident. Wesley would not deliberately kill anyone!" Naomi asserted, and she sounded completely sure of it.

"Well, I'm glad to hear this" Kas said, and tried to offer her a sincere smile. "However, Naomi, Wesley is not my client and he won't be my client until he reschedules an appointment with me."

Naomi's eyes darted around the room and Kas was sure there was more on her mind.

"There's something else" Naomi stated. "I came here today to tell you something else."

"I'm listening" Kas told her.

"Wesley saw your picture in the headlines of this morning's newspaper. He swears your daughter looks exactly like Caroline and I believe he is going to try to kidnap her!"

Chapter 61

Allen held the ticket to Kansas with one hand and a brown overnight bag with the other, as he scanned the arrivals and departures monitor on the wall above his head. Others in the bus depot were gathered around it, too.

Allen saw an older couple there who were holding hands. He watched them for a moment because they reminded him of the older couple on the mountain the evening of the inferno.

He turned his eyes away to concentrate on the screen again. Listed there was the departure time of the Greyhound bus which would take him to his destination. He noticed it was leaving the station in fifteen minutes.

Allen turned around and made his way through the crowd to a chair across the room. Just like airports, bus stations were obviously always busy, too, he thought as he took a seat at the end of a row of chairs.

He'd never gone anywhere by bus before. Once, when he was a kid, he remembered riding in a jet airplane to Kansas with Charlie and Harriet Carter. It was a long time ago now, though. It was when the only boogeymen he had to worry about were the ones underneath his bed.

Far away, in Kansas, he'd not be disturbed by any boogeymen. No, there all he would have to worry about would be getting along with his Aunt and Uncle, Harriet's beloved brother and sister-in-law.

People gave him the willies and he swallowed the lump in his throat. He knew he preferred the company of various boogeymen to trying to get along with people.

Some ghouls and goblins were actually quite harmless, he imagined. Some of them might even be humorous, at times. Although, not so humorous so as to ever forget their real identity and the fact they were notorious agents of doom.

Those on Mount Gaspar were especially bloodthirsty, though, and he understood enough about them now to know he had to escape them. After being released from the mental hospital, it became his main objective to put miles and miles between himself and the barbarians on Mount Gaspar.

Yet, the thought of staying with James and Ruth Davison brought him no internal calm, either, despite the medication he took to avoid the many fears which plagued him, the Paxil which was supposed to make everything feel so much better.

Two people, involved in an argument came to a halt right in front of him and Allen listened to their dispute. They didn't seem overly concerned about him hearing them.

The man, in dirty blue jeans and greasy white t-shirt, a mop of wild black hair on his head, held the beautiful woman by her shoulders while telling her in a desperate tone of voice,

"I'm a mechanic, Ira! It pays for the roof over our heads and the food we eat, but I can't afford a ticket to Kansas City, too! I wish I could, but I can't go with you, and if you board the bus for Kansas you will have to go without me!"

The woman started to weep and told the poor guy,

"I can't live here anymore, Pedro! I have to go to Kansas!"

She was sexy-looking and Allen noticed the seductive red dress she was wearing barely covered her. Her bosom was shapely and alluring, and Allen turned his eyes away. He gazed down at his empty lap and labored to hide his reddened face without calling attention to himself.

Allen had no one who loved him enough to weep over his departure. Once more, he felt his total isolation and he cursed his fears, particularly those which kept him from ever forming an association with any one. His only comrades had been those he was now running away from, other than Charlie and Harriet Carter. They were dead, though, and despite all of Daphne Orion's many stories about reincarnation, they were never going to return to him.

Allen tried concentrating on something else besides the aching loneliness he felt. He turned to his duffle bag, unzipped it and removed the peanut-butter sandwich he'd packed away to save for later. The sandwich was wrapped in a colorful napkin, which he removed and placed on his lap so he wouldn't soil his clean slacks. Then he bit into the sandwich and chewed his food thoughtlessly, mindlessly.

Suddenly someone he recognized came through the door and he cringed. It was Wesley Versuch and Allen didn't have any idea as to what he was doing here. He thought about hiding, but it was too late. Wesley had already spotted him, so he waited until the fierce-looking rebel made it through the crowd and over to where he was sitting. Then Wesley stood over him with a dejected look on his haggard face.

"Allen," Wesley exclaimed, as if he was relieved to discover him there. "They told me you were released from Saint Vincent's," he said, his Austrian accent giving a crispness to the words. "They also said you had purchased a one-way ticket to Kansas, but they didn't tell me when your bus was leaving."

Allen had no time for Wesley and he wasn't interested in whatever he had on his mind or his reason for being there. He imagined it had something to do with the occult, though, and he'd made up his mind he was never going to return to the occult. He wasn't the least bit pleased about an affiliate of the esoteric society turning up here now. He set his jaw, and his coffee-colored eyes glanced up at the brute who towered over his chair.

"Did they send you here to bring me back to their beserk organization? Well, you can tell them I'm never, ever, going to return! This is a total waste of your time!" Allen said, and he was adamant about it.

"Yeah, I know." Wesley sighed heavily, and dropped down in the empty chair beside him. "I hear ya," he groaned. "I'm not going back there either. I'm burned out with all of their brutality. They've poisoned the sky with their chemtrails and have finagled the world into thinking they're just a bunch of peace-loving hippies, sorely misunderstood." Wesley shook his head as though to rid himself of the memories he harbored.

Allen glanced at him again, doubtful Wesley really meant what he said.

"If you dislike them so much, then why are you working for them? I know the reason you're here and, like I said, it's a waste of time!"

Allen sounded angry, disgusted by what he suspected to be another trick.

Of course, Wesley would deny it, he told himself. He'd peacefully try to coax him back to Rattler's social order and, when this didn't work, he'd get hostile with him and there would probably be a lot of blood, both his and Wesley's, and this was exactly what Allen sought to avoid. He lost interest in his sandwich.

Wesley sank down in the chair, crossing his legs and resting his chin in his hand, and then he said,

"I've always liked you, Allen. You're not at all like the others. There's always been something clean,…and even…noble, about you," He seemed to be struggling with words to express his emotions.

He paused to glance at the young man beside him. He was older than Allen by about twelve years, and much more mature and worldly. He'd learned a lot through hardened experience and he leaned foreward as though to bestow some of this knowledge on the young man.

"There's a lot about me you don't know," he told him.

"I know enough," Allen replied quickly. "I know all I want to know about you." He was candid and unflinching with his answer.

Wesley tried to laugh but it sounded a lot more like a cheerless groan to Allen.

"You didn't know I was married once and I had a little girl." Wesley confided in him. "Her name was Caroline, and the Delphian's chemtrails killed Caroline. The chemtrails caused her leukemia which eventually took her life. She suffered a lot before she finally gave up the ghost."

Allen saw Wesley's eyes grow misty as he doubled his fist. This was a surprise to him. He'd never thought of Wesley as anything but a trouble-maker.

He knew he'd been raised in the occult, and that his great-great uncle was the banshee, Leopold Versuch. He didn't think there might be anything human about Wesley, though, or he might have some redemptive qualities.

"I'm sorry to hear this." Allen replied sincerely.

"Yeah," Wesley said, shaking his head, "But your apology doesn't bring Caroline back, does it?"

Allen knew there was nothing he could say to cheer him, so he remained silent, but he was listening now.

"The older couple who adopted you, what were their names?" Wesley asked him, as though it really mattered to him.

"Charlie and Harriet Carter," Allen said.

"I bet they did things with you, you know, average kinds of things, customary things?" Once again Wesley struggled to express his thoughts.

Allen nodded,

"I guess," he said, confused by his questions.

"They took you places too, right? Places like Disneyland, Sea World, you know, ordinary places?"

"Yea, we used to go fishing a lot, and camping. Is that what you mean?"

Then Allen saw Wesley actually grin.

"Exactly," he exclaimed. "I bet you had a great deal of fun, too?" he said, and he seemed almost excited over the thought.

"I guess….," Allen said, still rather cynical. "What's the point in all of this?"

The beam on Wesley's face disappeared and once more he declined in his chair.

"The banshee, Leopold Versuch, raised me in the occult. They were and are a bunch of satan-worshippers and well, I don't have to tell you, what kind of esoteric activities they engaged in. I never knew anything even remotefully normal not until, Caroline was born and then Naomi, my ex-wife and Caroline showed me a whole different world. I guess it was pretty run-of-the-mill, atleast, most would call it this. I thought it was totally amazing, though. The best time in my life was with Caroline and Naomi!" Wesley divulged while tears ran down his cheeks. "The occult ended my life and I wanted to die with Caroline," Wesley told him. "Can you comprehend this, Allen?"

"I guess…." Allen answered him but, mostly because he didn't know what else to say.

There was a long silence between them, during which Allen heard Wesley sniff and saw him rub at his nose.

"Did you know Rattler Mackenzie is Kastanje Scott's old man?" Wesley asked him. "Or, the spirit of her dad?"

"No," Allen shook his head. "No way," he exclaimed. "The Pastor's wife?"

He couldn't envision it but he thought Wesley had been truthful with him up until now. How could he make something like this up, and for what reason, he wondered. Wesley nodded

"It's true," he told him. "It's the honest to god truth," he lifted a hand as though he was prepared to swear to it.

Allen was speechless. He was so upset and naucious by this bulletin, he tossed his sandwich into the wastebasket beside him.

"Rattler Mackenzie has decided his daughter should reign over the free world, starting with the state of California! He's behind the movement to make her the Senator now." Wesley continued. "It looks like the Pastor's wife has collaborated with the occult and the state is singing her praise," Wesley said, and looked and sounded extremely upset over this. "I would hate to see Cadence Scott become an intrinsic part of the cabal, wouldn't you?" He glanced at Allen.

Still speechless, Allen nodded. She was an adorable little girl, he thought and so was Erin. It disturbed him deeply to think their family might become involved with the society he struggled to escape.

It angered him to imagine Rattler Mackenzie would seek to detrail Harriet's Pastor and his whole family this way.

Mrs. Scott must have been a real philanderer to ever go along with the cabal and accept their assistance in order to become the Senator of California, he thought and he wondered about this. Suddenly, he jumped out of his chair, and with a worried expression on his face, he exclaimed,

"There must be something we can do to put an end to Rattler's blueprints!"

"There is, Allen, there is," Wesley assured him.

Chapter 62

All day long Archie had felt like there was someone looking over his shoulder, or lurking behind him. In fact, he turned around several times during the day just to make sure he wasn't being followed.

He had accompanied his crew to lunch because he couldn't stand the thought of being alone. He knew if he was alone the apparitions might really disturb him then.

Sometimes Archie felt like he was losing it; like he was snapped together piece by piece and some of those pieces were beginning to losen. There had been other apparitions several times before but none of these had remained around long, and when Archie compared them with those Barry had told him about in private, he thought he was fortunate.

Barry had been hounded by a hellion who left bloody cyclopean footprints behind. Archie suspected one of those terrible phantoms had caused Barry's fatal accident, when his car collided with an eighteen-wheeler and brought Barry's life to an abrupt end.

As Archie drove his hunter-green Saturn Ion down Foothill Boulevard, on his way home, he felt antsy, despite the loud music which filtered through the car's amplifiers and surrounded him.

America sang, *Ventura Highway* and, usually, the music carried him away to far off places like the Carribean, places he could never afford to go, but had always dreamed of visiting. Now, nothing soothed his frayed nerves. America, the Bee Gees, or Iron Maiden did nothing for him, nothing but add to his aggitated state of mind.

He turned his thoughts away from the music to think of Jesse and how much he missed her. He recalled the morning he followed her as she walked from her apartment complex to the library. This was when she encountered the retarded guy, Reuben Neely, the one whose home was destroyed by the explosives Archie had planted in Neely's kitchen cupboard. He had done it to scare her, to convince her to keep her mouth shut or there would be even more destruction, and more than just Neely's dog would die.

If she went to the police and ratted on him, they'd come after Archie but not before he'd destroyed her landlord and his wife, Rachel; not before he'd ravaged her home and killed the son of a bitch who was sleeping with her.

He suspected Jesse needed more convincing though, and this was where he was headed now. He was going to ransack the place where she worked, Pet Emporium, located just off of Foothill Boulevard.

In spite of the fact the radio station he was tuned to was located in Althea, and he was on the outskirts just minutes away from Althea right now, Archie began to hear only static, a disgusting cutting, crackling noise. It was as though there was something else in the air, some force which was interfering with the radio's ability to transmit. He had heard it before, but it had never seemed so all-encompassing. Now it seemed to him as though some strange invisible discord cloaked everything.

Archie felt his heart begin to pound with an overwhelming fear. He was very near the area where the bloody event had taken place, when he had taken an AK-47 and shot holes in the car Jonathan Wright was in.

Heavy compact clouds hung low over the field where the blue Chevrolet had careened into after he'd shot at it. The car had come to a sudden stop in the baked soil, surrounded by nothing but cactus growing in the abandoned field.

Archie had achieved Rattler's desires then, in spite of the back seat passenger's arguments. Although, Gage had fussed and grumbled like a wimp, Archie had killed Jonathan Wright and took his grandson, Gregory, out with him.

Daphne was ecstatic, though, as she'd pressed down on the gas pedal and they'd sped away while enclosed in some kind of supernatural rainbow-colored light.

The light had vanished from the area now, and the scene had reverted to it's usual dismal-looking nothingness, a perfect place for banshees. In fact, a banshee is exactly what Archie saw in the desolate field.

The apparition, cloaked in black, floated about, in and around the enclave in which she had once existed before the occult had raised her from the dead.

She hung around the spot where the Chevrolet had wound up and she appeared hopelessly bedraggled but Archie recognized her. It was the demon known as Deedra, *the sorrowful wanderer.*

Deedra was a thin, whispy female, youthful and pretty in a darkly grotesque way. Her short black hair was a startling contrast to her ivory skin which peaked from areas uncovered by the bleak silk evening gown she wore.

It seemed long ago she had resigned herself to the morbid ambiance in which she always appeared. Now, she lingered beneath the gray, gloomy cloud as though grieving for Jonathan and Gregory and their sorrowful demise.

Archie was stunned and the hair on his neck bristled when he heard the commotion on the radio, like the loud and mournful sound of Deedra's dirge.

He pulled hard on his wheel to prevent colliding with the hoary man at the side of the highway who looked like he'd been injured. He swerved into the next lane and, to his utter surprise, he heard the loud blast from a car's horn….*beep, beeeeeep!*

Archie now realized how intoxicated he had become with evil spirits. In fact, so intoxicated he was a menace on the highway and he figured he'd better pull off rather than being hit and killed.

He slowed his car down and stopped on the shoulder of the road. He stayed in the car, fighting to control his nerves as he watched the apparition in the distance, but Deedra paid no attention to him.

He reached to turn off the radio, which had now gone silent anyway. The air was permeated with a frightening electricity, the electromagneticism of fiends from the abyss, he imagined.

He glanced at his image through the rear-view mirror and thought of Barry. Perhaps it was a similar encounter with evil spirits which had brought the poor bastard's life to a swift end, he thought.

Apparently Barry hadn't demonstrated the good sense to get off of the road and wait, though.

But wait for what? Archie wondered. These spirits cared nothing about time. They weren't burdened by the sand left in the hour-glass of time. They could be present in this location for hours, or even days and months, and now Archie worried about being trapped.

Once more, he looked in the rear-view mirror and noticed how much he had aged. His eyes were bloodshot and there was a permanent crease in his forehead along with lines around his mouth. He looked like he'd spent the better share of his life scowling.

He couldn't sit on the side of a public highway for long before the police would show up, and he didn't like the cops. Besides, he'd be the only one hampered when the damned cops arrived. The police couldn't restrain spirits, or throw them into the tank. The banshees were just as animated around cops, too.

Lost in his thoughts, Archie was startled to hear loud banging on the passenger's side window. He saw it was the old man he'd thought had been injured, but he was so severely burned he looked like he'd been attacked by a blow-torch.

"Let me in!" the raspy voice shouted.

Despite his noxious appearance, Archie recognized Jonathan Wright and he locked the doors, despairingly hoping the apparition would return to where it came from.

"Let me in!" the ethereal being howled at him again, rattling the car as he labored to open the door.

"Go away!" Archie shouted back, and pushed himself against his backrest, himself could vanish instead of being an easy victim for every rogue the occult had ever called up. Archie knew before long Jonathan would realize he didn't have to beg for entrance. He had an easy admission….he could float through metal.

Although Archie had turned the radio off, some invisible finger had pushed its buttons and turned its dial, and there was ear-piercing static. Then he heard a diabolical voice on the radio say,

"You can't just sit here, man! They're going to come after you and put you away if you stay here any longer!"

Archie already knew this. When a cop stopped to see what the trouble was, it would take nothing more than one quick call to his division in order to discover Archie Petersen was wanted for Jonathan Wright's murder. Without cooperation from the occult, the strongest alliance in the nation, they would pick him up and incarcerate him.

He weighed this heavily, then finally unlocked the doors, leaned over to open the door, and invited the demon inside his vehicle, which was exactly what the ghost of Jonathan Wright figured he would do.

As Jonathan got into his Saturn, Archie imagined he was knocking on death's door, seeking admission. There was very little else he could do but pick him up, though, and if he somehow managed to live through the confrontation with the banshee, then he might be able to persuade the apparition to cooperate and pillage Pet Emporium right along with him.

"It was nice of you to pick me up." Jonathan told Archie, as they sped down the road going as fast as the speed-limit allowed.

Jonathan reeked of smoke sulfer and burning flesh. He was a beastly sight; his facial features ran together like melted wax. His right eye and nostril seemed to be fused together.

"I said it was nice of you to pick me up." Jonathan repeated himself.

"I heard you" Archie sputtered. "I didn't have any other ulternative, though, did I? For the future, you should file my advice away," Archie generously offered his counsel. "You can ooze through any material in your present state, Jonathan. You don't have to knock, or even open doors, any more." Archie accorded him a slight smile.

Jonathan was one grisly gob, burned and rearranged, but at least he was dead and could float through walls now.

"Yeah, that's real nice" Jonathan answered him, "But I still miss my daughter and my grandson, Gregory. God took Gregory and I wound up a brick layer in hell."

"I'll bet hades feels your absence, then." Archie told him.

They'd never been so friendly to each other when Jonathan was alive. The old man had been one of the occult's informants but Archie had never liked him. He thought of him as a crotchety old man. It seemed to him like maybe death had softened Jonathan a bit around the edges, though.

"I have to be honest, Jonathan. I think this new role fits you," Archie said, and slapped his shoulder. His hand went through air.

"I'm glad to hear you appreciate my conversion, since you're the one who put me in the grave!" Jonathan said, angry at the fat man over what he'd done to him and the horribly permanent situation he was in.

Archie heard the animosity in Jonathan's voice. His stomach turned and he felt feverish.

"Am I going to die?" he gasped.

Jonathan lifted his head, pleased with the fear he heard in the stout man's voice as he recognized his power now.

"Every one is going to die sooner or later, Archie." He enjoyed the idea of ending Archie's life. Nothing would bring him more pleasure and it seemed, somehow, to be only fair.

"You won't die today, or even tomorrow, maybe. It depends on how long it takes us to finish the assignment Daphne Orion has given us to do."

Archie swallowed hard and tried to accept the fact of his own death, but first he'd try to accomplish one more feat for the cabal, something Daphne expected of him, as well as the banshee, Jonathan, whom she'd called forth from hades. In return, perhaps Jonathan might do him a favor.

"I figured you had a reason for being here and you didn't just come to chat."

Archie told Jonathan, as he veered his car onto the offramp, sped across the bridge and waited for the traffic light to turn green at the busy intersection. The banshee didn't complain. As a matter of fact, he said nothing as Archie took it upon himself to change his course and head for the pet store.

"So, what is this thing we've been given to do?" he questioned the demon.

"We are to kidnap Daphne's adversary, Kastanje Scott, and take her to Mount Gaspar." Jonathan informed him.

Archie said nothing but listened carefully and tried to envision it.

"Daphne said she will meet us there." Jonathan laughed and it sounded strange to hear a banshee laugh. Most of the banshees Archie knew never laughed at anything. Jonathan made a coarse noise, like he wasn't accustomed to it either. "At Mount Gaspar, we'll have the pleasure of watching two females fight to the death!"

"Live mud wrestlers" Archie muttered with anticipation. "The women wear those blouses and when they're wet, you can see their hooters!" He acted as excited as a kid who was looking forward to the sport.

Jonathan nodded at him,

"Exactly! Only, this will be ten times the amount of fun because there will be a lot of black magic involved!"

"Care to place any bets?" Archie inquired as he made a sharp right turn into Pet Emporium's parking-lot. It was dusk and the store was closed so the parking-lot was empty.

Chapter 63

Cody parked his Dodge wagon at the curb in front of the high-rise where *Scott & Spencer's* Law Firm was. He hurriedly got out and closed the door behind him.

There were pedestrians everywhere on this particular weekday afternoon. He saw two men dressed in business suits standing near the fountain, outside the superstructure, smoking cigarettes. He noticed the sign on the building which told him this was a smoke-free facility. He went inside.

To his left he saw the enclosed glass business office with the sign *Panorama Landscaping* above the glass façade. Scenic pictures were posted everywhere on the window.

Cody watched an attractive young woman get off the elevator. She had long, dark hair and sad, blue eyes which were swollen as though she'd spent the biggest share of her morning crying, he thought.

Although he was almost the length of the hall away from her, he impetuously called out to her, waving his hand and shouting,

"Hi! I wonder if you could tell me something?" She gave him a suspicious *who me* look and, upon approaching him, replied in a soft girlish voice,

"What is it you want?"

"I've never been here before," he answered her, and gave her a genuinely friendly smile.

"Could you tell me if there's someone who sort of manages the entranceway here? You know, directs foot-traffic, this kind of thing?" he asked.

"I haven't seen anyone…," she replied and looked around.

"Oh," he said with an intense nod. Then he turned and motioned to the door through which he had just come in, and by which she was leaving, he surmised. "I saw two chaps outside who looked as if they might work here, but they were far too preoccupied to lend me their attention," he grinned. "I suspect they were on a cigarette break. You don't smoke, do you?"

She shook her head.

"It's a bad habit and takes too many years from your life," she informed him.

"Yes," he agreed with her. "That it does," he said. She seemed like a nice sort, quite considerate and not artificial, he thought.

"My name is Cody." he finally said, reaching forth his hand to her. "Cody Baldwyn," he added.

"I'm Naomi," she replied shaking his hand. She didn't offer him her last name.

"Hi, Naomi," he said, and smiled at her. He looked down at the pad of paper he had with him. "I'm on my way to see the Defense Attorney, Kastanje Scott. Do you have any idea what floor she's on?"

"Yes," she said and flashed her eyes at his notepad. "Her office is on the fifth floor," she directed him, and then asked, "Are you a cop?"

She surprised Cody with the question.

"Wow," he laughed. "You're good," he teased her. "Did I give it away, though?

Straightaway Cody saw her button up. It was as if she had something to hide, he thought. He'd have to ask Kas if she knew anything about her.

"So, the Attorney is on the fifth floor?"

She nodded her head and looked around her as if she expected the boogeyman to leap out at her from his hiding place simply because she'd spoken to a cop.

"I have to go," she told him in a hushed voice.

"Okay," Cody answered her. "Thanks!" he said, backing his way to the elevator. "You've been a great deal of help!" and he watched as she hurried to the door and raced from the building.

Kas stood at the door after Naomi had left her office and thought back on the woman's troubling report of how Wesley Versuch planned to kidnap Cadence. Worried, she thought of calling Paul and letting him in on Wesley's devious plan. As she walked back to her desk, she decided against it, though. Instead, she leaned over the phone on the desk and pressed the button to speak to her secretary.

"Graham, would you place a call through to Lieutenant Cody Baldwyn at the precinct in Althea? Tell them Kas wishes to speak to the Lieutenant."

"Of course," Graham answered her, being very efficient and then he informed her,

"There is someone here to see you, Counselor. She says her name is Jesse Petersen. She's not alone; there's a man by the name of Hank Maddox with her."

"Send them in," Kas told him. It had been a while since she'd seen Jesse Petersen and she had wondered where Jesse had disappeared to, and why she had left Archie. She knew nothing about Hank Maddox.

Minutes later, Graham opened her door and Jesse came through it, followed by a brawny, good-looking man wearing a tan sports coat over a brown t-shirt.

Jesse looked delightful. Kas realized in a minute this was an altogether different Jesse than the one who'd left Archie. She rushed to greet her with opened arms.

On his way out, Graham, wearing a black suit, an earring in his ear, and another one fastened to his tongue, turned at the door and informed her,

"The precinct says the Lieutenant isn't in now. Should I continue trying to reach him?"

"Please," she requested of him with an urgent tone of voice. Then she turned her attention to fully concentrate on the revamped Jesse Petersen. At five-foot-seven, Kas was taller than Jesse and this was obvious when she embraced her. Gazing down at her with a broad smile, she inquired,

"Where have you been?"

Jesse didn't answer her but, instead, went to Kas' desk and placed a yellow manilla envelop upon it. Then she turned to Kas again and with a serious look she asked,

"Has Reuben Neely contacted you?"

Taken aback by Jesse's bracing appearance and purposeful manner, it took Kas a minute to respond.

"The young man whose dog was killed in the explosion? Yes, yes, he did. No more than an hour or so ago…," she told her. "He needs an Attorney," she further explained.

"Good," Jesse said. "I'm glad he called you. I have something I want to show you, something I think will help you proceed with Reuben's case."

"Okay," Kas answered.

She glanced at the big man who accompanied Jesse and noticed the stony expression on his face. For heaven's sake, he might well have been Jesse's own private bodyguard, she thought. The room took on a more serious aura.

Jesse returned her attention to the envelope as she labored to open it. Kas stood right beside her as she inspected the pictures Jesse removed from the envelop and arranged for her to see, placing one beside another in a vertical row. There were five pictures of Jesse, shot from an angle behind her so Kas saw only Jesse's back.

"Hank and Lacy had my car, so I jogged to work that morning. I was unaware someone had followed me and was snapping pictures!" Kas heard the definite sound of dread in Jesse's voice. "The last picture was taken while I was at the library, and after coming across Reuben Neely sitting on the library floor with the giant book in his lap." Jesse said, pointing her finger at the last picture of herself with Reuben.

Kas motioned to the first photo.

"Is this you in front of the complex where you live?" she wanted to know.

At times she'd wondered where Jesse might be staying while she was away. Judging from the woman's response, she now knew it was an apartment complex across town. The plants she saw in the picture were similar to ones which blossomed in this area of Althea.

"Very nice," she sighed.

"Thank you," Jesse answered, weakly.

Kas picked up the last picture in line and gazed at the young man Jesse claimed was Reuben Neely. From the cap he wore which read, Ask me about my Dog, and the children's book he held in his lap, she guessed Reuben was mentally challenged.

"This was taken before the explosion?" she asked.

"Yes," Jesse replied.

"Counselor," the huge man spoke up, "I know who took those prints." he said, and he sounded angry.

She put the picture down and turned her attention to him,

"Who might that be, Mister Maddox?"

"Jesse's husband, Archie Petersen," he answered her. "He took the photo of Jesse and Reuben together!"

He seemed all too quick to accuse Jesse's husband, she thought, and she gave him a curious look.

"This is an interesting premise, Mister Maddox. Did you and Mister Petersen have a quarrel?"

Hank quickly saw through her vaneer and he hesitated a bit before stating,

"Archie Petersen is a violent man and I've had firsthand knowledge of this."

"I've very few doubts, you do." she admitted to him with a smile.

Hank flashed Jesse a look, trying to hide his embarresment as he said,

"I get your point, Counselor. It's my connection to the culprit's wife which is in question here?"

He seemed innocent of any wrongdoing and he was quite sincere, too, perhaps to his own fault, Kas thought, before telling him,

"Until there's some tangible proof as to Archie's guilt, I'm afraid you'd make a poor witness, Mister Maddox."

"Hank," he told her, feeling somewhat intimidated by her.

"Hank," she said with amusement, "You may say whatever you'd like about Mister Petersen as long you say it outside the courtroom," she counseled him.

Jesse wasn't so quick to cooperate, though. She was sure Archie was responsible for the bomb which had killed Reuben's Labrador and destroyed his house. She'd come here to convince Kas of Archie's guilt and she wasn't going to turn around and leave now.

"I left Archie after he tried to kill me, Kas. The paramedics came to the house and took me to the hospital by ambulance because, during one of his séances, the banshee Archie conjured up convinced him to beat me to death. If the Lord hadn't intervened, I would have been dead." Jesse attested to her husband's destructive actions.

"Owww-eeeh!" the Detective exclaimed when he saw the gold post implanted in the secretary's tongue. He pointed at it.

"Does it bother you when you eat? I would think it would annoy the heck out of you when you eat," Cody said, mildly tweaking Graham.

The young man, whom Cody figured must have been all of twenty, shook the dark bangs out of his eyes and admitted to him,

"It doesn't hurt a bit. Now who would you be and which attorney are you here to see?"

Cody leaned against the desk watching Graham flip through the appointment book in front of him. Finally he said helpfully,

"I'm not on your list."

He thought of his own son who would have been about Graham's age right now, had he not been murdered.

"I don't have an appointment with the Attorney, Kastanje Scott, at all." he told him, as he watched the young man with a bit of amusement.

Graham's boyish charm and the retainer anchored to his lower front teeth were interesting, to say the least. He introduced himself.

"I'm Cody Baldwyn, but more importantly, though, who are you?"

It sounded to Graham as if he was truly interested.

"I'm Attorney Scott's private secretary, Graham Steeple." he answered him, and Cody saw the optimistic gleam in his eyes. "We tried phoning you at the precinct but they said you were out, and now you curiously turn up here."

Cody shrugged, and with a laugh he responded,

"Call me psychic. No, don't call me psychic, those blockheads are obnoxious. Have you ever met a real fortune-teller?" He enjoyed trying to converse with the boy.

"A real one?" Graham asked him, and shook his head. "No, but I've met plenty who claim to be clairvoyant. Just a minute, I will page the Attorney for you," he said.

Cody gazed around at the foyer while Graham beeped Kas. So avant-garde, he thought. It was white with black and white pictures of zebras, orangatans and apes on all of the walls. She was really into these mammals, huh? he wondered.

Finally, Graham told the Detective,

"You may see her now."

Cody nodded and his heart leaped into his throat, just thinking about actually being around her again. The allure of her soft fragrance, her energy and her very own unique chemistry.

He went to the door, knowing it was hers without being told because he felt the pull of her magnetism, and then knocked softly before entering her office.

She was exquisite, he thought, even while she stood and talked with her visitors. In spite of the others in the room with her, he envisioned her alone with him. When she turned her azure-blue eyes on him, he felt completely alive.

"Cody," she said, "This is Hank Maddox and you've already met Jesse Petersen."

He nodded, and remembered they'd met at the precinct. Jesse didn't look nearly as exhilarated to him then, though. No, then Jesse Petersen had seemed quite frail and weak, as though she should have been in the prime of her life but she had one foot in the grave already.

He exchanged greetings with them, uncertain whether to be blithful or sedate. He took his cue from her and smiled broadly.

"You know the man, Reuben Neely, who was on the news today? The guy the police presumed had killed his dog and destroyed his own house with a bomb?" Kas asked him. She was passionate, like an investigator when he or she is on the verge of cracking a big case, he thought.

"Yes, they have him at the police station now." Cody answered her. He remembered
seeing the police bring Mister Neely in. He was handcuffed as they lead him down the hall and to the interrogation room.

"Jesse has reason to believe he didn't do it," Kas contended, "She has reason to believe her husband, Archie Petersen, a devout follower of the occult, committed the atrocity, instead." she told him.

Cody studied the couple. The brawny man wearing brown slacks with matching pullover, and a tan sports coat, had a serious look on his face. He was bigger and taller than Cody. The woman beside him, in a salmon-colored blouse and coffee-colored capris, had her eyes riveted on him. It was as though they both expected some brainy solution to issue forth from him. He turned to Kas, who also gave him an expectant look.

"Your client, Gage Petersen, admitted to the police his Dad was the one who shot at the Aveo on Foothill Boulevard, too," Cody said, and when he saw the dismay in the Attorney's eyes he added, "I have a hunch Mister Petersen leaves a long trail of blood behind him."

Jesse nodded and struggled to hide her growing faith in the judicial system, a newly-found faith, a faith which hadn't yet developed its wings or its capacity to fly. Hank pulled her to his side and gave her a reassuring smile.

"This is just the beginning of a long drawn-out process," she told him, "of getting Archie committed to a cage, where he should have been all along."

Kas turned away from them as if detaching herself. She was struggling with her feelings and was unaware of Gage's confession. She was Gage's Attorney and should have been there when he made his confession, she chided herself. In fact, she should have been the first one he confided in, when he accused Archie Petersen of murdering Jonathan and Gregory Wright.

"I had no idea Gage confessed already," she sighed. Then she gave Cody a cold look as though blaming him for the failed communication.

"Why wasn't I told about this sooner?" she appealed to him. "Why didn't the department fill me in?"

Hank and Jesse exchanged uncomfortable looks, realizing this was a personal matter which no doubt should have been discussed privately between the Attorney and the Detective, so they headed for the door with Jesse offering a polite,

"Good luck, Kas, on your way to the Senate!" She put her heartfelt wishes into words, "We want you to know, we're behind you all of the way!"

She attempted to be cheerful, but caught the dejected look in Kas' eyes and immediately dropped the subject. Hank held the door open for Jesse but, before leaving, she requested of them,

"Call us and let us know how you decide to handle the matter; the sooner the better! Lieutenant, it was good seeing you again." she added, and smiled at him.

Cody tore his attention away from Kas in order to answer her.

"I'll be in touch." he told Jesse, and watched as Hank guided her through the door and shut it behind them.

Alone now, Cody looked at Kas, resting in the chair at her desk. He was confused by the tears which filled her eyes and spilled down her cheeks. He waited to see if she'd explain her tears to him.

She labored to put her heart-sick feelings into words.

"Oh! Cody!" she cried. "I've lost everything because of Rattler Mackenzie; EVERYTHING!" Detressed, she exclaimed. "My house, my marriage, being at home with my girls, and now even the ability to carry out my tasks as an attorney for the defense!"

Cody was deeply moved by her heart-wrenching agony.

"The last thing I relish is this damned nomination to Senate! Damn him, Cody! Damn Rattler's demands on me! I don't want to be the Senator of California!" she asserted."I want my life back! I want to be the phenomenal lawyer I was before Rattler capsized me!" she said, and she was furious.

Cody perched on the corner of her desk, his steel-toed shoes firmly planted on the floor, stared blankly down at his feet and shook his head with disappointment.

"This is exactly why the station didn't report it to you when Gage made his confession." he said, and gazed at her again.

He was angry with himself for her unhappiness and for the hurt reflected in her eyes. He was upset with his decision to exclude her in these matters. He'd been concerned for her personal welfare so he thought it better not to tell her.

The rattlesnake, too, seemed to want to protect her, though. He contemplated this now. He'd noticed how everytime someone had threatened her, they wound up dead, killed by the rattlesnake.

"I'm sorry Kas," he apologized to her. "I will personally see to it the precinct doesn't exclude you again," he promised her, but he understood this would hardly solve their dilemma.

"The Western Diamond Back Rattlesnake goes to any and all lengths to protect you, though!" he murmured and watched her leave the chair.

"They weren't thinking of me when they destroyed Neely's house." she argued.

"Are you sure?" he asked.

She walked around her desk and picked up the manilla envelop Jesse had left for them. She stood beside Cody as she handed the envelope filled with the photos to him.

"These were shot several hours before the explosion. The message is clear and strong, and the photographer meant to scare the living daylights out of Jesse."

He got to his feet, opened the envelop and examined the pictures. Finally, he said,

"He was sure Jesse would bring these to you, though."

He was still set on the idea she was the reason for this. He focused his attention on her, positive the occult's actions always had something to do with her. All along, their intention had been to manipulate her. He was thinking outloud as he said,

"A member of the occult moved right next door to you and your family on Victoria Street. Their son and your daughter almost wound up married, and probably the occult had a hand in moving their relationship right along," he informed her. "Remember how Daphne told you the occult was absorbed with every facet of your life, involved in every relationship? How they are in contact with every shred of your existence, she said, yet you were unaware of their presence; Do you remember how she told you this, Kas?"

"Yes, I recall what that witch told me!" Kas replied, annoyed at her memories of her conversation with Daphne.

"Here you are, a Defense Attorney in California," Cody said, simply telling her what she already knew. His words made her wonder at his purpose, though.

"It's no accident, Kas! You've been oblivious to the fact the occult has groomed you for this particular space in time when you would be made the Senator of California!" Cody was convincing.

He went on, and Kas felt pulled in by his deliberation. She peered into his dark green eyes which made her think of some isolated lagoon and she found him totally hypnotizing.

"That morning at the French Beagle when your uncle told you, you had been given a global federation. Some things are just destined to happen, Kas!" He was laboring to persuade her, but he really didn't have to work very hard at it. She believed what he told her was true.

"The one thing you did to overturn them was when you married the Pastor. This so upset them, for a time they gave up on their plans, until they discovered a way around what they deemed to be a disaster. They manipulated a way to tear you and Paul apart."

She was beginning to understand. This was why she'd married Paul. She'd joined herself to him in marriage to put an end to the occult's control over her. At one time Paul's love for her was stronger than the cabal. His conviction indestructible, his God omnipotent. When she married the Pastor, she had liberated herself from Rattler Mackenzie and his evil society.

"The only defense you ever had against the occult was your marriage to Pastor Scott," Cody explained to her. The truth hurt him sorely because he wanted her more than anything he'd wanted in quite a long while. He hesitated for a moment and then, with mixed feelings of both pain and pleasure, he continued,

"Yet, here we are, the two of us, and I'm so completely attracted to you right now, I can't think of anything else except how good it would be to kiss you!"

She trembled, teetering on enticement, unable to resist the treacherous urge to kiss him too. Softly, she said,

"I should warn you, should you kiss me right now, nothing will ever be the same."

Before they plunged to disaster, she closed her eyes in anticipation.

"I think we're way past that point," he said. "Things haven't been the same for me since I met the Mackenzies," and he gave in to temptation as their lips met.

Seconds later, Kas swore she heard bells and whistles, and she was quite sure it was not because of his kiss.

She thought she recognized the melody. It was *Ghost Busters* playing on Cody's cellphone and she watched him respond to it.

As he spoke to whomever it was, she stood close beside him and pondered the merit of one kiss. She'd traded everything else for just one kiss as though it were a jewel of infinite value.

Chapter 64

Daphne Orion paced back and forth in her cell. She was like a wild-cat or a she-devil, completely unprepared for confinement in a cold prison cell. Four walls, three of them scratched up and urine-stained, and the fourth was steel bars, which she rattled now.

"Let me out! Do you hear me? Let me out!" she yelled.

"Shut up, Witch!" came the sharp response from the cell across from hers. Daphne couldn't actually see the female prisoner, but she heard her. "Conjure up one of your evil spirits from the abyss to help you escape, you Sorceress!"

"I've already tried, to no avail." Daphne sighed, as she leaned against the cold iron bars in misery. She'd already tried to bring forth a specter, appealing to several of them, but she guessed none of them opted to be released from the abyss in exchange for a cheerless prison.

She'd tried to bring up the spirit of Jonathan Wright, but clearly that was a fiasco and either it hadn't worked or Jonathan had been elevated to their sphere and chose to appear some place else. Perhaps some place where he could feel the wind whip through his hair and see the stars above him and feel like he was free.

She turned from the bars and ran her hands through her long, curley red hair. She didn't need a mirror to tell her she was a mess. *Mirror,* mirror, on the wall who's the fairest of them all? Surely not you, not on this night and in this booby-hatch.

"Be quiet, Lizzie, or she'll turn into a goat!" another jailbird in another cell said as she giggled. "A real live goat, or is that a goatee?" the convict laughed.

"Bitch!" Daphne screamed, still thinking about her antagonist, the enchantress who was being heralded even now. Kastanje was preferred by the rattlesnake, Daphne's own beloved Rattler Mackenzie, the apostate reptile whom she'd always treated so fairly, and for whom she'd done so many, many favors. Tears made their way down Daphne's cheeks, feeling abandoned and helpless.

"Who you calling bitch, cupcake?" the woman in the cell across from hers clamored, itching for a fight.

Then, outside of her cell, beneath the light in the hallway, Daphne saw something. She paid close attention to whatever it was. The shadow moved closer to her cage.

The girls in the other cells apparently were not aware of it, and yet, it was no figment of her imagination. There was something in the hallway and, as it moved closer to her chamber, she recognized it and hurried to the bars, overjoyed by his appearance.

The banshee clothed in black robe, with a hood over his head, was no ordinary apparition. It was Leopold Versuch.

"Leopold!" Daphne whispered with excitement. "I tried to raise poltergeists and thought I had failed!"

She would never have expected the archangel and lead demon, Leopold Versuch, to answer her and appear outside her cell. His character and control were renowned. He had inordinate global persuasion.

She saw the small, gold key he held in his hand and she watched him slide it into the lock of her prison cell, giving it a twist. At once the door opened.

She tried to plunge forth to freedom but he obstructed her passageway and pushed her back into the dismal cage. Then he entered the jail cell along with her and she saw the door, all by itself, close behind him. He was not trapped, but he had prevented her escape to freedom.

She stood close enough to smell his scent which wafted through the air; the smell of burning incense, sandalwood combined with other eastern herbs and plants.

He was no taller than she was, but he possessed enormous power and strength. Daphne shivered with anticipation and the dreadful thought he might not free her, after all.

"Daphne," the great dignitary addressed her, "Why are you here?"

Almost babbling, she began pouring out the story, but he abruptly interrupted her and said,

"What flaw in your character caused you to be locked inside this dungeon?"

Leopold was ridiculing her, and she wondered if he already knew the answer to his question.

She imagined Versuch would not appreciate her reasons. The spirits did not indulge in feelings. They were beyond frivolous feelings like jealousy which had possessed Daphne, and which was the actual reason she was here. Embarressed by her emotions, she turned away from him.

"I wanted to see her, and to examine her face to face." Daphne said, barely above a whisper. "Rattler McKenzie is so intrigued with her, I couldn't help myself." she confessed. "I wanted to learn what Kastanje has which excites him so."

He shook his head at her, and she could see his displeasure, which made her feel quite immature.

"And what did you discover?" he asked.

She thought about it. Kastanje Makenzie Scott intrigued her. She was beautiful and bewitching, and Daphne didn't have to try very hard to imagine what a radiant she-devil she must have been in her zenith. She envisioned Rattler's daughter cloaked in a black robe with holly strewn the length of her glistening long, blonde hair. Oh, yes, indeed, Daphne loathed Kastanje because she was so brilliant and seductive. Yet, she was actually no more beautiful than Daphne Orion.

"She's nothing, Leopold," Daphne fibbed, and tried to convince herself it was true. "She's a yellow-bellied whimp, just a soft fragile female, one I could easily dispose of, but first I need someone to liberate me!" she appealed to him.

He made his way to her, wafting through the air, his feet not even touching the ground, and he said,

"Then you obviously didn't look close enough, Daphne."

"I did, Leopold, I did!" she insisted. "She's a wash-out, a has-been. I am fifteen years younger than she is, and I'm planning to coax her to the mountain, Mount Gaspar. Once she's there I will dispose of her for good, and then I'll have earned a lofty position in our regime." She was desperate enough to attempt it, but she failed to convince Versuch she would succeed with her endeavor.

He balanced himself and reached forth to take her hand, grasping it firmly in his.

"Do not be so quick to think you will overthrow her, Daphne, or the rattlesnake."

The contest could involve the deadly Western Diamond Back Rattlesnake, she supposed, and she was no match for him.

"Rattler would not turn against me," Daphne contended. "He couldn't, Leopold! I created him and he owes me!" she argued, and made herself believe

Rattler would eventually come to his senses and realize he owed his life to her. Then he would protect her.

When Versuch floated away from her, toward the steel-barred door of her cell, refusing to discuss the issue with her any longer, she was afraid he was going to leave her behind.

"Leopold!" she hollered at him, and saw him turn around to face her. "You can't leave me here, Leopold!"

"You are right." he answered her. "I cannot leave you here for, you see, the contest you speak of has already been arranged." Leopold sighed as though he was fatigued with the age-old battle of evil versus decency and fair play.

She saw the door open and, without another word or further delay, Daphne raced through the opened door and left the prison cell behind her.

Chapter 65

Cody convinced Kas to go home with him which she preferred doing to staying there, alone in her office, with the pesky fly and her morbid thoughts.

Cody's home was small, but pleasant, with a white picket-fence around the yard and well-trimmed shrubbery. They went in the back door and through the utility room. When they entered the kitchen, a white Persian cat raced across the black and white tiled floor and leaped into Cody's arms.

"Hey there, Tchaikovsky!" Cody said, and scratched his ears.

"Tchaikovsy?" Kas questioned him, and smiled at Cody and his prized cat. "Who else might spring upon you? Chopin or Gershwin, maybe?"

"Nope, there's just Tchaikovsy," Cody answered, returning the cat to the floor."He's my attack cat," he smiled as he took off his blue sports coat and hung it up on the over the door metal hook beside him.

Cody rolled up his sleeves and removed an apron from the round Soda-Shoppe-red dinette table with matching chairs. The apron was black with the words, *Grill Master, the Man, the Myth, the Legend* printed on it in white letters. He turned to look at her.

"Are you hungry?" he asked.

"Starving!" Kas said with a straight face. "What do you have in mind, Grill Master?" she inquired, and watched him stroll to the plain white refridgerator and open the door.

She spotted the picture of the pizza on his wall, beside the refridgerator, and she read the words: *I Support the 4 Basic Food Groups: Mushrooms, Tomatos, Pepperoni and Cheese.* She also saw the fridge magnet which read, *I Put Ketchup On My Ketchup.*

"Then I'll scramble us some eggs, and if you don't mind, you could cut up some potatoes and dice an onion. We'll have a simple dinner of scrambled eggs and fried potatoes with onions," he said, and added. "Does this sound good to you, too?"

"I thought for a minute we'd have grilled chicken and mushrooms," she answered him. She took the Idaho potatoes and the onion he handed her.

"Pay no attention to the idiot in the apron," he laughed, as he retrieved a cast-iron frying pan from a cabinet and went to work at the stove.

"Where are your knives and potato peeler?" Kas asked, looking around at the interesting items in Cody's kitchen.

There was an empty John Deere napkin-holder setting on top of one red cabinet. Also setting on top of the red and white cabinets, as if on display there, she noticed a particularly interesting spoon-rest made of earthenware and shaped like a chili pepper. Beside it was a sock elephant, gray with red ribbon around its neck, looking quite out of place among the kitchen novelties.

Cody turned from the eggs he broke over the frying pan, long enough to point her to the cabinet with drawers in it, beside the double-basin stainless steel sink.

She opened a drawer and found it filled with fascinating items which would take someone weeks to sort through. She was surprised to find a knife and potato peeler on top of the pile.

She took the potatoes to the cabinet where she'd left the vegetables and where the wastebasket was placed, across the kitchen from Cody. Somewhat fascinated with the wastebasket's décor of city streets, she started peeling the potatoes.

"How many? she asked, feeling somewhat inept. This wasn't something she practiced often.

"What, potatoes?" Cody asked, not turning around to look because he was diligently tending to the eggs in the frying pan.

"Yes," she answered him.

"Several…," he muttered.

"Several?" she echoed, wondering exactly what he meant by several. Three, or maybe no more than four, at the most, she guessed.

Cody was quiet and she found the silence nerve-wracking. She was accustomed to the babble and noise of a big house with three growing girls and their many friends, so she sought to fill the lull.

"We were amazed to find property with a mountain view twenty-one years ago when we first purchased the house on Victoria street," she told Cody.

"Really?" he said.

"Long ago we took the girls to the mountain too!" she said, and let her mind wander through a long range of memories.

The mountain view from their bedroom window was a major attraction the first time they had looked at the house. She remembered when their Real Estate Brokers showed it to them. It was the first time they had ever met Charlie and Harriet Carter. Both husband and wife were Real Estate Agents who operated their own business.

It was at a time when lots of people were relocating from crowded cities to the barren desert, and real estate was a lucrative adventure in the San Bernardino and Riverside desert.

It was before the infernos of Riverside County when homes and property were destroyed and people realized it was too dangerous to reside in the hot, dry desert. Many of them left for other locations, although others stayed behind. They were among those who stayed because they enjoyed the rugged environment and the uncluttered open space.

"The mountain appeared so magestic to us. Paul referred to it as the benchmark which indicated to him we were home."

She fondly recalled their snowball fight on Mount Gaspar. It seemed like eons ago to her now. Paul had lead her to believe she had the best of him and he was simply no competition for her until he snuck up behind her and buried her with snow. How she missed those happy-go-lucky days and wonderful adventures now.

"I always wondered how someone like you ever wound up married to a Pastor?" Cody questioned her from across the room.

"I guess you might say the Pastor made an honest woman out of me," Kas answered him with a laugh, but her memories were far too precious to scoff at.

"We met when were seniors in college," she told him. "He was a shy, awkward kid with dreams of being a Pastor and sharing the Word of God. He was focused, even then," she remembered.

"He grew up in Sibambe, Equador, just across the Equadorian Andes. That was where Paul's mother, Sarah Scott, died and was buried. Later, they came to the United States and lived in Michigan, in the upper peninsula area."

She'd never been there and now she wondered why they'd never taken the time or made the effort to visit Paul's older brother and his family there, in upper Michigan. She continued,

"It was with grave difficulty John Scott came to America with his two sons, Matthew and Paul. He lived with them there in Michigan for five years before he suffered a heart attack. He left instructions to take him back to Simbambe and bury him beside his beloved Sarah." she told him.

"Fascinating," Cody said. "So," he searched for the words to express his thoughts,

"quixotic?" He turned to glance at her and saw her nod at him with a smile on her lips.

He turned the stove off and put a lid over the frying pan. Then he moved to the cupboard to get the plates.

"What would you like to drink?" he asked her, and saw her shrug. "Coffee, tea, ice water?" He stood at the cupboard and gazed at her. "It's not the type of dinner which would go with pink champaigne although I have some, if you'd rather have that?"

She shook her head.

"No, ice water sounds fine," she told him.

"Ice water it is then," he smiled. "You still haven't answered my question, though. How did you wind up married to a Pastor?" He encouraged her to continue with her account, which he found interesting, to say the least. Cody found a couple of candles in one of the drawers. The tapers were red, white and blue with peace signs sculpted into them. "These will have to do," he sighed.

He took the potatoes and onions she'd prepared and tossed these into another frying pan on the stove. He added a sufficient amount of salt and pepper. As she helped him set the table, she continued with her story.

"I was reluctant to date him at first and explained to him my reasons, which he said were absurd."

"You didn't tell him your Dad was a Satanist, the high priest of the satanic occult?" he questioned her, with an addled look. "I think this might have given him second thoughts."

"I told him my Mother taught ballet and my Dad was the High Priest of the occult but, I don't think he heard me. He was too busy looking at my legs," she explained.

"He was dumbfounded?"

"He said God had brought us together."

"Did he say this while looking at your legs?"

"Sometime afterward…," she told him.

Seated across the table from each other, the lit candles lightened the darkness. The flames danced and flickered in their vases.

"Any way, I had all of these wild ideas of traveling the world and makeshift addresses at places like the Swiss Alps, Mozambque and the Riveria. I told Paul I was going to be rich. Back then, I suspect I would have put my all into the race for Senator of California, had I the chance, and I would have done so for financial acquisition and prestige."

She set her fork down, sipped from the glass of water in front of her and shook her head.

"I was egotistical and selfish then, before I fell inlove with Paul Scott and before our girls were born to us." Her eyes gazed absent-mindedly at her empty plate. "I thought I had rebelled against my father and everything he subjected me to, when, really, all I was doing was following his footsteps. I'm sure I wouldn't have found my way out of the rat trap without Paul."

Seconds later, when she gazed at him, he thought he saw in the candlelight more devotion for the Pastor mirrored in her blue eyes then he could ever hope to muster up within her for him.

"How so?" he whispered.

Her smile resonated her peace of mind,

"The saintly Pastor showed me the way." she said. She put her elbows on the table and rested her chin in her folded hands. "So how did you and Belle ever get together?"

He shrugged and swallowed a mouthful of water.

"Like you, it wasn't love at first sight," he admitted. "I arrested Belle and a couple of her girlfriends for illiciting a riot, and threw them into the can."

She laughed.

"Oh! no, you didn't?"" she said between gasps of laughter

"I did," Cody smiled. "Belle hated me for it, too. The day after when she was bailed out, she told me to go jump in the ocean." He said and he laughed now too.

Chapter 66

Kas had returned to her office and spent the night on the same pink sofa she had slept on the night before. When she awoke the next morning, to her dismay, she found her back ached and her head pounded.

What she needed was a firm mattress and what she craved was to be home again in her beautiful cherry-wood bed and locked inside Paul's powerhouse grip. She always slept better this way.

People had habits, she told herself, and some of those habits were impossible to part with. She would never adopt to this type of lifestyle, of being on her own, without Paul and without their girls, miles away from home.

Still drowsy, she stumbled to her desk and to her handbag on top of her desk. She rummaged through it for the bottle of asprin.

Then she went to the bar and let the faucet run, while she pulled a Dixie cup from the dispenser and filled it with water. The bottle was one of those child-proof containers. She wrestled with it and mumbled a few swear words before she finally succeeded to open it.

She criticized herself for using foul language and told herself she was a very poor candidate for a Pastor's wife. Paul might look for someone more suitable for the task, she thought. No one would blame him, as the spawn of the occult's high priest was an inappropriate role model.

She went to the window and opened the curtains to peer out at a city which seemed committed to making her the Senator of California.

The telephone on her desk rang and she went to pick it up, with thought of how miserable she was on her mind.

"Hello?" She questioned her caller.

"Kas, someone has made a total wreck out of Pet Emporium!" Cody groaned.

"What do you mean, a total wreck?" Kas asked, even more unquieted by Cody's abrupt report.

299

"I mean someone, or something stole into Pet Emporium sometime last night and completely overturned it!"

She had to see for herself.

"I'm on my way!" Kas said and hung up.

Cody was inside Pet Emporium. Those who had destroyed it were obviously some kind of sick lunatics. There was blood smeared on all of the walls, but on one wall, written in huge bloody letters, he saw the words,

'Keep your mouth shut, Jesse! Or, Hank is next!"

Police worked to lift fingerprints and collect other samples from the mess the lunatics had left behind them. Hell, The whole despicable occult could have been involved in this barrage.

Cody saw birds had flown their cages and now perched in the rafters atleast twelve feet above his head. He wondered who had opened their cages and let them out, and why.

A couple of colorful parrots were perched in a plastic tree. They chattered and what they were saying was very telling:

"Rattler reigns…Daphne rules…squawk, squawk." the parrots cackled noisily.

Puzzled, Cody wondered who'd taught them to utter this abominable declaration. He made his way carefully and cautiously toward the door he saw down one aisle. He paid extreme attention to the wall he followed upon which was a long row of pictures, the same photographs Kas had shown him the day he showed up at her law firm. Pictures of Jesse, one taken of her together with the mentally challenged young man, Reuben Neely, the one whose dog and house were destroyed by a mini-bomb.

The birds and their fowl descant led him to believe the fiends might have visited the pet store on more than one occasion and mingled with the birds. They may have carefully concealed their identity and had become regular customers.

Finally, Cody reached the opened door and made his way into the deserted room, unaware of the creatures who trailed him. The four wolves who were mean and vicious-looking. Their mouths hung open, displaying long, sharp blood-stained teeth, intent upon human blood to satisfy their appetites and they now persued Cody.

The Detective carried his gun with him but wondered if it would do him much good. He turned the corner and entered the dimly lit space.

He canvassed the room, cluttered with empty discarded boxes of all shapes and sizes. He stood over the desk and gazed down at the mess, papers strewn all over, a half empty cup of coffee. Atleast he assumed it was coffee. He picked it up, jounced it around and smelled it. It looked and smelled just like strong coffee.

He went to the filing cabinet. The drawers weren't locked so he opened the top one and leafed through the files. The villians names might have been scribbled down at one time, and stuck into the cabinet.

He heard a distinct rattle, an all too familiar sound. Instinctively, he knew what it was. The Western Diamond Back Rattlesnake was somewhere in the room with Cody.

He looked straight ahead and finally spotted the snake at the window. Part of its body seemed to be twisted around the blinds, but the greater part of it was laying along the window sill. He swallowed hard and attempted to hide his horror, remembering the snake was attracted to horror.

"Hello there, Detective," Rattler greeted him. "We've no appointment, but I'm thrilled you stopped by!" the snake greeted him, contemptuously.

Cody looked death in the face and managed to reply,

"Why am I not surprised to find you here, Rattler?"

"My Kastanje will win the election and be made the Senator of California in less than one week! We've no need for the likes of you now, Cody!" Rattler bragged.

"You're Kastanje?" Cody challenged him. "She doesn't consider herself to be your Kastanje, Rattler. As a matter of fact, you've done her so much harm, she'd love to see you returned to your crypt and sealed inside it!"

"You're a sore loser, Detective," Rattler chided him. "Besides, she will soon work for me! Kastanje will perform the tasks I assign her and before long the entire country will be christened into the cabal while you will be dead, nothing more than a bitter-sweet memory in Kastanje's pretty head!" the skilled archbishop and master of black magic delightedly informed him.

"It will take more than a snake to kill me, Rattler," Cody calmly told him. However, when he heard the door behind him close and lock, and then heard the phantoms growl, he lost his nerve.

"My hounds, which I have brought with me from the abyss will help me do you in," Rattler warned him, "The way you and your gun killed me, once upon a time."

He said as he slithered down from the sill and elongated himself up onto Keith Campbell's desk. "Get him, fellas," he charged the creatures.

Cody turned and saw Rattler's dogs advance toward him with blood in their eyes. He fired his gun but, in his frenzy the bullet only hit the floor and nothing else. He didn't hear the banshees whelp or mourn and he knew no bullet fired from a nine millimeter gun could kill them.

"Oh, God," Cody said. "Dear God, receive my life today!" he pleaded with his Maker.

The creature's sharp fangs tore at his limbs, mutilated his body, and one of them fastened his mouth around his neck and tore into his jugular vein, ending the Detective's life.

Chapter 67

After turning the knob and finding the door wouldn't open, Kas began to pound on it and call out,

"Are you in there, Cody? Cody, let me in!"

One of the Police Officers noticed the Attorney standing there, desperately trying to get into the room, and he left what he was doing and hurried over to her. Kas recognized the young cop when he asked her,

"What's the problem here?"

"Officer Newlyn, Detective Cody Baldwyn is trapped inside this room," she told him, as she pointed at the door and gave him an anxious look.

"How do you know he's in there?" Dell Newlyn asked, his hand on the door knob. He pressed his ear against the door to listen for voices or activity.

"He called me and I know he's there," she answered him impatiently. She didn't have time to explain it to him. She just knew Cody was behind the locked door and needed help.

"It's bolted shut," Dell muttered. "Move back," he told her.

Kas moved away from the door and expected him to kick the door down, which is exactly what Officer Newlyn did. Then he entered the room before her.

He let out a loud groan and Kas raced into the room. The cop stood looking down at the blood-soaked floor and Cody's lifeless body laying in a heap, so badly mangled it was hardly recognizable. However, she could identify Cody Baldwyn and so could Newlyn.

"What happened in here?" Newlyn uttered. "I saw the Lieutenant only minutes ago; couldn't have been more than a half hour ago at the most! He arrived sometime after we did."

He glanced at the woman beside him, in tears now, and he knew this was the lawyer the Detective had talked about.

"There's been no vicious animals on the premises who could have torn the Lieutenant's body to shreds like this! Not since we arrived!" Newlyn insisted.

"Police have blocked this area off, in fact! I don't even know how you managed to get in here!" he exclaimed, giving her another glance.

"This whole affair is satanic, Newlyn." Kas was trying to control her agony at the cabal's ugly disposal of Cody. She turned to the Cop and said, "Be sure to write this up! Be sure you record the Delphians are responsible for this destruction, and specifically Rattler

Mackenzie. I'm positive he killed this man! Got that, Newlyn?" She was consumed by anger.

He nodded at her, but he was still baffled. He'd seen no vicious animals anywhere around the area. No wolves anywhere nearby. The only animals able to destroy a man in this ruthless fashion were on the mountain, on Mount Gaspar, he thought.

Kas slid into her Viper, turned the ignition and started the engine. She had reluctantly tore herself away from Cody's mangled body and hurried out of the blood-stained store. She refused to gaze, again, at the one wall which bore Jesse's name in big vital-fluid letters.

She'd managed somehow to ignore those birds, too. Those eerie feathered creatures who squawked awful things to anyone within ear-shot. She'd moved numbly, in a daze, and had stumbled her way to her car, but now, in privacy, she lost it. Her tears flowed like a faucet and she whispered,

"Oh, Cody! I'm so sorry."

It felt like her heart would burst. She clasped her hands around the black steering wheel and gunned the engine, squealing tires on her way out of what was once Pet Emporium's parking lot.

If instead of having a nice quiet dinner together last night, they had made mad passionate love, if she'd shown more interest in him, if she'd thrown herself at him, would he still be alive today? She wanted to turn back the clock. She wanted one more chance to show the serpent she was earthy. But did this really matter to the serpent or had Rattler Mackenzie destroyed her dear friend for the pure enjoyment of it? Kas made it through the yellow traffic light before it turned red, and then another one, until she was merging with traffic on the freeway, all the while lost in her misery.

She had no clue as to where she was headed. It was Cody who had told her the only one who could save them from the evil plans for them was the Pastor. The devils had out-foxed Paul, though, and now she didn't hold out much hope he'd come to their rescue and, now with Cody dead, they were helplessly on their own.

The police, whatever honest cops remained on the police force, those who weren't loyal members of the occult, would attempt to uncover what had happened at Pet Emporium but there would be few of them who'd stay the course until the mystery was solved.

There was no one else committed to the task like Cody Baldwyn had been. Rattler must have known this, she told herself and once more she desperately pleaded for him but to no avail,

"Cody!"

Through blinding tears she saw the beggarly man on the road in front of her. A horrible sight. He looked like he'd been baked in some inferno.

She swerved into the next lane to keep from hitting him. Even then, she felt an awful thump beneath her wheels and she had the gut-wrenching thought she'd hit him.

Her tires squeeled as she sped into the next lane. Gazing into the rear-view mirror, she saw a huge semi overtaking her too fast. The truck slammed into the back end of her Viper and her car spun around.

The gigantic truck forced her down the road as if her Viper was only a plastic toy. It was like a bulldozer forcing her down the highway, and there was no escape.

Her car smashed into the viaduct and was being crushed by the heinous beast. Then, as though there was no more damage he could do to her, the semi moved on, disappearing down the road, but she was too disabled to even move.

Blood dripped from her nose and she caught it with the sleeve of her shirt. After she'd hit her head against the steering wheel, there was a deep gash on her forehead too, and leaning her head back, she stared at the ceiling of the wreckage around her and wondered how she had ever survived.

She must have fainted, but when she opened her eyes again she counted three separate abnormalities. She would have sworn these hideous entities matched the profile of Gollum of Lord of the Rings, with their round heads, ugly mugs and pointed ears. They were inside her car and tugged at her as they muttered,

"Oh!", "ah-huh!" and "Hmm?" They scrutinized her. "Look-see!" One of the creatures pointed at her with his finger, an unkept and unsightly long nail attached to the end of it. "Precious!" he exclaimed, as he lifted the necklace from around her neck and fondled it with his contorted hand.

These beings may well have sprung from middle earth after they'd found some hole through which they could ooze.

They grew noisily alarmed when they heard the human voice, and amidst their groans of "Hurry!" and "Oh-oh!" she recognized the the voice too.

"Jonathan, let's grab her and transport her to the mountain!" She heard Archie Petersen communicate to someone else and then she blacked out.

Chapter 68

They were minutes away from the ballpark. Wesley remembered being at the ballpark when he first saw Cadence Scott and he hoped she would be there again today.

He drove his blue 2000 Dodge Avenger to a stop at the intersection and gazed at his passenger. Allen Carter was bosom buddies with the raven. They'd been a regular twosome on Mount Gaspar, an irksome fissure in Daphne Orion's scheme. Wesley asked Allen about the bird.

"Have you seen the raven around lately?"

"Not since the night of the inferno on Mount Gaspar," Allen admitted, naively.

Wesley appreciated Allen's innocence. Others mocked him, claiming he was simple-minded. Wesley, though, found his demeanor expedient, and he was determined to use Allen to lure Cadence to him.

"Was the bird, what did you name him, following your commands that night?" Wesley asked him.

"Screech," Allen said. "No, he wasn't. We talked it over before hand, but it was more Screech's idea than mine."

It was a bright sunny morning and Wesley enjoyed looking at the scenery as they drove along. It was a perfect day to play ball in the park.

"The raven likes you. Apparently he's made an alliance with you." Wesley offered as a casual comment, but Allen sounded offended by this observation.

"What, because he talks to me? If others would listen he might talk to them, too."

Wesley shook his head, confident he wouldn't.

"I know something about the raven. I know he's no ordinary raven. I also know where he's from and why he frequents the occult on Mount Gaspar."

Allen flashed Wesley a surprised look and asked,

"What do you mean, you know where Screech is from and why he hangs around the occult?"

"Surely you know he's not a part of their organization," Wesley chided. "Oh, com'on, Allen! Does he behave anything at all like the others? You must have realized by now, Screech has an altogether different agenda."

"Of course, I've noticed!" Allen answered Wesley.

"So, then, can you give me an explanation as to where he's from and how he got there? Has Screech told you this or, like every one else, do you just have some lame-brained opinion concerning him?" Wesley challenged the younger man beside him.

"How is it you know so much about him?" Allen asked. "I would imagine he's some part of Chimera," he said.

"You're a quick study," Wesley grinned, and leaned over to pat him on the shoulder, a sort of you-catch-on-real-quick slap. "You see, Allen, it's people who've turned Chimera into something evil," Wesley explained. "The occult latched onto the idea of Chimera and raced with it, but just like most everything else, there are two sides to Chimera as well!" Wesley endeavored to enlighten him.

His passenger was silent. Maybe he was dumbfounded, Wesley thought. Allen might be blown away by this concept, but Wesley couldn't drop it. It was essential he explain these things to him for they would very soon be a part of the world he attempted to describe.

"Look," Wesley continued. "How can there be anything evil or wrong about Utopian daydreams?"

"I s'pose this depends upon whose daydreams you have in mind." Allen said, vocal again.

No doubt Allen thought the notion was a bunch of nonsense, Wesley suspected. At first, it might well sound like nothing more than foolishness, but it wasn't. There was a world of chimera and there had always been a world of chimera, and it was less than a day's trip away.

"What is awry about a child's dreams of Atlantis?" Wesley challenged. "What is immoral about a child's escape to the imaginary world of fantasy?" he asked, but didn't wait to hear a reply before he proclaimed, "Nothing! Absolutely nothing!"

Wesley brought his car to another standstill at the traffic light and they watched an old woman, bent over and worn by age, clinging to a walker which she slid along the crosswalk. It was a depressing sight.

"Watch!" Wesley exclaimed as he pointed the index finger of his right hand at the crosswalk, and at once there were four yellow birds with orange bills who followed after the woman. The one right behind her was big and noisy.

"Quack! Quack!" The duck prattled and three baby ducks followed her. Wesley laughed.

Then a middle-aged woman, also in the crosswalk, who was shaped like a butterball and wearing a flowered dress and a floppy straw hat, exclaimed,

"Oh, my lord! Would you look at that! Where did those ducks come from?"

"Shoo! Shoo!" An old man in suit and tie, chased after them, waving his fedora at the web-footed birds.

Wesley was laughing so hard he was in tears.

"Is this so awful Allen," he asked between gasps of laughter. "Now this is Chimera!" he exclaimed.

As the light turned green and they slowly proceeded forward again, they spotted the same aged woman on the sidewalk, now with the duck in her arms and three baby chickies wobbled noisely around her feet.

"You know what happens when evil people grab hold of chimera?" Wesley asked, and he believed he'd succeeded in making his point. "Other people wind up a calamity, sometimes slaughtered. Occasionally it's nothing short of a bloodbath, a holocaust!"

"It's been fun, Wesley," Allen admitted. "But what's your point?"

"I'm glad you asked me this." Wesley sat up straight, more sure than he'd ever been of his plans to kidnap Cadence. "There's a wonderful world of chimera on the opposite side of the mountain where Cadence Scott will be completely safe," Wesley told him. "Will you help me coax her there?" he said, looking directly at Allen.

"If it's the sort of place you've explained to me," Allen considered it, nodded his head and continued, "Yes, I will do it. However," he added, "If there's ever any time when I decide it's not how you described it, then I will take Cadence home with me."

"By all means," Wesley agreed, cheerfully, "It's a deal!"

As Wesley had hoped, there were kids in the ballpark, and as his Avenger came to a stop in the parking lot adjacent to the baseball diamond, both he and Allen saw the small crowd of kids wearing their caps and red and white uniforms. Their Coach, Tim Bailey, didn't appear to be anywhere around them, though.

Wesley saw the little girl, all alone, on a wooden bench outside of the ballpark. She was like a sitting-duck for any one in the occult, too accessible to them, and Wesley was moved with anger.

He could scarcely believe the adults were so negligent when there were dangerous crackpots on the prowl, and not just those of the occult, either. He opened his car door but felt something pull on his arm before he could get out.

"Wait," Allen tugged at him, "If anything should happen, you promise me, you will let me take Cadence home? If you don't, Wesley, so help me, I swear I'll…"

Wesley didn't let Allen finish his thoughts before interrupting him.

"I promise!" he said, and his anxiety for her safety was reflected in his eyes and voice. "If we don't do something soon, Allen, then Cadence might very well be injured or killed!"

He pointed to the little girl they could see through the car window.

"You see how thoughtless they are of her! Any nut-case could snatch her from that bench!" he said, as he jerked his arm away from Allen and bounded from the car.

Allen raced to catch up with him and they sauntered together over the park's luscious green grass toward Cadence Scott, who sat on the bench scratching her head.

When she saw them, she waved at Allen. Wesley's heart leaped in his chest and he knew he was smart to coax Allen into going with him.

Cadence seemed pleasantly surprised to see Allen. As they approached the bench, the little girl gave him a big smile and merriment shone in her blue eyes.

Wesley waited for Allen to say something, hoping he'd carry out their design to spirit Cadence away with them.

"Hi," Allen answered her. He sat down close beside her and Wesley waited for Allen to introduce him.

"Cadence, this is my friend, Wesley," he said, pointing at him.

Wesley offered her a big smile and answered,

"Hi Cadence!"

Cadence didn't respond right away but, instead, she gave him a once-over glance and said,

"Your hair is long."

Wesley wasn't sure whether Cadence approved of his mop of blond hair or not. He laughed and asked her,

"Do you like it? I just had it done! They call it winter meltdown." he joked, hoping to win her approval.

She laughed along with him. He compared her laughter to sweet music and wanted to take her in his arms and carry her safely away with him, but instead, he asked,

"How come you're not over there running those bases with them?" He gestured toward the ballpark and saw her older sister, Erin, wave to them. He waved back and glanced down at Cadence again. "I was here the other day when you made it to first base. They tagged you before you could reach home-plate, but I couldn't help notice what a fast runner you were, a regular Speedy Gonzales!" he praised her.

"Thanks," she said, but Wesley saw the frown on her angelic face. He was amazed how, close up, Cadence looked even more like the little girl locked away inside his mind.

"Erin says I can't play with them today. She says this is serious practice for the big game." Cadence admitted to him.

"Oh,no," Wesley groaned. "Erin isn't very smart not to let you play. You've got to be the fastest runner I've ever seen," he sympathized. "Why I bet even though I'm wearing my new tennis shoes, you might easily beat me, even!"

"Want to race?" she needled him with a grin. Excitement lit up her face as she jumped to her feet. She was no more than three and a half feet high, wearing blue jeans and t-shirt, with her curly blond hair stirred by the breeze. She gazed up into his eyes trustingly.

Kind eyes, both kind and playful eyes, she thought.

"You're on, Cadence!" Wesley accepted her invitation with a handshake.

Her little hand wrapped around his big thumb and he grasped it. He'd made a priceless connection with her and was determined to cultivate their friendship. He saw a Dogwood tree a half a block away and it's explosion of creamy white blossoms set it apart from all of the other trees growing around it.

"I will race you to the Dogwood tree over there," he said pointing to it.

"The Dogwood tree?" Cadence questioned him.

"The tree with white flowers." He pointed her attention to it, watching her carefully, happy to be holding her attention.

"I see it!" Cadence exclaimed. "I'll race you to the Dogwood tree," she repeated him.

"Allen, tell us when to go," Wesley called to him.

"Okay, go," Allen said and he sounded somewhat disinterested.

Wesley let Cadence take the lead. He would have let her win, except it would have served no purpose. He reached the Dogwood before she did, but not much ahead of her. Then with pretended glee, he jumped up and down and shouted,

"It's these new tennis shoes!" He laughed and fell on the ground beside her, where she lay breathing heavily, noisily gasping for air. Cadence had tried so hard to finish first.

He stretched and grabbed his feet and examined his shoes as though it amazed him.

"They told me when I bought these shoes, they'd make me run so fast nobody could ever catch up with me!"

"No way," she wheezed.

"No, really," he insisted. "I think these shoes must be magical or something! How else could I outrun you?" he asked her with a wide-eyed look. She sat up and stared at his shoes as though there might be something to what he told her.

"I have a brilliant idea!" he said, noticing Allen had crossed the park and now stood a few feet away. The question on Cadence's angelic face made him aware she hung on his words.

"How 'bout if we go pick up a pair of these for you?" he asked. "If you had your own pair, you'd be the fastest runner around!"

She shook her head at him.

"Why not?"

"Those shoes are too big for me," she announced. His shoes were so big she could almost swim in them.

He stood up and extended his hand to her, pulling her up onto her feet. Then he laughed and said,

"They come in little girl's sizes too! I saw a pair there just your size."

He saw her glance at the baseball diamond. Her sister had thrown another ball. There wasn't a chance their game would be over any time soon.

"What about Erin," Cadence questioned him. Her eyes went from Wesley's face to Allen's.

"We'll be back here before Erin even realizes we've left," Allen answered her, glancing at Wesley, who was grinning.

"That's right!" Wesley was excited as he got on one side of her with Allen on the other side. They gently lifted her in the air, on their way to Wesley's car.

Before Erin pitched another ball to the player on home plate, she glanced in the direction where she'd seen Allen and another man with her sister. She panicked when she realized they were gone.

Chapter 69

Tim Bailey sat at Paul's kitchen table and sipped the cold glass of iced tea Paul had made for him. He watched his Pastor and closest friend round something up for them to eat.

"Paul, you're the best preacher I've ever heard, the most charismatic pastor I've ever met, a compelling soul-winner and a compassionate shepherd." Tim praised his Pastor.

He had something on his mind, something he had to share with Paul for he disagreed with the way his Pastor handled his personal life and he was intent upon telling him so.

"But sometimes," he said, and made up his mind not to beat around the bush, "I swear you can be a pompous jackass!"

He nervously swallowed his iced tea and silently cringed for being so blunt. He glanced at the t.v. beside the toaster in the kitchen. It was on and he saw several kids circling a go-cart, something they'd had the ingenuity to create.

Meanwhile, Paul crossed the room and set a platter of Ritz crackers, cheese and slices of pepperoni on the table. Tim looked at him and thought he'd seen him looking better. There were dark circles under his eyes and a five o'clock shadow on his face.

"What's on your mind, Tim? Whatever it is, speak up, I need to hear it."

Paul sat down in the chair across from the elder of his church, his confidant, Tim Bailey, the man he trusted more than he trusted himself even.

"Pastor Guire managed somehow to convince you Kas was the ring leader of that esoteric society," Tim began. "He somehow made you believe she was a mole the occult had planted among us. However, if she was a mole, she surely kept it a secret all of these years." Tim ridiculed the whole far-out idea, finding it hard to believe Kas could ever be so two-faced.

Paul stared at the glass of iced tea setting in front of him, untouched. He shook his head.

"I've been thinking about it, dwelling upon it, and I've found lots of reasons to believe, otherwise. Things I never thought about at the time. You know, she was always reluctant to become involved in the church." he admitted to him with a frown.

"So, she seldom attended a pot-luck or a business meeting," Tim said, as he put slices of pepperoni and cheese between crackers. "She didn't head the women's missionary league and she seldom attended a prayer fellowship." After he'd prepared his food just right, he wolfed it down.

Paul interrupted him,

"It's more than that, Tim! You know it's far more serious…." Once more, for the umpteenth millionth time, his eyes filled with tears and he turned his head away, ashamed to show his emotions. "She's Rattler Mackenzie's daughter," he said, and his voice broke.

"So, you knew this when you married her," Tim argued with him.

"She never told me her father raped her and she'd had a child by him, Allen Carter, for crying out loud," he exclaimed, his voice growing louder. He put his fist over his mouth in an attempt to stifle his emotions.

"Yes, and instead of showing her any compassion you've thrown her out of her own house." he said, shaking his head. "We have far more regard for heathens and illegal aliens in this country than what you've shown toward Kas!"

With that said, he put together another bite-size snack.

"You make it sound like I'm to blame, like I'm a monster, or something," Paul sighed, heavily.

Tim looked right at him, nodded his head and answered,

"Yes, I do and this is exactly how it appears, too, Paul. Some twenty years ago, when you first came to Victoria Street, it was Kas who had the money to swing the deal on this house. Do you know why she left it behind? It wasn't because you threw her out, Paul…."

"What do you mean," Paul asked.

"Well, Kas left because it was the only thing she could think of to do to protect the girls, your daughters, Paul. The occult is after her and she left to protect you and the kids." he told him.

"Oh, no," Tim groaned, and turned his attention to the t.v. Paul's back was to it so he stood up and turned around to see what Tim thought was so deplorable.

There was a picture of Kas' car on the News, deserted and smashed. The newscaster explained it had been hit by an eighteen-wheeler. Some hit-and-run driver had demolished Kas' brand new Viper.

"Wonder who let this leak out?" Tim exclaimed. "This is going to cost her the election!" he added, and shook his head.

Under the circumstances, he was way off the mark and he surely sounded shallow, but the occult couldn't have known they would show this tragedy on the five o'clock news, he reasoned.

He saw Paul turn pale as he leaned against his chair, shattered by the catastrophe he saw on t.v.

"Where's Kas?" he muttered.

Chapter 70

When Kas opened her eyes, she was flat on her back on the cold, hard ground, staring up into something similar to Tolkien's rendition of a mythical entity called "Gollum".

The creature's insane-looking eyes bulged at her, and then dangled before her the golden heart-shaped pendant it had swiped from around her neck.

"Mine!" it told her, and folded its greedy fist around her necklace, then pressed it to it's bare chest.

"You son-of-a-bitch!" she breathed, surprised to find this thing, whatever it was, wasn't a nightmare, but it was much worse because it was real.

It put it's grotesque finger over her mouth and brought its ugly mug close to her face,

"Shush!" it had the audacity to tell her, "Daphne is coming." Then it withdrew its head and trembled. Or, at least, it looked to her like it quivered. She couldn't see very much in the dim light which enveloped them and her vision was further impaired by the wound on her forehead, she suspected. The gash she'd received when the eighteen-wheeler had smashed her automobile. Things looked fuzzy to her.

Apparently, Daphne had escaped her prison cell and was on her way to this eerie cavern, she guessed.

"Oh oh," the little thief who stood beside her breathed and she glanced at him.

Troubled by the others hostile actions, it crept backward, when the others surrounded it. Its fingers folded tightly around the necklace. Kas squirmed.

"Compromise," it appealed to them. "Balbo make deal!" It offered them a cut of its find.

"No deal!" The consort and spokesman for the others replied, shaking it's head vigorously. Greedy Balbo wasn't about to relinquish his jewels.

Kas felt some curious affinity for the bandit beside her. She couldn't have explained it if her life had depended upon it, but she felt the burden to defend Balbo against his gold digger relatives.

"Look, guys, it's costume jewelry," she said, and attempted to persuade them. "It's not worth the squabble," she impressed upon them.

She was caught right in the middle of their family feud so she tried to convince them to settle things without a lot of ruckus.

From far away, outside of the excavation, there was a swooshing sound, a noise which started as a low buzz but then grew louder. It wasn't her imagination because the others heard it too, and they reacted to it.

They seemed to forget all about the bargain-basement necklace and, as the whirling noise increased, they turned to each other with scared looks on their grotesque faces as they whispered to each other,

"Aurelius is coming, Aurelius is coming," repeatedly. "Hide!" They urged each other.

"No place to hide from Aurelius." Their leader, the one who'd been ready to kill Balbo for the cheap pendant, told his hearers.

"Who's Aurelius?" Kas asked Balbo.

Balbo glanced up at her and shuddered,

"Aurelius Numen, all-knowing, all-powerful Numen!"

"Aurelius is your god?" Kas inquired, and was taken aback when the blazing light suddenly occupied the trench. She heard a loud thump, followed by another one, and then another, Aurelius descending, clamboring down the stairway.

The enormous creature from another dimension or planet finally appeared, clothed in a bronze coat of armor, with a red cape around the shoulders. He was gigantic, and resembled the other beings, only much larger.

His size made him look more authoritative, too. He surely intimidated the creatures for they made not a sound. They stared at him in awe, and fell to their knees, prostrating themselves around Aurelius Numan's feet, which were shod in iron-hard footgear.

"My expedition through the elliptical galaxy has brought me here, at Rattler Mackenzie's request." he stated.

His eyes changed from the sapphire blue Kas had seen on all of their faces, to a fiery red, as though Aurelius's disposition had turned foul. Kas caught the frightened sighs of his devotees.

"What dilemma have you birdbrains come across which would make the rattlesnake imagine he could ever call upon me, the eminent Aurelius?" he inquired with a booming voice. It was obvious he lacked any consideration for his lowly subjects if, indeed, this was what they were.

Kas watched these creatures timidly point to her. She stood detached from their assemblage, yet, they seemed positive she was the reason the rattlesnake had contacted

Aurelius and interrupted his travels.

She gazed up at this gigantic brute before whom she appeared so feeble and, swallowing hard, somehow she managed to say,

"I'm sorry we disturbed your expeditions, Aurelius."

This one who explored their spiral galaxy made her realize how astronomical and all-encompassing the art of black magic had become.

"You are Rattler Mackenzie's progeny. The one whose destiny is to rule over this tiny planet," Aurelius proclaimed.

It may have been small but it was the only planet she knew about. She'd never seen the entire galaxy as this Herculean had and she had very little desire to see it now. Although, it would have been interesting had she been able to comprehend the enormous affects the occult had over space, every mile and inch of it. The thought horribly intrigued her.

"Have I no decision in this matter, Aurelius?" she appealed to the demonic sage.

Daphne staggered with amazement when she saw the behemoth spaceship, the vehicle she knew Aurelius had disembarked from, and she knew he was now in the underpass which had once been a shelter for the Delphians.

She knew she was not welcomed by this company of diabolical beings. They would not indulge her. It was appalling to find the fallen angels had dropped anchor inside the tunnel and now one of their own crowned heads was in there with them.

She stood amidst the ruins which was once Chimera, surrounded by mounds of clay, the graves of her poor, misfortunate followers who'd been killed by the inferno. She shivered to think what the serpentines would do to her if they discovered she lingered nearby.

She wondered who was behind their hostile incursion here. She had a sneaking suspicion Kastanje was somewhere about, probably down there in the tunnel with them. After all, she'd soon be their affiliate in a manner of speaking. *Roll out the old and ring in the new*, Daphne thought, filled with animosity toward Kastanje.

Suddenly, she heard a noise. Dangerously, nearby she heard someone whisper,

"All hell has broken lose, Jonathan! We're in one heap of trouble now!"

She easily identified Archie's voice, and the ghost of Jonathan Wright must have been somewhere nearby, too. Concealed behind an upright slab of what once was their headquarters, Daphne gazed around to see if she could spot Archie.

Finally, she saw him in clear view, standing amongst the ruins with an astonished look on his face. She remembered Archie had never seen Aurelius, or his spaceship, before and he looked shocked to see the saucer now.

Archie was astonished. So much so, he forgot everything else, where he was and what he was doing there. This was the first starship he'd ever encountered.

He was unaware these things truly existed. Although he'd heard about the Project Daedalus and Project Longshot, too, he thought they were just tales of something which could be available sometime in the distant future. He'd never dreamed he'd actually see a flying object so close up.

"It must be a faster-than-light ship, Jonathan," Archie muttered. "Transcending our current understanding of physics." he said, finding it impossible to take his eyes off of the enormous ship. A spaceship this size must have carried a lot of passengers, he imagined.

"Psst!"

He heard someone call, and suddenly he became aware of his precarious situation, a visible object to whatever had landed in their midst.

He turned his head away from the huge machine to look about, finally spotting Daphne Orion cloaked in obscurity.

Inching backward, step-by-step, until he finally reached her, his eyes still glued upon the extraordinary UFO, he asked,

"What is going on?"

"What's the sense of hiding if you're going to shout?" she chided him.

"What on earth is that thing?" he demanded.

"It's Aurelius Numen's spacecraft," she explained to him. "I imagine someone signaled him, although I can't imagine who?"

Daphne looked around to see if they still remained undiscovered. When she saw the strange-looking men, or robots, dressed in bronze suits, covered from head to toe, she released a horrified sigh. The three barbarians were headed in their direction and she was beyond being scared. She told Archie,

"You're about to find out…!"

Chapter 71

"When I consider Thy heavens, the work of Thy fingers, the moon and the stars, which Thou hast ordained; What is man, that Thou art mindful of him? and the son of man, that Thou visitest him?"—Psalm 8:3-4

Upon the wood, in calligraphy, these words were scrawled.

The old woman went to work removing the loafs of bread from the ancient potbelly stove. Her aged hands wrapped in oven gloves, carefully took the twelve loafs of wheat cakes from the oven and then set these on the couner and allowed the oven's door to slam shut.

She wouldn't horde her scrumptious handiwork but share these with the creatures who also occupied a space on the mountain. The animals were her furry friends and good company, as well.

Turning around she surveyed her cabin. Yes, it was just a cabin, although, old world, it was cozy and the yellow curtains on the small windows made it seem more cheerful, too.

She was surprised to find she was not alone as she had imagined, though. On closer scrutiny, she saw three individuals, two men and a little girl at her door, who had let themselves in.

"Well, you may as well come the rest of the way inside," she told them. "Come in, Wesley," she called to him. "Bring your little troop with you so I can get a closer gander at them," she requested.

"Daisy O'Brien!" he exclaimed, dancing across the crickity old floor followed by Allen and the beautiful child.

"Daisy, ole girl, I've never seen anyone able to hide from you!" he laughed merrily, as he lead his friends to her. "She claims to be as blind as a bat," he cupped his hand over his mouth and whispered to them.

"Blind, perhaps, but I'm not deaf, Wesley," she admonished him, and once he was within her reach she threw her arms around his shoulders and pulled him closer to her.

Allen and Cadence gaped at the woman who gave Wesley an affectionate squeeze. Her white hair was piled high upon her head, fastened there by numberous bobby pins. The woman, in dress and apron, seemed incredibly sharp and healthy, there was no doubt about that.

"Let me look at you!" She pulled away from him and examined his countenance and then frowned, maximizing the crinkles around her mouth.

"You haven't changed, not an iota, Wesley," she murmured. "Not an iota," she repeated. "Still the very same Wesley!" she chided him, and patted his cheek with her hand, still covered with the glove she'd worn to remove the loafs from the oven.

"Child!" she gushed, and gazed down at Cadence, cupping her hand beneath her chin. "You are every bit as lovely as I had imagined!" she insisted.

Bending over, she looked the little girl in the eyes and said, "You must be Cadence Scott!"

Cadence nodded, surprised by Daisy's amazing insight.

"How did you know?" Cadence asked her.

The old woman straightened her posture and patted her head with her gloved hand.

"Why, it's all in here, my dear! It's all in here," she stressed. "and this is just where it's going to stay, too."

Then she turned her attention to Allen.

"Allen Carter!" she beamed at him, and put her arms around his shoulders while placing a wet kiss on his cheek. "The raven you call Screech has told me all about you," she divulged. "He says you are woefully out of place, lost in a jungle of corruption, is what he claims. Is this true, Allen?" She gave him a hard look. Wisdom sparkled in Daisy's eyes.

"Not any more, Daisy." he meekly confessed.

"Good," she retorted, "See that you stay away from that sordid gang. You'll be much better off if you do," she admonished him.

"Come, now, I've made bread and I still have enough honey and homemade blueberry jam tucked away. Just enough to fill your empty stomachs," she said, and she escorted them to the table and cheerfully waited on them.

The aroma of Daisy's bread filled the house and made their stomaches growl. As sunlight danced upon Daisy's table, they ate the delicious bread and Wesley told her what he was doing there and why he'd brought Cadence, as well as Allen, to her.

"So, you can see, Daisy," he finished his explanation and popped another piece of the warm bread covered with blueberry jam into his mouth, "We came to you for advice."

He told the old woman all about Cadence's troubles in words he knew the little girl couldn't possibly comprehend. There was no way, after he'd delivered his spiel, the little girl could know the height or the depth of the kind of trouble she was in.

When he had finished, Daisy nodded with understanding. She patted him on the back and said,

"A hideaway, some ivory tower, just until so much strife should blow over."

She eyed the beautiful child beside her who was on her knees on the chair licking the blueberry jam off the slice of bread.

"These little ones whose angels always behold the face of God," Daisy hummed, as she brushed Cadence's long curls away from her face.

She folded her arms on the table and shook her head with dismay.

"There's no way my granddaughter, Daphne, is going to accept defeat, not without causing some major disturbance."

Allen looked at her with surprise.

"Daphne Orion is your granddaughter, Daisy?" he inquired. He was shocked by this information for he couldn't imagine Daisy and Daphne had anything in common with each other.

"I'm afraid so," she said, "Of course, she's changed her last name from O'Brien to Orion, said it had something to do with astrology and new age." She then stood up to clear the table, collecting all the saucers and taking them to the double-basin sink. "The Lord God knows how to humble this old soul," she said. "Like a thorn in my heart, that one!"

She immersed the dishes in a sinkful of lukewarm water and soap-suds. Leaving them to soak, she removed the towel from the bar to dry her hands.

"Desmond Papers is Daphne's errand boy. Yes ma'm, no ma'm, whatever you wish ma'm. Desmond is nothing but Daphne's toy, her marionette." she said, expressing her grief over the sort of alliance Daphne had with the present Senator of California.

"Blood is thicker than water and I imagine the grody old snake will go to any lengths to establish his daughter in the senate, though."

Rowr, came the growl at the window, so blatant and chilling it made everyone turn their heads.

"It's just a bear!" Cadence shouted, and the bear, separated from them only by the thin wiry screen, cast its dark round eyes at the child.

"Jaban is one of four cubs born to Amarisa just last spring," Daisy explained to Cadence, who'd never seen a real bear anywhere else but at the zoo. That seemed like a long time ago to a little girl who adored animals of every type, shape, shade and color.

"Alright, Jaban," Daisy called to the cub. "You'll get your share of bread in a minute." she promised him. Then, turning to the little girl whose eyes were round saucers and shone so sweetly, she added, "Would you like to help feed the animals, Cadence?"

Allen, though, became frightened for their safety. Jabin's Mamma, he imagined, would be nearby and most likely even bigger and more rowdy than her cub.

"Are you sure it's safe?" he asked, and turned to look at Wesley.

"I'm sure," Wesley smiled, and patted his arm. "Daisy and the animals in this area are buddies! They share a healthy respect for each other," Wesley said, while rising from his chair. He followed the females to the door and motioned for Allen to tag along, too. "This is something you've got to see to believe, Allen!" he exclaimed.

Just outside Daisy's door there was a field of abundant grass. They followed the old woman as she pursued Jabin, a timid animal, Daisy said, and explained how he had never come to her house to beg for food before. According to her, Jabin was the shyest of all four of Amarisa's cubs; Zimbri, Solomon, Uriah and Jabin.

Allen knew they were following Jabin straight to a den of fierce bears, and he wondered if they weren't being somewhat foolish.

As they made their way around blossoms of yellow show, orange desert mariposa and purple sand verbena, though, he was elated with the natural beauty around him. It was much more lovely and peaceful than the crowded city streets and the busy cluttered gridlock of the valley. He'd never guessed such tranquility could thrive almost next door to the Delphian's snake pit.

How had Daphne ever been so sidetracked? he wondered. This was far more like the stories she'd told him about Chimera. It was a Shangri-la, similar to the Garden of Eden.

Cadence lost her awareness of the others as she pursued a Monarch butterfly.

"Screech!" Allen shouted and he pointed to the sky. The raven was soaring above their heads. Then he almost stumbled over the cub bear, Jabin, who'd stopped directly in front of him.

Jabin called their attention to a spot of earth. Buried in blood-stained grass,they found Jabin's brother, Solomon. At least, what remained of Solomon after something had mangled the bear to pieces.

Daisy groaned. Something or someone had invaded paradise. The old woman almost lost her balance. She dropped her bread and leaned heavily upon Wesley.

"There's never been a vicious animal around here, ever," she fretted, as tears filled her eyes. "Something must have followed you here, Wesley," she said, and torment rang in her voice.

Chapter 72

Cadence took Wesley's hand. The hours had raced away and it was long past time for her nap. Much had happened during the day and she was exhausted, although she'd never admit it.

They'd kept her from seeing anything of Jabin's brother's mangled body. She'd watched Wesley, with shovel in hand, bury poor Solomon, so she knew he was dead, though. Poor, poor Solomon, what an awful way to end up.

Jabin hadn't come to Daisy's to beg for food, but to share his tragic loss with her, and to alarm her to whatever danger now lurked about.

Cadence laid down on Daisy's bed, still clinging to Wesley and unwilling to let him go until she was fast asleep.

"I want to pray for Jabin!" She looked into his loving eyes. "Jabin has a mammoth ache inside him now," she struggled to explain as she pointed to her heart, expressing her own feelings over her loss, being pulled apart and separated from her parents and her sisters.

"I think this is a good idea." Wesley encouraged her, and he knew she wanted to pray for Jabin right then so he lowered his head, closed his eyes, and listened to her sweet voice appeal to whatever force might care enough to listen.

"Dear God," Cadence said, "Repair the terrible wound in Jabin's heart after losing his brother, Solomon today."

Wesley thought it might be crazy, and he'd surely never admit it to anyone, but it felt to him as though her prayers went somewhere, some place he had only heard about and entertained no thought of ever going.

Wesley quietly closed the door behind him as he left the bedroom. Daisy was sitting at one end of the table, beneath the glow from the ceiling light, while Allen leaned against a yellow bamboo hamper on the opposite side of the room.

"She's asleep," Wesley reported to them.

"Poor girl," Daisy murmured, and her voice was filled with pity. "The tragedy she's been exposed to is something she'll never forget. It might even affect the rest of her life," she added, with much concern.

"Wesley and I made a deal before coming here." Allen said, and referred to the agreement they'd made concerning Cadence's safety.

Wesley shook his head and his eyes went to the floor, his mind crammed with difficult thoughts.

"Daisy, I've been less than honest with you," he confessed.

"Go ahead, Wesley, I'm listening," the old woman replied.

The look she gave him sent shivers down his spine. Daisy was wiser than most. He suspected, right from the beginning, Daisy knew what real motives drove him, in spite of the way he had tried to manipulate her, tried to convince her he had only Cadence's safety in mind.

Now he paced the floor with discomfort as an inner voice badgered him.

"I tried to make you believe I was only trying to protect the child." He glanced at both Daisy and Allen and then quickly turned his eyes away from their faces. He couldn't look at them and confess to being fraudulent too.

"My real motives were selfish, though," Wesley said. "What I really wanted was several more hours with Caroline. Just enough time to bring her here, to show her this amazing place. Therefore, I went to great lengths to deceive you both." He paused and gazed at their crestfallen faces.

Allen shifted his gaze, painfully aware, once more, someone had taken advantage of the good faith he had put in them. He eyed Daisy and wondered how she would respond to being lied to and manipulated.

Allen saw her wipe a tear from her cheek. Then gently confide in her young friend,

"I knew this, Wesley. Not for one minute would I allow you to ever deceive me. I only prayed, eventually, you would 'fess up, admit to your wrong-doing."

However, despite the compassion in Daisy's eyes, Wesley told himself she would never forgive him if she knew the depth of deceit he'd exposed her to and the murder he'd carried out.

"Wesley," once more a distant voice, somewhere beyond his present surroundings called to him. He recognized the voice, it belonged to Carla, the woman he had killed.

He was sure Carla had something to do with Solomon's death, the cub's mangled body. Now Carla wanted him, perhaps to mutilate his body the same way.

The banshee would gain what she sought. Insanity would give way and allow her access. One could play-act at something, pretend to be something they weren't, even deceive others, but in the end truth would prevail.

He hurried to the chair next to the old woman and sat down beside her. There was some comfort beside Daisy. At least, for now, he was safe from the demons which plagued him.

"Daisy, remember when I was a boy, not much older than Cadence, when I first came across Chimera, tucked away and surrounded by desert willows and beautiful plants? Do you recall when I followed your husband, Titus, around everywhere?" Wesley enquired of her with excitement.

"I remember," Daisy nodded at him. "Even then you were less than truthful." Daisy said."I warned you then, against deceitful ways!" she scolded him.

She took both of his hands with her own and grasped them tightly, so tightly Wesley felt trapped.

"God doesn't care for deceit," she argued. "Come clean, Wesley, there's blood on your hands!" she badgered him for a confession.

He pulled away from her, got up and marched across the room. Allen stood beside the door. He had half a mind to block Wesley's exit. Later he would wish he had done so.

"Take Cadence home with you, Allen," Wesley knuckled under, believing, after all, he had no solutions for her. He wasn't innocent like Allen and he wasn't judicious like Daisy. He was no role model for Cadence or Caroline, he thought, turning once more to the old woman.

"I will face the devil alone, Daisy!" he told her.

Finally, he left the shelter of Daisy's small and durable cabin to answer the banshee's summons.

"Over here, Wesley…," the voice called to him, luring him onward through the lengthening shadows of nightfall. Wesley pursued the voice through the thick grass, some of it waist high. Then he heard the devilish utterance.

"Why did you kill me, Wesley?"

The voice was impossible to pinpoint. Carla's bitter call sounded from every which way. Seemingly from behind the Juniper tree he heard her say,

"Don't give me the idiotic account you have told every one else. I was there, I remember, Wesley!"

He stumbled along, haunted by the banshee's bitter words. His bizarre bout with an avenging spirit who stabbed his conscience.

"I trusted you, but just like the little girl and the old woman, you fooled me, too."

The voice drew him onward and pinned him to the Juniper tree. Pressed against it, he could go no further, and then he was conscious of eerie growls; fierce phantoms; white wolves with blood in their eyes.

Their swift feet trampled the grass, and left footprints behind. The wolves leaped upon him and knocked him to the ground, diabolical beasts turning this portion of paradise into hades.

Their knife-like teeth tore at his flesh. He writhed in pain, trying to fight them off. Now, remembering Daisy's admonition but it was too late. As the phantoms with their sharp teeth pierced and sliced at him, tearing him apart, Wesley wished he hadn't lied to Daisy.

Carla's spirit stood over the mutilated dead body, staring at what remained of her old lover after the wolves had destroyed him.

As though proud of their handiwork, the wolves gathered around her. They were as devoted to her as Cinnamon had been, except the wolves were vicious.

She turned away from the bloody carnage and gazed around her, and at the old woman's cabin across the field. The smoke from Daisy's furnace arose from her chimney and whirled into space. This place gave Carla the creeps.

The awful stench of honor and principle, like logs burning in the old woman's stove, except their smell was obnoxious to her. They couldn't stay here, she thought.

Daisy sat in her rocking chair, with the child bundled in her arms, and rocked back and forth while she hummed, *'Eidleweiss'*.

Just outside of her small home there arose a loud clatter. It wasn't the sound of the wind whipping through the trees which produced the unearthly racket.

It was the noise of Deedra's dirge and Daisy knew enough to grasp the state of affairs. There was a foul odor in the air, the scent of murder and Deedra lamented the awful bloodshed.

The wolves howled with delight and Deedra wept. The louder the noise grew, the more stubbornly Daisy repelled the disorder. She fixed herself to the chair, kissed the child's brow, and continued to hum and rock.

Allen paced the floor, treading across the crickity old boards until, finally, he couldn't take any more and he turned to look at Daisy and Cadence.

"I'm going to see what's become of Wesley." he anxiously told them.

The old woman didn't answer him. Cadence stirred in her lap and Daisy hummed but did not acknowledge him.

As he left her hut, he heard Cadence ask Daisy where he was going and he heard the old woman tell her,

"He'll be back, Dear."

Daisy's response gave him the courage he needed to investigate.

Chapter 73

Pastor Paul watched Erin closely, and tried hard to understand as she struggled to explain what had happened,

"I saw Allen and another guy with Cadence, just before they disappeared." Erin went on. "I've looked everywhere, the park is empty, no one is there and Cadence is gone," she cried. "I know I shouldn't have let her out of my sight!" She was a basket case.

Crystal arrived home and, with a grimace, she opened the sliding door.

"No sign of Cadence anywhere," she reported to them.

She had combed the neighborhood in her car, stopping to ask neighbors and friends if they'd seen her sister. No one had seen her, but many of them had seen her mother's crushed automobile on the t.v. news, and those who had were sympathetic.

Tim was glued to the t.v. set as he watched CNN tally the votes. Despite the awful dilemma, Kas maintained a leading edge over Desmond Papers.

He found it almost unbelieveable how, less than an hour ago, the station had slipped and shown a picture of the nominee's wrecked car on the freeway, but still the race for the senate continued without interference, as though her presence was unnecessary. In fact, it looked to him, like Kas didn't even have to be alive in order to win the race for Senator of California.

"How are they going to conjure up a representative once Kas wins?" Tim muttered, baffled by what he saw on the t.v.

It was obvious to him she was, indeed, going to win for the results were almost all in. Either they knew where she was, and they could somehow exhibit her when the time came for her acceptance speech, or those sorcerers would conjure up a close carbon-copy of her.

"I'd wager to bet the occult knows where both Kas and Cadence have disappeared to!" Tim said, and elbowed the Pastor. "Paul, look at this, this is outlandish!" he exclaimed.

330

"Not now, Tim," Paul answered, panic-stricken over both his wife and his little girl, their adversity, and the disaster which had fallen upon his family.

Suddenly, there was a pounding noise at their front door and they exchanged anxious looks. Paul suspected it might be the occult and they might have more esoteric activities planned for them. He didn't know whether to answer the front door, or direct all those inside to attempt a quick get-away through the back door.

"Dad, someone has to answer the door," Crystal appealed to him.

Whoever it was, whatever it was, now rang the doorbell over and over again. Finally he made a decision, left the kitchen and went to the front door, followed by his two daughters.

Concealed behind their father, the girls watched as he opened the door. Standing there was a uniformed policeman. He tipped his cap at them and said,

"I'm Officer Dell Newlyn. May I come in?" He directed the question to the Pastor, who wore a five-o'clock-shadow on his face and a fretful look in his eyes.

Paul opened the screen door and made way for Officer Newlyn to enter his home.

As the policeman entered, he removed his cap and said,

"Pastor, there's no easy way to tell you this, but your wife's car, a silver Viper registered to Mrs. Kastanje Scott, was located on the freeway about an hour ago, abandoned and showing significant damage."

"Yes," Paul concurred, "I know. We saw it on the news, Officer Newlyn." Paul was being stoic and managed to conceal his terror-stricken state of mind.

Officer Newlyn caught a glimpse of Erin behind her father and nodded to her.

"Are you also aware, Pastor, only minutes ago, one of our officers came across your little girl, there," he pointed to Erin. "and she reported to him how her sister was missing? Has she been recovered yet, Pastor Scott?" Newlyn asked him.

"No," Paul answered with glazed eyes and unsteady voice.

"Then we have two major dilemmas on our hands, don't we, sir?" Newlyn said, taking a couple more steps into the room. He gazed around and immediately spotted the picture on the wall, a framed photograph of the Pastor and his lovely family.

"Is this the little girl we're looking for?" Newlyn asked, and directed their attention to the picture.

"Yes," Paul answered him.

Paul recalled what Tim had told him only minutes ago, how he believed the occult had managed to take both Kas and Cadence. He also remembered Roosevelt Shuyler and Lorraine Martin at one time had claimed the occult's headquarters was located on Mount Gaspar.

"Sir," Newlyn said, and interrupted Paul's musing. "I saw your wife at the Pet Emporium just before the accident on the freeway occurred." he informed the Pastor.

"The Pet Emporium," Crystal whispered. "Jesse Petersen works there."

Newlyn recalled the foreboding threat scribbled in blood-red letters on one wall of the pet store,

"Keep your mouth shut, Jesse, or Hank is next!"

He went on to inform them,

"Your wife directed my attention to a locked door behind which we, both the Attorney and I, discovered Detective Cody Baldwyn's body, torn to shreds by some mysterious predator." He drew a long breath before adding, "Attorney Scott claimed the occult was behind the

Detective's dreadful death and demanded I write it up, how the occult had murdered the Detective."

Cody Baldwyn was dead, Paul thought and shook his head with remorse.

"Officer Newlyn, I believe the Delphians, on top of Mount Gaspar, now have my wife and my daughter, and it's crucial we should go there at once!" Paul had made up his mind. He struggled to explain his reasons,

"It seems Daphne Orion has raised my wife's dead father from the crypt! Mackenzie turned himself into a rattlesnake, and the whole thing is so weird it boggles one's mind to contemplate it! However, I believe we'll find those sorcerers on top of Mount Gaspar. And I also believe my wife and daughter are being held there, too!" He was determined to rescue them before it was too late.

Tim came into the living room, a shocked look on his face, and reported to Paul,

"Desmond Papers just conceded his race for the senate and says he will now put all of his effort into supporting the new Senator of California, Kastanje Scott!" He glanced at his watch and said, "Yet, there are still three hours before the polls even close!"

He shook his head and wondered how in the world someone in Kas' situation could run the state of California. She couldn't, he concluded, and someone else would. Those devil worshippers whose headquarters was on Mount Gaspar would do it.

Chapter 74

The bondsmen who worked for Aurelius were extremely rough with Daphne, hoisting her through the air and down the stairs, followed by several of the banshees. All at once Daphne's scream,

"My water has broken!" rang through the air.

Kas heard the screams, and saw through the light which radiated from Aurelius like a fluorescent aura, the two whisps of vapor, or spirits. Both ghosts appeared to her to be females.

The cyborgs in copper suits and helmets dropped Daphne on the cold hard ground and left her there for the banshees to watch. They were brutal and inhumane with their captives, both Daphne Orion and Archie Petersen.

Archie fared even worse than Daphne. The androids who'd captured him chained his body to the wall and allowed Balbo and his relatives to take turns throwing darts at him.

"Missed!", "Try again," Kas heard their grunts and shrieks.

This hole was nothing less than hell, Kas thought. So far, though, no one but Balbo had attacked her, and all he wanted was the pendant she wore around her neck, which he still clenched in his grisly little hand.

Daphne had been left on the ground like a sack of grain, and her screams echoed through the cavern. The two feminine phantoms established their intentions. One of them said loudly enough for everyone to hear,

"Hell wants your baby, Daphne."

Like midwives from another world, they went right to work, collecting what they had come for from Daphne's womb, even as she moaned and screamed for them to go away.

"You can't take my baby! It's mine!" she yelled at them.

She sounded a lot like Balbo and the noise he'd made over the heart-shaped necklace.

Meanwhile, Aurelius looked on with a sour face and Kas could tell he was unhappy over the entire chaotic situation. He still seemed confused as to why the rattlesnake had interrupted his travels aboard his spaceship for what he concluded to be worthless human activities. There were other spheres, Mercury and Venus to explore, galaxies where no man had gone. Such distant places filled his mind and he had no time for petty pursuits.

More cyborgs came down the stairs and they had Allen Carter with them. The moment Kas saw the young man her heart went out to him.

"Allen!" she cried, and was prompted to tell these cybernetic organisms to release him.

They wouldn't have listened to her, though, or might rough him up even more, just out of spite. They seemed to understand nothing but barbarity.

When they set Allen down on the ground, Kas hurried to him. She touched his arm, and then smoothed the hair back from out of his eyes, examining his face.

"Are you alright?" she whispered to him.

"Fine, I think." he replied.

She imagined he'd seen this underpass before, and may have even helped build it. After all, he'd been a member of the occult. She was still upset with him over his involvement with this depraved crowd. She realized she was feeling like a mother with a wayward child, and resolved to guard her emotions.

Aurelius turned and gave him a long, piercing look, as though contemplating what to do with the young man, and if he might hold any value to him. Kas was horrified by th thought she might lose Allen as abruptly as she had gained access to him.

"Have you seen these foul creatures before?" she whispered to him.

"Only Daphne and Archie," he replied, and then added. "I wish the Pastor was here."

"Me too!" Kas answered, and her heart ached for Paul. She wondered if they'd ever be together again.

Things changed when a scream rang through the tunnel. Daphne's baby had arrived, and the outcry which followed astonished them. Apparently it was still undecided as to whether Daphne would be allowed to keep her baby, or if the unearthly midwives would take him from her.

"His name is Brutus." One of the spirits divulged as she wrapped him in blankets.

Aurelius sauntered over to the other-worldly female and demanded she hand the baby over to him.

Listless, and lieing in a pool of blood, Daphne reached for her baby and weakly called for him.

"He's mine," she pleaded with Aurelius and the ghost, but both of them ignored her pleas.

Obviously, the female spirit felt she was no match for Aurelius and she handed him Daphne's son.

With the tiny baby cradled in his powerful arms, mighty Aurelius turned and started toward the stairs. His cyborgs followed him and so did Balbo and his allies.

"You can't leave me here!" Archie entreated him.

Archie was still chained to the wall. The darts the miniature monsters had thrown at him were scattered on the ground around his feet. A couple of the little devils had been lucky and managed to hit their target. Blood issued forth from Archie's forehead and left shoulder.

"Take me with you aboard your spaceship, Aurelius," he begged him.

Aurelius turned around to look at him and then, with an arrogant sneer, he replied,

"What need has the all-sufficient Aurelius for a potbellied pig?" and without a second thought he added, "Kill him, Zorian!"

The android left his Captain's side and strolled over to where Archie was bound. He withdrew his long, sharp knife from its sheath at his side and drove the blade into Archie's stomach. Kas turned her head away, repulsed by the blood which oozed forth.

Archie shook his head and sadly whispered,

"I wish so much things had been different!" Kas was moved by his dying words and bowed her head.

Then Aurelius cast his gaze on Allen. No stone could be left unturned. Allen seemed to interest him and he told his androids.

"Bring the young man, too. I think I will make a swell captain out of him," he said, with as much glee as Aurelius could ever be expected to display. His slaves quickly moved to obey their master's orders.

"No!" Kas shouted at them. "Take me, instead!" she beseeched him.

"Take her, Aurelius," Daphne concurred. She seemed to have regained enough strength and realized all she had left, now, was her strong desire to rule the world without interference.

Aurelius laughed at both women.

"Leave the young man behind to be pampered by the females, then. He'll soon learn it's a fate worse than death," and he laughed again.

"Balbo," he turned to the little elf who followed him like a faithful pet. "You stay here," he told him.

Balbo seemed shocked by this bizarre change of plans. He'd been all prepared to board the spacecraft and travel to unknown galaxies with his kinsmen and his heroic Captain.

"Balbo go too, Sir!" He stamped the ground, flapped his arms and petitioned him. However, Aurelius would not be swayed.

Kas almost felt sorry for the small beastly creature. She heard Aurelius issue still another order.

"Elias, take the jewelry Balbo has in his hand. This will teach the imp to share with others."

"No, mine!" Balbo backed away from them. "It's mine!" he insisted, and made as much noise over the cheap jewelry as Daphne had when Aurelius took her son.

"Wait," Kas shouted. "Hasn't Balbo suffered enough? You're leaving him stranded here! For pete's sake, let Balbo have the cruddy old pendant! How is this going to hurt the mighty Aurelius?" she mocked him.

The Captain shook his head at her and proclaimed,

"This is exactly how you will lose your position in the global plan. You've lost the ability to take orders!" he admonished her. However, Aurelius turned his attention away from Balbo and continued up the stairs, his crew following in the footsteps of their Captain.

As they disappeared through the narrow doorway, Kas and Allen realized there was no one to stop their flight now. After waiting another few minutes, they raced up the stairs.

Something, or someone, fell upon Kas and knocked her down. Her feet flew out from under her and she slid the rest of the way down the stairway with Daphne right on her back.

"Bitch!" Daphne yelled at her with so much hatred. "I've lost my son and I'll be damned if you will make it out of here with yours!"

Kas threw her off of her back and got to her feet. Allen watched, dazed by the words

Daphne had hurled at the Pastor's wife.

Kas turned to look at Daphne,

"Where you're going, they won't let you keep your baby, anyway, Daphne!" she lashed back. "Which is a good thing, because you'd soon kill him for fussing! Brutus is safer with Aurelius on his spaceship then he'd be with you," she asserted.

"I came here for one reason and that is to get rid of you!" Daphne shouted, losing all control. "I will rule over the new world! Me and not you!" she swore.

At that moment it seemed a bolt of electricity struck Daphne, sweeping through her body and flowing out to strike Kas, hurling her through the air. It shot her backward like a bullet and slammed her body against the wall. Her head struck a protruding boulder which knocked her unconscious.

Allen looked at Daphne, enraged at what she had done to the Pastor's wife.

"You killed her, Daphne! You killed her and you will pay in hell for her death too!" he screamed at her.

She laughed at him,

"Do you think your threats bother me, Allen?" Her face took on a hateful expression as she pointed to Kas and sneered, "There's your dead biological mother! She bore you and now you can bury her!"

Balbo made his way to Kas, gazing down at her as though considering her plight. She sat upright but her body looked limp and lifeless.

He couldn't understand the meaning of many words human beings used, words like 'death' baffled him. No one ever died in the world he was from. Balbo was already thousands of years old.

He opened his clenched fist with the golden necklace in his palm. Slowly he bent over and offered it to her, wishing she would open her pretty eyes and take it from him. He would gladly surrender it to her then.

"Yours," Balbo appealed to her.

Chapter 75

As Paul's Lincoln Navigator wound it's way up Mount Gaspar, he turned a sharp curve and those inside his van saw the aerial phenomena hover over the mountain.

In the dusk, they could see the millions of lights which circled the manned spacecraft, and could hear the swooshing throbbing noise its engines made as the bronze saucer hung there, suspended in flight.

They followed close behind Dell Newlyn's marked vehicle and Tim stuck his upper torso through the opened window to get an even better look at the strange craft. He was dizzy over the sight, the enormity of it.

"I've heard of these things," he shouted to the others in the car. "I've never seen one, though!"

Paul swallowed hard and gripped his steering wheel with apprehension.

"I hope Mom and Cadence aren't inside that thing!" Crystal exclaimed from the backseat. She remembered the awful way she'd treated her mother the last time she'd seen her. Now she wished she could relive the episode.

The UFO hovered over the mountain for only a couple of minutes before it darted off, through the heavy criss-cross clouds, and into space. Paul knew if Kas and Cadence were inside of it he likely would never see them again. What an awful fate, he thought, and kept telling himself they weren't on board the spaceship.

Tim returned to his former position and, settling into his seat again, he jabbered nervously,

"I wish I'd had my camera! I'd like to have taken a picture of it and shared it with Chenoa and the boys!"

Dell's car slowed and came to a standstill near where the UFO had been when they saw it. Paul parked his van beside the car and watched Dell get out. He turned his head to tell Crystal and Erin, in the backseat,

"Be careful and use your heads. If something looks suspicious to you…stay away from it. I suspect there are a lot of suspicious looking things around here!" He gazed around at the barren scene. The whole thing certainly looked unwelcoming to him.

Inside the dank, dark tunnel, Balbo heard the chilling hiss of a rattlesnake. It terrified him for he recognized a common enemy. Snakes didn't like Hobgoblins any more than Hobgoblins liked Snakes and this was no ordinary garden variety Snake.

Once more, he turned his attention to the lovely creature who sagged against the wall and hadn't moved since the she-devil put her there.

There was one dismal chance in hell the snake, who was now on its slippery way toward the beautiful blond, might awaken her but Balbo wasn't about to stick around to find out. Not when his chances of leaving this disaster behind seemed pretty good at the moment.

He folded his fingers around the heart-shaped pendant and scurried to the stairway, pausing to look back one more time. The snake was close beside the woman now, and surprisingly, he heard it speak to her,

"Sweet Pea, you won! You won the race for senate by a landslide! You are the new Senator of California!"

Balbo shook his head with pity at the woman's predicament, and her anguish too, if by some miraculous fluke, she ever woke up.

Then he proceeded up the stairs and poked his head through the open doorway and looked around. His heart was beating like a trip-hammer, and his adrenalyn soared.

Outside of the tunnel he saw the wreckage of Chimera, the chunks of cement, burnt wood and the piles of worthless junk. Then he saw metal machines on belts of black rubber, with people similar to the humans inside the tunnel standing beside them.

As Balbo took in the carnage, he saw an aged human come out of the woodland with a little girl in her arms. The woman was wrapped in radiant light and the sight of her distressed him deeply. He knew he had no other choice, now, but to escape while he still could, before it was too late. Before the radiance which surrounded the woman moved closer and enveloped him in it's snare.

Balbo moved quickly through the wreckage, made his escape, and sped to freedom.

The Pastor stood right behind Officer Dell Newlyn as Dell loaded his gun. Crystal and Erin carefully got out of their dad's van, questioning whether they would find their mother here.

Crystal was awe-struck by the horror and devastation. Few people would even think to look for their mother at such a place as this. Erin was scared the UFO had taken both Cadence and her mother, and where they would wind up was impossible to try to imagine.

As Dell loaded the clips into his gun he sensed an extraordinary presence nearby, and then felt a fleshy hand against his sleeve. With alarm, he looked around and saw the lined face of the old woman who held the Pastor's daughter in one arm and a battered black book in her other hand. She was surrounded by a radiant light which seemed to spread out from around her.

"Put your gun away, Dell," the woman instructed him with a clear tone of voice. "It will do you no good here." she told him.

"Daddy!" Cadence yelled, as Paul took a step forward. The old woman gave him the child.

Paul seemed stunned as he wrapped his arms around her, but then he pressed her to him as tears flooded his eyes.

"Cadence!" he cried with happiness, and hundreds of pounds of deadweight slid from his weary shoulders. Crystal and Erin gathered around them with delight.

Holding his daughter in his arms, Paul finally gazed into the bright blue eyes of the aged woman, the Good Samaritan who'd delivered Cadence safely to him.

"Thank you!" slipped from his lips, and he was never more sincere.

Daisy nodded and was pleased to see Cadence's daddy loved her very much.

"This is the only object needed here," Daisy informed the Pastor and the Policeman,as she held the Book up for them to see. It was the Ancient Scriptures, the Book of Prophecy, both the Old and the New Testaments.

Dell was prepared for another Bible thumper. They meant well, he suspected, but much of the time they only got in the way and obstructed the path to justice. Officer Dell Newlyn was obsessed by his own desire to see that justice prevailed.

"The only question is, does the Pastor have the conviction to use it?" Daisy asked, and the look in her eyes stabbed Paul's conscience.

He was speechless, and overcome with guilt. He reckoned he'd been a very poor steward of God's Word. Instead of going to the Word for instruction, he had allowed an heretic to deceive him. He suspected none of the atrocities spread around them would have prevailed if he had consulted the Word like a truly caring and devout Shepherd of God's flock. If he had only applied the Word of God things would have been different, he now realized. He bowed his head before looking Daisy in the eye and answering her penetrating question.

"I have failed at my post, and I'm afraid I'm in no position to function as an Ambassador for the Most High now." He was painfully honest with Daisy.

He put Cadence on the ground and Crystal took her hand.

"I'm Daisy; Daisy O'Brien," the woman introduced herself. "We're going in there," she announced. "If we're ever going to come out, we won't need a gun, but the Book, as well as believers in the Book. Are you with me?" she asked the Pastor.

"With all of my heart, Daisy" Paul answered her.

Dell put his gun away, but kept it close beside him, in case they might need it and he strongly suspected they would. He followed the Pastor whom Daisy lead into the bowels of trouble, under the ground, inside the tunnel. The Pastor's daughters trailed after them.

The old woman stopped when she reached the hole which would take them down into the underpass. It was dark and treacherous inside, lit only by dim flickers of light. Daisy looked at the Pastor.

"I'm an old woman, Pastor Paul," she confided in him. "I will need your help going down the stairs," Daisy told him and she took a hold of Paul's arm.

The snake hid underneath the stairway and stuck his head out, to watch and maybe even to bite one of them if the opportunity was handed to him.

Paul helped Daisy and she leaned on him as they made their way further and further down the stairs and into the dangerous tunnel the others following close behind as the snake waited for them.

Without much of a warning, only a hiss and a short rattle, Rattler attacked, piercing Paul's thick leather boot with his fangs. Paul was not hurt but the snake was disgraced and furious over his attempted failure. He would have made more of a fuss if his cantankerous green eyes hadn't settled upon the old woman who filled him with horror. It wasn't bad enough the pious preacher had dropped in but he'd brought Daisy O'Brien with him, Rattler was agitated by what he perceived.

The snake glanced at Daphne who made a painful sound when she saw her grandmother in the dark cavern which was lit by a couple of lanterns pinned to the walls of bedrock.

"Wait a minute!" Paul said, "There's a snake down here too!" He cautioned the others when he realized what vicious crime the rattlesnake had just committed against him.

"Rattler Mackenzie, your wife's father, Pastor Paul," Daisy whispered to him.

Paul shivered, appalled by the fact this rattlesnake was a close relative, the progenator of the woman he loved. When his eyes adjusted to the light, he saw Allen Carter crouched beside Kas, Kas' limp body was stationed against the barricade. Moved with anguish when he saw her, Paul forgot himself and he left every one behind as he hurried to Kas and crumbled to his knees beside her debilitated body.

"O, Babe, I'm so sorry!" he cried as he touched her hand and kissed her forehead, afraid to move her, fearful he would worsen things if he did. "Kas," he called to her. "Please, Kas, don't die!" He pleaded with her, fearful he was too late.

He saw Crystal and Erin kneel beside their mother too. He blamed himself for their mother's awful situation. If only he'd listened to her instead of listening to a dissident convince him, because she was a rare find she was somehow evil.

"O, God," Paul prayed, "Don't take her away from us! Crystal, Erin, Cadence and I need her so much!" he pleaded with God.

Daisy was filled with sympathy as she witnessed their pain. Her granddaughter and the snake had brought the Pastor and his little family so much misery, and Daisy felt nothing but malice for Daphne and Mackenzie now. She was ready to take them both on.

"Daphne despises the Book I hold in my hands, don't you, Daphne?"

Daisy called her attention to the Holy Scriptures and watched Daphne drop to the floor, then scoot away from her like some scared beast.

Rattler hissed at Daisy. He grasped the type of unwavering faith the old woman had in the Book she clung to, and it's Author. She displayed more faith in this special Book than any one had ever put in magic.

"Shush, you grody old snake, or I will read the Living Word to you too!" She threatened, as she rifled through the Book's pages, turning them swiftly with her fingers. "How 'bout if I read to you how God has given me power over the serpent? Would you like me to read this to you? Or, how 'bout I tell you what's written down concerning your fate?" Daisy asked him, with vehemence.

Rattler knew he couldn't do a thing to the old woman. Her faith in her Omnipotent God far exceeded any puny beliefs he had ever clung to.

"Daisy O'Brien!" he said with seething hatred. "I cannot damage your faith, but I can devour your granddaughter," he told her.

"I believe you have already done this, Mackenzie," she snapped at him. "Look at her! She's no more my granddaughter than you are Kastanje's father," Daisy informed him.

"Then you won't mind if I have my way with her, will you?" he hissed.

Daisy remained speechless as Rattler Mackenzie made his way to Daphne Orion. He slithered over the ground on his way to the red-head. Once he reached her, without a pause, he started up her dress. Once inside of her garments, he climbed up one leg and then over her abdomen. Daphne was too weak and fearful to move, or to make any fuss, and the snake took advantage of her delicate situation.

Cradled in Paul's arms and surrounded by their daughters, Kas finally opened her eyes and gazed at Daphne and Mackenzie. She groaned when she saw the emboldened snake slither over Daphne's plump breasts.

Inches from her face now, the snake smiled into her green eyes. Then he stretched his neck, opened his mouth and devoured her head. Daphne's headless body descended onto the floor, and the snake quickly disappeared as though he had never been there.

Chapter 76

Paul had never felt so happy as he did that day, with both Kas and Cadence restored to him. They had a brand new lease on life now, he told himself.

"I love you!" he told Kas, as he embraced her and gently kissed her lips. "I will spend the rest of my life trying to make up for the harm I brought you when I was too blind to believe in your integrity, Kas," he told her.

She put her finger to his lips to interrupt him.

"Sshh," she whispered, "Just kiss me again!"

The girls gathered around them on the cold hard ground and loudly applauded their parents.

With Paul's kiss, Kas felt as if new life had been breathed into her. Now she remembered well the infinite value of one kiss. There was a remedy for her injuries. The cure was her husband's arms, she thought, and smiled at him.

"You can start making up for your past failures once we get home!" She gave him an alluring look. "Would you be good enough to help me to my feet?" she inquired of their daughters.

The girls labored to stand the new Senator of California on her feet.

"Let's get out of here!" Crystal made the brilliant suggestion.

"Wait a minute," Kas told her as she gazed at Allen. She saw his handsome face and his expressive brown eyes. He smiled at her almost timidly.

"I guess you realize by now," she said, "I'm your mother."

She destested the way he'd acquired such important knowledge, though.

"Rattler was my father?" he questioned her.

She nodded at him,

"He was, but not any more," she said, with a shake of her head. She pointed to Daisy and said, "That lovely old woman managed to return him to his grave."

"I'd be glad to be a substitute," Paul offered.

"Really?" Allen grinned at him. The thought of living up to the type of example Pastor Paul set was a real challenge, but he'd try to measure up, he told himself. To the Pastor he said,

"You're on."

The girls included Allen in their circle as they helped their mother out of the tunnel.

Daisy stood watching them with a blissful look on her crinkled face. Kas stopped when they reached the aged woman. She looked somehow so familiar.

"Do I know you?" she asked her.

Kas had the overwhelming feeling, they'd met before, many years ago and somewhere else.

"I was there when you weren't much bigger than Cadence," Daisy told her and pointed to the little girl who clung to her mother's side. "Back in Nevada when you would visit me from time to time, and we'd have milk and cookies together. 'Course I was much younger then," Daisy laughed. "I don't think either one of us could ever have guessed you'd be the Senator of California, though, as you are today." She smiled at Kas.

"Daisy!" Kas said with recognition. "I could never forget my Daisy!" she told her, and folded her arms around the old woman.

There were heroes in life like Daisy, Kas thought. There were brutal beasts but, then, there were heroes too. She'd known several excellent role models. She thought of Cody too. Then she turned to gaze at Paul and he gripped her hand. She was not just the Senator of California but she was the Pastor's wife. This thought pleased her very much.

FLASHES OF SOMEONE ELSE
by C.C. Colee

Joining her friends, Maria Diaz and Rhannon Estrella, for a vacation in a quaint village in France along the Mediterranean Sea, Catherine LaRue was wondering why she agreed to the trip. The moment she arrived, she felt like a fifth wheel. While waiting in the lobby for her friends to arrive, her interest perked up as she watched a handsome man check into the same hotel. Coincidentally, the handsome man she saw that day was also a friend of Maria's who introduced himself as Cory Vann. Despite Rhannon's instant dislike to Cory, Maria continued with her silly plan of trying to play matchmaker to Catherine and Cory. It turned out to be futile as they came together without her meddling. Everything was going along just fine until one morning Catherine went off alone and took a fall. That fall would forever change her life—and that of her friends.

Paperback, 259 pages
6" x 9"
ISBN 1-4137-9166-2
Retail Price $27.95

About the authors:

Cody Lee and Chris Cole (C.C. Colee) met in the seventh grade. They have been friends for over thirty years and have always shared a love of writing. Their other works include *RB: The Widow Maker*, *RB: The Enchantress*, *RB: The Game*, *Sweet Christine* and *Casey's Soul*.